© Sophie Davidson

Melissa Fu grew up in Northern New Mexico and now lives near Cambridge, UK, with her husband and children. With academic backgrounds in physics and English, she has worked in education as a teacher, curriculum developer, and consultant. She was the 2018/19 David TK Wong Fellow at the University of East Anglia. *Peach Blossom Spring* is her first novel.

Praise for *Peach Blossom Spring*

'I absolutely adored this novel about love and war, migration and belonging. Melissa Fu portrays the time, the culture, the place and the struggles of this family so vividly, with nuance and colour and life. Her writing is subtle and powerful, it stays with you. This is such a stunning achievement.'
Christy Lefteri, author of *The Beekeeper of Aleppo*

'What an immersive, expertly plotted and elegantly written novel. In its sweep and scope, it would appeal to fans of Madeleine Thien and Min Jin Lee and its lyrical voice – championing the vitality and ingenuity of the immigrant experience across three settings – confirms Melissa Fu as a writer to watch.'
Sharlene Teo, author of *Ponti*

PEACH BLOSSOM SPRING

MELISSA FU

WILDFIRE

First published in 2022 by
WILDFIRE
an imprint of HEADLINE PUBLISHING GROUP

First published in paperback in 2023 by
WILDFIRE
an imprint of HEADLINE PUBLISHING GROUP

1

Cataloguing in Publication Data is available from the British Library

ISBN 978 1 4722 7757 2

Offset in 11.09/13.10 pt Ehrhardt MT Pro by Jouve (UK), Milton Keynes

Map Illustration © Tim Peters

Printed and bound in Great Britain by Clays Ltd, Elcograf S.p.A.

Headline's policy is to use papers that are natural, renewable and recyclable
products and made from wood grown in well-managed forests and other
controlled sources. The logging and manufacturing processes are expected to
conform to the environmental regulations of the country of origin.

HEADLINE PUBLISHING GROUP
an Hachette UK Company
Carmelite House
50 Victoria Embankment
London
EC4Y 0DZ

www.headline.co.uk
www.hachette.co.uk

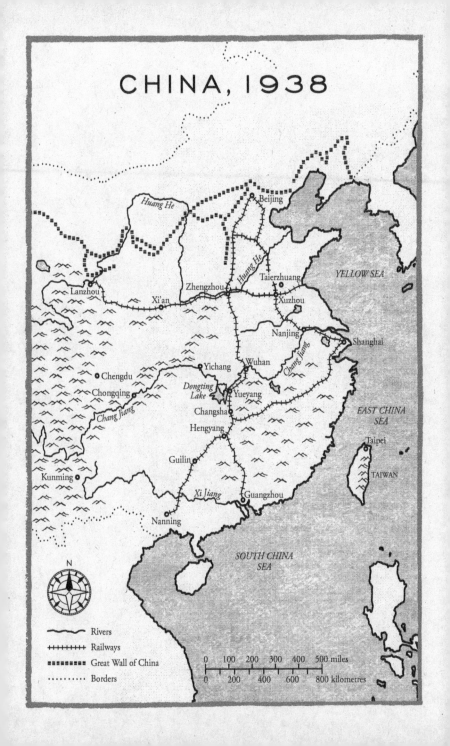

For my family, and in memory of 傅惠民 (1932–2019)

Origins

Tell us, they say, *tell us where you're from.*

He is from walking and walking and walking. He is from shoes filled with holes, blistered toes and calloused heels that know the roughness of gravel roads and the relief in straw, in grass. He is from staying each night in a different place, sometimes city, sometimes country. From roads that wrap around mountains and dip through valleys. From waterways shrouded in fog and mist.

He is from walking across China.

Tell us your memories, they say.

He remembers kerosene lamps burning low, the smell of woodsmoke, cold stone floors under his bare feet. Urgent voices, the rasping of coins, carts creaking at night. He remembers a sandalwood puzzle picture. One way up, there were one hundred monkeys. Turn it over, there were ninety-nine. How did that monkey appear and disappear? He is from this mystery.

Tell us more, they say as they nestle by his side. *How did you come here?*

He crossed rivers. He crossed oceans.

He carried a watch bought from a sailor, a letter to open doors. A suitcase, a packet of light blue aerogrammes, a single pair of wool socks.

He went towards the call of a beautiful country, a beckoning dream, a promise made of air. Towards wingbeats of birds, kaleidoscopes of seasons he'd never imagined before.

And now, they say, their eyes clear and voices playful, *tell us a story.*

To know a story is to stroke the silken surfaces of loss, to feel the weight of beauty in his hands.

To know a story is to carry it always, etched in his bones, even if dormant for decades.

Tell us, they insist.

To tell a story, he realises, is to plant a seed and let it grow.

PART ONE
1938–1941

Chapter One

Dao Hongtse had three wives. Their names are not important.

The first wife had the first son, Dao Zhiwen. This boy was too wild. He grabbed his first-son privileges with one hand and cast away his first-son duties with the other. He changed his name to Longwei and swaggered out of the house and into the streets. He gambled and won, then gambled and lost. Longwei loves tobacco, whiskey and women.

The first wife had two more children: a girl who grew into a sallow, thin woman whom no one wanted to marry, and a son who died at five months. With a heart bound by grief and feet bound by the old traditions, the first wife is now little more than a wraith lost in folds of opium smoke. She only ventures out of her chamber to refill her pipe and condemn the rest of the household.

Hongtse's second wife works hard. Her back is broad and her hands are rough. She lives in fear of the shrieks and howls of first wife. Hongtse doesn't love her, but he depends on her. Yet the second wife bore only daughters. Their names are not important. They married young and produced sons for other families.

His third wife was the favourite. Hongtse even loved her. She will be forever beautiful because she died in childbirth, bringing Hongtse his youngest son, Dao Xiaowen.

Dao Hongtse's business, Heavenly Light Kerosene and Antiques, has been passed down from father to son for generations. Kerosene is a good business: everyone needs heat, everyone needs light. Hongtse's customers are Nationalists, Communists, merchants, peasants, farmers. One day, Longwei will inherit the business and its responsibilities.

Up a narrow staircase, in a room above the kerosene shop, Dao

Hongtse also trades gold coins, jade, antique carvings and hand scrolls. Easy to move, hard to trace, always valuable. He has trained Xiaowen in the art of discerning between that which is of lasting value and that which is of momentary delight.

Between his eldest and his youngest sons, Hongtse covers all possibilities. Where Longwei is street-smart, Xiaowen is book-wise. If Longwei offers bluster, Xiaowen articulates with a fine brush. What Longwei settles by force, Xiaowen negotiates. As the years pass, Longwei has only daughters, but Xiaowen has a son.

Xiaowen's son is called Dao Renshu – *renshu* meaning benevolence, kindness, not *renshu* meaning to concede, to admit defeat. Dao Hongtse makes sure his grandson knows the difference. Renshu is Hongtse's only grandchild who is the son of a son. The boy carries the family name. Above all, he must be protected.

It is a late afternoon in early spring. The air tingles with freshness, shaking off the last chill of winter and hinting at blossoms to come. Tiny leaves are opening on the trees, and each day the sun offers a bit more light. Inside Dao Hongtse's kerosene shop, the wooden floorboards are swept clean, the counter is clear. Dao Hongtse can be seen speaking to a young woman who wears a simple, dark green tunic. Her hair is pulled back in a bun. Though it is clear he is her superior, both in age and position, there is an air of mutual respect. Their relaxed postures suggest familiarity, even affection. He delivers news that illuminates her face. Although she doesn't embrace him, her elation is clear.

Then he hands her a small silk bag and says something as she looks inside. She listens carefully, then responds. He considers her answer before replying. They nod in agreement. She offers a half-bow and turns to leave the room.

A light goes on in the room above the kerosene shop.

Soon, the profile of the woman can be seen in the upstairs window.

Shui Meilin records the new inventory in her ledgers, her slim, quick fingers working the abacus. Lately, many of her father-in-law's customers have been trading gold and jade for kerosene.

Everywhere, cash is scarce and prices have been rising. Dao Hongtse instructed that these particular jewels are to be put in hock. The tearful customer who traded them for a week's supply of fuel pleaded with Old Dao not to sell them to anyone else, hoping to soon be able to buy back his heirlooms. Both Meilin and Hongtse were perturbed by this deal, yet another sign of the encroaching war with the Japanese, but Hongtse accepted the treasures for payment, of course. He is, after all, a businessman.

Meilin rises to put the valuables away, moving through the room as if by memory. After closing and locking the glass display cabinet, she looks out the window. The sun is setting, her work is done for the day, and she feels hopeful. Dao Hongtse has just told her of the Chinese army's triumph at Taierzhuang. Both Dao Hongtse's sons are expected home soon, given leave after a bloody but victorious rotation.

Meilin last saw her husband, Dao Xiaowen, and his brother Longwei nine months ago. After the Luguoqiao incident up north, the brothers had left home to join the fight. Meilin and her sister-in-law, Xue Wenling, had been proud their husbands were protecting the future of the Republic. The family awaited news from the faraway frontline, but weeks passed, then months, and none came. Though disappointing, this was understandable; the post was sporadic and troops were constantly on the move.

Yet waves from the war began to push into the city of Changsha. At first it was just a trickle: hotels and guesthouses filled with wealthier people retreating from the turbulent east. Wenling remarked that at least she could see the Shanghai styles sooner. Then more refugees arrived. Shops were busier than ever, as disrupted supply lines along the rivers and railways drove prices up. The streets and markets clamoured with rallies against the Japanese aggressors. But despite these gallant displays of patriotism, the Japanese advance continued. It wasn't long before Shanghai fell, and by December, the Imperial Japanese Army had overtaken Nanjing. With Chiang Kai-shek's Nationalist government relocated to nearby Wuhan, a steady stream of evacuees is now pouring into Changsha.

Hongtse's news of the victory at Taierzhuang is most welcome.

The resistance was strong, the Japanese were humiliated. This, everyone is certain, will be a turning point. Best of all, Meilin can count on one hand the days until she will be able to hold her dear Xiaowen again.

Meilin's thoughts are interrupted by shrieking and giggling, followed by the sound of footsteps running across the courtyard. They thump up the stairs and down the corridor. Renshu and his cousin Liling burst into the room. Breathless and laughing, with messy hair, the two demand snacks. Renshu is three and a half, and Liling is five. Renshu's legs, still chubby, struggle to keep up with his adored cousin. Liling's face is so full of warmth and cheer that Meilin finds it hard not to smile when seeing her. When Renshu smiles, his solemn, round eyes crinkle into crescents, and the dimple in his left cheek reveals itself. Both children are flushed from racing around the compound. They have barrelled through the house, knocking on the doors of the scary nainai, the ugly nainai and the dead nainai, running away before anyone could catch them. After chasing the cats into corners, up the walls and out into the streets, they'd teased Yeye's goldfish in the pond by making shadows on the water and tapping the surface with sticks.

Now, they dig through Meilin's sewing basket, looking for the sweet lotus seeds she hides for them in the folds of cloth. Once the treats are devoured, Liling roars at Renshu. She chases him around the room, past the display cabinet, until he crouches behind a carved rosewood folding screen. When she holds her arms out, fingers wiggling to tickle him, he runs to the bedroom and hides under the bedclothes, knocking a pile of neatly folded laundry to the floor.

A sharp and impatient knock comes at the door. Liling dashes under the bed and Renshu pretends to sleep.

Meilin opens the door to Liling's mother, Wenling. Though it is nearing the end of a long day, Wenling's appearance is immaculate. For as long as Meilin has known her, Wenling has eschewed traditional dress and insisted on ordering the latest Western fashions. She is always careful that her oval face shows no blemishes, although it may boast the occasional beauty spot, depending on the trends. Today she wears her hair in glossy finger curls and exudes glamour with her dark mascara, black eyeliner, and scarlet lipstick. Sometimes Meilin is a bit intimidated by her sister-in-law's sophistication. Meilin has never bothered with the fashions. In place of powders, her nose is spattered with freckles, and her heart-shaped face suggests a radiant, rougher charm. Shorter than Wenling, she doesn't wear heels to make her any taller or tiny shoes to make her more feminine. Xiaowen has always said she is beautiful exactly as she is, and Meilin believes him.

As usual, Wenling is cross. Without bothering to acknowledge Meilin, she shouts for Liling to come out now, to stop playing, it's time for her bath.

Liling and Renshu stifle their laughter.

Wenling storms into the bedroom and stoops to look under the bed. She pulls Liling out by the ankle. When Liling stands, Wenling fusses about the line of dust on the front of her dress, glaring at Meilin. As Wenling drags her daughter downstairs, scolding her, Liling looks back and makes faces at Renshu.

Meilin motions for Renshu to tidy the mess. He tries his best, but soon tires of wrestling with the bedclothes and wanders back out to the front room to sit by his ma's side.

'Time to calm down now. You and your cousin are too naughty!' she scolds, shaking her head, but there's a lightness in her voice that suggests amusement more than reproach.

After Renshu's dinner and bath, Meilin readies him for bed. Since his birth, Meilin's days and heart have been full. She loves Renshu, not because his birth raises her place in the family, to the mother of a son of a son of Hongtse, and not just because his eyes and nose remind her of Xiaowen. She loves him because his laugh sounds like the wind playing temple bells in spring. She loves him because he fills her with a joy she hadn't known existed before he gave her his first smile. Having married late, at twenty-one, there were times she wondered if she would ever be a mother. She sings him to sleep with the 'Song of the Fishermen'. His eyes flutter closed; rest smooths his brow.

She will do anything for this child.

*

In the quieten darkness of the room, Meilin sits for a moment, a long absent happiness rising through her. Xiaowen will be home soon. She can almost feel him in the shadows. She closes her eyes and recalls the eve of his departure.

They had returned to their rooms after the last family meal to enjoy their final evening alone. Two-year-old Renshu was sitting in his father's lap, roaring like a tiger, excited from the novelty of staying up late. Xiaowen beamed to see his boy's spirit.

'Look at this boy. He has grown fierce and strong like his ma.'

Renshu squirmed off Xiaowen's lap and roared again.

Xiaowen scooped Renshu back up. 'You take care of your ma, yes?'

Renshu nodded.

'I have to go away, but I will return soon. Right now, it's time for this baby tiger to sleep.' He squeezed Renshu tightly, and the boy's brow momentarily wrinkled. Xiaowen kissed his son's head.

After settling Renshu in the back, Meilin had come out again to the very room where she sits now. Xiaowen was at the table, a narrow wooden box in front of him. Meilin put her arms around him and kissed his neck as she sat beside him. He handed her the box, indicating she should open it.

Inside was a roll of silk brocade: creamy peony blossoms climbing a green lattice against a dark background. Gold threads traced an auspicious cloud pattern along the edges. Meilin caught her breath and stared at Xiaowen in disbelief. A hand scroll. Xiaowen nodded, encouraging her to examine it more closely. Meilin brushed off her hands, lifted it, and loosened the red tassel. Slowly, slowly, she unrolled the silk to reveal the first painted scene: ancient, silent mountains, a rushing blue-green river, a group of travellers.

She leaned forward to examine the delicate strokes, mesmerised by the fine detail of each bird, stone and tree, the distinctions between the travellers' faces. It was astonishing. Finer work than any Meilin had ever seen.

'When did you find this?'

'Years ago, while scouting for antiques for my father.'

'And you didn't give it to him?'

'No, not this one,' he said, his fingertip tracing the swirls of the clouds. 'I wanted to save it.'

'It must be worth a fortune,' she murmured.

'Meilin, it is for our future. When the war is over and I return, we can use it to open our own shop.'

'What about Heavenly Light Antiques?'

He shook his head and smiled. 'Old Hongtse will be just fine with Longwei's help and Wenling's meddling. Let's dream of something else. China is changing. We don't need to follow every old tradition. Imagine a speciality antiques shop, just for you and me.'

Meilin threw her arms around her husband, marvelling that she had married a man who could envision such a future. Something of their own. They would build something of their own.

'Meilin, you must promise me two things: take care of yourself and Renshu, and keep our scroll safe for our future.'

'I promise.'

Side by side, they sat late into the night, taking in the poetry of each of the scroll's scenes. After they put it away, they lay together in the dark, tracing the curves of arms, legs, faces. They spent the hours before dawn memorising the shape of each other.

Meilin sits at the window in the upstairs shop, waiting. Xiaowen's regiment is expected back today.

It was nearly five years ago that he'd walked into her family's antique shop in the western city of Yichang with a magnificent Tang sancai camel figurine to sell. Despite its age, the green, tan and cream glazes were clear and unchipped. On its back sat three musicians. The details were uncommonly delicate. Meilin immediately knew she wanted it for their collection. As they bargained for a fair price, she was delighted to discover that she shared with the young man not just a love of old treasures, but also a passion for the ideals of the new China.

Meilin's parents, early supporters of the May Fourth Movement, believed in women's rights and other reforms for the new republic. They had brought up all their children to know the value of education, hard work and economic independence. Occasionally, though, they despaired that Meilin, their youngest, was *too* independent; she had already scared off many potential matches and refused several others.

However, Dao Xiaowen, this new trader from Changsha, kept returning. Sometimes to buy, sometimes to sell, but always seeking out Meilin. Haggling over trinkets evolved into heated discussions about replacing the old traditions with the rigours of Mr Science and Mr Democracy, and dissections of the finer points of Dr Sun Yat-sen's Three Principles.

After several months, no one was surprised when Xiaowen and Meilin fell in love. To her parents' delight, she agreed to marry him, two years her senior by age, but her equal in intellect and outlook.

In her new home, Meilin quickly settled into Dao Hongtse's upstairs antiques shop. Hongtse marvelled at how easily she learned the location and provenance of every item in the inventory. He was quick to notice the flawless sums in the ledgers were always in her hand. Hongtse jests, with fondness, that Meilin is, without doubt, the finest treasure Xiaowen has ever found.

Whether through business acumen or canny foresight with regard to his daughter-in-law's strong personality, Hongtse had given his blessing for Xiaowen and Meilin to live in the rooms behind the antiques shop. While still in the Dao family compound, Meilin and Renshu live apart from the rest of the family, separated by the courtyard. In this way, Meilin can slip away from a household filled with mothers-in-law, elder sisters, nieces, nephews, and a revolving collection of cousins, uncles, aunts and other distant relations who continually appear with hopes that Hongtse will share his good fortune.

Now, Meilin's ears prick up as an army jeep turns and heads down the road, slowing as it approaches the compound. She cries out in excitement and runs downstairs to greet it, arriving before any of the others.

When the door of the jeep opens, Longwei gets out. He wears his olive green service uniform with gleaming brass buttons, and black leather boots that go up to his knees. A thick, dark brown leather belt cinches his waist, and a smart cap emblazoned with the Republic's Blue Sky with a White Sun sits on his head. He grabs his duffel, then straightens his tall frame, holding his head high. He salutes the driver, and the jeep drives off.

'But – where is . . .?'

Longwei's normally imperious eyes look mournful.

'Xiaowen?' Meilin's voice sounds small and not her own. A strange silence descends.

'He was a hero,' Longwei says at last. 'He was a hero at Taierzhuang.'

'Where is he?'

Longwei repeats it once more. 'He was a hero.'

There must be a misunderstanding. Meilin spins around, looking for another jeep. The road is empty. Where is Xiaowen? Both the brothers were expected. Hongtse said both. He must be coming soon.

'He was a hero at Taierzhuang,' Longwei says again, in a voice marked with pride, disbelief and, most of all, sorrow.

'Stop saying that. *Hero* means nothing.' Her voice rises to a shriek. 'Did he die? Tell me!'

But Longwei only lowers his eyes and shakes his head.

She flies at him, hammering her fists against his chest. 'No! No!'

He catches her arms and holds them. She is sobbing, sobbing. She feels her body collapse into his. The coarse weave of his coat is rough against her cheek.

'I don't know,' he says quietly. 'I didn't see him again.'

A cold cough sounds behind them. She can barely lift her head to look up. It is Wenling. Longwei gently steps back from Meilin to embrace his wife.

Now the rest of the household has come out to greet Longwei. Meilin watches their reunions as if they are actors on a stage. Every part of her feels stunned, and the question *Where is Xiaowen?* echoes in her head, its answer unthinkable: *No one knows*. Through the rest of the afternoon and into the evening, everything is muffled, numb. *Where is Xiaowen?*

Grateful for Longwei's return, Hongtse's household is enveloped in sombre celebration. Victory is costly: many families have no sons returning. At least they have one.

Somehow, Meilin makes it through the day to dinnertime. She is grateful for the distraction of routine, helping to bring a multitude of dishes to the table as wives and children start to congregate. She hears Wenling calling to her girls.

Wenling has a voice like porcelain. It slides over the ear, leaving the listener aware of their own rough surfaces. As Wenling walks down the corridors, her jade bracelets clink with each step, announcing her approach. When she enters the dining room, stepping over the high threshold, she nods in Meilin's direction without making eye contact, and surveys the table, checking the number of place settings, counting the dishes and bestowing smiles or censure among those gathered.

Working in his father's kerosene business, Longwei had spent years travelling the Chang Jiang between Wuhan and Shanghai, collecting shipments and supervising distributions in towns and cities along the river. It was on one of these journeys that he found Wenling. The daughter of a prominent and rich Nanjing businessman, her elegance and pedigree enchanted Longwei. He courted her with an ambitious, acquisitive passion. They soon married in great ceremony, with hundreds of guests and an elaborate banquet. As her ageing mother-in-law has grown more reclusive, Wenling has become the taitai in the house, domineering and idle. It suits her.

All the women and children are now at the table except Wenling's own daughters, Lifen and Liling. She calls for them again, impatient. Although Wenling seems all smooth surfaces, cracks show when she speaks to her daughters. Lifen slinks in the room, eyes lowered, but not apologetic. The girl has all her mother's mannerisms, but not her devastating beauty. Instead, the seven-year-old's face echoes her father's features, the strong nose and heavy brow that speak authority in a man but will one day cause people to describe Lifen as 'striking'. She has broad shoulders and a short back. Her ear lobes are too long, and her arms and legs too short to move with Wenling's grace, but she already bears the same air of expecting much more than that which has been offered to her. Two steps behind Lifen is Liling, with untidy pigtails and ink spots on her face. She has Wenling's delicate build and bones, her smooth skin and clear eyes, but somehow the allure seems washed away, as if the child is aware of the perpetual disappointment she represents to her father for not being a son, and to her mother for being too dreamy and soft-hearted.

Throughout the meal, Wenling fawns on her husband, periodically tracing the red insignia with three gold triangles on his lapel. His daughters cling to his sides. Dao Hongtse gives Longwei a rare and grudging nod of approval. Meilin tries to be happy – she *is* happy for Longwei – but what about Xiaowen? When Renshu asks for his ba, Meilin holds him close and murmurs on the top of his head that his ba is a hero. And maybe his ba will come home with the next group of soldiers. Meilin glances up and notices Dao Hongtse listening to her. When their eyes meet, she sees his are filled with worry and fear for his lost son.

Meilin makes it through the evening, holding her composure. But in the quieten of her rooms that night, after Renshu has fallen asleep, she takes out Xiaowen's scroll and weeps until dawn.

The summer passes in a blur of sorrow and disbelief. Xiaowen doesn't return with the next convoy, or any after. The wives and sisters, intending kindness, pressure Meilin to move to the big house, but Meilin refuses. She wants to stay where she and Xiaowen set up their life together. Maybe he will still come home. Hongtse, broken by the loss of his youngest son, lets her do as she wishes.

The leaves turn to gold and red, and Xiaowen still doesn't appear. Without him, Changsha no longer feels like home. Meilin writes to her family in Yichang, begging them to let her come home and bring Renshu with her. Yet, for all their progressive views about New Culture, they adhere to the tradition that she is now a member of the Dao family. She and her son must stay.

Besides, they plan to close their shop and move to their ancestral compound in the hills above Yichang. Given all the turmoil in the east, it is a necessary precaution.

Yuelu Mountain, Hunan Province, China, October 1938

Meilin strikes a match. It flares, then fizzles in the damp, drizzly air. She sighs.

'Maybe we shouldn't be burning paper money for Xiaowen. What if he isn't really dead? What if all these riches show up for him in the afterlife and he isn't there?'

'I don't believe any of that.' Longwei scans the families walking the path up Yuelu Shan, here to revere the tombs of their ancestors and remember the lost. Even with the uncertainties of war, people have still come out for the Double Ninth Festival. Perhaps during these times it is even more necessary to hold on to celebrations. Longwei seems to be searching for someone. Meilin wonders who. Not his wife and daughters, certainly. Wenling was quick to excuse herself when the morning arrived with heavy clouds spitting rain. Suddenly maternal, she pointed out Lifen's delicate nature and Liling's fading cough, claiming the cold air would make them suffer. She said she'd stay home to supervise the Chongyang cakes for later. Besides, Wenling sniffed, it wasn't *her* husband who was probably dead.

Their coats rip and flap in the wind. Meilin tries again. The matchstick snaps in half without lighting. She drops it on the sodden pile of yellow and brown leaves at her feet.

Nearby, Hongtse and Renshu launch bamboo boats on a small pond. Hongtse has promised Renshu a gold coin for the one that carries the most stones without sinking. They have spent the morning lining up boats, trying to decide which could balance speed and seaworthiness while maximising cargo. Children from other families have wandered over to join in, fashioning makeshift boats from twigs and dry leaves.

'On the other hand,' she muses, 'maybe it's like filling a bank account for the future. If he does arrive in the afterlife, he will find that he is already a rich man.'

When Longwei doesn't answer, Meilin glances over at him. He is monitoring the edges of the cemetery, noting who comes in and out. Since his return from Taierzhuang, Longwei hasn't worn a soldier's uniform. He says he has been promoted. Whatever his new role, Longwei is no longer strictly a military man. Most days, he stations himself in Hongtse's kerosene shop. Men come and go. Sometimes they wear the leggings and uniform of the Kuomintang. Sometimes they wear Western suits or traditional scholars' robes. They are not Hongtse's usual customers. They are a rougher sort, hissing names of towns and crossroads. There seems to be a lot more arguing than kerosene selling. From a chair in the corner, Hongtse scowls and mutters about filial piety, but Longwei ignores him. Eventually, he quiets and listens to the harsh, urgent words that pass between Longwei and these men. Longwei calls them his brothers. They are, none of them, his brothers.

She studies Longwei's profile now. He could be a younger, more ruthless Hongtse. Both are over six feet tall, but Longwei's broader shoulders suggest a dominance, a forcefulness the old man lacks. He is muscular where his father is lean. A long scar runs down his left forearm. Is it from a fight? She squints to see any traces of Xiaowen in him. No. There is nothing to suggest these two shared a father.

As if he can hear her thoughts, Longwei turns to face her, eyes glittering. He bares his tea-and-nicotine-stained teeth as he takes a cigarette from a packet and holds it in his mouth. When he strikes a match, it catches instantly. He lights his smoke, then flicks out the flame.

'My brother was a fool.'

Meilin is taken aback. Had she spoken aloud?

'Xiaowen was a good man,' she counters. 'He wouldn't play mahjong and chase singing girls in the teahouses. He wouldn't deal with those thugs of yours who come and go from the shop all day long.' She pauses. Longwei still watches the ground, but his jaw has stiffened. Although she is usually cautious, the rustle of activity in the kerosene shop over the past weeks, and Long-wei's preoccupation today makes her bold. 'He wouldn't cheat his own father of shipments and gloss the books.'

Meilin expects a reprimand, a denial, or at least some kind of justification.

Instead, Longwei drops his cigarette on the ground and crushes the embers underfoot. He inhales deeply, blows out through his teeth, then stares hard at Meilin. He steps closer. She holds her ground and stares back.

'A good man,' he sneers. 'Good men die or disappear. Haven't you noticed by now?' He is about to continue when Renshu runs up, holding the champion bamboo boat in one hand and a new gold coin in the other. Longwei's expression shifts from spiteful to welcoming. He gathers Renshu in his arms and lifts him to his chest. The boy squeals, kicking his legs and laughing. Unease swims through Meilin's stomach.

'Soon, the grain will shed its husk and come forth,' Longwei says to the boy as he sets him down. Renshu ignores his uncle's words and races back to Hongtse. Longwei turns to address Meilin again. 'Change is coming, Meilin. It's barely been ten days since Guang-zhou fell, and now this defeat in Wuhan. It's been our good fortune to avoid bombings so far, but Changsha is no longer safe.' Longwei grasps her shoulders and looks directly at her, face to face.

The strength of his grip is unsettling, his usual smugness is gone. Why didn't he argue back when she challenged him?

'Be ready. For anything. Understand?' A peppery, tobacco-tinged heat radiates from him. He lifts his head, gazes past her. Whatever he's been looking for, he finally sees it. After giving her shoulders a firm squeeze, he drops his hands and walks away.

Meilin swallows. She massages one of her shoulders.

A family of three has assembled at a tomb nearby: two parents and a young girl. They carry willow baskets filled with flowers, incense and other offerings. The father uses his coat to shelter his family from the wind, and the mother kneels and sets up the shrine. The girl places a wreath of zhuyu twigs on the ground, the red berries a bright spot in the dull day. Together, mother and daughter arrange a stack of oranges and place a small flask of chrysanthemum liquor alongside. A perfect pyramid of devotion. With a fine-tipped brush and a pot of red paint, the mother refreshes the faded inscriptions while the father winks at the girl. Finally, she lights the incense, and all three stand and bow. A thin wisp of smoke rises, then drifts away in the wind.

A sudden gust scatters the paper money Meilin holds loosely in her hand. She rushes to gather the soggy scraps, now crumpled and soiled.

Changsha, Hunan Province, China, November 1938

Today, everything feels different to Renshu. The voices from the shop downstairs are louder than usual. The door opens and closes every few minutes. A parade of heavy footsteps pounds in and out.

He settles into a familiar activity: as his ma sews, Renshu takes apart the three stacked sections of her sewing basket, sifting through the spools of thread, looking for his favourites. Peacock blue, emperor's crimson, gold like a cup of oolong. He bites his lip in concentration, lays them lengthways, side-by-side on the wooden floor. Then, with a long slat of wood, he gives them all an equal push. The coloured strands unwind like a wobbly rainbow. Some days, the winner is the fastest. Others, it's the one that rolls the furthest. He winds the threads back up and races other colours, other combinations, looking for the champion.

When he tires of the game, he sorts through the carved cinnabar box of jade charms, golden bells and silver coins that sits by his ma's side. Every so often, she picks up a coin and continues sewing. It seems like she's been doing this for weeks. He likes to examine the jade pendants: a plum, a serpent, a buddha. He holds them up to the window, one at a time, and watches the sun's late light stream through, revealing white veins in the green stone. His favourite is the three-legged toad with a gold coin in its mouth. The best part is that the coin rotates. Renshu spins it with his index finger, watching its uneven rattle and whirr until it slows to a stop, and then he spins it again.

When they hear the stairs creak, Meilin's brow creases. She shushes Renshu and takes the treasures from his hands, slips them back into the box, closes the lid, and puts it in the bottom section of her basket. She folds her sewing over the box. Sensing her urgency, Renshu lines up the basket's middle section and presses it down snugly. Meilin rests the last basket, the one with spools, needles, buttons and scissors on top. As she picks up her knitting, she releases a long, careful exhale, and the line of worry across her forehead fades. Renshu fills his hands with buttons to show to Uncle or Yeye, or whoever is coming along the corridor.

It is Uncle and two big men. Although Renshu usually jumps into Uncle's arms when he sees him, the men make him shy, so Renshu stays quieten. The men carry a large wooden crate. They have a leathery, smoky smell that Renshu isn't sure about. One of the men has big boots, and the other a long beard and moustache. Uncle and his ma start arguing.

Uncle waves at some of the antiques and the men open the crate and start loading things into it: lamps, paintings, small sculptures. At first they pack carelessly. Renshu's ma says some sharp words and reaches behind a counter for a stack of soft cloths. Uncle barks at the men and they take all the pieces out, one by one, and start over. This time, they use the cloths to wrap each item. Uncle goes over to a pot in the corner that holds many scrolls. He grabs an armful of them and asks Ma something. She's not happy. She scowls and gives him a box of charms, but not the one in her basket. The men have filled the crate with treasures. Now they knock nails in the top to seal it up. Once they've shouldered the crate and left, Ma lets out a big sigh and slides down to the floor with her back against the door.

After a few moments, Meilin rises and goes into their bedroom. Renshu hears her moving furniture. She returns holding a narrow wooden box. She beckons him to sit by her side at a low wooden table that, until moments ago, held dragon lamps and phoenix carvings. She invites him to open the box. Inside is a scroll. Renshu lifts it up. He loosens the tassel. Meilin leans forward to help him lay it flat on the table. When the first scene is fully revealed, she places one hand on his to stop him unrolling it any further. Her other hovers over the columns of characters as she reads aloud. This, she tells him, is a story of travelling scholars. Here they start with strong legs and bright eyes. They will follow the river and the sun.

Below them, the kerosene shop boils with arguments and rough laughter that carries no mirth. Worried words fog the air: *The Japanese approach from the north and the south. Like a pincer.*

Renshu prods Meilin. He wants to see more. As he unrolls the next scene, Meilin rolls up the section they have just read. Once more, she stays his hand when the full scene is revealed. Again, she reads the poetry, conducting its music and story. For the rest of the afternoon, they journey through the scroll, scene by scene, discovering details and making up stories. Guiding Renshu, she shows him her favourite parts: here, the tiger sleeps and the travellers pass without harm. There, in the crowded market, the cleverest scholar wins a game of chance and wit. On narrow bridges over mountain streams, travellers contemplate the constancy of ever-flowing motion.

'Renshu,' whispers his ma, 'have you noticed that none of the travellers face backwards? They move forward through the landscapes and never look back.'

Cigarette smoke and the rattling of kerosene bottles float up from the shop. Talk of bridges, railroads and rivers creeps along the walls. *Leave nothing of value behind.*

Remember, she says, these travelling scholars carry everything they need on their backs. They leave behind anything that weighs them down. Remember, she says, that regret is a heavy burden. And as she puts an arm around Renshu and points at the traveller resting underneath cherry blossoms at the end of his long journey, she whispers, 'Remember that to have an orchard is to honour the generations that came before and will come after.'

He nods. He will remember.

That night, when a hand grips her shoulder and shakes her awake, Meilin is not surprised. Longwei's voice is low, but the urgency is unmistakable.

'We need to leave. Now. Go out the back.'

She blinks in the night and sees his silhouette disappear through the doorway.

Though it is quieten and dark, if she strains, she can hear rustling across the courtyard, in the house.

Meilin pulls her sewing basket close, unstacks the layers, checks that the box of coins and charms is still at the bottom. From under her bed, she retrieves the two silk jackets, one large, one small, that she has been padding with notes and coins for weeks. The lumpy bundles in her hands offer a cool, soft reassurance. She puts them aside; they will wear them. On the floor is the box containing the scroll. She wraps it in cloth and puts it in her basket. Her heart thuds and tears smart behind her eyes. More sounds of muffled, hurried movement disturb the house. Meilin reassembles her basket. She tugs the handles together. The basket is heavy, but there is nothing in it she wants to leave behind.

A cart rolls by. Outside, a few lights still blink in the houses and streets. She stands and watches Renshu, his eyes closed, his breath unhurried and warm. Another cart stops outside and she hears fierce whispers. She waits another thirty seconds in absolute stillness, inhales deeply, and cups her hand around his small shoulder.

In the cart, Renshu stretches his legs, pushing against her sewing basket. Just as they've left their street and are approaching the market, an explosion rocks the air. Renshu twists and arches his back to see, but Meilin tightens her grip to block his view. She gives him a wooden puzzle, tells him to count the monkeys. Absorbed in his task, she keeps him facing forward.

Heat and brightness light the night. Flames crackle, shouts carry on the wind. Meilin's eyes sting from the smoke, and her heart is racing. When she turns and looks back, she gasps: Hongtse's shop is burning.

'What is it, Ma?' Renshu asks, wriggling.

Meilin swallows her fear, steadies herself, 'Shhh, it's okay,' she tells him.

Han, the servant who pulls the cart, turns down another alleyway.

'Where are we going? What about the others?' she asks.

'Big fire, ma'am, big fire! To the meeting place,' he says, and continues.

Alarm bells are clanging. They pass structure after structure blazing in the night.

It wasn't only Dao Hongtse's shop.

The city is a sea of flames. The roads are filling as others flee the blaze. Some in carts, some in wagons filled with families, furniture, pots, sacks of grain. Many people are on foot, balancing shoulder poles with hastily packed and overflowing baskets. And there are some who escaped with only their nightclothes and whatever they could grab. Army jeeps weave through the masses, headed against the flow, towards the burning city. A few motor cars, caught in the snarl, honk their horns and rev their engines. The fire alarm bells clang over the continuing smoke and flames.

The cart jostles over the bumpy road, making Meilin's teeth chatter. Han rushes around a corner, and Renshu is flung out of Meilin's arms, towards the edge of the seats. 'Ma!' he cries out in alarm. Meilin pulls him back on to her lap and leans forward to shield him, covering his ears and eyes.

Another explosion, like thunder in her lungs. Cases fall off the back of the cart, but Han doesn't stop. A whoosh of hot wind engulfs them, blowing smoke and cinders into the night.

Meilin glances over her shoulder once more. Although the flames make the air shimmer, chills run down her arms. She won't look back again.

Chapter Two

Towards the interior, China, November 1938

At the train station, Han tells them to get out and wait for the others. It is only when Han taps her shoulder, then shakes it, that Meilin realises she has tensed up, her jaw clenched, her hands balled into fists. Despite the waves of heat and flame, Meilin is shivering. Han wraps a blanket around her.

Before Meilin can ask any questions, he hurries off. Meilin looks around, stunned. The station is already crowded with other families. She sees an empty alcove and steers Renshu towards it.

'Ma, what's happening?' Renshu asks.

'We're waiting for everyone else. Here,' she says, lifting him on to a wall so he can see over the crowd, 'can you see Uncle or Yeye coming?' She makes her voice calm, bright.

He cranes his head back and forth, keeping watch. Every so often, he reports that he doesn't see them yet, then he resumes his lookout.

When he can't see her face, Meilin drops the smile. A squall of questions flurries through her mind. Did Longwei know the fire was going to happen? Is this what he was warning her about? Why so many fires? Around her, rumours rustle: *The Japanese set Changsha on fire. No, it was the Kuomintang, anything to stop the enemy from advancing. No, it was bandits who love chaos for its own sake. It was the Generalissimo's orders. No, he would never betray us like that.*

Renshu looks down at Meilin and shakes his head, tearful. 'I don't see them, Ma.'

'It's okay, they'll be here soon.' She helps him off the wall. Renshu sits on her lap and leans into her, the top of his head just under her chin.

'Ma, where's my yeye?'

'Don't worry, he's coming.'

A few minutes later: 'Ma, why did we have to leave the house?'

'Shhh,' she murmurs.

'I want to go home.' He climbs out of her lap. 'Why are there so many people? I'm cold. I want Yeye. Ma.' He sticks his face right up close to hers. 'I want to go home.'

'Stop it!' she snaps.

He is taken aback. Tears spring to his eyes and he starts to wail.

Meilin curses herself. She didn't mean to sound so angry. She pulls him into her lap and rubs his back, shushing him more gently. Renshu's sobs quieten.

Where are they? What if they don't come? Should she go back? Back to what? Where are all the other people going? Should she follow? No, she'll wait. If Longwei told Han to leave them at the train station, he must have a plan. She fingers the hem of her jacket, tracing the embedded coins. What will they do if the others don't come? Fire alarm bells clang over the shouts and commotion.

'Meilin!' Longwei's voice carries above the noise. Longwei, Wenling and the girls have finally arrived. Climbing out of their cart, Wenling looks flustered and the girls are wide-eyed and unusually quieten. Longwei starts to unload suitcases.

'You are safe, you are safe!' Meilin slides Renshu off her lap and jumps to her feet. Renshu grabs her hand and burrows into her side. She puts her arm around him. 'The others? Where are they?' Meilin asks.

Longwei pauses. 'They aren't here? Han was supposed to get them.'

Meilin shakes her head. 'He didn't come back.'

Longwei looks around. It is as if he registers for the first time all the people, the noise, the despair.

'Han . . . he . . .' He leaves his sentence unfinished and keeps searching the crowds. 'They'll be here soon.'

Longwei starts waving at someone. He rushes off into the crowd. It must be Han. But no, he is heading towards an officer standing alongside a military jeep. The officer starts speaking and hands him some papers. Longwei pages through the documents, says something, then gestures towards the city. They confer, they look at the tracks, they scan the crowds. More than once, Longwei draws himself up tall and nods.

He returns, waving the papers. Something in his nature has changed after his exchange with the officer. 'Train tickets.' His voice is sharp. 'A train is coming soon. We have to go.'

'But what about the others? Shouldn't we wait?' Meilin asks.

Longwei ignores her. He points at the luggage and tells his family to repack. A single suitcase each. Leave the rest with Xu, he says, gesturing at his driver. Cowed by the strangeness of the situation and the harshness of Longwei's tone, Wenling and the girls start sorting through their cases, bickering and agonising over what to keep. Renshu stands near Liling and Lifen, picking up and putting down the things – books, small dolls, wooden combs, silk dresses – that they must leave behind.

'Did you know about the fire?' Meilin challenges Longwei.

'I told you to be ready for anything.'

'What about the rest of the family?' Meilin persists.

'Xu will look for them. My colleague will send them on another train. We cannot wait, we need to go.'

'Where?'

'The Japanese are coming down from Wuhan. Some say they are already at Dongting Lake. More enemy troops advance from the south, from Guangzhou. We are being squeezed.' He holds his hand up to show his index finger and thumb coming together. 'There is no time.' He is curt. 'We need to leave.'

She looks at him in disbelief. 'But your father, you're leaving—'

'I'm not leaving him behind. I told you, Xu will look for them.'

There is the whistle and screech of the train arriving. Wenling and the girls stand silently, holding one suitcase each. Renshu comes back to Meilin's side.

'You *are* leaving them,' Meilin insists.

'Why are you arguing?' Longwei shouts. He glances across the throngs of people, then to the train. 'My father,' he says slowly, looking at Meilin, then at Renshu, then back at Meilin again, 'my father would want to know that the family name is safe.'

People are gathering possessions and moving towards the platform.

'Where are we going?' Meilin asks again.

'Chongqing, the new capital. The train will take us to the Chang Jiang, where we'll take a steamboat west, to the interior. The government is relocating. We'll follow.'

Meilin looks again at the crowds, hoping to see Hongtse or the rest of the family.

'What are you waiting for?' Longwei says. 'The city is scorched; the shop has burned down. This is our chance. *His* chance.' He gathers up Renshu with one arm and his suitcase with the other and starts walking away.

Sick with disbelief and dismay, Meilin grabs her basket and hurries after him.

On the crowded train, Renshu sits on Meilin's lap. Despite her initial misgivings, Meilin can see they were lucky to get tickets. Longwei has the right friends, the right kind of influence.

The train crawls north. At each station, no one gets off and more people squeeze on, their arms laden with tattered suitcases and awkward bundles. Those fleeing the fire are joined by others abandoning their homes and cities to the Japanese. The air in the coach is close and stale with the odours of too many bodies, with camphor and cooking oil. Renshu's face is flushed and blotchy. He must be itchy and sweaty underneath all his clothes. Eventually, he nods off into a fitful, uneven doze. The train overfills and people climb on to the roof, bracing themselves against the biting November winds.

That night, in the darkest hours, the train comes to an abrupt stop, nowhere near a station, jolting people awake. *What is it? Where are we?* Meilin tries to shake off her drowsiness. She rouses Renshu.

'Wake up,' she whispers.

His head rolls away from her and he leans into Wenling, who stiffens and stands. Renshu's body, heavy with sleep, collapses into the warm spot she left behind.

'Renshu.' Meilin jiggles his arm, tries to lift him. 'Renshu, we have to go.'

'Ma?' he blinks.

Once Meilin finally manages to get Renshu on his feet, she grabs her basket. Still half-asleep, Renshu stumbles waywardly along the aisle, and Meilin helps him off the train.

People stream out of the passenger cars and continue to walk north, deserting the silent hulk of the engine. Renshu lags behind. Meilin tries to keep the silhouettes of Longwei, Wenling and the girls in sight.

She glances back at the train. Rising to the horizon in the distance, the tracks are parallel lines gleaming in the moonlight. She looks ahead. There is no gleam. The tracks are missing. On this bewildering night, it seems like every time she turns around, something else is torn away, something else is lost.

'What happened to the tracks?' someone asks, and Meilin leans forward, desperate to catch the answer.

'Damn Japs took the tracks!' a man responds.

'No, it was the army,' someone else argues. 'They took them away to slow the enemy advance.'

'But what about us?' the man asks.

The response is unintelligible.

Through the night, they walk and walk. When the children are too tired to go any further, they shelter under a grove of trees for a few hours. Worrying about Hongtse and the rest of the family, uncertain of what lies ahead, Meilin can't sleep. Renshu shifts uneasily in her arms, looking for comfort. Eventually he nods off and Meilin dozes lightly, alert to the sounds of other families nearby.

With daylight, Meilin wakes to find that Longwei is not there. Where has he gone? Across a field, she sees a small village. In the dark last night, they didn't realise how close it was. Wenling and the girls huddle together, still asleep. When Meilin stirs, Renshu wakes. Meilin rubs his cold hands with her own, trying to warm them up.

'Where is Uncle?' he asks, surveying the groups of people struggling along the road, some walking, some riding in carts or rickshaws.

'I'm not sure. He'll be back soon,' Meilin says.

But then he starts in again with his questions: *Where's my yeye? Why did we leave him behind? What happened to the train? Why did we sleep outside? Can we go home?*

Meilin doesn't know how she'll explain any of this to Renshu. How she'll explain any of this to herself. He is quieten for a few moments. Then: 'Where's my monkey puzzle?'

At last, a question she can answer. Meilin finds the puzzle in her basket and gives it to him.

By the time Renshu has counted sixty-seven monkeys, she sees Longwei heading back across the field. He rides with a farmer in a blue cart, pulled by a donkey. Renshu drops the puzzle and runs to meet Longwei. 'Uncle!'

His shout wakes Wenling and the girls. In the stark morning light, Meilin sees that Wenling's face is smudged with traces of old make-up. Wenling reaches for her suitcase and takes out a small mirror and cosmetics case, wiping away yesterday's grime.

Longwei explains that the farmer, Hu, and his donkey will help them. In the cart are a few blankets, bamboo mats to cover the ground, and a bag of sweet potatoes and cabbages.

They eat, then pile their cases on to Hu's cart. The children take turns riding and walking. So it goes. Walking, riding, walking, joining the constant and slow-moving procession of carts, trucks, convoys and people on foot trying to make it to the Chang Jiang. At night, they shelter together near the cart or under trees. When they pass through a village, they venture into the markets to bargain for food. With each day that goes by, feet and tempers become more sore. With each night, the hope of reuniting with Hongtse or anyone else diminishes. Even if the family did survive the fire, how would they ever find them?

It's been a week since they left Changsha. They are not far from the city of Yueyang when a military personnel jeep drives up and an officer gets out to speak with Longwei. The two move out of earshot, but Meilin watches. Longwei's posture is slightly reserved, as if he is sizing up the man and his message. Then Longwei's eyebrows rise and his eyes open wide. She catches the word 'Generalissimo'. Longwei nods vigorously and gestures towards Meilin, Wenling and the children. The officer glances over and shakes his head. Longwei frowns. The officer salutes, gets back into his jeep and waits.

Longwei comes over and says he must go south; he is needed at an important conference in Hengyang. They must continue on without him.

'You're leaving us behind?' Wenling sputters.

His eyes flit towards the waiting jeep. 'It's too dangerous for you to come. You and Meilin go on into Yueyang and wait. I will send someone who can take you to Yichang. I'll join you there after the conference.'

'But what if the city is occupied?' Meilin blurts, saying aloud what they have all been fearing.

'Oh!' Wenling shrieks. 'The Japanese bandits will torture and kill us! You're a selfish bastard to leave your wife and children.' Her voice rises in desperation. 'Take us with you or stay. We need you!'

Longwei draws himself up. 'My country needs me,' he says, in a measured voice.

Wenling and Longwei lock eyes.

'Go,' Wenling finally says, her voice ice cold. Her hair is unkempt and her face sallow. Over the past few days, she has given up trying to put on make-up in the mornings. 'Go get yourself killed and be a dead and useless hero, just like your brother!' She walks away. Lifen follows.

'I have no time for your nonsense, woman!' Longwei shouts after her. Brushing aside her outburst, he pulls his suitcase off the cart. He sorts through a few belongings, then speaks to Hu.

Renshu and Liling have burst into tears, and Meilin hurries to comfort them. She settles the kids on a bamboo mat and gives them the buns she had been saving for today's journey. Their faces are tear-stained and dirty. 'Eat slowly,' she says. 'I'm going to speak with Uncle. Whatever happens, I'll keep you safe. I promise.'

When she approaches Longwei, he turns and looks at her with such intensity that goosebumps rise on her arms. In his hand, he holds a fat envelope of cash.

'Meilin, after I leave, Hu is going to take you to what looks like a deserted donkey track. He'll show you a way through the fields, and then he'll leave. At dawn, take this shortcut into Yueyang and go to this house.' Longwei rests the envelope on his suitcase, draws a rough map of the city on the back, and marks an 'X' on one of the side streets. He adds a name and an address. 'Wait there for an escort.' He hands Meilin the envelope.

Meilin says the name aloud. 'Liu Shufan.'

'Trust me, Meilin. Shufan will look after you.' He says Shufan's name softly.

Meilin glances at Wenling, who stands sulking by a bush. 'Wenling is right. This is madness. You know what the Japanese soldiers did in Nanjing. How can you think this is safe?'

He shakes his head. 'I never said it was safe. But it is our best choice. If I don't go to Hengyang, I will lose this opportunity for all of us.'

'And will you go back to Changsha and look for Hongtse? Will you leave a message for Xiaowen, in case he comes home and can't find us?'

Longwei's expression softens. 'Meilin,' he says gently. 'My father, my brother . . .' His voice tapers off.

Meilin can't bear to think about what he's not saying. 'It's too risky to separate, Longwei. What if something goes wrong? How will we find you in Yichang?'

He studies her, then puts more cash in the envelope. 'Always thinking, aren't you? It will be fine, just wait in Yueyang for the escort. But if something goes wrong, there should be enough here to get you to Yichang, and we can meet at Huangling Temple.'

'When?'

'Two, three weeks? If I get there first, I will wait for you. If you get there first, wait for me.'

He hands her the envelope just as Wenling and Lifen return. The heft of the cash in Meilin's hand is reassuring. It acknowledges an agreement, an understanding, between Meilin and Longwei. Wenling is silent. Longwei tries to reach out to her, but she moves away, refusing his touch. He gives his daughters distracted hugs and Renshu a squeeze.

'Stay together. Promise?' He waits until both Wenling and Meilin nod. 'I will see you in Yichang.'

He picks up his case, and heads over to the jeep.

After Longwei leaves, Meilin relays his instructions to Wenling. She listens without interrupting, but fear and anger spread across her face. When Meilin finishes, Wenling purses her lips into a thin line.

'Fine,' Wenling says. She starts to paw through her suitcase, shaking out and refolding a silk dress, a pair of trousers. She picks up and puts down her hairbrush, then digs out a pair of gloves and pulls them on.

'Big sister, I'm sorry that—'

'Don't.' Wenling cuts her off, holding up a hand but not looking up from her suitcase. 'Don't think that we're friends. Don't think you can fix this horrible situation. Just don't.'

Meilin feels as if she's been slapped. 'Wenling.' Surprised to hear the tremor in her own voice, she steadies herself. Then her anger flares, and in a stronger voice she continues, 'Wenling, the most important thing is to get to Yueyang. We don't have to like each other, but we have to help each other.'

Wenling looks up at Meilin with the attitude of a cornered and furious creature. Meilin doesn't say another word. Wenling rearranges her things once more and closes her case.

That night, Hu leaves them under a large tree, where they wait. In the early hours, when movement along the main road has stilled, they wake the children. Meilin shushes their questions and reassures them they will be fine, feeling the burden of their trust in her. By moonlight, they head silently across the fields.

As they approach Yueyang, Meilin sees that many houses and buildings are flying a Japanese flag. Her heart falls. She motions to Wenling, pointing them out. The city is occupied. Now what?

'Find Liu Shufan,' Wenling mouths.

Meilin nods and pulls out the envelope. Staying within the shadows, they soon find their way to the house.

Meilin draws a deep breath before knocking softly.

They wait.

At first, the woman inside only cracks open the door for long enough to say, 'Go away.'

Meilin tamps down the curl of fear in her belly and knocks again, insisting that Dao Longwei sent them. At this, the door is thrown wide and the woman ushers them in, quickly.

'Dao Longwei, eh?' she says, chuckling to herself. 'That rascal, he knows I'd do anything for him. And which one of you is the wife?'

'I am,' Wenling says.

She looks Wenling up and down. 'Of course you are. He always did love a pretty face.'

Wenling scowls.

'And you?' Shufan asks Meilin.

'He's my brother-in-law.'

'Ah, yes.' Liu Shufan seems to recall something. 'You must be Xiaowen's wife. Longwei spoke of you.'

At the mention of Xiaowen, Meilin's eyes fill. She cannot speak.

'What has happened to the Dao brothers that they would send you here?'

Wenling stammers out an explanation while Meilin holds back her tears.

After fussing over the children, Shufan serves them bowls filled with more rice than they have seen since leaving Changsha. Then, she pours water into a big copper basin and sets it on the stove. They are to have a wash, and afterwards, a rest. While the water heats, she shows them a room whose door is hidden behind a cupboard in the kitchen. In the room are clean straw mattresses covered with coarse, worn cloth. There are no windows, but Shufan lights a small kerosene lamp and the space feels warm and safe. Once everyone is clean and dry, Wenling says she'll stay in the room to settle the children.

Out in the kitchen, Meilin helps Shufan clean up.

'How do you know Longwei?' Meilin asks.

'I've known Longwei for many years.' Shufan looks at Meilin

with an expression that says more than any explanation could. 'We're old friends,' she concludes. When Wenling comes out, all three sit down.

Shufan pours three mugs of tea.

'Did you see anyone when you came through the town this morning?'

Meilin and Wenling both shake their heads.

Shufan stands and goes over to the window. She peeks through the closed curtains. The street has come alive. People are up to feed their animals, set out night soil, get water for the day. 'These damn Kempeitai patrol the streets every morning and afternoon. It's good no one saw you.' She turns to the women, her voice firm. 'As soon as it's dark tonight, I'll show you the path out of Yueyang.'

'But Longwei said to wait with you until the escort arrives to take us to Yichang,' Wenling protests.

Shufan furrows her brow. 'You can rest in the back room. Maybe someone will come for you during the day.' Then she shakes her head and holds up her hands. 'Either way, you can't stay. Once it's dark, you'll need to keep moving.'

Wenling turns pale. Her fury bristles just under the surface. Hands shaking, she puts her tea down and goes into the room with the children.

Meilin turns to Shufan. 'Please, will you let us stay a little longer? I'm certain no one saw us. Longwei will send someone, I know he will.'

'I can't risk compromising the network. Longwei knows that.' Shufan's voice is firm.

Under the table, Meilin tugs at the cuff of her jacket. She wiggles her fingers to loosen the threads and frees a gold coin. She puts it on the table. 'Please.'

Shufan hesitates, then takes the coin. She turns it over in her palm, spits on it and rubs it until it gleams. Finally, she bites it and inspects the tiny dents left behind. Satisfied, she pockets it. 'One extra day only. And then, even if no one has come, you must leave. If you stay any longer, someone will notice. Someone always notices.'

'Of course,' Meilin agrees.

The next day, Shufan goes out early in the morning. Meilin keeps the children amused and quieten in the back room, reassuring them that either someone will come or they will go and find a boat to meet Longwei. Wenling, skittish, hovers around the window. When Shufan returns, she scolds Wenling, fearing she's been seen. The day passes and no escort arrives. Shufan is adamant. They must leave that night. Meilin presses a second coin into Shufan's palm. 'Sister, will you help us get some supplies?'

The two women confer and Shufan leaves the house again. She comes back with fresh bamboo sleeping mats and a padded coverlet for each of them, an enamel pot for washing and cooking rice, second-hand trousers for the children – these are a bit too big, but the extra cloth will be helpful – a small bag of rice, a packet of salt and a bottle of oil.

After two days of rest, warmth and generous meals, it is time to go. Meilin thanks Liu Shufan. Wenling says nothing. At nightfall, they head out of the city, taking a lesser-known donkey path to the road that goes along the Chang Jiang.

Chapter Three

By dawn, they have reached a river town big enough for ships travelling upstream to stop for passengers and supplies.

'I'll see about tickets,' Wenling says, setting off towards the docks.

The children trail behind, tired from walking through the night. After Meilin gives them some breakfast, they become more animated. Liling and Renshu begin to play. Lifen tries to join in, but they ignore her. Anger flashes across Lifen's face. 'I don't want to play your baby game anyway,' she says, and sits, turning her back to them.

Meilin surveys the crowds camped out near the docks. They can't all be waiting for steamboats, can they?

Wenling returns with a gloomy face. 'Boats don't come often, and when they do, there are hardly any tickets.'

'How much do they cost?'

Wenling names an astronomical sum. Meilin hands her Longwei's envelope of cash. Halfway through counting, Wenling stops. There's no way they have enough.

'We'll have to walk,' Meilin says.

'Walk?' Wenling wails. 'All the way to Yichang? How will the children cope?'

Meilin considers her stash of coins and treasures. Wenling must have some, too. If they pooled all their money, would there be enough to buy tickets? And then how would they pay for food or supplies? It's not worth the risk.

'Look at all these people.' Meilin waves at the crowds. 'It would be foolish to wait for a boat that might not even have space for us.'

Despite Wenling's protests, Meilin prevails. They walk. Over the next few days, Meilin and Wenling reach a cold understanding. They have no choice but to rely on one another. Most travellers they pass are families like themselves, but bandits and thieves are never far away. Meilin swings between exhaustion and vigilance, grateful for each day that brings them closer to Yichang and, she hopes, a reunion with Longwei.

The days pass in a blur of towns, villages and countryside. Meilin loses track of how long it has been. They walk past shapes by the side of the road that reek of urine and rot. There are abandoned bundles of soiled clothes, stained mats. They improvise places to sleep, they bargain in markets for small, mouldy sweet potatoes. Though the nights are cold, they don't make any fires after dark, not wanting to attract Japanese planes. Any cooking is done quickly, in the day's early light, making enough for several days' rations.

So it goes: a jade bracelet for a bag of rice, a gold earring for warm lodging, silver coins for oil. Once Longwei's cash is gone, the coins, notes and charms that Meilin had sewn into the jackets and that Wenling, too, had hidden in her belongings emerge to be traded away for the day's necessities.

Sometimes, even if they have money, there is nothing to buy. They take what's left from previous days and mix it with edible roots or leaves they find by the road. Pulled in too many directions, with no relief, Meilin's weariness becomes bone deep. Both Renshu and Liling are constantly sniffling, and Renshu has a hoarse cough. Their cheeks and fingers are red and chapped from the bitter winds. It will be December soon, and on cold, clear nights, the temperature drops. She hopes they can make it to Yichang before the frosts arrive.

'What's that?' Renshu asks one morning near Jingzhou, still many li from Yichang. He points at a group of boys in uniform marching up the road. The youngest ones are not much older than Renshu; the oldest are nearly young men. Each has a small bag slung over his shoulder, and they sing as they march.

'It must be a school,' Meilin says.

She hurries Renshu and Liling closer so she can hear what they are saying. Soon, she catches the words: they are reciting verses from the *San Zi Jing*. Meilin murmurs along with them, saying the familiar triplets. Forming the words on her tongue summons up a different time, a different world. She remembers learning them from her father, a verse at a time, as a child. Part of her wants to reach back in time and become that child again, away from this war, this wandering.

'What are they saying, Auntie?' Liling interrupts her thoughts. 'How do you know the words?'

'It is the *San Zi Jing*. My baba taught me,' Meilin says, almost to herself.

'Teach us, too, Auntie?' Liling asks.

Of course! Why hadn't she thought of it before? They are just the right age to learn this poem.

'We say the *San Zi Jing* three characters at a time. It's a very old poem. Learning it is important. It teaches us morality, history, science and good conduct.'

The children look alarmed.

'Oh, such serious looks! Don't worry, it's not too hard and it's fun. Each day, we'll add a few triplets and soon, you'll know it all by heart.'

'Like you?'

'Like me, and like those boys.' Meilin nods towards the students who are now out of earshot. 'Just repeat after me:

'People at birth.'

'People at birth.'

'Are naturally good.'

'Are naturally good.'

'Their natures are similar.'

'Their natures are similar.'

'Their habits become different.'

'Their habits become different.'

'Again.'

They repeat and repeat, until the first verse has sunk under their tongues. Listening to them, Meilin realises that, in spite of all that has been left behind and all the unknown that lies ahead, they have, in this moment, discovered a small island amid the chaos. She cannot promise them external safety, but she can help them create their own internal reserves of beauty.

Meilin and Wenling both quickly recognise that the school group provides security and the possibility of companionship. For the following days and nights, they stay close to the teachers and students. On nights when the school finds shelter in a barn or abandoned structure, Meilin and Wenling camp nearby. Lifen even befriends a few of the younger students. The teachers don't seem to mind. Perhaps they see how vulnerable the women are. Sometimes Wenling chats with a few of the women in the group. Meilin, grateful for the space, keeps an eye on Renshu and Liling.

Each day, as they get closer to Yichang, Meilin searches the horizon for familiar landmarks. For nearly a week, fog and low clouds have made the distances hard to measure. But this afternoon, the sky is clear, the air is calm, and Meilin can see the ridges of Yellow Ox Mountain rising to the west. They are only a day's walk from Yichang. When the school group stops at a temple for a few extra days, Meilin and Wenling decide to continue alone. They are so close. Surely Longwei will be there and waiting.

The next morning, they start off together. But two or three li down the road, Renshu says he needs to poo. Meilin stops to help him. Wenling, annoyed with the boy, with Meilin, with the entire situation, continues ahead with the girls, refusing to wait.

By the time Meilin realises that Wenling has taken the bag with all their food, they are nowhere in sight. She curses Wenling for her selfish impatience, then curses herself for being so foolish as to put everything in one bag. She should have known that Wenling wouldn't wait. Blinking back tears of frustration, she looks at the hills. At least she knows where she is now. A rebellious thought crosses her mind: she and Renshu could go to her family's compound instead of Yichang. It's not far from here. Wenling can fend for herself.

'Ma?' Renshu tugs at her hand.

'What is it?' she snaps, still annoyed with Wenling.

'What's that noise?' he asks.

'What noise?' she says.

A strange droning overhead cuts the air.

There are shouts. *Run! Take cover!* People start scattering in all directions.

Meilin looks up. A Japanese plane swoops down, its force blowing her hair and clothing back. She would be able to see the gunner's face if it weren't for his goggles. For a moment, she is paralysed with disbelief. Through all the miles and hardship, she had never imagined the Japanese would attack civilians. Is this plane really shooting at her? At Renshu? And yet the *ratatatata-tatat* of machine-gun fire pierces the air.

Chaos abounds. Carts are overturned as people flee, abandoning their belongings.

'Ma!' Renshu's voice snaps her into action.

She shepherds him to the edge of the road and they dive under the cover of the foliage. Meilin pushes him ahead, ignoring the branches scratching along her arms as they bury themselves deeper. Crouched in the leaves, heart pounding in her chest, alert to all movements, she holds him. *Please, please, please, let us survive.*

The plane swings back around, targeting anyone left on the road. A barrage of bullets sprays overhead. Cracking and crashing splinter the air as debris and branches rain down. Renshu screams. Meilin throws herself over her son, shielding him. He trembles underneath her, sobbing.

Again and again, with sickening, merciless indifference, the plane thunders back and forth. *Was this what it was like for Xiaowen in his last moments?* The thought pops into Meilin's mind, bringing to the surface what she has known but has been unwilling to admit. Xiaowen is gone. Fresh grief erupts and she squeezes her eyes shut. Meilin embraces Renshu tighter, praying for the ambush to cease. When it appears no one is left standing, the plane finally flies off.

For several seconds, Meilin doesn't move. Then, slowly, she lifts her head. All is quieten. She shakes off leaves and branches, and stands. Heart racing, legs trembling, breath ragged, she pulls Renshu to his feet. He's shaking and pale with terror, but alive.

'Are you okay? Does it hurt anywhere?' She frantically searches for any injury, any harm to her boy.

He buries himself in her side.

She squeezes his arms and legs, checks his torso, wipes the blood from several small scratches. The feel of his warm limbs in her hands reassures her that he is okay.

They emerge from the bushes. The road is littered with bodies. Bullet holes mark the dirt where they stood only moments ago.

Slowly, Meilin leads Renshu through the wreckage. She almost can't bear to look for Wenling, Lifen and Liling, but knows they must. She has to know if they are unharmed. And if they aren't, if they have suffered the worst, she must get to Yichang to tell Longwei.

'Liling! Liling! Where are you?' Renshu calls and calls until his voice is hoarse and weak.

All around, people are struggling to find their families, struggling to collect what remains of their belongings and continue towards the west. Had the plane attacked a few minutes earlier, or had they gone for the bushes on the other side of the road, they might well have been killed. Meilin knows they are lucky, but she doesn't feel it.

She feels, instead, a profound sense of helplessness. Until now, there was always something she could do to protect Renshu, always some way she could make things a bit better. She has always believed that eventually, everything would be okay. The fire in Changsha? At least they escaped alive. Longwei leaving them behind? There was a plan to meet again. All those days on the road? It was a matter of putting one foot in front of the other. As long as they were moving away from the war and towards Yichang, they would eventually find safety. But she had never dreamed that they themselves would be attacked. She is struck by the sobering realisation that, despite her fierce intentions, she can't promise to always keep Renshu safe.

It shouldn't be this way, she wants to shout. She wants to blame someone. Longwei for leaving them behind, Wenling for being so selfish, the war, the Japanese. A rage begins to boil in her. How could—

Renshu is tugging at her. 'Ma, what's she doing?'

Meilin shakes herself from her anger to see what Renshu is pointing at. A woman holds the body of a young girl in her arms. She shakes the child, crying and cursing.

'Why doesn't the girl wake up?' Renshu asks.

The woman's fatigued face sags with despair. Her wail crescendos into an uncontrollable keening. Renshu grips Meilin's arm, bewildered.

Meilin says, gently, 'The little girl must have died. The bullets must have hurt her too much to get well again.'

Renshu looks up at her. 'Died? But why won't she wake up?'

'She can't. She can't do anything anymore. She's dead.'

His face is solemn. Neither of them knows what to say. They begin walking again.

'Ma?'

'Yes?'

'Does everyone die?'

Meilin bites her lip. These questions. She should have known they would come.

'Yes, Renshu,' she says. 'Everyone does.'

'And what about us? Will we die, too?'

'Someday, yes. We all will.'

'When?'

It takes a minute for Meilin to grasp what he is asking. 'I don't know. No one knows when they will die. But not for a long time, I hope.'

'My baba is dead.'

Meilin stops and puts her basket down. She closes her eyes, covering her mouth with her cold hand. To hear Renshu say this so clearly, so simply, crushes her. Opening her eyes again, she exhales slowly. She takes the sleeping roll from him and sets it on the ground so she sees his face. 'Yes, Renshu, he is. But you must remember that your baba was a good and kind man.' Grasping both his hands, she asks, 'Do you remember him?'

The boy's eyes fill and he shakes his head.

That Renshu no longer remembers Xiaowen hurts more than any cold or ache she's ever known. A terrible, raw emptiness eats at her last reserves of fortitude. She squeezes his hands, then rubs them with hers, trying to warm up his fingers.

'What about Yeye? Is Yeye dead?'

Meilin thinks of the flames, the night of the fire. She nods.

'What about Liling? And Auntie and Lifen? Uncle? Are they all dead, too?' An avalanche of fears tumbles from his lips, and Meilin cannot stop them. 'Everyone is dead? Everyone is dead!' Renshu shrieks. He won't calm down, he can't calm down. Meilin can't bear to hear his words. What if they are true?

'Stop it! Stop it!' Meilin lashes out, slapping him before she realises what she's doing.

He freezes mid-sentence. Two, then three seconds pass, and he begins to bawl again. Meilin wants to cry, too.

'I'm so sorry.' She gathers him into her arms to calm him. His arms and back feel bony through his thin padded jacket. His hair, matted and dull, hangs in his face, and his cheeks are gaunt. What has happened to her chubby, giggling troublemaker who rushed through the courtyards in Changsha?

The glowing embers of a small fire, left behind by other travellers, catch her attention. An idea occurs to Meilin. Though only a small thing, it feels like a wellspring of hope after days of despair. She nudges Renshu towards the fading coals and they warm their hands. Meilin unrolls their bedroll on the cold, packed dirt and sits. She pats the soft cloth next to her, motioning for Renshu to sit, too.

'This,' she gestures at the landscape around them, scarred with burned fields and abandoned, bombed-out structures, the river crowded with boats of all sizes heading upstream, and people walking with forlorn burdens, 'this is just one scene. It's like our scroll. We can only unroll it one scene at a time. We have to keep going to see what the next one is.'

He sinks to the ground, his sobs lessening into sniffs and hiccups.

She opens her basket and reaches for the scroll. When she opens its box, she almost bursts into tears to see the bright red tassels she'd fastened with such care on their last night in Changsha. In the past, she never would have touched the scroll with unwashed hands, but right now, she runs her fingers along its length. The fine threads of the peonies on the silk casing are a comforting caress. That this treasure is intact, untouched by all the wreckage around her, feels like a message from Xiaowen. Although he is dead, he is not gone.

She unrolls the scroll to show a flourishing farm and a nobleman with a grey beard sitting astride a stallion. Renshu leans into her, looking at the horse. She knows this is one of his favourite scenes on the scroll.

'There was once an old man from the frontier who had a great stallion,' she begins. 'It was dark brown, glossy and strong, with a long black mane and a wild look in its eye. It was known to be the most gallant horse in all the neighbouring towns and villages.' As she tells the story, she feels herself relaxing into its rhythms, letting the images carry her away, however briefly, from her own despair.

'Everyone said he must be the luckiest man to have such a noble beast. It was the envy of all. But one day, the stallion ran away. Of course, everyone said this was a great tragedy. What terrible luck!'

Renshu groans in sympathy.

'But the old man didn't despair. Instead, he said, "What makes you so certain this isn't a blessing?" A few weeks later, the stallion came galloping back home, followed by a beautiful wild mare. Soon, there was a colt. The three magnificent creatures brought pride and prosperity to the man. Everyone said this was cause for great celebration. But the old man said, "What makes you so certain this isn't a curse?" The villagers couldn't believe he'd say such a thing, but a few days later, the man's only son fell while riding the stallion and broke his leg. With the harvest coming in soon, this doubled the old man's work in the fields. "Oh, such misfortune!" said the villagers. But the old man said—'

' "What makes you so certain this isn't a blessing?" ' Renshu finishes.

'Yes, that's exactly what he said,' Meilin smiles. 'Not long after, a battle broke out between neighbouring warlords, and all the men in the village had to go to fight. Except for the old and the infirm. Because of his broken leg, the man's son was spared. The fight was bloody and vicious. None of the men who went came back. It was only because the man was old and his son was lame that they survived to take care of each other for many years.' Meilin pauses for a moment. 'Within every misfortune there is a blessing, and within every blessing, the seeds of misfortune. And so it goes, until the end of time.'

'But Ma, what's the blessing in all this?' Renshu stares at the swarms of people, the wagons, and the tired donkeys and oxen trudging along.

Meilin is quieten for several moments as she rolls up the scroll and reassembles her basket. They both get to their feet. She rerolls the bedroll and helps Renshu put it on his back. She dusts off her trousers and picks up her basket.

'I don't know,' she says, finally. 'I'm still looking.'

Maybe the blessing is that she is close to home. Maybe it is that she has found, through the scroll, a way to connect Renshu with Xiaowen once more. Maybe it is that, soon, the road makes a few bends, and Meilin sees a city wall. Yichang.

Chapter Four

Once in the city, Meilin heads towards Huangling Temple. If they find Longwei, she'll have to tell him they all got separated in the attack. But maybe Wenling and the girls will be there already? Maybe they will be safe. And if no one is there? Maybe it's a terrible blessing. Maybe Meilin will take Renshu to her family's compound in the hills. She will go home.

As they get closer to the temple, Meilin feels the pull of her family's antique shop. It's on the way. She knows her family is gone, but she wants to see it.

'What are we doing?' Renshu asks once they are standing outside the shop.

A massive chain secures the handles of the wooden doors. Meilin peers through the windows, dusty from neglect. Inside, the shelves are empty, the walls are bare, a few stray pieces of paper litter the floor. It is the very same space where she spent childhood days listening to her grandmother's stories, where she learned how to differentiate between the fine and the mediocre, and where she met and fell in love with Xiaowen. Though she knows her family left for safety months ago, she could never have imagined that it would look so cold and soulless without the bustle of her parents and all the treasures inside.

'Just looking,' Meilin says. She glances up at the rooms above, where she and her family had lived. The windows are shuttered and there's no sign of life.

'Do we know who lives here?' Renshu asks.

'No, not anymore,' she murmurs.

She takes his hand in hers and they continue on to the temple.

*

They arrive at dusk. Though there are many people sitting on the steps, and even more sheltering inside, none is their family. After buying some sweet potatoes from a vendor, they eat, and fall asleep, exhausted, on the temple steps.

Through the night, Meilin keeps waking, adrenaline pulsing through her limbs. Several times, Renshu cries out in fear, babbling about the plane. Each time, she soothes him back to sleep and stays awake, watchful, until her bleary eyes finally close.

'Renshu! Auntie!'

Meilin shakes herself. She must still be asleep.

'Renshu! Wake up, it's me!'

He rubs his eyes. 'Liling!' he shouts, and jumps up, hugging her. 'I thought you were dead,' he says.

'Dead? No, no we're not dead. We're with Baba!'

Meilin is not dreaming. It is Liling. Her niece is there, messy pigtails and all. And coming up the steps, just behind her, is Longwei.

Longwei looks at both Meilin and Renshu as if drinking after a long thirst. Renshu runs over and Longwei gathers him in his arms. The boy rests his head on his uncle's chest.

Longwei looks strong, filling out his smart suit. His face is full of colour and health, as if he has been thriving over the past month. Meilin feels teary, and her cheeks grow warm. She hadn't expected such emotion. She glances down at his feet: new leather boots.

'Meilin,' he says, putting Renshu down and extending a hand to help her up.

She rises, but she doesn't take his hand. 'Big brother,' she replies, dipping her chin, but not lowering her gaze. 'How long have you been here?'

'Nearly a week. I've been coming to the temple every day, hoping against hope that you'd appear. When I heard that you left Yueyang without the escort, I despaired. I could only imagine the worst. But when I got here, I resolved to wait a week, even two. Yesterday, I found Wenling and the girls. They said you got separated on the road.'

'Where are Wenling and Lifen? Are they safe?' In her relief and gladness at seeing Longwei, she forgets her anger.

'They are at the guesthouse, resting.' His voice wavers, and he pauses. 'I knew you'd come. I knew you'd make it, Meilin.'

He motions again for her to take his hand.

She relents and grasps it.

'Come,' he says, walking down the steps, 'let's go to the guesthouse.'

At the guesthouse, there is fresh rice and fish, hot tea, and oranges for them all. After giving Renshu a hot bath, Meilin rubs him dry with a coarse cloth towel, gaping at the dark grey water left behind in the metal tub. His hair is slick and his cheeks glow for the first time in weeks. Exhausted and relieved, he sleeps through that afternoon and into the night.

Wenling is thinly kind and says she's glad they are all safe. After a night at the guesthouse, her face is freshly washed and made-up, but she can't conceal the shadows under her eyes. She doesn't apologise for leaving Meilin and Renshu behind. She explains that since Meilin said they were so close to Yichang, she thought they would be fine. And after the attack, she just wanted to get the girls to safety. Halfway through her excuses, Meilin stops listening. She has no energy to be angry, and anyway, it doesn't matter. They are all together again.

Longwei reports that his meeting at Hengyang went well. Meilin wonders if that is a blessing or a curse. With his promotion and new responsibilities, he assures them, they can all travel together up the Chang Jiang to Chongqing. He promises that they will have a place to stay, schools for the children, some stability.

In the morning, Longwei goes out to make arrangements for the next leg of their journey. When he returns, he produces silk stockings and cosmetics for Wenling, mooncakes for the children, and a bolt of dark blue silk for Meilin. He says there will be space on a boat for them the next day.

That night, Meilin holds the silk to her cheek, its smooth weave comforting and soft against her skin. She thinks of what she can make with it: a new lining for her jacket, warm undershirts for Renshu. Every scrap will patch something torn or broken. She thinks of her earlier impulse to return to her family. Now, she wavers. She doesn't know for sure if her parents are at the family compound. Renshu is only four and so fatigued already by the journey from Changsha. Could he make the additional trip up the hills in the winter weather? What if they arrive and no one is there? As much as she longs for her family, right now it is safer to stay with Longwei. She'll come back to Yichang later. Maybe by springtime, the war will be over. It will be warmer, Renshu will be bigger and stronger, and they can find her family then.

Chang Jiang, westbound, Hubei and Sichuan Provinces, China, December 1938

At the docks, workers load factory machinery and equipment on to a small steamer. Abandoned possessions lie scattered around, left behind to make room for more passengers. There are abandoned people, too, who have run out of resources and influence. Refugees have poured into Yichang from across the troubled eastern provinces. They come on the river in boats big and small, in steamers, junks and sampans. They come on foot, through the mountains, on the roads, looking as weary as Meilin feels. A few arrive in trucks or cars. Everyone wants to get to the new capital, Chongqing. To get there, everyone has to go through Yichang, this bottleneck of desperation.

At Yichang, the Chang Jiang changes its nature from a wide and generous waterway to a snaking, treacherous river that winds between the Dabashan and Wushan mountain ranges, sudden cliffs and gorges rising from its banks.

The family boards an old junk. The sailors raise and lower the tattered and patched sail, tugging it back and forth, trying to harness the wind when it blows helpfully and to streamline their momentum when it doesn't. Along with the captain and oarsmen, there is only enough room for a few dozen passengers, who gather under a sheltered area at the back. When Wenling baulked at the size and condition of the boat, Longwei barked that they were lucky to get tickets. Her other option would be walking through the mountains. Meilin thinks to herself how quickly the couple's warm reunion has cooled as Wenling retreats into her customary sulk.

The passengers huddle under the shelter, where the roof is too low to stand upright. Meilin is queasy. Wenling and Lifen both look green. The younger children stumble and fall back down each time they try to stand. At first, it is a game – who can stay upright the longest? – but soon the waters toss the boat too roughly and they only sit, clinging to each other. When the boat tips or jags, belongings slide across the floor and everyone scrambles to retrieve them. The other travellers keep to themselves, squatting low or sitting on bamboo mats wrapped around coverlets and blankets.

After a few hours, Meilin stands and staggers towards the opening. She needs fresh air; it is too close in the hold. She steadies herself and works her way towards the front. At least outside she will be able to see what is coming, instead of feeling victim to unpredictable waves.

'Welcome to the Gates of Hell,' says one of the oarsmen as she emerges. The brightness outside dazzles her, and she feels both dizzy and blind until her eyes adjust.

'Xiling Gorge,' he says, as she turns her head from side to side.

Looking up, Meilin sees a sliver of sky framed between two tall cliffs. Around them, rocks jut out from the banks and the riverbed like teeth, threatening to puncture the boat's wooden sides. Whirlpools froth on either side. Icy waters toss the boat up, down, up, down. Although it seemed bright when she first came outside, Meilin soon sees that they are deep in shadow down in this gorge.

'How long does it take to get to Chongqing?' she asks.

He guffaws. 'What, are you weary already?'

'How long?' she repeats.

He squints up the river, shrugs. 'Depends on the water, the traffic, the weather – so many factors. Maybe three weeks, maybe five?'

Five weeks? Right then, the captain shouts and the oarsman turns back to work. Meilin steadies herself and heads back into the hold, glad there are still many verses of the *San Zi Jing* left to teach Renshu and Liling.

A few hours later, the junk bumps up against the bank, under the shelter of trees. The sun has set and little light is left. They will stay here for the night. Too wave-tossed and nauseous to eat or rest, too frightened to ask questions, they pass the night, rocking in the side currents.

When morning comes, whatever sleep anyone found is chased away by feet pounding the deck outside the shelter. 'Out! Out! Everyone out! Get your things and get off!'

Confusion spreads through the hold. Dazed, passengers collect their belongings in the dim light.

'Out!' the crewmen repeat, rapping on the wall to wake anyone still sleeping.

Outside, they explain that because it is winter, the water is low. The passage is especially tight in this section. River trackers will pull the boat through, but all passengers must traverse a footpath along the cliffs and meet the boat further upstream. In the cold dawn, fingers numb and bodies aching, they follow the crew, determination propelling them forward, up, up and around.

The path is not too long, but there are many other boats ahead of theirs – gunboats, small steamers, sampans, fishing vessels – so they must wait. Meilin sits, Renshu dozing at her side, watching the river trackers balanced on the precarious walkway cut into the cliff edge.

The trackers strain against the current, towing the boats, step by precarious step, over the rocky shallows below. Over years of this dragging, their ropes have cut deep grooves into the rock. They lean forward, their chests almost parallel to the ground, hands grasping at the sides of the cliffs to wrench themselves forward. Some wear turbans around their heads. Despite the cold, most are naked, sweat steaming from their toiling shoulders. *Hey zo, hey zo*, they chant, their muscled legs working in tandem.

Eventually, one tracker loses his footing on a slippery section.

He doesn't release his harness quickly enough and the three trackers attached to the same rope are pulled down with him. The group of four is lost, whirling white waters consuming them and carrying them away. Meilin cries out, shielding Renshu. The other trackers pause briefly, but no one stops. They cannot risk it; they must carry on. Startled awake, Renshu asks what happened. Meilin shakes her head, says it was nothing.

When their boat is ready again, they board somberly. The danger isn't over, it never is, but at least they have passed through Xiling Gorge.

Gradually, the river widens and slows. Every few days, the boat stops at small villages where farmers sell dried fish and oranges. Range after range of the Wu Mountains appears and disappears in the mists to either side. When the mists lift, they leave dustings of snow high up in the hills. *Ma, it's like the mountains on our scroll*, Renshu whispers one morning. *Yes*, she murmurs, *it is*.

A few weeks into the journey, as has become their habit, Renshu and his ma stand on the deck in the fresh air, watching the water.

Renshu loves looking for interesting shapes among the stone cliffs. He spots a pair of peaks that he says look like wolf ears. His ma points at a rock column, seeing a graceful goddess that keeps watch on the valley below. He's squinting, trying to see this too, when Liling runs up, her face tear-stained. Her ma must be cross again. Since getting on the boat, Auntie is always scolding Liling, telling her she is naughty or too wild. Whenever her ma shouts at her, Liling comes to Renshu and his ma.

'Liling, come watch the river with us,' his ma says.

Ahead sits a small city on a hill. Unlike many of the other riverside villages they have passed, this one rises from a bit of land that reaches out towards the water. 'White Emperor City,' announces the captain. 'White Emperor City is the home of poets and heroes. Centuries ago, Li Bai and Du Fu lived there when they wrote some of their most famous poems.'

'And,' a low voice adds, 'this is where the great Zhuge Liang is honoured.' Renshu grins to see that Uncle has joined them. Soon, Longwei is telling Liling and Renshu age-old tales of the

Three Kingdoms. They howl with glee at the story of Zhuge Liang winning 100,000 arrows with twenty straw boats. Ma says she's heard these old stories of blood brothers, treachery and trickery too many times. But Renshu can tell she still enjoys them by the way she watches Uncle. Liling and Renshu giggle at the scary faces he makes, and everyone cheers when he raises his voice in song, booming out across the water. At the end, Renshu and Liling beg for more, but Uncle says not now, maybe later.

'I can tell you a story about bravery. Real bravery,' Ma says to the children, as Uncle strides to the edge of the boat and joins a group of men smoking cigarettes and sharing a bottle of brandy.

'Real bravery?' Liling echoes.

'It's a story about serpents.' Ma opens her basket. From the bottom section, she lifts the wooden, rectangular box. The hand scroll. Renshu grasps Liling's hand and jumps about, excited. The two children crowd around Meilin to look more closely. As his ma unrolls from the left and rerolls from the right, the figures on the scroll are even more enchanting than Renshu remembers. He can almost hear the cormorants screeching above the painted fishermen as they dip their oars into the water. In a hunting scene, he is certain he feels the thunder of a stallion's hooves. Liling exclaims again and again with delight at each detail she discovers. The flowers! The birds! The colours of the mountains!

Finally, his ma pauses at a scene showing houses, gardens and temples nestled in foothills. 'Once, in this small village,' she begins, gesturing at the scroll, 'there was a girl named Li Chi.' She looks thoughtfully at Liling. 'Her name was not so very different from yours, Liling. Maybe her nature wasn't, either.

'Li Chi was the sixth daughter of a poor farmer who lived in a village below the Yung Mountains. Way up near the mountain peak, there lived a fearsome serpent. One night, he appeared in all the villagers' dreams and demanded that he be given a thirteen-year-old maiden every year on the eighth day of the eighth month. Otherwise, he would ransack the entire village.

'Naturally, everyone lived in fear of the beast. So the village magistrates took it upon themselves to sacrifice the daughters of crooks and thieves. Over nine years, nine young girls were given to the greedy serpent. But on the eve of the eighth day of the eighth month of the tenth year, Li Chi went to her parents and said, "Let me be the one who goes to the serpent. You have more daughters than you need and the magistrates will give you a small sum for me, as you are neither crooks nor thieves." '

Liling, listening intently, leans closer onto Meilin's lap.

'Do you see Li Chi?' Meilin asks.

Renshu points to a girl standing apart from where the children are playing. A dog sits by her side. Liling points to a solitary figure in a cape, heading up the mountain path.

Renshu nudges his ma to continue.

'Well, of course, Li Chi's parents said no! But Li Chi, though the youngest and the smallest, was also the bravest and most stubborn of all her sisters. She went to the magistrates anyway. "As my parents are neither crooks nor thieves, will you give them a small sum for me?" The magistrates agreed.

'The next day, Li Chi headed up into the mountains with a sharp sword, a snake-fighting dog, and a basket of sweetened rice balls. She was frightened, but she was also determined. These two feelings always go hand in hand.'

'When Li Chi reached the mouth of the cave, she spread the rice balls on the ground and called out, "Oh Serpent, don't you want to eat these delicious rice balls before you devour me?"'

'The serpent, that gluttonous beast, came rushing to the front of the cave and lowered his head to gobble the rice balls. And at that instant, Li Chi released her snarling dog. He leapt and sank his teeth into the back of the serpent's neck. Caught off guard, the serpent reared up in pain and surprise. Seizing her chance, Li Chi drove her sword into the serpent's chest, deep and true. The serpent howled and writhed and moaned, until finally he collapsed at her feet.'

'Hooray!' shouts Renshu.

Liling's eyes are as big as the full moon. 'Then what?'

Ma's voice becomes a whisper. 'After she was sure the serpent was dead, Li Chi crept into his cave. Pew-ee! It smelled terrible! And in the very back, she found nine skulls lined up along the wall. "Oh my darlings," she said, picking up each one in turn, "for your timidity you were devoured. How pitiful!" Then she retrieved her sword and her dog, and marched down the mountain, back to her family and the grateful villagers. After much celebration, she was lauded as a heroine for ages to come.'

Renshu and Liling clap, happy with the tale.

'Oh my darlings,' says Meilin to the children, 'whatever serpents wait ahead for us, let us be bold like Li Chi.' She gives each a kiss on the head and rolls up the scroll, tucking it back into the bottom of her basket.

Later, as the boat continues towards Chongqing, under the cover of darkness, Meilin stands once more on the deck and looks upriver. It's been days since she's heard the drone of a plane or the squeal of air-raid sirens. The mountain peaks have become a little less dramatic, like the hackles of a fighting dog that has lain down. They have travelled so far, they must be safer. She cannot imagine the enemy making it this far. Yet even if the cliffs and gorges hide their boat from Japanese planes, the river is a dragon that breathes its own rushing, crushing rapids. While not an enemy, it can be just as dangerous. Even in peacetime, travelling through the gorges is precarious. Her plan to return and look for her parents in the spring now seems naive. Foolish, even. Meilin wonders if she was mistaken to hesitate in Yichang, if she should have taken the opportunity then. Had she, like Li Chi's darlings, been too timid?

Chapter Five

They arrive in Chongqing to find a city shrouded in cold and mist. The buildings, piled on top of each other, cling to the sides of the hilly Yuzhong peninsula. If the land were to shrug its shoulders, everything would tumble into the rivers below.

Nearly three months after fleeing Changsha, it is not so much relief as numbness that Meilin feels, stepping off the junk and gazing at what must be hundreds of steep steps leading from Chaotianmen dock up to the streets. Everywhere among stacks of crates and luggage stand new arrivals as dazed and travel-worn as she. They mix with beggars in rags hoping for handouts and hawkers shouting in an unfamiliar dialect. Porters with bulging shoulders and calves climb up and down the steps in a steady stream. They haul everything imaginable, from sedan chairs holding those who will not or cannot walk, to baskets overflowing with goods and equipment, to creaking bamboo shoulder poles laden with buckets of water, splashing with every step.

A young man in a soldier's uniform and a cloth cap comes to greet Longwei. After a brief exchange, he signals to a porter to transport their cases up the steps. Meilin carries her basket herself. The young man leads them up winding passageways to a small flat in one of the hillside houses. There are three rooms: one for Longwei, Wenling and the girls, a smaller one for Meilin and Renshu, and a third that functions as kitchen, wash area and common space. There is a tub filled with water, a table with two long benches, and three small kerosene lamps. Though it is smaller than the servants' quarters in the compound at Changsha, Meilin is grateful. These are rooms, not barns, shacks or makeshift shelters under trees. Despite the cold draughts from outside and the racket and cooking odours from the surrounding flats, it is infinitely better than the dank and close hold of the junk.

That night, Meilin tries to sleep, but when she closes her eyes, she feels like she's still on the water. Renshu is fitful, starting at every scuttle in the walls or thump from above. When he finally slumbers, Meilin lies on her back, flattened with exhaustion. A whispered but fierce argument between Longwei and Wenling in the next room penetrates the walls.

'What good is this so-called promotion of yours if we have to live in a squalid flat in this backward, dirty city? There are rats in the walls, and bugs crawling along the floors.'

'You have a place to live. We have water, food, warmth.'

'Can't we at least live somewhere with electricity instead of this filthy hovel?'

'All you do is complain. We are fortunate. I need to be here for my job.'

'Your job? What is your job? You say you're not a soldier, but military personnel turn up wherever we go. Are you an officer? Why don't you have a uniform? Are you a spy? I don't even know who you are!'

'Enough, woman!' he hisses. 'You should be grateful I provide. If you're so miserable, leave.'

Just then, one of the girls cries out, waking from a bad dream. Meilin hears Wenling cross the room to calm the child. Eventually the room quiets.

In the cold, under a thin coverlet, Meilin puts her hand on Renshu, and the rise and fall of his back lulls her to sleep.

Once they have settled in, Meilin writes to her parents. Her letter is short: she says they are safe in Chongqing, Renshu is growing. She misses them and hopes to see them soon. While there's no guarantee that a letter will reach anyone in China, she still writes. Not writing would be giving up.

Longwei never does explain his work, but it is clear he has made himself useful to the Kuomintang. As shady as ever, he comes, he goes. Sometimes he's away for days at a time. Whatever his role, no one bothers them in these rooms. Each morning, a porter brings buckets of fresh water for the day. Longwei is always able to produce what the family needs: rice, salt, oil, cash.

In the periphery of Meilin's days, an immense grief looms. The grand, collapsed visions for her life with Xiaowen, their dreams of a thriving business and family, of China growing into democracy. Her sadness comes in smaller ways, too. She mourns the absence of Hongtse's brusque kindness, the sight of Renshu's hand in Xiaowen's, the daily ritual of closing up shop and updating her ledgers. The shadow of her loss is so overwhelming that she fears if she looked at it directly, it would engulf her. She cannot allow it to overcome her – there is too much to do to keep everyone fed, safe and well.

In truth, she welcomes the distractions of shopping, cooking and washing. After only a few visits to the market, Wenling now refuses to help with errands, saying the noise and stench give her headaches, so Meilin leaves her sister-in-law to mope in the flat and criticise her daughters. Initially, Meilin is sapped by handling so many tasks herself. She feels unused to such physical labour, and is still exhausted from their long journey. But with time, Meilin comes to relish the freedom of being out in the bustling city and away from Wenling's misery.

In March, the Japanese troops advance to Nanchang. As refugees continue to flee to the interior, housing in Chongqing becomes even more limited. Hastily built structures made of wooden boards and bamboo held together with wire and mud spring up. Meilin feels less and less like a newcomer. She now knows the streets and alleyways of the Yuzhong peninsula, and has begun to pick up the Sichuanese dialect. In the market, she recognises the faces of her favourite sellers, and she thinks they recognise her, too. Even Wenling has found a few shops set up by relocated Shanghai families that keep her satisfied with magazines and small luxuries.

Renshu doesn't mind the chaos and noise of Chongqing. He likes the new voices, languages and smells. He likes the roads that lead up to steps, around and about into unexpected doorways. Every turn holds a surprise, a different family, a different dwelling.

Though still foggy and overcast, some days are warm enough

that Renshu and Liling can go with his ma to the market. Ma works her way through the stalls, in search of the day's best bargains. Renshu and Liling trail behind, carrying her cabbage greens, onions and fruit. Once, they almost lose her after pulling faces at a baby boy riding in a basket on his ma's back. A sharp, peppery smell tingles Renshu's nose whenever they pass the bamboo vats as big as he is, filled with chopped chillies, garlic and Sichuan peppers. When his ma lets him taste a tiny bite of the chilli paste, the spices catch in his throat and he howls, not yet used to the fiery foods of Chongqing.

Other times, they spend afternoons with Uncle Longwei in the park. He stops to buy cigarettes and chat with the seller, who has a peacock named Man Zi. Many other children gather around to gawk at the bird. Renshu and Liling join in as everyone clucks and coos, trying to get Man Zi to show his brilliant tail. When he does, they cheer and he flutters. The best treasure to find in the park, on the paths or under the bushes, is one of Man Zi's plumes.

After stocking up on his smokes, Uncle crosses over to the mahjong games. Clusters of men guffaw at jokes that Renshu doesn't understand. A constant percussion of hacking and spitting rises above the cigarette smoke, the shuffling and stacking of tiles on tables. Renshu and Liling keep an eye out for Old Catfish. Bald on top, with long, silver whiskers, he hovers over the table, belching and rubbing his belly. Whenever he's around, he fumbles in the pockets of his too-tight jacket and tosses the children a few coins. They rush to the mahua vendor nearby to buy long twists of fried dough. Hours pass while Uncle shares cigarettes and news.

Renshu's favourite days are when Uncle takes them down to Chaotianmen to meet the weary new arrivals, wobbly legged on the long flights of steps. There is always something to see. Steamers, junks and sampans docking and embarking, the workers loading and unloading, builders repairing sails, hammering new siding on to wooden boats. Near the tip of the peninsula, Renshu and Liling stand and watch the muddy brown Chang Jiang mix with the fast-moving jade-green current of the Jialing.

Although it's only been a few months, it seems ages since they arrived. Even further away is the memory of the cold winter on the road. Spring is coming, the fogs are lifting, and Renshu has stopped being scared at night.

It is the beginning of May, a day full of sun, with a promise of spring blossom in the air. Meilin has finished her shopping and, because the weather is so glorious, she agrees to stop by the park. Renshu wants to show her Man Zi and, as always, he hopes he'll be lucky enough to find a feather. On the way, they linger outside a newly built bank, where Renshu admires a black rickshaw with gold trim. Meilin dismisses the painful thought that, had the war not come, he would have always travelled in such style. Maybe when this is all over, they will again.

'Ma, a red ball!' Renshu points up at something outside the bank.

Meilin looks. It is not a ball, but a red lantern. At the corner, another red lantern is hoisted up a pole. All along the street, more and more lanterns appear.

In the clear sky, Meilin can see a dark 'V', like birds in strict formation. Dismay spreads through her body. The Japanese have reached Chongqing.

On the street, the crowds are dispersing. An air-raid siren begins its wail: low and slow at first, then building in pitch and volume until it reaches an ear-splitting shriek. It stops to reset and starts again, insistent. It's too loud. The helplessness and fear she'd felt during the strafing attack outside Yichang, absent for months, now return and overwhelm her. She can't think. She can't move. People are running past, *hurry, hurry, take cover.* Now the planes are so near she can see the brilliant red circles on their wings. Shop doors are closing. Shutters rattle down. Renshu begins to whimper. A man carrying a toddler shakes Meilin's shoulder, breaking her paralysis. He gestures down the street. *Go to the Great Tunnel. The Shibati gate is over there.* With her basket in one hand and Renshu's fingers clasped in the other, she follows. They descend a staircase that disappears into the ground just as the gates clang shut behind them.

A whistling shears the air, wind gusting at their backs. Then, a deafening explosion. Renshu screams and Meilin pulls him closer. The ground trembles. Inside the tunnel, bare light bulbs flicker and sway. Frightened eyes gleam in the light. More whistling and echoing explosions. Again and again. The lights blink once more, then go out. All around, people are crying and shouting. Renshu begins to sob. Meilin wraps her arms around him. Skin to skin, she tries to soothe him, soothe herself. She tries to rub away the sickening sense of defeat. This mountain city was supposed to protect them. They had been so safe. In the dark, tears slip down Meilin's face. They wait. She loses all sense of time. The walls of the tunnel weep too, releasing moisture. Has it been minutes? Hours?

Occasionally, a torch or candle flashes in the darkness. The tunnel is dotted with the red glow of cigarettes producing too much smoke. The air is sour with the reek of garlic and tobacco. People push and jostle, trying to make more room. Renshu coughs and Meilin tries to breathe through her mouth. The thunderous explosions don't relent.

All around Renshu, fingers poke, hands grope, knees knock into his legs. Other people's hips and bellies bump too close to his neck, his ears. He can't breathe. His head hurts and he feels dizzy. He wants to get out of this tunnel. Someone shouts that the doors are open, and people scramble to get outside. Someone shoves him from behind, and Renshu loses his ma's hand. A wave of people carries him away from her.

'Ma! Ma!' His shouts are lost in a crush of shoulders and elbows.

The instant Meilin feels Renshu's hand drop away, she starts shaking. Panic shoots down her arms. If she can't get to him, he will be trampled. She pushes back against the surge. People curse and push and move around her. She doesn't hear them. She must find Renshu. Nothing matters more.

There! He has fallen. She kneels to get him. He has fainted.

She lifts him and carries him, stumbling forward, now moving with the motion of the crowd, until they are finally, finally outside. Clutching Renshu, she crumples against a wall, gulping in big lungfuls of air.

*

Dusk has dulled the sky, but flames burn brightly in every direction. Sulphur curls around piles of rubble. Cinders float by. People emerge from shelters in stunned silence, walking slowly. Cries begin to rise from every direction as loss after loss is discovered. Some hurry towards the sounds of distress to help dig out those buried in debris; others wander in disbelief, choking and coughing. Although the sirens are silent and bombs no longer whistle down, there's a constant crackle of flames, punctuated by the splintering creak and crash of collapsing buildings.

Entire blocks have been demolished. Craters as wide as houses mark where the bombs exploded. Among the wreckage are fragments of snapped furniture, overturned tables, flattened bookshelves. Shopfronts wobble, their facades cheerfully advertising cigarettes or tailoring. Behind lie only piles of broken masonry and shattered glass.

A few blocks away, in the middle of the street, they see the fancy rickshaw again, overturned. One of the wheels is still spinning, squeaking. The black lacquer and gold trim is spattered with blood, dust and bits of white and pink. Meilin nearly retches. She swallows back her nausea and drags Renshu away before he can see what she has: a hand attached to an arm attached to no body.

In the park, the cigarette seller's stand is an ash heap. When Renshu sees the scattered peacock plumes but no sign of Man Zi, he again bursts into tears.

Back in their rooms, Meilin has never been so relieved to see Longwei, Wenling and the girls. Somehow, they, too, have survived. Longwei says they sheltered in another public tunnel, closer to home. While Wenling complains about how uncomfortable, dark and dirty it was, Meilin despairs. How could the Japanese have made it all this way? Through the winter and early spring, the fogs and mists were so thick they'd kept the skies quieten. She had begun to believe they might have escaped it all. She'd trusted they'd be safe in the interior. Now where is there left to run?

Through the night, the city blazes and no one sleeps.

The next morning dawns clear and bright. It is the anniversary of the May Fourth Revolution. Of all days, today is one to celebrate the Republic, the spirit of the Chinese people. Meilin rallies. Determined to find something to brighten the family's day, she and Renshu head back to the market. Meilin is heartened to see that the shops which are still standing raise their shutters and open their doors. In the streets, people are clearing the rubble, speaking of resilience.

At five o'clock, the air-raid sirens start up once more. *Again?* Meilin despairs. In the sky, a swarm of flies approaches. The optimism of moments before is crushed. Meilin and Renshu shelter with the family in the public tunnel closest to the flat. They endure the raid by repeating verses of the *San Zi Jing*, over and over. Even Wenling joins in.

Finally, the weather turns cloudy. A respite from the bombings follows. The days are spent looking for survivors, helping the wounded, pumping water to put out fires. Monks from Arhat Temple circulate among the debris, chanting, conducting rituals for the dead. Carts and baskets fill with limbs. Bodies are laid out in neat rows, so that people can recognise loved ones. Only a few are claimed and taken away for proper burial. More are left, and soon maggots nest and feast on the rotting flesh. In the depths of night, when the streets are empty, rats and vermin scurry.

The clear skies of summer become an invitation for more Japanese planes, and Meilin loses track of the days they spend crouched underground. When autumn comes, while it's clear the war is far from over, Chongqing has become a city of resistance, and somehow life continues. Wenling and Longwei enrol the girls in boarding school in Shapingba, a neighbourhood about fifteen miles away. Wenling pleads to move to Shapingba too, but Longwei refuses. They are lucky to have the rooms they do, he says. She always expects too much, she's never satisfied, he grumbles. When Longwei suggests that Renshu go to school too, Meilin protests that he's only five. She'll teach him herself. What she doesn't say is that she hates becoming even more beholden to Longwei. She's never sure when his goodwill might run out, or if he's expecting something in exchange for all his munificence. Is his charity still an act of filial piety, honouring his lost father and brother? *Family stays together*, he says. But she doesn't trust him. She knows too little about where he spends his days.

Soon Wenling befriends some of the mothers at the girls' school. They are wives of bankers, businessmen and high-ranking officials. Wenling begins taking a sedan chair to their houses in Shapingba a few times a week to gossip or play mahjong, claiming she needs to be near the girls, and frequently stays the night.

Meilin, too, has made new friends among her favourite vendors in the Shibati market. There's Auntie Deng and Uncle Liang, who bring in beautiful produce from Chengdu. Uncle Liang has a soft spot for Renshu and always slips him extra fruit. They both poke fun at Meilin's smattering of Sichuanese mixed with Mandarin, but they also encourage her. Since their arrival last February, Meilin's fluency has improved greatly. Meilin grows to know other familiar faces, too. Mr Huang, who runs a restaurant, also likes Auntie Deng's produce. Grandma Xi, who sells cloth, admires Meilin's handiwork with her needle. More than once, they have all had to flee to the Great Tunnel together during an air raid.

With the girls at school and Wenling frequently away, Meilin and Renshu are often on their own. During the quieter days, they unroll the scroll and linger over scenes, telling each other the old stories and making up new ones. Each time Meilin unfastens the tassel, the scent of the sandalwood rollers rises like a ghost and she inhales deeply. It is as if, with just that single breath, Xiaowen has returned. The gold threads along the edges glint a greeting. Without fail, Meilin always finds something new to admire in the details she has treasured for so long. The scroll – its miraculous existence, its never-ending beauty – is a well of hope.

Renshu's favourite scene is the marketplace. They like to see how many cheats and rascals they can spot. Look! A boy steals fish from a bucket while the seller haggles with an old woman in a shawl. Over there, behind the chickens in wicker cages, a tall man slips eggs into his deep pockets. The sorghum seller's scales tilt at a dishonest angle. See, below the table, his son – already an expert swindler– pulls a string to indicate an apparent balance well before the sides hold equal weights. And everywhere, pick-pockets help themselves to the baskets of the naive country folk who, having travelled far to sell their harvests, celebrate their earnings with too much plum wine. Even the dogs are thieves in this market, snuffling their noses along the tables to snatch a bun or a pork roll before someone chases them away.

In the corner is a fortune-teller. Meilin and Renshu are unsure whether she is a fraud. Some days, they decide she is the only true and kind person in the market. Her tea-leaf divinations and *I Ching* readings are known for miles. People trust her to utter chants that cure illnesses, to tell them what sacrifices will honour the ancestors, and to read their children's stars in hopes of aus-picious beginnings. But on bad days, they say she is the worst crook of them all. She sells shoddy promises, which is far worse than peddling cheap cloth or using faulty scales. The damage she does is unforgivable because it hurts their hearts.

Sometimes Meilin wonders what comes next in their story. How long will they be in Chongqing? Everyone is waiting to go home. But Meilin is no longer sure where home is. No replies come from her letters to her family. In the spring, she decides, she'll enrol Renshu in the local school. Without the company of his cousins, she worries he'll lonely. And while he's at lessons, maybe she can find some paid work nearby. She doesn't want to stay in the shadow of Longwei and Wenling forever.

Chapter Six

Chongqing, Sichuan Province, China, June 1941

In early June, the girls return to Chongqing for a short stay. With them back around, Wenling is happier to be home, and she is civil, even conversational, with Meilin.

Lifen, now eleven, is helping Wenling make tea for the family. The steam rises from the pot as she pours hot water over the leaves. Wenling arranges five teacups and some plates of peanuts and melon seeds on an enamel tray. When the tea and snacks have been distributed, Wenling nods to Lifen, who returns to her book. Wenling picks up the newspaper with great interest.

Meilin watches Liling and Renshu chattering away in the corner. They sit together on a quilt. They have put their cups and snack plates on a stool as if it is a small table, and sit cross-legged on either side. Meilin notices Lifen eyeing them over the top of her book.

'Lifen,' says Meilin, 'tell me about your school in Shapingba.'

The girl, grateful to be included, joins Meilin at the table. They chat about teachers, friends, favourite subjects. Eventually the talk turns to air raids.

'Auntie,' Lifen addresses Meilin. 'In my school, even when we run to the shelters, we still do our lessons.'

'That's good, learning is important,' Meilin says, wanting to praise her niece, who has always seemed caught between childhood and maturity.

'Yes, it's very good, the school,' Wenling remarks, looking up from the paper. 'Their bomb shelters are equipped with seats and lights for studying. When the sirens sound, the students take their books and run to the caves.'

'Here in the city,' Meilin gripes, 'the tunnels are cramped and stuffy and hot. And now that even more refugees have arrived, they are so crowded. Everyone has assigned shelters, but when the air-raid sirens go, there's not always time to reach them. People just squeeze into whichever one is closest.'

'I've heard that there are special shelters for bureaucrats and officials,' Wenling comments. 'With bars and provisions. These guys spend the air raids enjoying cards, dancing girls and drinks.'

'Dancing!' Meilin exclaims in disbelief.

'It's true,' Wenling insists. 'One of the school mothers told me.' She sighs and looks around the room. 'I wish my husband would get us transferred to Shapingba. There are fewer bombings, and the shelters are better. My friends hide in caves dug into the sides of the hills. They store mats there so they don't have to sit on the cold ground.' Wenling lifts her teacup to take a sip and grimaces. She spits it back into the cup. 'Too cold!' She rises. 'Lifen, Liling, come along. We need to go to the tailor's to choose fabrics for your summer dresses.'

Lifen, happy for the attention, starts to get ready. But Liling ignores her mother and continues playing with Renshu.

'Liling!' Wenling repeats, clapping her hands.

'I don't want to go,' Liling mutters.

'What?' Wenling says, her voice dangerously quieten.

Liling turns her face up towards her ma. 'I want to stay here with Renshu and Auntie. I don't care what my dresses look like,' she declares.

'Liling!' Wenling steps forward, hand raised to strike.

'Wait,' Meilin cries out instinctively.

Wenling turns on Meilin. 'Don't interfere. This is none of your business.'

'No, of course not, big sister.' Meilin retreats. 'But I'm happy to look after her if you want to take Lifen. It's so hot out and with her short legs and sour mood, she'll only slow you down. Why don't you two go ahead?'

Wenling fumes briefly. 'Fine,' she finally says. 'It's easier without you, Liling. Just don't you dare complain if you don't like your dresses.'

Liling has been shifting her gaze between Meilin and her ma. When Wenling relents, Liling smiles at her, a little too sweetly, and goes back to playing with Renshu.

Once Wenling and Lifen have gone, Meilin puts away the tea things, then gets her sewing basket to do some mending.

Renshu and Liling are talking about their schools. Liling likes hers, but Renshu's not so sure about his. It's hard to sit still. And repeating his brushstrokes hundreds of times to practise characters is dull.

'Renshu,' Meilin interrupts, hating to hear him complain. 'I cannot change your teachers or their methods. But I can tell you a story.'

'A scroll story?'

'Yes, a scroll story.'

Renshu's face lights up and he goes over to her basket to take out their treasure. Meilin puts away her mending, and Liling and Renshu sit by her side.

'Can you find a hermit in a thatched mountain hut, a busy city down in the valley, and a palace, with horses and soldiers and banners flying in the wind?'

They pore over the scroll, unrolling and rerolling it, section by section, searching for the scene she has described. When they find it, Meilin begins:

'There was once an emperor who loved roosters. One day, he asked his advisors, "Who is the finest artist in the land?"

' "Your excellency," they said, "by far the most talented artist of all is Master Wen, who lives high in the hills of Dabashan."

' "Bring him here!" boomed the emperor.

'So the emperor's men went into the mountains, searching along old trails almost lost to time until, at last, they found Master Wen. They explained that he must come see the emperor at once.

'Master Wen lay down his brushes and put on his shoes. He wrapped his robes around himself and, without a word, followed the emperor's men down the mountain and into the palace. Such riches! Such gold! They led him along a corridor lined with one hundred soldiers and one hundred glittering dragon lamps. At the end, Master Wen bowed to the emperor, who sat on a sumptuous golden throne.

'"They tell me you are the finest artist in the land."

'Master Wen stood up straight and nodded.

'"I want the best painting of a rooster the world has ever seen. Just for me. I commission you."

'"Of course, your excellency. But I need two years."

'"Two years?" sputtered the emperor, turning a bright red. The emperor was not accustomed to waiting two minutes for anything, let alone two years.

'The one hundred soldiers stared straight ahead. No one blinked or uttered a word.

'But Master Wen simply held up two fingers.

'"Very well, take two years, then return with my painting. If it is as marvellous as I expect, then you shall have all the tea and ink and scrolls you desire. You may spend the rest of your years writing poetry, practising calligraphy and painting landscapes."

'There were quieten murmurs throughout the hall.

'"But," thundered the emperor, holding up a hand to make his conditions clear, "should you fail to produce a painting that pleases me, then the painting will be burned and you along with it.'

'Master Wen nodded and returned to his hut.

'Two years passed, and the emperor's men came again to the mountains. Master Wen's moustache and beard had grown longer and greyer, but his eyes were as sharp as ever. He greeted them at his hut, then picked up a scroll, his favourite brush, his inkstone and an ink cake.

'"I am ready."

'Back down the mountain, back into the city, to the palace, and down the same long corridor with one hundred soldiers and one hundred glittering lamps. This time, the emperor, who had grown even fatter, sat on silk cushions in robes of red and gold.

'Master Wen bowed.

'"Where is my painting?" boomed the emperor.

'Master Wen unrolled the scroll, and to everyone's shock, the silk was blank.

' "May I have some water, your excellency?"

'A servant hurried forward with a flask.

'Master Wen took the water, poured it in the well at the bottom of his inkstone, unwrapped his ink cake, and began to scrape the cake against the well, mixing ink. A wonderful scent of camphor, pine and fresh flowers filled the air. When he was satisfied with the ink's consistency, he dipped his brush into the dark pool and lifted it out, careful not to spill a single drop.

'He touched the brush to the scroll and the ink began to bleed on to the silk. His hand moved deftly, pausing here, accelerating there, sometimes making the stroke thick, sometimes thin. The brush danced with agility and grace. And before everyone's eyes, a rooster appeared. With the last bit of ink in his dish, Master Wen added a final flourish on the coxcomb.

'For some time, the hall was silent. Finally, the emperor spoke.

' "Master Wen, that is, indeed, the most astonishing rooster painting I have ever seen. You shall have your tea and ink. But first, I must know: that took you no more than three minutes. Why did you need two years?"

'The artist dried his inkstone with the hem of his robe and wrapped his ink cake in silk, tenderly wiping his brush clean. When he had finished, he beckoned for the emperor to come close.

' "Come visit my workshop," he whispered in the emperor's ear.

'When the emperor and his men arrived at Master Wen's home in the mountains, they found stacks and stacks of paper, covered with sketches and studies and partially finished paintings of roosters. Roosters and roosters, reaching all the way to the ceiling.'

Renshu and Liling laugh. That is what Meilin hoped for, what she always hopes for, when she tells them a story. If they laugh, they'll remember it. And if they remember it, they'll always have this piece of home, of her.

A few days later, Meilin, Renshu and Liling are in the market, visiting Meilin's friends. Renshu and Liling sit on an upturned crate, each eating a stem of longans from Uncle Liang. Auntie

Deng is making a fuss over Liling, saying how pretty she is, what a doll. Liling smirks. She's more of a tomboy than a doll, Meilin thinks, but over the past two years, the girl has grown into a real beauty, with a striking resemblance to Wenling. Meilin wonders if this is behind their increased battles.

Liling, increasingly rebellious, has been arguing with Wenling throughout their summer visit, wanting to spend more and more time with Renshu and Meilin. Today's outing, of course, provoked another confrontation. Finally, Wenling had thrown her hands up, saying, 'Go! Go run around in the dirty market with your cousin. I'd rather have the peace and quieten anyway.' Liling had screamed back, 'And I'd rather be with Auntie and Renshu. I wish you weren't my mother; I wish Auntie was my ma!' At this, Wenling slapped the girl, hard, and left the room. It took most of the morning for Liling to calm down. Determined to keep Wenling and Liling away from each other for as long as she could, Meilin has stayed in the market far longer than necessary.

But the sun is setting. They should go. As much as Meilin dreads facing Wenling, she needs to start preparing the evening meal. Longwei is expected back from meetings in Guilin and the whole family is meant to be together before the girls return to school. Meilin glances up at the sky. Perhaps they can linger for just a little longer. It's been days since the last airstrike.

At the onset of the war, the Japanese army had boasted that it would take over China in a handful of months. It has now been nearly four years, and China still holds the aggressors at bay. But this is cold comfort. By now, Meilin and Renshu have survived hundreds of bombings. Still, Meilin's uneasy. Clear skies are always the worst, the most dangerous. They shouldn't stay out in the open.

Auntie Deng is telling a story when the moan of the air-raid sirens begins. She stops mid-sentence. Renshu scans the sky for the incoming formation. Liling looks at Meilin, eyes wide.

'Auntie, I'm scared,' she whispers.

'It will be okay, Liling,' Meilin reassures her, trying to sound calm. 'We'll go in the Great Tunnel. It's nearby. Stay close with us.'

'I want my ma,' the girl wails, bursting into tears.

'Here, hold my hand, little one,' Uncle Liang says to Liling. 'I'll keep you safe.' He takes her small hand and they start running towards the Great Tunnel.

Meilin hurries Renshu along, but he tugs back.

'Hurry!' she says. 'It will fill and we won't get in. We need to go now!'

But Renshu is obstinate. No. He won't budge.

Families rush by. The sirens roar. Meilin shouts, 'Renshu! There's no time to argue!'

The fleet swarms closer; Meilin catches glints of sunlight reflecting off their wings.

Doors are shutting, merchants are abandoning newly repaired stalls.

Finally, Meilin tries to scoop her son up. At six years old, he is too big to carry. He kicks at the air and flounders out of her arms. 'I hate the tunnel! The air is bad. I won't go!' Meilin sees a new stubbornness and deep fear in his eyes.

She stumbles. Renshu wrenches free and starts to run in the opposite direction.

'No! Come back!' she shrieks, but he is too quick.

Three blocks later, Meilin catches him, but they have lost sight of Auntie Deng, Uncle Liang and Liling. Scolding Renshu, she struggles to drag him back. Halfway down the steps to the entrance, she sees the gates have closed. The officials refuse to let them in. *Too crowded, already full,* they say, implacable. Meilin looks past their shoulders. The tunnel is heaving with people, more crowded than she's ever seen it. They crouch outside the gate, under the partial shelter, hoping it will be enough.

For hours, the planes circle overhead. Without thick walls to muffle the explosions, each window shattered or wall crumbled vibrates straight into Meilin. Her ears ring and her body shudders with the aftershocks. Expecting each moment to be their last, she hovers over Renshu, who cries and cries.

With the fall of darkness, fewer bombs land, but the fearsome drone of the planes continues. Hours after dusk, Meilin raises her head. It finally sounds like the planes are growing more distant. Maybe soon the all-clear signal will sound and the gates will open. She helps Renshu to his feet and they venture up the stairs.

Then, shouts from the tunnel behind them: *The lamps are going out!*

There's not enough oxygen for the flames. Which means there's not enough oxygen for the people. Turning back to look down at the entrance, Meilin feels a new kind of terror.

Despite the increasing calls for help, the guards still refuse to open the gates. They insist they must wait for official instructions.

Pandemonium erupts in the tunnel. People are screaming, pushing, moaning, trying to get out. They are clawing, tearing at their clothes. *Open the gates, open the gates!* Was it a blessing to be denied entrance after all? Meilin wonders, then is shocked by her own thoughts. Auntie Deng, Uncle Liang and Liling are trapped inside. One wooden gate opens partially and the crowd begins to pour out like a torrent, a stampede. Meilin clings to the side of the steps, shielding Renshu as people surge by, tripping, stumbling, trampling over those who have fallen. Auntie Deng staggers out, gasping, her clothes torn. Meilin feels the fist around her heart begin to loosen.

Meilin helps Auntie Deng over to them. Her ankle is sprained. The three make their way up the stairs to wait for Uncle Liang and Liling.

'Where's Liling?' Renshu asks.

'They were right behind me,' Auntie Deng pants. 'They'll come out soon.' But after that first wave, although the blood-curdling shrieks continue, people stop emerging. Some of the young men who have escaped the tunnel try to re-enter to aid those still inside. Their efforts are futile. When they climb back out, they say that the tunnel has been blocked by the bodies of those who have fainted, or worse, suffocated.

Meilin keeps her eyes locked on the tunnel's opening, her guilt and dread growing as the hours pass. Renshu, frightened into silence, clings to her. Though exhausted, wariness keeps him alert.

'Liang! Liang!' Auntie Deng paces back and forth, her own injuries forgotten as she calls.

Through the night, the other gates to the tunnel stay stubbornly closed. The officials haven't sounded the all-clear. Without instruction from higher-ups, the wardens refuse to budge. No rescue teams arrive. Thousands remain stuck in the unbearable heat and toxic air.

It is only after daybreak that officers come – not to rescue, but to clear the corpses.

Among the bodies are those of Uncle Liang and Liling.

In the weeks following Liling's death, everyone reels with grief. Longwei funnels his anguish into his work. Through official channels, he tries to find out what went wrong in the chain of command. He reports back that the Generalissimo was distressed by the disaster, and the Air Defence Commander and Deputy Air Defence Commander will be relieved of their duties. He testifies before a committee that the higher-ranking officials failed to protect the public.

In contrast, Wenling retires to her bed, hardly eating or speaking, her eyes swollen and face bare, uninterested in visits from her Shapingba friends. She barely protests when Lifen refuses to return to school. Renshu, too, stays home, not wanting to go into the city. He tries to play with Lifen, and though she is sometimes kind, it's not the same. No one else is like Liling.

Desperate to keep the household running, Meilin tries to maintain her usual routines, but inside, she feels wretched. The tragedy is her fault. It's the Japanese army's fault. It's the officials' fault. The wardens who were blindly obedient. The engineers who designed the tunnels. It's no one's fault. It's everyone's fault.

Attempting to escape this vortex of helpless regret, Meilin tries to comfort Wenling. There are no words that can soothe this loss, so Meilin prepares Wenling's favourite dishes.

Today she has brought back fresh greens and a small amount of pork. She has spent hours cooking. When Meilin serves the food, Wenling pushes away her bowl in distaste. 'Stop trying to make things better. Everything you do just makes things worse.'

'We're all grieving,' Meilin murmurs, exhausted, then immediately regrets it.

Wenling lifts her head, her eyes glittering with hostility. 'You were supposed to look after her,' she says.

Meilin wants to sob. She can't deny it.

'Why did I trust you? You had been poisoning her against me ever since leaving Changsha. If you weren't here, none of this would have happened.'

'I'm so sorry, Wenling. I'd do anything to change that day. I'm—'

Wenling cuts her off. 'For years, my friends have asked me why I let my family be dragged down by my dead brother-in-law's widow and son. Why I didn't stand up for myself and demand you leave, find a life of your own. But I always said, *No, my youngest loves them so much.* And now this softness of mine has resulted in her death. I should have insisted you go your own way ages ago. I should have been stronger. You have brought nothing but misfortune to us. Because of you and your son, my child is dead.'

'It was an accident!' Meilin's temper flares, then fizzles when she sees the sharp pain on Wenling's face. Wenling has lost a child. There is nothing Meilin can do to change that. 'I don't want to fight, Wenling,' Meilin says. 'I, too, feel as if I have lost a daughter.'

At this, Wenling shrieks. 'No, no, no! She was not your daughter. How dare you! You who have taken her life, now you also try to claim her in death?'

'What can I do?' Meilin asks, exhausted.

Wenling stares past Meilin, looking at the wall. 'I want you and your son to get out. I want' – she looks up at the ceiling, and her voice is unsteady – 'I want to never have to see you again.'

Meilin has known derision, scorn and contempt from Wenling. She has been the recipient of her mockery and impatience, but underneath it all, Meilin has always believed there was some kind of bond, some sense of family, however minute.

But this is different. In Wenling's voice, there is no trace of warmth or grudging kinship. Only a cold and certain hate.

Renshu and Lifen have stopped eating, watching their mothers in a frigid silence.

'Come,' Meilin says to Renshu, putting down her chopsticks and bowl. She gets up from the table and goes into their room.

Though it is Chongqing's steamy summer, Renshu doesn't protest when Meilin tells him to put on all his clothes, as many layers as possible. He doesn't say a word when Meilin packs their most precious belongings into her sewing basket. Despite its age, it is still strong and holds all that they need. Solemn and silent, he understands that, once again, it's time to go.

When they leave, Wenling doesn't even look up.

PART TWO
1941–1948

Chapter Seven

Chongqing, Sichuan Province, China, August 1941

'This loss should bring your family together, not tear it apart,' Auntie Deng mourns.

Meilin wipes away the tears rolling down her cheeks. Not knowing where else to go, she'd come to the market.

'So, you need a place to stay?' Auntie Deng asks.

Meilin nods.

'Stay with me for a little while. Without Liang, I could use some help here in the market. Let's see what happens. Maybe we all need some time to heal.' Auntie Deng squeezes Meilin's hand and gives Renshu a hug.

'I don't want to go back,' Meilin whispers, surprising herself.

It only takes a few days before Longwei comes to the market, looking for Meilin.

Renshu sees him first and runs to his uncle, giving him a great embrace and chattering excitedly about how they've been staying with Auntie Deng. When Meilin comes out from behind the stall, where she's been helping to unload a fresh shipment of greens, Longwei sets Renshu down.

Longwei's cheeks look hollow and he is unshaven. His grief is still raw.

'What happened?' he asks Meilin, holding Renshu close to his side. 'Wenling wouldn't tell me. She just said that you left.'

Meilin looks away, refusing to make eye contact.

'Meilin, listen. After Liling . . .' He trails off and tries again. 'Meilin, my request to transfer to Shapingba has been granted. We're moving to where we'll be safer. Will you come with us?'

'Elder brother,' Meilin says, 'Wenling doesn't want us there. And she's right. We have relied on your kindness for too long. We need to make our own way.'

'And how will you do that?' he asks, his voice tinged with disbelief.

Meilin bristles at his tone. True, she has relied on him until now, but she can take care of herself and Renshu. After all, that was her promise to Xiaowen.

Longwei picks up an orange, passing it from hand to hand. Meilin turns away to help another customer at the stall.

'You want more oranges?' Auntie Deng limps over to him, collecting more and putting them into his hands. 'Very juicy, very tasty.'

When the customer is gone, and Auntie Deng has sold Longwei many oranges and a half-dozen persimmons, he says to Meilin, 'We are leaving the apartment at the end of the month. At the very least, you and Renshu can stay there once we're gone.'

Meilin doesn't say anything.

He sighs, says goodbye to Auntie Deng and Renshu, and tells Meilin to think about it. Then he leaves.

'Meilin!' Auntie Deng says, as soon as he is out of earshot. 'You can go back now. See, it's going to work out.'

'But I don't want to. Don't you still need our help here, Auntie?'

'Meilin,' Auntie Deng tuts. 'Don't be foolish. They are your family.'

'No, not anymore. Look, you've got a customer.' Meilin nods towards a woman browsing the sweet potatoes.

But later that week, Auntie Deng tells Meilin, 'When the summer ends, I'm returning to Chengdu. You and Renshu have been a great help, but it's too hard to be here without Liang. It doesn't feel right.'

Although Auntie Deng rarely shows her grief, Meilin has heard her weeping at night.

'Besides,' Auntie Deng continues, 'my daughter has a new baby, she needs help with the other children.' She holds up her hand before Meilin can protest. 'At the end of the month, when I leave, if you still won't join your brother-in-law, then go back to that apartment. If it stands empty, someone else will move in and you'll lose this chance. Put away your pride and anger, Mei-lin. Things are hard enough already.'

In September, as the heat subsides, Meilin and Renshu return to the vacated rooms. During the day, they stay at the apartment, so that when the air-raid sirens start, they can rush to the smaller shelter nearby. Of course, Renshu is terrified of this tunnel, too. Every time, Meilin must convince him it is the only safe choice. They avoid Shibati altogether. Without Auntie Deng, the market becomes only a reminder of that terrible day in June. Renshu's playfulness has dimmed. In its place is a protectiveness of Meilin and a new wariness. Although he misses his uncle, auntie and Lifen, he seems to have sensed the rift and doesn't ask about them.

Most of all, though, Renshu misses Liling. Every night, he cries and cries until he falls asleep. His fears flare up in night-mares and Meilin's nights are broken, too, as she tries to coax him back to sleep. He says he wishes he would wake up to find Liling there, laughing, asking him to play, telling him a funny story or sharing her sweets with him. But no matter how hard he cries, or how much he wishes, nothing brings her back.

With October, the fog returns and the bombings finally lessen. Meilin gets Renshu back to school. Routine helps them both. Yet in this quieter season, Meilin's unhappiness and loneliness cut deeper. When Renshu is at school, she finds she cannot stop weep-ing. A dam has burst, and years of grief flood through her. For so long, Meilin has held her sorrow at bay. There was always some-thing more pressing than grief: a need to find food and shelter, to attend to the family's feelings, to simply survive the day. But now, without the pressure of immediate crisis, without the constant daily tension of navigating between Longwei and Wenling, her vigilance shifts to melancholy. In the wake of so much loss, she mourns not only the life she'd intended for Renshu – stability and safety, an untroubled childhood watched over by Xiaowen – but also all that he has experienced that she cannot undo. Even if the war were to end tomorrow, he'll inherit a country of burned cities, displaced people, broken families.

In her despair, Meilin discovers something else, too: anger. Anger at the damage that has been done. Anger that so many possibilities have been taken from her son, futures erased. Anger at how helpless she feels. It is from this fury that a determination begins to take root. A determination that the circumstances that have destroyed so much of Renshu's childhood, so much of her life, will not also steal the last of their hope. She resolves to imagine a new future for him. A future of stability, learning, health, prosperity. He will grow strong and attend university. He will become a scholar, follow a life of the mind. He will move forward. He will even, one day, be able to forget all these sorrows.

Chongqing, Sichuan Province, China, February 1942

Although she wasn't expecting him, Meilin isn't surprised when Longwei appears shortly after the New Year, bringing rice, oil, salt and cloth. She accepts his gifts; she'd be foolish not to. These essentials are still hard to get and precious.

'Meilin, you've had your time. Come live in Shapingba now.' His haircut is neat and his face newly shaven. He stands tall, almost restored to his old commanding presence, but there is a flicker of uncertainty in his voice.

Meilin doesn't say anything.

'Look, America has joined the war. This is a turning point. Soon the Chinese will be victorious, I'm sure of it. We can rebuild our nation, we can rebuild our family. Come back, Meilin.'

'No, Longwei. Wenling's grief is too great. She blames me for Liling's death. Our being there will only torment Wenling more.'

'Wenling's anger is not my anger. We share our sorrow, but not our anger. Come back,' he appeals, this time more gently.

'Elder brother, I give you my respect and thanks for the many ways you've helped me and Renshu, but we will not move to Shapingba with you. Go home. You have a wife and daughter to comfort.'

Finally, seeing that he will not convince her, he turns to leave, muttering, 'How did I end up caught between the two most stubborn women in all of China?'

The next time Longwei comes, it is the height of summer. Longwei brings Renshu a small toy car. Amazed at his good fortune, the eight-year-old accepts the gift with glee. Meilin scolds Longwei for spoiling him with such extravagance, but Longwei waves her protests aside. He rumples Renshu's hair and the boy goes off to play with his new treasure.

'You don't have to keep coming up here, Longwei,' Meilin says. 'We're fine.'

'I know.'

'So why do you?'

'I must check in on my only nephew and my brother's widow. For family. Family stays together.'

'How are Wenling and Lifen?' she asks.

'Lifen is well. In school, studying hard. And Wenling, well, she has plenty of friends with whom she can complain about her husband.'

Meilin purses her lips, hiding a smile. Longwei glimpses her amusement and breaks into a loud guffaw.

Meilin pulls back, alarmed at their slide into conviviality. She dons a formal face and thanks him, saying, 'Elder brother, you have been too generous. I imagine you must have important work to do. We won't delay you any longer.'

And, as if remembering his role, his expression sobers, and he nods. Soon after, he leaves.

As the years pass, Meilin just manages to keep Renshu fed, clothed and safe. She finds small jobs at his school or with some of the women's aid organisations, collecting blankets, medical supplies and clothing for soldiers at the front. Sometimes she helps at one of Madame Chiang Kai-shek's schools for war orphans, sewing clothing and looking after the smallest children. In conversations with the other women, Meilin comes to form her own views on the war. She begins to nurture two dreams: a better future for Renshu and continued independence for herself. As much as she hates all that the war has taken from her, this new-found self-sufficiency, however modest, is precious and powerful.

A pattern emerges: Longwei visits twice a year, with gifts of rice, oil and salt. Sometimes he includes cloth or wool. It is usually around the New Year and then, later, close to a festival or holiday. He never stays long. Gradually, their conversations evolve away from their shared grief and towards the state of the world, the hope for peace, and the victories and losses of the Chinese forces. Meilin is surprised by how much she comes to relish her talks with Longwei. They remind her a little of her youthful discussions with Xiaowen. But Longwei is grittier, more realistic, and these days, so is she.

Chongqing, Sichuan Province, China, February 1945

This year, when Longwei comes, in addition to his usual gifts, he brings new shoes for Renshu and a package of tea for Meilin. Meilin is grateful. All arms and legs, and nearly eleven years old, Renshu is constantly growing out of his clothes. Over the past few years, not only has he grown in stature, but he's grown in personhood. He's become an imaginative problem-solver, much like Dao Hongtse. Renshu loves to show the other children at school how to make boats from leaves and twigs. He's a hard worker and does his lessons diligently. Meilin swells with pride when she sees Longwei look at him with admiration.

'Thank you,' Meilin says, putting away the gifts and taking down two teacups. She opens the package of tea and shakes a handful of leaves into a tin teapot. She lights the kerosene stove and they wait for the water to boil.

Pouring them each a cup, she sighs. 'Why is this war still dragging on? It's been three years since the Americans joined, and still no victory.'

Longwei blows on the surface of his tea and shakes his head. It's been a grim year for the Kuomintang. The Japanese now control provinces on both sides of the Yellow River and continue to advance into the interior.

'I even heard that the loss in Henan was because the Chinese people revolted. The peasants wanted revenge against the Kuomintang for breaching the river, and the famine and floods that followed,' Meilin remarks.

Taken aback, Longwei scowls. Then he sits up straighter. With both reproach and pride, he responds, 'It was, it still is, a time of national sacrifice. We must trade parts of this country for time. To do so, we must destroy any assets that could be used by the enemy.'

'Like the fire in Changsha?' Meilin asks, the words slipping out. She's long wondered. 'You knew beforehand, didn't you? The Kuomintang burned the city down on purpose.' She watches as Longwei refuses to meet her eyes. 'And what's worse,' she says, 'the Japanese didn't ever actually attack. Your Generalissimo doesn't value human life, just his own legacy. People are tiring of his carelessness.'

'You don't understand what decisions a leader must make,' he growls.

'I understand that he sacrifices his people without a second thought. I understand that trains and trucks and boats carry government files and equipment when they could carry families to safety.'

'You should be more careful in what you say.'

'Why? Am I wrong?' she challenges.

Longwei sputters, shaking his head, caught off-guard by her forthrightness. Recovering himself, he says, 'We will be victorious, Meilin. Soon.'

He leaves abruptly. For about a week, his gifts go untouched. But then Meilin, determinedly practical, uses them.

By the spring of 1945, the Nazi hold on Europe is weakening. The allies turn their attention to Japan, firebombing the cities of Tokyo, Nagoya and Osaka. In China, battles rage even as all the armies – the Nationalists, the Communists and the Japanese – are depleted and near collapse.

After more than eight years, the people of China wake one

August morning to hear that America has dropped fearsome bombs on two cities in Japan, bombs named Little Boy and Fat Man. The mushroom-shaped clouds they formed in Hiroshima and Nagasaki were immense. Loss radiated outwards, blooming for miles and miles, and stunning the Japanese into a quick surrender. They have put down their guns and grounded their Zeros. The War of Resistance, at long last, is over.

Chongqing, Sichuan Province, China, August 1946

It is the close of the Hungry Ghost festival, and Meilin kneels at the river, lighting small lanterns in paper boats and setting them adrift on the water. With each one, she thinks of an ancestor or a lost loved one and murmurs a small blessing. She watches as they join scores of other boats bobbing along in the dusk. Further down, out of earshot, but still in sight, Renshu and a group of boys launch boats of their own into the crowded river.

Despite the return of peace, Meilin feels further than ever from the life she once hoped to build when she married Xiaowen. Those dreams belong to someone else. She's not who she was. Not so willing to follow all the old ideas, the new ideas or any ideas, just because they were her father's, her father-in-law's or her husband's.

Her thoughts have instead been returning, again and again, to her family in the hills above Yichang. She wonders if their remote settlement has carried on quietly through the usual shifts of the seasons, undisturbed by the violence of the cities. Any shame she might have once felt about leaving her late husband's family to return to her own seems irrelevant now. She wants to be among those who have always known and loved her. She wants a chance for her boy and her parents to know and love one another.

'Do you still believe in hungry ghosts?' The voice is deep, gravelly and mocking. Though it's been well over a year, she knows that voice.

She glances up. Longwei. When did he arrive and why is he

here? He looks down at her with a mixture of amusement and contempt.

'Yes. Especially those who had no proper burial.' She gets up and straightens her tunic and trousers. 'At least I believe in something.'

'I believe in something.'

'What?' She expects he'll say gold, or power, or the gullibility of others. Or that he believes in strategy: that there's always an angle from which you can see how to win.

'China.'

She studies him, looking for sarcasm in his expression. Long-wei's face is serious. Not a trace of ridicule lines his eyes or twitches at the edges of his lips.

How can he mean this? Though the end of the war initially gave Meilin hope, China's peace has been short-lived. After the Japanese surrendered, there was brief cooperation between the Chinese Communist Party and the Kuomintang. Mao Zedong and Chiang Kai-shek even signed a pact of solidarity in Chong-qing. But this was just a puppet show, both sides stalling while they regathered troops and strength. Only ten months later, the truce had collapsed, and fighting between the Nationalists and Communists had resumed by June.

Even Old Hongtse had believed in wealth and oil, not patriot-ism. Could his mercenary son truly have an allegiance to something as insubstantial as a mouthful of slogans?

'What is China?' she finally manages.

'China' – he inhales, lifts his chin, arranges his shoulders as if in salute and looks into the distance, as if he could see the Gen-eralissimo himself approaching – 'is ours.

'She does not belong to the Japanese, the Imperialists, the for-eigners who rolled into Shanghai. She is not the warlords', the emperors' or the Americans'. She is for the Chinese people. One people, one country.'

'Longwei,' Meilin interrupts, 'why are you here? Why aren't you with your wife and daughter?'

'China has become a chessboard.' Longwei continues, ignor-ing her questions. 'Borders are being re-established, territories drawn.'

'Pah! A country is not a chessboard!'

His raised eyebrows prompt her to continue.

'A country is a place to make homes, to grow families and towns and cities,' she says. 'It is not some exercise in military prowess.'

'No, Meilin. China is a chessboard and the players are the white and the red. We must demonstrate our worth to the players or become pawns.'

Meilin knows that he's not wholly wrong. But she doesn't think he's completely right, either. 'Why are you here?' she asks again. She is in no mood for metaphor.

'We have to move. We are going to Shanghai. You will come with us.'

'Shanghai! Wenling must be thrilled! Why?'

'I have a new post. Civil servant with the Kuomintang.'

'So now you have a title? You must be very important. This war has been good for you, hasn't it?' she taunts, not bothering to hide her contempt.

He ignores her. 'You will come with us.'

It isn't a question.

Meilin wants none of this. She is not interested in games of chess, or chance, or whatever Longwei wants to call it. All she wants is enough peace and stability for her boy to grow, to understand that the world is not always at war, that loss and flight are not life's primary experiences.

'Meilin, I am here because family stays together. You will join us.'

'Why do you think we will come with you?'

'Family stays together!' he says again, as if repetition was the same as explanation. She stares at him, and he starts to cough that smoker's cough. Phlegm gathers in his throat, and he hacks, then spits it out. Longwei clears his throat again and takes out another cigarette, offering her one. She shakes her head in disgust.

The red tip of his cigarette glows in the deepening dusk. More lanterns float by, their orange and yellow flames reflected on the waters. As they stand in silence, her own family comes to mind. She has no desire to rejoin Longwei and Wenling. But the possibility of going back to her parents, which has seemed like a fantasy, begins to glimmer with potential.

What can she trust about this man? She can trust his hunger for power. She can trust his ambition to get to Shanghai and 'demonstrate his worth', as he says. He wants to be valuable, not as a sacrifice, but as a strategist. His determination is growing. The war *has* served him well.

'I insist. You and Renshu, come with us,' Longwei repeats. Meilin is no stranger to strategy, either. Any boat that travels down the Chang Jiang must stop in Yichang. Knowing Longwei, knowing Wenling, in Yichang, they will probably transfer to a larger, more comfortable steamer that will take them on to Shanghai. This steamer will be big enough that it must sail when scheduled, regardless of whether or not all the passengers are on board.

Meilin keeps her gaze straight ahead. She doesn't want her eyes or her voice to betray her thoughts. 'When?' she asks.

'We'll sail at the end of the month.'

Meilin looks once more at Longwei and slowly nods. 'Okay,' she agrees.

Longwei grins; he has finally clenched a long-desired victory. He thinks that she wants and seeks his protection, that she will be grateful for his generosity. As a nod to Meilin and her ghosts, he picks up the last of her lanterns, lights it and sets it afloat.

But he's wrong. Meilin doesn't want his protection. She wants a spot on the boat.

Chapter Eight

Chang Jiang, eastbound, China, September 1946

Eight years ago, Meilin and Renshu travelled up the Chang Jiang in a fog of worry and anguish. Going downriver now, Meilin is less desperate, more hopeful. Instead of the adrenaline of immediate need, she begins to feel the qualms of daring to look forward, to dream. In some ways, she's not sure which is more frightening.

The river is crowded with boats going east; everyone is trying to get home. Meilin sits alone on deck, thinking about the village in the hills. Once the idea to return to Yichang took hold, she could see Renshu with her father, tending the radishes and sweet potatoes. She could feel her hands massaging her mother's back, rubbing away the tension of washing and beating out clothes. If she could imagine these moments so vividly, how could they not be possible?

'You're lucky my husband takes pity on you.' Wenling's voice cuts into her reverie. Over the years, it has become brittle and harsh. She is still beautiful, but a frailty has taken hold of her. No matter how elegantly dressed or expertly made-up, her refinement floats only on the surface, unable to conceal a brokenness beneath.

This is the first time Wenling has spoken directly to Meilin since leaving Chongqing. So far, she has refused, looking past Meilin and Renshu, or referring to them as if they aren't there. Longwei hasn't seemed to notice. Either he is blind to her animosity, or he dismisses it as an annoyance. But Meilin sees that time has neither dulled Wenling's resentment nor softened her grief.

'Had it been up to me, we would have left you behind.'

Meilin presses her lips together. Instead of responding, she studies the mountains. The changing leaves splash the hills with reds, oranges, yellows.

'You and your boy stay away from my family. You've only ever brought trouble. Leave my husband alone.'

'Big sister,' Meilin starts, but Wenling has turned away. Meilin watches the angry woman retreat back into the hold. She considers whether to follow and appease. Perhaps at one time she would have tried. But it would feel like an empty gesture now.

A few moments later, Renshu joins her. At twelve years old, he is taller than she, his long legs and lean build predicting a swift stride as a man. Xiaowen's cheekbones and strong jaw are starting to echo in Renshu's once rounded face.

'Ma, I miss Liling. I always miss her, but being with Uncle, Auntie and Lifen makes it hurt all over again.'

Meilin puts her hand on his and squeezes in agreement. 'It's okay to still be sad,' she murmurs. 'Our sorrow reminds us of all the joyful moments, too.'

The boat has slowed. Wu Gorge lies ahead. River trackers prepare ropes to guide the boat through the rapids. Although they move with the water's flow this time, it is still a hazardous journey. Passage through the gorge may take hours, or even days if many boats are waiting.

'Ma, do you remember telling me and Liling that this river was a serpent and the mountains were dragons?'

Meilin nods.

'Remember telling us "Li Chi Slays the Serpent"? Tell me another story?'

'Aren't you too old for my stories?'

'No, Ma, never too old for stories.'

For an instant, Meilin sees the small boy with chubby legs and a happy laugh.

She looks along the river, then up at the cliffs. She notices a small crevice in the hillside. She begins to pull together the pieces of a story she once knew. How did it go again?

Out comes the scroll, and she unrolls and rerolls until she reaches a section where a fisherman steers his small boat through a bed of reeds. Above him rise blue-green mountains whose tops disappear in swirls of clouds.

'This is the story,' she begins, 'of Peach Blossom Spring.

'Once, not far from here, there was a fisherman, called Old Zhu from Wuling, who lost his way.'

'When?' interrupts Renshu.

'A long time ago.'

'When the Qing still ruled?' Renshu has become so precise. He wants to know exactly when and where things have happened, are happening, will happen.

'Way before that.' Meilin waves her hand as if to brush away the centuries. 'Many, many empires ago.'

'How many?'

Meilin considers his questions. She worries the war years have made him wary; he is always collecting information, as if he knows to be on the lookout.

'I think it was the time of the Jin. Yes, the Jin. Enough questions, now listen. Old Zhu, having had no luck with the fish that day, had closed his eyes and fallen asleep. He floated down the river and when he woke, he discovered a wondrous sight: a grove of peach trees in full bloom! Wanting a closer look, he dragged his boat ashore. Their beauty drew him forward and he walked deeper and deeper into the forest. The bloom was so abundant that the ground was covered in fallen blossoms. He picked up a handful and inhaled, the soft, silky petals tickling his nose.'

Another passenger standing on the deck is listening. Meilin can tell by the way he adjusts his stance to lean closer. Perhaps he, too, is a fisherman. She raises her voice a little and continues.

'At the end of the grove, there was an opening in the mountainside. Like that.' Meilin gestures at the dark crack she'd spotted earlier. Renshu cranes his neck to see, then turns back to her.

'What next? Did Old Zhu enter?'

'Of course he did! Wouldn't you? At first, the opening was big enough for him to reach above his head, and to stretch out his arms and not touch the walls. As he walked, however, the cave became smaller and smaller. Though it felt like the walls were closing around him, he still went forward.

'Finally, when the cave was so small that there was just enough room for the height and width of a single man, he stepped out the other side. Aha!' Meilin opens her arms wide. 'Before him lay cultivated rice and tea fields, people working and laughing, children and dogs playing. Well, Old Zhu thought he must be dreaming. He hadn't seen such harmony and calm in years. Nevertheless, he continued down into the village. If he was dreaming, he hoped not to wake any time soon.

'He approached a group of people dressed in a style he had never seen. They asked where he had come from. As he explained, he learned that the people of this plentiful valley had never heard of the Han or the Wei, let alone the Jin. Their forefathers had fled the chaos during the age of Qin. They have lived there ever since, cut off from the outside world.

'The villagers brought out wine to toast their guest and killed a chicken for a feast, entreating Old Zhu to stay. There was singing and merry-making into the night.'

Meilin pauses. Renshu looks expectantly at her. The passenger turns around. He has long whiskers and merry eyes. Liver spots speckle his cheeks. He takes out a cigarette and listens openly, leaning back on his elbows.

'Then what?' Renshu asks.

Meilin stalls, remembering now more clearly how the story goes. Making a decision, Meilin concludes, 'After several days and several feasts, Old Zhu decided to stay in the village and make it his home. He was happy in Peach Blossom Spring. Why would he want to leave a land of peaceful plenty?'

'Really? That's a strange ending.' Renshu is sceptical.

'What do you mean? It's a nice ending.'

'It seems like one more thing should happen. A joke or a tragedy or a lesson?' Renshu suggests.

Meilin shrugs. 'No, that's it. The end.'

Renshu narrows his eyes. 'Maybe I am getting too old for your stories, after all,' he says. He rises and goes towards the other side of the boat.

'There is more to that story, you know,' murmurs the passenger, putting out his cigarette.

'I know,' sighs Meilin. Then she gathers her basket and walks away.

The river is widening, pushing its banks back, changing into the broad waterway that expands across the plains, stretching to the east. Meilin hasn't told Renshu her plan. He is young, and she knows how secrets can leak even from closed mouths. It's better if he only knows once it's happening.

At Yichang, they disembark. Again, all around are groups of exhausted, thin faces, surrounded by meagre possessions. Longwei is arranging tickets for the next steamer. Wenling and Lifen sit on their cases, listless. As no one is watching her, Meilin starts sorting through her basket. She lifts her box of jade charms and coins, trying not to make a sound. She opens it. Only a handful of valuables remain, enough to cover the bottom of the box. To muffle their jingling, she crams in some scraps of cloth. Her hand rests on the scroll's box at the bottom of the basket. Squinting at the cold, clear sky, she puts on a jumper, her thickest socks and a hat. In the spaces she's vacated, she stows a box of matches, a small sack of rice and a block of tea. In the middle section of the basket, she folds a warm coverlet. The top, as always, holds her spools, needles and scissors. Once again, she's ready.

Meilin picks up her basket and goes to Renshu.

'Come, let's go to the market. Wear your coat, these days turn cold quickly.'

'Why do you have your basket?'

'We'll get oranges for the journey. Put your coat on,' she repeats.

Their conversation has caught Wenling's interest.

'There is no time for a market trip!' grumbles Longwei, who has just returned with a fistful of tickets.

'It's been such a long time since we've had oranges,' Wenling wheedles. 'And everyone knows Yichang oranges have the best flavour.' Sensing Longwei's resolve weakening, Wenling tries another tactic. 'Meilin knows the city; she can be quick.'

Meilin stays silent as Longwei considers. She is counting on Wenling's fondness for fruit and Longwei's tendency to indulge her.

'Don't delay.' He scowls. 'The steamer will arrive soon. If you're late, we'll leave without you.'

'I know,' says Meilin.

Once in the city, Meilin finds that her feet remember the short-cuts to the market. She moves quickly. Renshu struggles to keep up. She doesn't want to pause. She fears if she lets herself see what has been damaged, what has been lost, she will lose focus. At a fruit stall, she buys an armful of oranges. 'Here,' Meilin says, handing Renshu a tin pot she has just purchased from a neighbouring stall. 'We'll carry them in this.' Then she bargains with a man selling snow pears. Once she has filled the few remaining gaps in her basket with pears, she studies the hillside.

'Will we go back now, Ma?'

'Soon,' she murmurs, and starts walking across the market, away from the docks.

He looks back at the boats, then hurries to catch up to her. 'Ma, we need to go back.'

'The boat's not here yet,' she says, without turning to look. 'I just want to see if I can find something.'

'What are you looking for?' He has now caught up. 'Ma, a big steamer has reached the port. Look!'

Meilin glances. 'Yes, but it will take time to dock and then unload and load. It might not even be our boat. We've been on the water for so many days, let's stretch our legs a little longer.'

She walks faster now, and turns on to a road heading uphill.

'Ma,' Renshu grabs her arm. 'We have to go. We have to go back to our family.'

Meilin twists her arm free. When did he become so strong?

'Renshu, you have family here. My parents. Your wai gong and wai po.'

'Wai gong? Wai po?'

'You don't remember them, but they met you when you were little, with your baba. When the war came, we couldn't see them again. Now that the war is over, let's go find them.'

His mouth drops open in disbelief. Meilin keeps talking.

'We need to let Uncle and Auntie and Lifen go to Shanghai. We—'

The boy's eyes brim with tears as he takes in what she is saying. He starts running down the hill towards the docks. Oranges bounce out of the pot as he goes. He hunches his arm awkwardly over the top and continues, but when the steamer's horn signals its departure, his shoulders drop and he slows, bursting into sobs.

Meilin runs after him, gathering the fallen fruit. When she reaches him, she drops the fruit and folds him into her arms, caressing his hair. She doesn't say *we'll see them again* or *it's just for a short time*, or give any other sort of false comfort. She just lets him cry until he exhausts his tears. Then she puts the oranges back in the pot, one by one.

They watch in silence as the steamer heads downriver with Longwei, Wenling, Lifen and many others, but not with them.

Meilin hopes she's made the right decision.

'Come, Renshu.' Meilin picks up her basket and hands him the pot. 'We need to keep going.'

The dirt road rises into the hills. The day is warm and the path is steep. With each step, Meilin's sense of cautious optimism grows into elation. Finally! After all these years she has been bold, not timid. She is on her way home. Her heart is glad.

Renshu drags behind, kicking at the dust. After twenty minutes, he says he's tired and hungry.

She sits down on a rock overlooking the valley and pats the spot next to her. They have climbed far and quickly. It's good to rest. Meilin reaches into her basket and offers him a snow pear. He won't meet her gaze, but he does take the pear. It is round with tiny white freckles on a golden translucent skin. He takes a bite. Crisp like water chestnuts. Meilin takes one for herself. The sweet juice slakes her thirst.

'Save your seeds,' she instructs.

They follow a winding path through a thick bamboo forest, clacking a welcome in the wind. Soon, Meilin recognises a grove of trees. She rushes to examine them. Among the stumps, a few still grow. Meilin tugs down a branch and pulls off a stiff, waxy leaf. It is red, mottled with spots of green and yellow.

'Camphor,' Meilin says. 'We use the oils for medicines. Also good for keeping away moths.'

'Why have some been cut down?'

'It's a tradition to plant a camphor tree each time a baby girl is born. The tree and the girl grow together. That way, with a glance, the village matchmaker sees how many daughters a family has, and will know when they are old enough to be married. When one of the daughters gets engaged, the family cuts down the tree to make a trunk for her wedding dowry.'

'Did you have a camphor trunk, Ma?'

'Yes, I did,' Meilin says, softly.

The landscape is calling to Meilin. She knows these hills and cliffs. Beyond are the mountains of her youth. As a girl, she spent many summers here with her grandparents while her parents tended the shop in the city below. She breathes in the scent of pines, becoming more and more certain that the thick tree cover will have shielded her village from any bombs. Every overgrown path assures her that the remote settlement would have been missed by marching troops. Her father will be outside, gazing up, not in fear of planes, but reading the patterns of the clouds. Her mother will be worrying over which greens to feed their oxen. They will welcome her home.

Yet something doesn't seem right. They haven't seen any others on this road. Meilin keeps expecting to encounter a goatherd and his flock, or to hear the uneven roll of cartwheels on gravel. The farms are still, the tea fields too quieten. Something is missing. It's been eight years of war, she reasons. Of course there will be changes. She's optimistic, but not foolish. But as they continue, her foreboding grows.

When they pass a dilapidated pig pen, Meilin realises: *The animals!* Where are the braying donkeys and grunting pigs? No whiff of male goats peppers the air. No chickens have been fussing and cackling in the road.

She fills the quieten with talk about her family's cottage, their livestock, the brook with sweet water. She tells Renshu about the *Thump! Thump! Thump!* she'd hear some mornings when Farmer Liao's wife beat out the rugs, looking for the coins that fell from his pockets when he drank too much wine the night before. She reminisces about weaving bamboo leaves into mats for drying tea, about the deafening rush of rainfall in these forests during monsoons.

Rounding the final corner, she sees scorched patches of ground where wooden structures once stood, only half their walls remaining. There are piles of rubble, but no people. She shakes her head in disbelief. Impossible. She must have made a wrong turn. This must be some other unfortunate village.

But when her eyes trace shape of the hills on the horizon and the bend of the river down below, Meilin sees the landscape she committed to memory years ago. Her mistake is not that she lost her way; her mistake is that she dreamed this place would be untouched. Her basket falls to the ground as her grip loosens. *Not here, not here.*

She races past the abandoned pens, beyond the shattered stone walls, to the ancestors' tombs. She can't see the shrines at the end of the terrace. There should be bright red lanterns hanging on poles, and banners flying in the breeze. Even if the fresh fruit and flowers aren't there, the banners will be. Even if no longer bright, but faded and threadbare, they will be there. But at the foot of the shrines, Meilin finds no flowers, no fruit, no banners.

The tombs and family tablets have been smashed to pieces, scattered into piles of rubble. She falls to her knees and combs through the wreckage, looking for fragments of a name, a character, anything. She digs and digs. Nothing has been left intact.

Her hands are chafed and bleeding from her efforts. Fury and grief surge through her blood, gathering in her throat. She bursts out, howling a pain beyond words. She forgets the boy, forgets where she is, who she is, and collapses to the ground. As long as this place was safe and her parents were living and the ancestors well-tended, Meilin could bear anything, travel any distance. But now, all is lost.

*

Renshu has been watching with dismay. The moment they rounded the corner and his ma fell silent, he knew something was wrong. His pulse had raced in fear as she turned in a slow circle. When she dropped her basket and ran towards the tombs, he followed helplessly. Now he stands, stunned to see his ma wailing on the ground.

Shaken, he picks up her basket. He brings it over and sits beside her. There is little light left; it's getting cold. From the basket, he takes out the wool coverlet and wraps it around her shoulders.

He has never seen her like this. In his memory, she is always humming, sewing, cooking, walking, telling stories. Even during the war, she always knew what to do next. For the first time ever, his ma looks small and sad.

Renshu rubs her back with his open palm, the way she would for him when he was sick or upset. As darkness falls, her sobs recede, but she doesn't speak. He reaches his arm around her to keep them both warm. It's cold, but the sky is clear. Above the silhouettes of the trees, he sees more glittering stars than he ever has before.

It has been two full days. Renshu watches over his ma as best he can, but she is locked in a grief he cannot penetrate. He has made a shelter near the ruins, a small area in which to sit and rest, using fallen branches for cover. From the stream, he collects fresh water and coaxes her to drink from a broken teacup he found in the rubble. Each night, he builds a small fire to cook rice and brew tea. The embers offer little warmth. Later, he holds her close, soothing her turbulent dreams. When day comes, he tries to give her the remaining oranges. She barely takes a bite before pushing the fruit away.

Though the sun is bright, the temperature is dropping. Soon, the first snows will arrive. Their padded jackets and coverlets won't keep out the frost. Their provisions are almost gone. They cannot stay. Renshu must find a way to get to Yichang. And then what? A boat downriver to Shanghai to look for Uncle? A boat back to Chongqing? He doesn't know. But they must go somewhere else. To a place where Meilin will wake from this trance and be his ma again.

This morning, she sleeps peacefully after another restless night. He covers her with his jacket and rises to stretch his legs. Usually when she rests, he doesn't venture far, wanting to be within earshot. But today, instead of turning back when he reaches the edges of the settlement, he continues into the forest. Light filters through the thick trees. A clearing lies ahead. Curious, he draws near and discovers a grove of ancient trees. Many are disfigured and bent with age, their branches wild and untended. Venturing closer, he discovers they are pear trees. Some still bear fruit. Renshu finds a few pears that haven't yet fallen. He will bring them to Meilin.

In his pocket, he fingers the small, brown pear seeds his ma told him to save on the way up. He pulls them out and studies them. They look like russet-coloured drops of rain. Or tears. On impulse, he grabs a stick, digs a small hole, and places the seeds inside. He covers them with soft earth and pats the ground. Kneeling by the stream, he cups his hands together. With dripping handfuls, he waters the seeds. He squints up at the sun. Then Renshu gathers his new pears and heads back.

Meilin is still asleep. Renshu opens her basket. Inside are their clothes, the scroll and her box of treasures. It is much lighter than he remembers. Inside he finds a handful of coins and charms. Meilin stirs. He pockets a few gold coins and a jade charm, then puts the lid back. It will be enough, he thinks.

When Meilin opens her eyes, he pours cups of water on her hands to wash away the dirt and dried blood. He moistens the cloth of his shirt and wipes her face clear of smudged tears.

'Drink.' He puts the cup in her hands. 'Eat.' He gives her small bites of pear.

She sits and shakes her head, staring at the remains of her home.

'Come, Ma,' he insists. 'We need to go where it will be warmer and safer.'

He helps her to her feet. He carries her basket and their bedding. She leans on him. She doesn't speak. He gently leads her away.

*

All the way down the mountain, Meilin follows Renshu. Although he doesn't know how to find Yichang, he figures that as long as they go downhill, they will eventually reach the river. There, he will buy boat tickets. They will find Uncle in Shanghai. He'll explain that they got lost in the market. He'll say they are sorry. Everything will be fine. They will be safe again.

By afternoon, they are in the city. He trades the jade charm for food for the journey. At the docks, he finds a man selling tickets. Renshu says they want to go to Shanghai.

'Tickets are very expensive,' the man says, and looks past him to the next customers.

Renshu stays there.

The man turns and sees him again. 'You still here? How much do you have?'

Renshu shows the man the two gold coins from his pocket.

The man's eyes narrow. 'Yes, yes, this boat will take you there,' the man says, snatching the coins and thrusting some papers into Renshu's hands. Boarding the boat, Renshu dismisses the nagging sense that he might have been cheated. It doesn't matter, he thinks, they are headed to Uncle.

Meilin says 'yes' to whatever Renshu suggests. Sometimes, without warning, she starts to sob. Then she'll remain mute for days. Renshu doesn't know how to comfort her. She doesn't look like his ma. She looks like a lost child, with her hair in oily strands falling around her shoulders, and her tunic torn and dirty. Her eyes, usually alert and quick, don't focus on anything. Renshu takes out the scroll. Opening to the mountain peaks, he invokes Li Chi and her bravery in slaying the serpent. Then he finds a lone fisherman on a river. This must be Old Zhu, headed to Peach Blossom Spring. But when he starts retelling the story about the man who lost his horse, Renshu cannot think of any blessings, so he stops. Meilin doesn't seem to notice.

One morning, Renshu wakes to the sound of clinking coins. Meilin is going through her box. Counting and recounting, muttering and shaking her head. She has washed her face and pulled her hair into a bun.

'Ma! What is it?' he asks.

'Two gold pieces are missing.' Her voice is clear. And angry.

'Ma,' he reminds her, 'I used them for the boat tickets.'

'Two pieces? Two pieces of gold? Aiee! That is too much!' she shrieks.

Renshu's stomach drops. He was trying to help. He was finding a way back to Uncle.

'You were cheated! No wonder that lousy thief was so quick to push us on the boat. One piece for both of us would have been more than enough.'

Renshu stutters, 'Ma, you, you said it was okay.'

'I said okay? No, I never would have said okay to such a swindle!'

'There was nothing else I could do. You were too sad and we had to get on this boat to find Uncle.'

Meilin counts her coins again. *Clink, clink.*

'Ma, I'm sorry,' Renshu whispers.

Meilin swallows her next sentence and drops the rest of the coins and charms back into the box. 'My jade eggplant charm is gone, too,' she grumbles.

Even though he hates it when she's angry with him, relief springs up in Renshu. If she's cross, she must be coming out of her sadness. His ma is back.

Chapter Nine

Shanghai, China, January 1947

Sailing into Shanghai, Meilin and Renshu gape at the European buildings along the shore. *The Bund*, one of the other passengers tells them. Even after a decade of war and occupation, and now, during its struggle to rebuild, the promenade's elegance and stature are striking. Meilin sees why Wenling loves this city so much.

Streets bustle with trolleys, shiny motorcars, rickshaws, jeeps. For the first time, Meilin and Renshu see people from all over the world: Europeans with light-coloured hair and eyes, Sikh policemen wearing red turbans, Americans, Russians. There are unfamiliar languages and accents to wonder at. Shanghainese is so different from Mandarin and Sichuanese that at first Meilin cannot understand it at all. Still, enough people from all over China have come to the city that Meilin can get by with a mixture of Mandarin, Sichuanese and careful gestures.

They spend one week and a precious gold piece to stay at an inn while they search for Longwei. It's overwhelming. All Meilin knows is that Longwei said he was now a civil servant. They ask at a few government offices. She is told 'civil servant' is not enough of a job title. Does she know what area he works in? Does she know who his superior is? Does she have any more information? The few facts she offers aren't enough. Meilin never knew what Longwei did. In truth, she didn't want to know. She only knew that he'd worked for – and revered – the Generalissimo.

It used to be that Dao Longwei had connections everywhere, but now, no one seems to have heard of the man. There is a whirlpool of suggestions, but no definite answers: if he is part of the government, won't he be at the re-established capital in Nanjing? Or maybe he went to Chengdu? Or he might have gone to Taiwan to work in the government after Retrocession?

Changing strategy, Meilin is certain Longwei wouldn't be able to stay away from the enticements of gambling and drinks. She turns her attention to some of Shanghai's seedier corners. One evening, she trails government workers and off-duty Nationalist officers to Madame Zi's Emporium.

Glamorous and sophisticated, Madame Zi's Emporium offers something for everyone: a teahouse by day, where deals of all kinds occur; a shulou in the evenings for storytelling and opera, boasting gramophones and dancing girls; and at night, there are rooms upstairs for pleasures with the changsan ladies.

Meilin has begun to see beyond the glitter of the wealthy for-eigners, beyond the chauffeurs at the Palace Hotel in their smart caps and suits, opening the door for ladies in furs. She sees beyond the Cathay Theatre's neon lights, even beyond the spark-ling, alluring strains of jazz spilling out of dance clubs and into the streets. Many here still struggle for survival. Everyday neces-sities are expensive and scarce. If they are going to survive, she realises, she needs to find a job.

The next afternoon, Meilin returns to Madame Zi's. The woman at the door is older, maybe in her early fifties, and impec-cably dressed. Her suit of rich, deep maroon brocade has that unmistakable Shanghai mix of Eastern and Western styles. Her permed and dyed hair contrasts with her puffy face and cheeks. Around her thick wrists dangle jade bracelets, while gold ear-rings glint from her ears.

'What do you want? This is a place for gentlemen,' she scowls at Meilin.

Meilin flushes and hesitates.

'Are you looking for someone?' the woman demands, made suspicious by Meilin's reticence.

'Are you Madame Zi?' Meilin falters. 'I'm looking for work.'

The woman's eyes slide over Meilin, assessing her. Meilin stands straighter and purses her lips.

Madame Zi shakes her head. 'You're too old. There's nothing for you here.'

At that moment, one of the girls inside complains that her

costume does not fit properly. Meilin notices some sequins have fallen off and the hem is fraying.

Madame Zi glares back at the girl and curses her carelessness.

'I can sew,' Meilin says. 'I can fix your costumes and keep them tidy.' She bends down to take a piece of embroidery from her bag. It's a small black silk square, something she did on the long boat ride to Shanghai. Without a plan, following the wisdom of her fingers, the embroidery had seemed to almost weave itself. Over the weeks of travel, a peach tree had appeared, in full fruit, with leaves in many different shades of green. She holds it out now to Madame Zi. The woman takes it, squints at it, runs her fat, soft fingers along the stitches. She hands it back to Meilin.

'What else can you do?'

Meilin looks beyond Madame Zi. Around the room are tables of men drinking and eating snacks. Several tables need clearing. 'I can prepare food, wait tables, fix costumes. I can do many things that will keep your' – she pauses, not sure what to call the place, then recalls the sign outside – 'Emporium running smoothly.'

Madame Zi eyes Meilin again. This time, when the woman appraises her, Meilin raises her chin. Her expression is respectful, but not subservient. She has offered Madame Zi something she needs.

'Come back tomorrow. I'll think about it.' Madame Zi is curt, but her tone has shifted from dismissal to interest.

They come to an agreement: Meilin will mend costumes, help supervise clients and look after the girls. Madame Zi can only offer a small wage, but Meilin and Renshu can stay at an apartment down the street in a shikumen building that she also owns. The flat is small: a room and a tingzijian, a tiny north-facing study, above a kitchen, cold and cramped. But there is a sink and electricity. Plus, she can use scraps of cloth from the costumes to make slippers, mend Renshu's coat and trousers, and occasionally, when there is enough, sew new clothes.

In their new rooms, Meilin and Renshu share leftovers from a banquet earlier that evening. Outside, people light paper lanterns and release them into the sky to celebrate the close of the New Year's festivities. It is the Year of the Pig, a symbol of wealth and plenty. They go outside to watch. As a surprise, Meilin produces two lanterns for them to light. It is a small extravagance so they, too, can welcome the new year, when hope is a habit.

'What do you hope for this year?' Meilin asks Renshu.

The boy is quieten. Meilin looks at him. He looks thin, too thin. Despite the hungry, restless days, he has grown. In Chong-qing, she had sewed him a padded jacket that she'd been sure would last. The sleeves were too long and he had to fold up the cuffs. Now it barely stretches around his shoulders. Once fluffy and full, the padding is wadded flat. Where the satin has torn, cotton filling pokes out. The edges are marked with oil stains, dirt from the road, smudges where he has wiped something up or dried something off.

'Books,' Renshu says.

'Books?' His answer surprises and delights her. 'What kind of books?'

'All kinds. I want to learn more. I want to take exams and go to university. Be a scholar.'

His wish waters her sadness for Xiaowen and her own lost family. They would all be so delighted to see the young man he is becoming.

'We'll find a school for you, then,' she says. Though her reserves are low, she still has some cash. Education is a kind of investment, she reasons, and one she's always wanted for him.

'What about you, Ma, what do you wish for?'

Meilin considers what to say, watching a lantern float into the sky. Each lantern that rises is a defiant answer to all the bombs that fell. The lanterns don't erase the loss, but they feel like a show of hope, of resilience. Though the Communists and Kuo-mintang are fighting again in the northeast, for tonight, at least, Shanghai feels peaceful.

What do you wish for? His question echoes in her mind. When was the last time, if ever, someone asked her that? When was the last time she asked herself? For so long, the answer has been one of immediacy: shelter, food, money, safety, cloth, wood, warmth.

She does need and wish for all those things. But New Year's wishes are a time to reach beyond the practical. Of course, there are the impossible things: for Xiaowen to have returned, to have found her family, for the war to never have happened. But what does she wish for that could still be possible? How might they not just survive, but flourish?

'An orchard,' she says.

'An orchard?'

'Come, let's go inside,' she says.

Back in their room, Meilin gets the scroll from her basket. It is her last connection to the future she and Xiaowen once dreamed of. She carefully shuttles the silk from one end to the other, as if enacting a ritual, to the final scene where the traveller rests under blossoming trees.

'This.' She points at the trees. 'This is what I want.'

Renshu smiles. Perhaps now is the time to tell her about the ancient orchard he'd discovered in Yichang, and the seeds he left behind there.

'Have I ever told you the story about the magic pear tree?' Meilin asks, breaking his thoughts.

'The magic pear tree?' He shakes his head. And before he can say another word, she starts.

'There was once a farmer from a town called Bailizhou, not far from where I grew up. One autumn, the farmer had a splendid pear harvest. He filled his cart with fruit and made his way to the market.'

As the music of the story flows from his ma's tongue, Renshu fills with warmth. The cold night disappears and he is transported into the world she conjures. She seems, for once, happy. He will tell her about the seeds later.

'At the market, the farmer was doing a fine business. He spent the morning exchanging those golden globes for silver coins. After each purchase, he imagined what he would buy: strong black boots, a fur coat for winter, maybe even another donkey or a new cart. As the day went on, his purse and his dreams were growing fatter and fatter.

'Along came a monk. The edges of his robes were dusty and

frayed. He had walked a great distance, having come over the mountains on his way to a sacred temple. Although the monk had forsaken most of his worldly desires and earthly belongings long ago, the pears looked so delicious and smelled so sweet that he hungered after one.

'Approaching the farmer, he said, "Please, good sir, in your benevolence and generosity, will you give a humble monk one of your sweet pears?"

'The farmer hesitated. If he gave the monk a pear, people might get idea that he would give his fruit away for free. But he knew he shouldn't refuse a monk, so he pretended he didn't hear and hoped the monk would wander away.

'"Dear brother," persisted the monk, "you would honour your family name if you shared a pear. You have plenty. Could you not spare just one?"

'At that moment, the farmer was selling pears to a rich family. After pouring coins into the farmer's palm, the mother gave each of her children a pear. The farmer turned his back to the monk and batted at the air with his free hand, as if swatting a mosquito.

'An old tea seller nearby had been watching. She knew something about the ways of monks, so she flipped a coin in the farmer's direction. "Give the old man a pear! Have you no shame?" The farmer caught the coin mid-air and slipped it into his silk purse. "Very well," the farmer said to the monk, "have a pear."

'The monk bowed to the tea seller. "Thank you for the kindness." Then he turned to the farmer's cart and selected a pear. He sat down in the middle of the market and bit into his pear with his eyes closed, humming with pleasure. In this manner, he ate the whole fruit, stem and all, except for one seed. Then, opening his eyes, he stood and said, "You have many pears, but I only needed one seed."

'Taking a small shovel from his sack, he dug a hole. He placed the seed in the hole and carefully covered it. He then took his begging bowl and went over to the tea seller, holding it out. Without comment, the tea seller filled the bowl.

'The monk poured the water where he had buried the seed.

By now, a crowd had gathered to watch. From the moist spot on the ground, a shoot broke through the earth. In front of everyone's eyes, it grew and thickened into a trunk. Within minutes, the trunk divided, and branches sprouted and began to wind their way up, like arms reaching towards the sky. Cries of astonishment rang out as buds burst forth, then blossomed into full splendour. Amazement followed unfurling leaves, the blossoms folding in on themselves so that fruit began to swell and ripen. When the tree was heavy with fruit, a strong, sweet fragrance tickled everyone's noses and newly sprung limbs bowed down under the pull of plump pears. The monk turned to the crowd and, with open arms and a deep bow, invited everyone to eat.

'Once everyone had enjoyed a pear or two,' Meilin continues, 'the monk clapped his hands twice. The pear tree's leaves began to change colour, then wither, dry and drop. When they had all fallen and the branches were bare, he took a small axe from his bag, chopped down the tree, put the trunk over his shoulder, and walked out of the market, his robes dragging behind in the dust.

'Throughout these antics, the farmer stood aghast, his back to his cart. When everyone rushed to eat the monk's miraculous pears, the farmer was stunned, at a loss for words. Once the monk was gone, the market resumed its usual hubbub. The chickens, who had gone quieten in their wicker cages, began to squawk again, the vegetable sellers began bargaining once more with the thrifty old women, and dogs went back to their scampering. The farmer was about to continue selling his pears when the realisation struck him like a fist in his stomach.

'He spun around. Sure enough, his cart was empty. Examining the front, he saw that the cart handle had been hacked away. Shouting and red-faced, the farmer ran down the street after the monk, his overfull purse spilling coins as he went. A trail of children followed behind, collecting the riches he left in his wake. When he rounded the corner where the monk had disappeared, the only thing he saw was his cart handle lying in the middle of the empty road.'

Renshu laughs. A thunderous boom breaks the air.

'Renshu, look!'

Fireworks! Beyond the rising lanterns, high up in the sky, a dazzle of sparks and spirals. Then another, and another. Again and again, the thump of the launch, the whoosh of the rockets, then a bloom of colour, lighting up the sky.

They watch until the final flash shimmers and only smoky ghosts of fleeting brilliance remain.

Each day, after Renshu goes to school, Meilin heads to the Emporium. In the mornings, she helps prepare food. In the afternoons, she serves customers tea. As the evening clientele float in, Meilin goes home to Renshu. She turns around the mending so quickly that Madame Zi has nothing to complain about. Although it's an unsavoury place, it's practical. It's strategic. If she's going to find Longwei anywhere, it will be here.

Meilin is starting to recognise some regular customers. Among the Emporium's patrons are literati, intellectuals and art dealers, alongside civil servants and off-duty officers. Whatever their politics, they all come to drink tea, eat snacks and debate. Frequently, the art dealers produce small treasures, fishing for a sale. Meilin has seen ornate jewellery, carved boxes, bright baubles and jade charms changing hands. One seller, Mr Li, often trades in scrolls. He wears gold-rimmed glasses and his slick hair is parted in the middle. Though he's articulate and well-mannered, he's not always honest. She lingers when he unrolls one of his wares for a prospective buyer, listening in on the negotiations. From what she's seen of his collection, she knows her own scroll is much finer.

There's also Mr Xu, a big man with a broad nose, silver-tipped hair and a smoker's cough. She's not sure what his job is, but he has a hearty laugh and is friendly to everyone. Most of the men don't even see her, but Mr Xu jokes with Meilin when she brings more hot water for tea or clears away the plates. Occasionally he winks at her. She has to admit she likes the attention.

Today, Mr Xu is arguing with Mr Li. She listens intently, hoping to hear a mention of Longwei.

'Now that the Kuomintang have captured Yan'an, no doubt the Nationalists will prevail. How can the Communists continue without their capital?' Mr Li says.

'The CCP still has great support among the peasantry. Many still haven't forgiven the Nationalists for their corruption during the war,' Mr Xu counters.

'But the Kuomintang have the treasury, the cities, even the army! Even if there's support for the Communists, they don't have the resources. It's inconceivable they could overcome the KMT.'

'Unlikely,' Mr Xu agrees, 'but not impossible.'

Mr Li scoffs and finishes his tea in a single gulp. He catches Meilin's eye and signals that he wants more hot water. She heads to the kitchen, leaving them to their conversation.

Months pass, but Longwei never turns up. Although Meilin doesn't stop looking for him, the hope of reuniting grows fainter and fainter. Still, Meilin and Renshu are making a kind of life here. Madame Zi's trust in and estimation of Meilin grows. Dancing girls, says Madame Zi, come and go like willow leaves blowing down the road in autumn. But a seamstress as good as Meilin, now that is a rare find. Madame Zi is happy as long as Meilin keeps the costumes bright and alluring. All that sparkle attracts men and their bulging wallets away from the troubles of the world outside.

Shanghai, China, April 1948

As the Year of the Pig turns into the Year of the Rat, whatever sense of security Meilin and Renshu have cultivated begins to disintegrate. Inflation has spiralled out of control. A black market thrives and frustration with the government's mishandling of the economy simmers. More and more protests spring up in the streets. Uneasy, and losing faith in the Nationalists, foreigners are returning to their homelands.

At the Emporium, business is starting to dwindle. Initially, Madame Zi broadcasts a brash confidence. 'Regardless of politics, all men have the same appetites,' she says.

But in the spring, when the Communists retake Yan'an and much of the north, fewer and fewer customers come through the door. The regulars become sporadic in their visits. When they do come, they tend to drink too much.

With each report of more territory lost, more soldiers fallen, Mr Li waves his hands in disbelief. 'The Kuomintang had the bigger army and better resources. How can they have lost their advantages?' he exclaims.

'Hah!' Mr Xu blusters, signalling Meilin to bring another bottle of brandy. 'It's because the KMT have left too much destruction and discontent in their wake. They have lost the people's allegiance.'

'Maybe in the countryside, but you can't really believe the Communists could gain the cities,' Li presses as he empties his glass.

'Not possible. Not possible,' Mr Guo, another regular, mutters.

Meilin lingers to hear more of the discussion, but is soon called away by other customers.

A few weeks later, Meilin and Renshu are walking back towards the shikumen. As they pass a fabric store, Meilin notices that the price on a bolt of red silk that caught her eye that morning has been crossed out and rewritten several times. It has nearly quad-rupled during the day. Renshu is talking about his school.

Last year, it was a haven. For a few hours a day, he could immerse himself in his learning and friends. But now, classmates are disappearing. They come to school one day and don't come back the next. Rumours say that those from wealthier families have been whisked away to stay with relatives in Hong Kong, Taiwan, even America.

A convoy of military jeeps pass, honking their horns to clear the way. Renshu watches thoughtfully.

'Maybe I should become a soldier,' he says. 'Some of my classmates have quit school to join the army.'

'Absolutely not!' Meilin cries. 'You're only fourteen. What are you thinking?'

'But Ma, you work so hard. If I joined the army, I could earn money to help. I'd have a good uniform, too.'

'Renshu, after all that we have been through, I can't lose you, too. We're okay here. We have food, we have a place to stay. It's not so bad, right?' She grasps his hand.

He shrugs and shakes his hand free.

Ahead is a crowded square. Meilin can see people handing out fliers. She doesn't know which side they are on – CCP or KMT. Either way, she decides to steer Renshu away. They take a short-cut through an alleyway and pass an antiques shop. Meilin recognises Mr Li inside. At the corner, she glances up to note the intersection and they continue home.

In the autumn, the government calls for all citizens to hand over any gold, silver or foreign coins in an attempt to stabilise the currency. While it's now illegal to have gold, this only makes people hold on to what they have even more tightly. The economy continues to deteriorate. The Nationalist government is losing what little control remains. Meilin hears that the CCP is recruiting new members, even as suspected Communists are shot dead, point-blank, in the streets.

It is as dangerous an atmosphere as Meilin can ever remember. Much more poisonous than the Chongqing days. At least then, it was clear who the enemy were: they flew planes with white flags and red suns. Now, it's not so easy to know. Last week, Meilin saw someone in a Kuomintang uniform knocking on doors all down the lane, collecting names, occupations and activities of residents. She didn't answer when he rapped at her door. Now many of those neighbours are missing. Some of them were even government supporters! Who knows who that man in the uniform was? When there are spies for both parties everywhere, the best strategy is to be invisible.

One morning in late November, Meilin arrives at the Emporium to a scene of chaos. Tables are overturned, girls are crying. Meilin drops the costumes she has mended and runs over to the wailing Madame Zi.

'What happened?' she cries.

'A raid! A raid! Oh my beautiful Emporium!'

'When?'

Madame Zi is cursing and mumbling and pacing around. After

many questions and half answers, Meilin pieces together that the night before, a group of CCP members burst in and dragged away many patrons, including some of the lower-ranking KMT officers. Their fate? Probably to be questioned, tortured and killed.

'How, who?' Meilin stutters.

'Mr Xu, that putrid festering pig testicle, is a Communist!' Madame Zi spits in disgust. 'He was spying on us all along.'

Meilin's stomach drops. Mr Xu?

For so long, Madame Zi has remained sanguine, but now she's hysterical. She's packing up, she's leaving her beloved city.

'Where are you going?'

Madame holds up her hands, bare of rings and bracelets. 'America. I sold my jewels for a ticket.'

Meilin doesn't have gold to sell like Madame. What will she do? 'Madame, can you help us, please?' she begs.

'I can't, I don't have anything to spare.' Then she pauses. 'When I got my tickets this morning, there were still some for the *Taiping* next week, heading to Taiwan. Maybe you can get some? Either way, you must leave Shanghai, Meilin. Mr Xu' – and here she lets off another string of obscenities – 'is sure to have marked this place, the shikumen, and everyone here. There is no time. Get out!'

After school, Renshu is heading home when someone calls to him, waving. 'Hey! You're Meilin's boy, aren't you?'

The speaker is a big man, with short hair. Silvery at the tips. A wide nose and a cough. Renshu doesn't say anything.

'Cautious? I like that. It's a good quality,' the man says. 'It means you're a good judge of character. But there's no need to be suspicious, I know your ma from Madame Zi's. Maybe she's mentioned me? I'm Xu Deming, Mr Xu.'

Renshu squints at Mr Xu. Isn't he the one his ma says will sometimes slip her an extra coin?

'See. I knew you'd know me,' Mr Xu says, his voice polishing over Renshu's uncertainty. 'I have an opportunity for you.' Mr Xu glances around. Renshu looks, too. There are few passers-by on the street. Mr Xu steps closer to Renshu. 'You know this civil war is very serious. We are fighting for the soul of our country. The Red Army is approaching Shanghai. Some say it's only a matter of days before they arrive and take control.'

Renshu nods.

'I can give you a job that will help you and your ma stay safe.'

Over the past few weeks, his ma has been increasingly worried as business has dropped off at the Emporium. 'What's the job?' Renshu asks.

'You'll be my assistant. You'll help make China strong again. Working with me would be a great act of patriotism. You're nearly a man now, you need to look after your ma.' Mr Xu smiles broadly and holds out his chubby hands. 'So, do you want the job?'

Back at the shikumen, Meilin is trying to calm herself and come up with a plan. Taiwan? Really? A tiny island Meilin knows nothing about? There must be other options. Hong Kong? Train tickets would be easier and cheaper to get; they might even be able to make it on foot, at least part of the way. No, no, Hong Kong is too risky. It would take too long, and traintracks are too vulnerable. Besides, in Hong Kong, they wouldn't have the ocean separating them from the Communists. Taiwan, then. Who knows? Maybe Longwei will be there, if he's still alive. But how is she going to get two tickets?

She goes into their small study and retrieves her basket from its hiding place. She opens her wooden box. All that remains is a single gold coin. It's nowhere near enough. She picks up the scroll.

'Ma? Ma, where are you?'

Renshu is home. She puts the scroll back in the basket and exhales, closing her eyes briefly as she prepares to tell Renshu they will, once again, be leaving.

'Ma! Ma! I have good news! Someone has offered me a job!'

Alarm bells go off in Meilin's head. This does not sound like good news. Any composure she had corralled moments before skitters away.

'What? Who have you been talking to? Don't you know not to trust strangers?'

'No, not a stranger, Ma. Your friend, Mr Xu. You said he was the kindest and funniest of all the customers.'

Meilin's mouth goes dry. 'What did you say?'

'He said I needed to talk to you first, of course. We agreed to meet again tomorrow.'

'Did you tell him where we live?' Meilin barely whispers. Her heart is thudding in her ears.

'He didn't ask.'

'Were you followed home?'

Renshu looks over his shoulder. 'I don't know. I don't think so. Ma, what's wrong? I thought you liked him. I can help us earn more money.'

'He's a spy!' Meilin is hysterical; she can no longer keep it in. 'He's a spy for the Communists! There was a raid at Madame Zi's last night and he was behind it.'

Renshu gasps.

'You are too trusting, Renshu. We've got to leave Shanghai, as soon as possible.'

'Because of me?'

'No, not because of you.' She reassures him, attempting to muffle her panic. 'Because it's not safe here anymore. Because it's time.'

That evening, Meilin puts on a silk qipao, borrowed from Madame Zi's costumes. It's plum-coloured, with peonies. Her hair is in a chignon, high on her head to show off the lines of her neck. In her basket, she carries the scroll.

'Renshu, stay here, in the study. Don't answer the door for anyone. Don't put the lights on in the main room – that window is visible from the street.'

'Where are you going?'

'I have a small errand. Promise me you won't open the door. Promise?'

He nods solemnly. Her outburst earlier has frightened him.

The streets are busy outside, night vendors frying eggs in hot iron pots, rickshaws rattling past, followed by the occasional car. Further out, Meilin can hear the shouts of the military troops. Lights flash. She heads for Mr Li's.

Inside, the shop is small but luxurious. Display cabinets are filled with delicate snuff bottles, serving platters, cloisonné vases, and carved wooden ruyi sceptres. Near the front counter, he has a display of jade charms that Meilin studies. In her finery, she is certain he doesn't recognise her. A few other customers browse the sancai ceramics and porcelain figures. One by one, they leave. When she is the only customer left, Meilin asks Mr Li if he has any hand scrolls or landscape paintings.

He glances out the window. It's dark, and the streets are emptying of possible customers. 'In my office,' he says, and motions for her to follow him to a back room.

The room has elegant tiled floors, a low, rosewood kang table in the centre, and a tall, black lacquer display cabinet with brass fittings at the side. On the walls hang several scrolls depicting landscapes. In one corner is a basket holding many more scrolls, rolled up. In the other, a fire crackles in a wood stove.

'Please,' he says, gesturing at the walls.

Meilin walks the perimeter, contemplating each scroll. The room is warm, so she takes off her jacket and drapes it over her arm, covering her basket. She considers a painting of pines on a riverbank, mountains towering behind. A peasant and donkey cross a bridge in the foreground. The artwork is good, but not as good as her scroll. 'What's the price?'

'I keep it simple,' he says. 'Pay me in gold bullion, any currency, but it must weigh two liang.'

She nods and moves on to the next painting, a crane standing in long grasses. 'And this?'

'Also two liang. Do you have gold?' His impatience cracks his veneer of refinement.

'Actually, I come to sell, not buy.' Her heart pings as she takes her scroll from her basket and hands it to him to inspect. He eagerly unrolls it until its ends dangle off the kang and touch the cold floor. She has never looked at it fully unrolled. It feels like a betrayal to see it fully exposed, all its mysteries laid bare. She wants to shield it from his eyes and hands, but she restrains herself. Despite his attempt at indifference, he cannot hide his admiration.

'Two liang,' he offers.

She scoffs. It is nowhere near enough. But this is only the beginning of the negotiation. They both know this.

'Pah! You must give me at least eight! Look at the careful detail, the quality of the silk, the excellent calligraphy. Are you mad? Eight liang is a bargain – I should be asking ten.'

He smirks, amused by her spirit. 'Three liang, but no more.'

Back and forth, back and forth. She bargains him up to four, but she knows she needs more.

'How can you say four is fair when you are asking two liang for those?' She waves at the scrolls on the wall. 'You know they are nowhere near the quality of mine. Mine is a much finer work. A fair exchange. All I ask for is a fair exchange.'

He tilts his head in recognition. 'I know you. You're from Madame Zi's Emporium!'

His expression has shifted from hard-bargaining art dealer to something else. She's seen this look on men who come to the Emporium for the changsan girls. He moistens his lips. She shivers as she feels his eyes gliding over her dress.

'So you want some gold for this scroll of yours, which is, I admit, very, very beautiful.' He comes around to stand right next to her. Fumes of tobacco and sweat rise from his skin. 'But we can't agree on a price. Hmm . . .' He turns, then traces a finger along her cheek and jawbone. 'For eight liang, don't you have anything else to offer?' Even though it's warm in the room, goosebumps prickle her arm.

She knows what he wants. Of course she knows. Some part of her knew when she walked into the shop, when she put on the qipao with the long zip and high leg slits, even when she discovered his shop weeks ago.

'It's nearly closing time. I will go get your money. I feel sure we are going to come to an agreement soon,' he says. She hears him in the front of the shop, pulling down the shades. Keys jangle as he locks the door.

Get out. Leave. There must be another way, a different way, to get what she needs. She kneels and starts to roll up the scroll, swiftly but carefully, not wanting to damage it. She keeps an eye on the door; she'll have to squeeze by as quickly as she can. As she's tying the tassel, a hand grips her shoulder from behind. Startled, she drops the scroll and it clatters to the floor, partially unrolling. He has entered the room through a different door.

Then he's grabbing her wrist and pinning her arm behind her back, his voice calm and genial. 'I think we've found a fair price.' He's pushing up the fabric of her dress, pulling her underwear down.

Pain shoots along her shoulder. She focuses on the pain, unwilling to acknowledge what else is happening. Just when she thinks her arm is about to snap, he lets go. Relief barely registers before her cheek is pressed hard against the rosewood she admired before. A strong hand holds her head down and another unzips her dress, pulls it off. He is groping her breasts, her buttocks, pulling her thighs apart. She wants to kick or scream or push him away. She can't. She's captured in her own body. Frozen.

Terror eclipses her pain.

Her pulse was racing when her head hit the desk, but now, everything slows. Her limbs are like a rag doll's. He flips her over and then he's on top of her. She turns her face away and stares at the motionless blades of a ceiling fan.

When he penetrates her, there is a sharp, piercing pain, then a terrible creeping coldness.

She is not here. She is not here.

He's grunting. Her back skids and chafes along the table. There is a rhythmic scraping of table legs on the tile floor. She still cannot move.

After a massive, rough shove, he shudders and groans.

He is spent, lying on her, trapping her.

Again and again, her eyes trace the shape of the fan blades.

Finally, he pulls away.

She drops back down into her body. Her back hurts, her thighs hurt, her arms ache, her groin is numb. She cannot stop shaking.

She hears him panting. She senses where he is in the room, but she can't – won't – look at him.

'There's your fair exchange,' he says, and she sees his hands pick up her scroll from the floor. She sits and cradles her face with her hand, touching her mouth, her cheekbones, her eye sockets, as if checking to see if she is complete. Still shaking, she grasps her hands together and blows on her fingers. It doesn't help. Her shoes are still on. She pulls her underwear back up, retrieves her dress. The fire snaps and sputters. Somehow she gets herself dressed, puts her jacket back on, finds her basket.

On the table, he sets down a silk purse. The coins inside clink. She reaches for the purse. It is nauseatingly heavy.

'Go now,' he says.

She watches her feet, willing each one to move. One step. Another step. She is concentrating on the designs of the floor tiles; she is almost at the door. The door squeaks as he opens it. There are rats scuttling in the alley. It is so cold outside. She retches against the building, shuddering, shuddering. Then, slowly, she makes her way back to Renshu.

Chapter Ten

Harbour of Shanghai, China, December 1948

They stand on the deck of the *Taiping*. People crowd in front and behind, making room where there is none. Renshu, a full head taller than Meilin, stays close, sheltering her, protecting their space. It would be easy for fingers to wander into pockets. A bag set down by one pair of hands is likely to be picked up by another.

Behind the drifting silhouettes of the sampans and fishing boats, lights glimmer on the shore. A never-ending crowd stretches from the end of the dock back towards the Bund. People cry and wail, begging for just one more boat to ferry them to the steamer. Earlier, on the small boat Meilin and Renshu caught, the boatman refused to leave until everyone discarded something from their suitcases. Clothing, books and mementos accumulated as families agonised over what to keep, what to leave. Anticipating moments like this, Meilin had tossed down a red satin bag of costume jewellery from the Emporium. A man, probably in cahoots with the boat's owner, gathered the castaway items. Even with the lightened load, waves still threatened to capsize the craft. Icy salt water sloshed over their shoes. Hurrying up a wobbly ramp, they boarded the *Taiping*. Meilin's gold had only been enough for deck spots; cabin tickets were too costly.

Most of the other passengers on the deck are male. The few families Meilin saw earlier have disappeared. Perhaps they were able to afford cabins. Feeling vulnerable, she scans the crowd. By the side of the boat she spots a young mother with three children. Meilin steers Renshu towards them. Each child has a bag, and the mother holds a baby in her arms. The silky tufts of the baby's hair stick up like thick wild grass. The children huddle near their mother: a boy, who could be about five, and two girls, identical twins, maybe a bit older, with glossy plaits and padded jackets. They peek at Meilin and Renshu, then whisper to each other. Meilin catches the mother's eye and nods. The mother smiles back.

The placid moment doesn't last long. The baby starts writhing in his mama's arms. Then he arches his back and kicks, pushing against her. The little boy is trying to get the twins to play, but they ignore him, so he pokes his ma, then pinches the baby. This sets the baby off into high-pitched shrieks. The boy pulls one of the twins' plaits, hard. She slaps him across the face. The other twin tackles him, and the mother shouts at them all to stop it immediately. Now they are all crying, and the baby screams even louder. The second twin shoves her little brother, and he stumbles into Renshu. All along the deck, people shout and shove back. In the ruckus, a man who reeks of alcohol loses his balance and falls on his backside. More embarrassed than hurt, he staggers to his feet and starts shouting at the young mother. She is apologising, the baby is howling, the kids are bickering, and the man is yammering at them in an unfamiliar dialect. Finally, the man says something in disgust and shoulders his way through the onlookers.

'What a bastard!' Meilin says to the mother. 'Do you want a hand?'

The woman's look of relief makes Meilin teary herself, and she takes the baby into her arms. Holding the squirmy bundle, she begins to sway, singing softly. This action soothes her own jangled nerves. The mother alternately scolds and comforts her other children, until they, too, calm down.

Meilin and the woman begin to chat. The young mother, named Zhao Peiwen, is from a small village near Wuhan. Her husband is in the army. He was able to procure boat tickets, but didn't have enough influence or cash for a cabin in the hold. Still, they are grateful to escape. There will be temporary housing for them in Taiwan, and he'll join them here when he can.

The baby has calmed. Peiwen takes him back, thanking Meilin again for her kindness. 'And you?' she asks. 'What is your story?'

After sharing their names, Meilin says they got separated from their family after the war. Before she can continue, the conversation is interrupted by more commotion. Alarmed, Meilin and Peiwen strain to see what's happening. A military police officer and one of the crew members are checking tickets, working their way along the deck.

'There are too many passengers to travel safely. Priority is for military and military families. Those without proper identification must disembark,' the officer intones.

'But I bought a ticket!' a man protests.

'It doesn't matter if you can't show proper identification.' The officer signals to a colleague to escort the man away.

Meilin lets out a slow breath, trying to contain her panic. The officer is getting closer. As he speaks with the passengers, people argue, waving papers and passports. More often than not, he shakes his head and they are pulled off the ship, dragged away. Someone worms through the crowd, trying to evade questioning, but this simply draws attention. Soon another officer catches him on the other side of the deck.

Meilin's heart is rabbiting. She has nothing. No gold, no jewellery, no cash. Should she and Renshu duck down and creep away?

'Papers!' a male voice demands at her side.

Meilin jumps. So intent on watching the first officer, she didn't notice this other one, closer.

She fumbles in her basket, reaching after papers that don't exist.

'Here.' Peiwen thrusts a bundle into his hands.

Meilin stares at her in astonishment.

While he checks the papers' validity, Peiwen shifts the baby from one hip to the other and makes the tiniest motion with her head, indicating that Meilin must stay silent. She grasps Meilin's hand to stop her frantic scrabbling in the basket.

The man peers at Peiwen and says her name. She nods.

He looks at the next paper and says two more names: 'Zhu Huifang and Zhu Huiqing?'

She indicates her twins.

'Zhu Huifei?'

She nods at her boy. Finally, she holds up the baby when the man says, 'Zhu Huibao?'

He shuffles the pages, and Peiwen gestures to Meilin and Renshu.

He looks at Meilin and says, 'Zhu Yuming?'

She nods.

Then: 'Deng Jinwei?'

Renshu takes his cue from Meilin and nods, too.

The man hands the papers back to Peiwen and continues to the next person.

'What did you do?' Meilin whispers.

Peiwen shushes her. 'Later,' she whispers. Meilin watches the unlucky passengers being escorted off the boat. She shudders to think how close she and Renshu were to being among them.

A long horn sounds. The boat finally begins to pull away. Passengers clutch their hats; scarves fly in the wind. People sob as they lose sight of family and friends on shore. The air is jumbled with dialects, but the cadence of disbelief and grief is recognisable in any language.

Meilin turns to Peiwen. 'Thank you. You saved us. How did you—'

Peiwen cuts her off. 'We were supposed to meet my sister-in-law and her husband in Shanghai. We were going to travel to Taiwan together, but they didn't turn up. I couldn't risk waiting. We had to leave without them.' Her voice falters, and she wipes her eyes.

'There are no easy decisions in difficult times,' Meilin murmurs.

'You needed two military travel permits. I had two to spare. That wasn't a difficult decision.'

Renshu is amusing Peiwen's kids. He is showing them the finger bomb game Meilin remembers from Chongqing. He wraps his fingers around each other to form a tangled nest and dares the kids to lift his fingers one by one. They giggle with nervous relief each time the finger stands up and the remaining fingers remain quieten. If they can raise all his fingers except for the trigger, they win. But if they raise the wrong one, he shouts 'Kaboom!'

Peiwen picks up the conversation again. It's been just her and the children for months. She tells Meilin they were all born during the war. Each time her husband came home on leave, it was a great celebration. And then, of course, nine months later, a baby. Happy to be distracted from her own thoughts, Meilin feels herself warming to Peiwen.

The boat navigates the Huangpu River, dodging carcasses of sunken ships and live mines still lurking in the river bed. On either side, the banks are littered with the wreckage of burned-out buildings, tangled barbed wire and rubble left from the decade-long struggle for control. Smoke rises off fires still smouldering from the latest skirmishes. This choked waterway is as different as can be from the swirling, treacherous waters of Xiling Gorge. But Meilin thinks to herself that this, too, is a passage through the Gates of Hell.

At last, they reach the mouth of the river and the boat moves into the sea. Vast open waters lie ahead. Meilin watches the shoreline recede.

'Where are you going once you get to Taiwan?' Peiwen asks.

Meilin shies away from the question. She's not sure how to answer what she hasn't even asked herself. She's relieved when one of the girls comes over and says she's hungry. The other kids soon flock around her. After raising her eyebrows to ask if it's okay, Peiwen hands Meilin the drowsy baby. Then she opens her bag and gives them each a red bean paste bun. She holds out the bag to Renshu and Meilin. The buns are one of Renshu's favourites. Meilin can't remember when they last ate. Her stomach rumbles, and she's sure his does too, but Meilin shakes her head, no. They have nothing to share in return.

'Go on,' urges Peiwen, holding the buns out closer to Renshu. 'You have helped us. Please.'

Meilin relents and nods at Renshu. He takes one and thanks Peiwen. Meilin says she's not hungry, save them for the kids, and look, the baby is finally asleep. When Peiwen takes the sleeping boy back in her arms, Meilin feels a momentary emptiness, a missing warmth, before she calls Renshu over to her side.

Peiwen's children have settled on the deck. The twins sit back-to-back, leaning against each other for support. Their little brother snuggles against his ma and the baby. All around, conversations are dying down. Meilin and Renshu sit with their backs to the boat's sides, arms wrapped around their belongings. Finally safe and with a moment of quieten, the enormity of the past week looms over Meilin. Her arm is still tender where Mr Li had twisted it. Everything is sore and it's hard to sit. Bruises bloom all along her legs and buttocks. A dull pain bites at her exhaustion, keeping her from rest.

'Ma?'

'Yes?'

'Ma, I'm sorry,' Renshu says to the dark.

'Sorry? Why sorry?' she asks back, also looking at the dark.

'About talking to Mr Xu. It's all my fault.'

Meilin closes her eyes and breathes deeply. She waits until she is certain she won't break down when she speaks. 'Renshu, it's not your fault.' She reaches up and puts her arm around him. It hurts to lift her shoulder, but she wants to hold her boy.

'We are together,' she says. 'We are escaping the fighting; we might even find Auntie and Uncle in Taiwan. So . . . so, what makes you so sure this isn't a blessing?'

'Your stories . . .' he starts, and then trails off, as if he doesn't know what to say.

'How about I tell you a new one?'

'From the scroll?'

Meilin pauses. 'It would be too dark to see the scroll right now, so you'll have to use your imagination.' She keeps her voice composed, hoping not to reveal how shaken she still is. This is her last story, the one she's been saving to tell when the time was right.

'Two monks were walking through the countryside on a spring day.' She feels Renshu's shoulders relax.

'Deep in conversation about what it means to become truly enlightened, they came to a roaring river. A peasant woman sitting on the bank called out.

' "Please, dear brothers, will you help me cross? I cannot swim and I'm afraid of the rapids."

'Without a moment's hesitation, the older monk bent down, lifted the woman and walked into the river. The waters swirled and tugged at his robes, but calm and sure-footed, he brought her to safety on the other side. He set her down on the shore and bowed.

' "Thank you, dear brother!" she said, bowing back. Then she gathered her slightly wet bundle and continued on her way.

'The whole time, the younger monk followed behind without saying a word.

'They continued walking down the road, now in silence. After some time, the younger monk began to sigh and wrinkle his nose. He became more and more agitated until he could contain his frustration no more.

' "Brother, how could you do that?"

' "Do what?"

' "Carry that woman! You know it is against the rules of our order to have any contact with females. Why did you break that rule?"

'The older monk stopped and looked the younger monk straight in the eye.

'They stood like that for a long time, neither speaking a word.

'Finally, the older monk said, "Brother, I set that woman down on the other side of the river. Why are you still carrying her?" '

Meilin takes her arm from Renshu's shoulder and turns to face him. 'Renshu, let's not carry anything that we've already left behind.'

Though no longer a boy, his eyes are full of a solemn, simple trust. It has been a decade since the night they fled Changsha. Now, more than ever before, a great unknown awaits. Regardless of what lies ahead, she promises herself, she won't betray this trust.

The sea is calm. The ship has turned off its lights to move stealthily, evading the wartime curfew. They fall silent. Soon, Renshu's asleep.

Meilin looks back. She sees nothing but dark water. During all these years of disruption, they have still always had China beneath their feet. Now as the boat sails further away, all that she has ever known, all that great excess and great loss, slips silently beyond the horizon. Waves lick the sides of the ship, voices murmur on the deck, and the steamer's engines churn. China is gone.

PART THREE
1948–1960

Chapter Eleven

Keelung Harbour, Taiwan, December 1948

They stumble into the port's stuffy, overcrowded offices. A queue of people sitting on battered suitcases or rolled-up quilts inches along as each group registers their arrival. When it is their turn, Meilin notices the braid on the official's hat is frayed, and his buttons have been polished so often that the shiny veneer has flaked off, revealing dull metal underneath.

'State your name, city, and province of origin.' The official doesn't look up, his pen poised to complete his form.

Without hesitation, Meilin says 'Zhu, Yuming and Deng, Jinwei. Wuhan, Hubei Province.' She has been practising the names since Peiwen insisted they come with her. *You have nowhere to go; I have no one to help me. Use my sister-in-law and brother-in-law's names. Use their ration cards. We have to help each other out in these hard times. Where will you live otherwise?*

'Identification papers?'

Meilin hands him the documents from Peiwen and watches him copy the information. He briefly raises his eyes to ask for her last place of residence. Meilin gives the address of Madame Zi's shikumen. Taking out a soiled handkerchief, he wipes his glistening forehead. He signs and stamps various papers, gathers them up and hands them all to her. He is explaining something, but Meilin is so relieved, she can't take anything in. He dismisses them. Renshu picks up her basket and their suitcase and they exit into the bright, cold air.

Outside, people mill around, waiting for friends and relatives. Others look uncertain; now that they have arrived in Taiwan, what next? A military transport truck with a canvas top rolls into the area and people start boarding. It soon fills and drives off.

'Meilin!' Peiwen calls. She and the children have just emerged from the offices.

When the next truck arrives, they show their papers to the driver, climb on and ride into Taipei.

It's a small city. There are only a few motorcars running among the pedestrians, bicycles, pedicabs and rickshaws. Traffic ducks in and out of lanes and down alleys that lead off the main roads. After the dense motion she'd grown accustomed to in Shanghai, Meilin welcomes the relative calm. Her eye wanders over the unfamiliar architecture of red and grey bricks. The buildings are shorter, few reaching above two storeys. Most people are wearing clothes in styles she's never seen, and Meilin can't understand the language. Japanese? Peiwen shakes her head. No, it's something else. They drive past people walking along the roads, carrying belongings, looking for places to stay. Locals jeer at the truck as it rumbles by. Finally, they pull up at a building that looks like a school. Through an open door, Meilin sees it is already overflowing with occupants. A small man in a khaki uniform rushes out, crying 'No room, no room!' and signals for them to drive on. At the city's outskirts, the truck stops again outside a massive, slightly dilapidated warehouse. The building's sides are made of corrugated steel. Weeds and yellowed grasses poke up between cracks in the concrete paving. A big man, also in a khaki uniform, comes over, confers with the driver, and then motions for everyone to get off the truck. They stand in a daze, surrounded by their few belongings. The uniformed man pulls the warehouse doors open and calls them inside.

It is as dark as a cave. When her eyes adjust, Meilin sees the warehouse has been divided into several small makeshift shelters, with thin walls made from bagasse boards that have been precariously nailed together. Each marks a living space for a family. A tarp slung over a rope functions as a door. As they follow the man, they pass some sections with this curtain pulled back. People gather around overturned crates or the occasional glow of a kerosene lamp. It is a tiny village contained inside this big building.

At the far end, people wait in a queue to use zinc basins for washing. The man points out a communal water tank where they can get an allotted amount each day. The kitchen is a long counter with small, coal-cake-fired earthen stoves. Outside, in a nearby field, the man shows them the toilet: a simple shack. Inside, there is a place to squat on rough planks set across a deep ditch. The stench is staggering. Flies buzz everywhere.

After this tour, each new family is issued a space of two ping for living, regardless of the number of family members. Then the man hurries off to attend to some other duty.

Once they have set their belongings inside, Meilin and Pei-wen send the kids off to collect water. Peiwen holds the baby and turns a slow circle, letting out a slow sigh as she looks at the stained tarp curtain, the flimsy walls, the concrete floor.

'It's only temporary,' Meilin says.

'We have a roof over our heads and a floor under our feet,' Peiwen adds.

They arrange their blankets into warm beds as best as they can. When the children return, they cook some of Peiwen's dwindling supply of rice. Afterwards, they sit side by side for warmth, still hungry and tired, but glad the sea no longer moves underneath them. Somehow, the afternoon and evening have passed in shuffling and worry, and now night has arrived.

The bare bulbs hanging above are turned off, and the weak light they offered disappears. Throughout the warehouse, kerosene lamps flicker, throwing shadows high up on the walls. Meilin hears many different accents and dialects. Everyone is from somewhere else. One by one, the lamps blink off and the talk dies down.

As they lie in their new shelter, this dank, damp warehouse on an island far from home, the cold from the floor steals through their bedding to settle directly on their skin.

'It's only temporary,' Peiwen says, echoing Meilin's earlier words.

There is rustling throughout the warehouse. Do mice scurry among the stores of grain? Wisps of conversation and cigarette smoke drift in from outside. Meilin stares up into the high rafters of the warehouse. It is like looking at a night sky in which all the stars have been extinguished.

Throughout the first winter, they bargain in the market every day for old vegetables. They look for scraps of bamboo and discarded wood for small fires. Because Peiwen's husband is in the military, the government gives them rations of flour, oil, salt. It is not enough, but it is something. Other families in the warehouse help them enrol the kids in the schools for military families, point them to the Native Place associations that have formed. Slowly, they begin to piece together a life.

One day, Meilin finds a newspaper, *Zhongyang Ribao*, left behind in the market. The front page shouts slogans about the Generalissimo, but Meilin turns it over and on the back, she notices the 'Missing Persons' classifieds. People are looking for relatives last seen on the mainland. Some ads give the name and contact details for the seeker. Others name and describe lost family members. For the next hour, she stands in the cold air and reads them. Each tiny box of text tells a story of huge loss and stubborn hope. Maybe Longwei, if he's here, will have placed one for her and Renshu? At the end of the last column, she sighs. No luck.

As winter turns to spring, whenever she can, Meilin gets a newspaper and reads every single 'Missing Persons' advert. She even places a few herself, naming Longwei, Wenling and Lifen. Where there's a chance, she must try. But she never hears back.

By March, the warehouse is full. Trucks filled with new arrivals are sent somewhere else. Although winds shake the walls and hailstorms batter the roof, the only things that fall on their heads are raindrops from leaks and cracks, not shrapnel. A buzz overhead signifies mosquitos, not airplanes. In April, headlines proclaim that the Communist army has jumped the Yangtze and taken Nanjing. When Shanghai falls in May, the classified sections swell, but there is no sign of Longwei.

In October, Mao Zedong proclaims the establishment of the Peoples' Republic of China. When Chiang Kai-shek retreats to Taipei in December with the last of his troops, declaring that the Republic of China will stage its recovery of the mainland from

Taiwan, Meilin stops reading the newspapers. She's too tired these days. She's been spending the evenings sewing. Though the weak light inside the warehouse strains her eyes, she embroiders tiny bats and peonies on purses she then sells in the market. Despite everything, Meilin insists on adding brightness and beauty.

It's been nearly a year since they arrived in Taiwan.

In early winter, Peiwen's husband, Yuping, sends news that a spot has finally opened up for them at a New Harmony Juancun, a military families' village. They leave the warehouse for a tiny two-room house. One room is for Peiwen and her kids, the other is for Meilin and Renshu, and the food and small stove they bought on the black market. Though cramped, their new place has solid walls. It is somewhere to return to at the end of the day. It can become a home.

Taipei, Taiwan, September 1950

At the juancun, Meilin's friendship with Peiwen strengthens. They continue to share the work of looking after the children, cooking and shopping. She is grateful the kids have school. The government rations of food and basic supplies continue. They are reaching towards stability.

Of course, military patrols are everywhere; that's to be expected. Everyone is preparing for when, in a few years' time, the KMT will retake the Motherland from the Communist bandits. There are American sailors, too, in Taipei. Since the outbreak of the Korean war, the US Navy's Seventh Fleet has been patrolling the Strait.

In the evenings and afternoons, when it's too hot to stay inside, people drag rattan chairs into the narrow alleyways between houses, chatting and reminiscing as they try to cool down. The atmosphere overflows with stories and songs in different dialects. Often, families prepare dishes from their hometowns to share. When people speak of returning to the Motherland, Meilin grows quieten. They long for families, homes, friends, beloved places. But when Meilin looks back, she sees nothing but loss, no one but ghosts.

Kids run wild through the compound, in and out of each other's houses, trading toys, food and swear words. Gossip travels across the alleyways and down the lanes faster than those gossiped about can get home to set the story straight. Meilin feels like she's a part of a big family.

Still, one must be careful. Ears and eyes are everywhere. More often than not, when Meilin looks out the window, someone else looks back in at her. Sounds, smells and conversations pass straight through the thin walls. Everyone heard Mr Chen the night he stumbled down the alleyways, drunkenly cursing the KMT, cursing the Generalissimo and even denouncing Madame Chiang. No one was surprised when the garrison command dragged him away two days later.

In Meilin's view, as long as you don't criticise the government or make anyone angry or jealous enough to falsely accuse you, it's possible to grow, even flourish, here. Besides, after the betrayals in Shanghai, Meilin has lost all appetite for politics. Instead, she focuses on Renshu. She tries to find something joyful in each day – making food that the children like, selling handicrafts in the market or bargaining for fresh vegetables – building a life on small but certain pleasures.

Today is Renshu's first day at Jianguo High School. His new shoes feel stiff. It's hard to concentrate because he keeps tracing his fingers along the clean, sharp cuffs of his shirt, and sneaking glances at the seams pressed into his trouser legs. Itchy as it is, he is proud to wear this new uniform. Last year, at middle school, he was glad to sit at a desk for lessons without the constant fear of air raids or emergency evacuations. He did well, and at the end of the year, his teachers encouraged him to go to Jianguo.

Now the teacher has put up a mathematics problem using terms and symbols that Renshu doesn't know. All his classmates are busy making calculations and drawing graphs. Renshu stares at the board. He is used to finishing top in his lessons. However fragmented his learning in Chongqing, Shanghai or even last year at the middle school, he has always shone. But now, he doesn't even understand the questions, let alone know the answers. He goes mute with shame.

That afternoon, back at the juancun, his ma greets him with a hopeful look.

'How was it?'

'Good.' He fiddles with the clasp on his bag.

'That's it? Nothing else?'

He looks at her and shakes his head. He says he needs to study. It's quieten in the house. Peiwen and the baby must be out. Thankfully, the kids aren't home yet. He sits on the settee and takes out some paper and a small, worn textbook. He pulls an upturned crate towards him and places his paper and pencil on top. Thumbing through to the page the teacher assigned, he balances the book on his leg, keeping it open with his elbow. With one hand, he holds the crate steady, and with the other, he works out the maths. He can hear his ma in the other room, cutting something on a chopping board.

She comes in with a plate of watermelon slices. He says he's not hungry, and looks at his paper again. Somewhere the calculation has gone wrong and he can't find his mistake. She sets the plate down and sits next to him, accidentally knocking the book to the floor. She picks it up and hands it back. He flips the pages until he finds his place again, and creases the spine to make the book stay open.

'What is it, Renshu? What's wrong?'

Renshu jams his pencil into the textbook and closes the cover. 'I'm so far behind everyone else. I'll never catch up. And' – he looks up at the door, his voice cracking in frustration – 'in two minutes, Peiwen's kids will come home. When will I study? How can I learn? At night there's not enough light; in the day, there's too much noise. And there's no space in this house.'

He scowls and kicks the crate, knocking over the watermelon slices. He starts to pick them up, but then, exasperated, he walks out, slamming the wooden door.

*

Meilin hasn't seen Renshu so angry in a long time. For weeks, he had been looking forward to starting at Jianguo. How frustrating it must be to begin at last, only to feel like he's falling short. Meilin looks around the small, cramped space. What can she do?

The voices of Peiwen's kids echo down the alley. Meilin quickly tidies the room and puts Renshu's bag away. She has just put fresh melon slices on the plate when the family bursts through the door.

The twins are arguing and their brother is whining. When they see the melon, all three drop their school bags to grab slices. They start eating right away, hardly stopping to say hello before heading back outside, spitting the seeds out in the dirt road.

Later that week, when Renshu arrives home, his ma ushers him into the back room.

'Here,' she says, showing him a small table she has made by placing a long bagasse board across the top of two wooden crates. She demonstrates how he can sit on the floor and spread his work out. 'I will take care of the kids after school. The girls can go to the market together and Huifei can help me.'

Renshu kneels and runs his hand along the surface of the board. A desk, a place to sit, time to study.

She says she traded a pair of embroidered slippers and a mended silk jacket he had outgrown for the crates and board. She shows him how she has tucked their bedding inside the crates, so the room feels both tidier and more spacious, even though it holds more things.

'I will make you proud, Ma. I will do my best.' His eyes fill, but he is too old to cry.

'You already make me proud. Look!' She points. Outside, a cock struts by, waggling its wattle.

'A rooster! A good sign, isn't it?' He laughs.

'Yes, practise your learning here. Your characters, your calculations. Study hard.'

'Ma, where is it?'

'Where is what?'

'The scroll, where is it?'

It's a question that's been on his mind for a long time. He hasn't seen it since before they came to Taiwan.

The first time Renshu asked Meilin about the scroll was when they were living in the warehouse. She had said that taking it out would attract unwanted attention. Though he promised he'd be very quieten, very gentle, she'd refused. After that, he asked a few more times, but she always said no. Once they'd moved to the juancun and had a room of their own, he asked again. His ma frowned, shook her head and carried on with her sewing. In that moment, he saw how much his question had troubled her. Since then, something has held him back from asking. But today, the rooster has reminded them both of the scroll, so he thought it would be okay.

A shadow passes over Meilin's face and she lowers her eyes. Her expression tells him the answer, even though she doesn't speak.

He suspected it might be gone, but her tiny gesture feels like a massive blow. He didn't realise how much he had hoped otherwise. 'What happened?'

'I sold it.' Her voice is hoarse.

'Sold it?' Renshu's voice rises with anger. 'How could you? It was our only connection to Ba. Why did you sell it?' He is fuming, surprised by his own fury.

Stricken, his ma takes in a sharp breath. 'I had no other choice. We had to get out of Shanghai.' Tears are rolling down her cheeks. He hasn't seen her cry like this in a long time. He tries to tamp down his dismay, angry at himself now for upsetting her.

'Ma, I'm sorry. It's just that we loved it so much. We've always had it.'

She's crying, and he doesn't know what to do. This was such a happy moment and he's ruined it. *What happened in Shanghai?* Those last days were so chaotic.

Finally, she recovers enough to speak. 'It was only an object, Renshu. Maybe it was never ours to keep. The important thing is that we have its stories.'

The front door bangs open and the noise of Peiwen's children fills the house.

She wipes her eyes, stands and nudges his bag towards him. 'Study now.'

Meilin's gift of time and space is a sanctuary for Renshu. For the first time, he can concentrate fully. He can study without needing to keep one ear tuned to the outside world, ready to relocate at a moment's notice. He falls in love with the elegance of equations, the properties of motion. He is amazed by how, given an object's initial conditions, he can predict where and when it might arrive elsewhere. There is an inarguable reliability in maths, in physics. Renshu comes to believe that, if he studies enough, anything might make sense. There is a comfort, too, in the realisation that nothing can take his learning away. Unlike land, gold, treasures, food, or even people, once he understands something, it is his to keep forever.

Taipei, Taiwan, May 1955

It has been a good day for Meilin. In the market, Luo was celebrating his grandson's birth, so he threw in an extra bundle of snow peas. Since the PRC's bombardment of the Kinmen and Dachen islands last autumn, even more Americans are stationed in Taipei. Missing their sweethearts and wives, they've bought all Meilin's embroidered silk purses. She never asks who the treasures are for. A bit of discretion makes her wares sell quickly, a lesson that some sellers with quick tongues have yet to learn.

Meilin walks home with a full basket: cabbages, carrots, onions, mangos, a pineapple and the snow peas. All this, and she still has some New Taiwan dollars folded in her purse.

A group of schoolboys works its way down the street like a khaki-coloured wave, searching for snacks and comics after school. The youngest are the loudest, with satchels slung over their shoulders, untidy hair, shirts untucked, lunch pails light and swinging. She keeps an eye out for Renshu among the older groups, moving with lower voices and longer strides, arms laden with extra books that won't fit in their bags. There he is. Laughing with his friends, he looks happy. There is a certain joy that arises when Meilin glimpses everyday contentment in her boy. Given all that they've been through, these small moments of ease feel like big treasures.

He catches her eye and nods. Says goodbye to his friends and heads over.

'A good day?' He eyes her overflowing basket and takes it from her, shifting his bag to the other shoulder.

'Yes, I sold out.' She holds up her bulging purse. 'And you?'

He nods. 'Teacher Liang has confirmed our places for the Joint College Entrance Exams at the end of summer. There's so much to study.' And he pats his bag, bursting with papers and borrowed books.

She smiles up at him.

Entering the juancun, they turn down a narrow alleyway, flanked on either side with simple, one-storey houses connected in long rows. At one end, workmen are repairing and rebuilding the corrugated tin and fibreglass walls. Every year, these houses are patched and mended to last just a little longer. Every year, the government says they'll be victorious in retaking the Motherland. But instead, every year, typhoons blow down more walls. Meilin hopes their current house will last another season.

The communal toilet block is not too crowded, so Renshu hands Meilin her basket and ducks in.

Meilin carries on. Vendors on bicycles wobble down the street, hawking snacks. From open doors and windows, people chat with neighbours. Closer to Peiwen's, she passes women lifting loads of washing from big willow baskets. They wring out the shirts, trousers and underclothes and hang them along bamboo poles to dry. Among the clothes are children's shorts sporting the Republic of China flag hand-in-hand with the USA's Stars and Stripes, sewn from the flour sacks given in aid by the US government. Some women also hang up US soldiers' uniforms to dry. Good money can be made by washing the troops' laundry.

As soon as Meilin opens the door, she senses something has changed. In the corner stands a new column of suitcases, bags and other luggage. She hears unfamiliar voices.

Blinking away the brightness of the afternoon, she sees the

outlines of three people crowded on the bamboo settee. Their backs are turned to her and they speak with a fourth person, who is sitting on a crate turned on its end. He wears the uniform of a middle ranking KMT officer and in his face, Meilin sees the lines of Peiwen's eldest boy.

'Hello?'

They turn and fall quieten. The man on the crate calls, 'Peiwen!'

Peiwen comes through the bamboo curtain, drying her wet hands on her apron. Her expression is a mixture of joy and nervousness.

'Meilin! Meilin! Such wonderful news, my family are here! This is my husband, Zhu Yuping.' The man on the crate scowls. Slightly flustered, Peiwen continues, 'And this is my mother-in law, and my sister-in-law, Zhu Yuming, and her husband, Deng Jinwei.' *Zhu Yuming* and *Deng Jinwei*, the names on the ration cards Meilin and Renshu have been using. Yuming turns around. She is younger than Peiwen, expecting a baby, and wears a look of travel-weariness that Meilin has almost forgotten. Jinwei, slouched in his seat, glances at Meilin with watery eyes and mumbles a greeting. At the end of the settee sits the silver-haired matriarch with her mouth drawn in, holding her lips tightly over her teeth.

Competing emotions rise in Meilin. Joy for Peiwen, sadness for her own lost family, worry about what this means. She masks her ambivalence with a smile and holds out her hands in welcome.

'I have – I have extra vegetables to celebrate,' she stammers, picking up her basket.

'Come.' Peiwen motions to her. 'Help me prepare; I will tell you all.' She pulls Meilin towards the kitchen. 'Yuming, the tea is almost ready. You bring it in and sit with the others. Big sister and I will finish the cooking.'

By the time Yuming has poured tea, Renshu has entered. After another round of introductions, Renshu joins them in the kitchen.

'Ma?'

'It's okay, Renshu. Go get the kids from school.'

'Ma, are they staying?' he whispers.

'Of course. They are Peiwen's family.' She sees him considering the implications this will have for the modest house that has sheltered them for the past five years. Meilin and Renshu have grown used to sleeping on the floor in the back room after all the dishes have been tidied, while Peiwen and her children squeeze across the front room in five sets of blankets and pillows they roll out each night and pack away each morning. Now they will add four more – with a baby soon to come. She pushes him towards the door. 'Go get the kids for me today. Take them to the market.'

He looks doubtful, but she takes a note from her purse and presses it in his hands. 'Here, buy some melon seeds or sugar cane stalks to celebrate the arrival of family.'

She watches him disappear down the alley. When she turns back to Peiwen, her friend's eyes are filled with tears.

'Peiwen, you must be so happy! This is great good fortune.'

'Of course, of course. I thought I'd never see any of them again. My husband found them all. And he got Deng Jinwei transferred here, too. Isn't it wonderful?'

'Yes, it's wonderful,' Meilin agrees.

'Someone must have told them how to find me. I am so happy . . .' Peiwen's voice peters out as her eyes rest on Meilin and Renshu's rolled up quilts and blankets.

Peiwen kneels to open a tub of rice and measures out cupfuls to pick through and rinse. The grains sound like rain as they slide over one another, out of the cup and into the enamel basin.

Meilin looks out the back door, to where Renshu and the children collected bamboo and scraps of wire to make a fence. Could they fashion a roof, too, strengthen the fence into walls and make a new room back there? Many other families have been building extensions. They could, too. She tries to imagine how to accommodate more people. How will they all eat? Where will they get more bowls, blankets, bedding? It's too hard to hold all these thoughts at once. She peers into the kettle. It is almost empty. She picks it up and heads out for more water.

Returning to the house, she pauses outside the back door. Peiwen and Yuping are arguing.

'They are like family. We help each other. That's how it works here.'

'But we *are* family,' he hisses back. 'Besides, we cannot risk having two people using the same ration cards. You have already given them more than enough!'

'But where would they go? Besides, Meilin has shared her earnings, Renshu has helped with the kids. We wouldn't have survived without them.'

'You wouldn't have survived without me! It is because I serve that we have all this.'

There is a clatter, as if something has been shoved across the counter.

'One week. Then, they go. This rice is for *family*, not *like family*.'

The bamboo curtains slide and swish. Meilin hears Peiwen draw in a sharp, ragged sob.

Again. They will have to move again. Where? They don't know anyone outside the juancun. Meilin swallows back her tears and pushes away her questions. It's still a happy day, a day of reunion.

When Meilin peeks around the corner, she sees her friend's eyes are red and she is picking up bowls from the floor, rubbing at the chipped edges.

'I'm sorry,' Peiwen whispers. 'I'm sorry.'

'It's okay.' Meilin puts the kettle down and embraces her friend. 'We'll find our way. Hey, look at what Luo had today.' She leans over to her basket, pulling out the pineapple. 'Let's celebrate the return of family.'

Peiwen wipes her eyes and picks up the kettle. She pours the water carefully over the rice grains, then sets the bowl aside to soak. Meilin takes the vegetables from her basket, peels the onion, inspects the cabbage leaves. The kitchen soon fills with the sound of chopping and the clink of bowls and dishes being stacked back into order.

Chapter Twelve

Meilin leans against an arcade column outside the newsagents with a copy of the *Zhongyang Ribao*. She and Renshu need a new home. Soon. She turns past the headlines with their empty promises about reclaiming the Motherland, thinking about how this temporary sojourn in Taiwan has become their most permanent home since Changsha. She skims the classifieds and stops at the 'Help Wanted' section.

She remembers overhearing two women complaining about the lack of good help during a recent festival at the Hubei Native Place Association. Meilin had stood quietly to the side as they gossiped about how another family had brought their nannies, maids and cooks from Wuhan, and that was why their children were doing better at school. One of the women lamented that she could only get local girls to help her. *Those maids don't know how to prepare braised eggplant properly, and they teach the children nasty habits. They don't even speak Mandarin.* The other added that, though she had expected a Benshengren girl to get better deals in the market, she suspected their servant just bought second-rate produce from her cousins and kept the extra money. *This island is such a nightmare. When are we going home?* On and on the two women had complained. At the time, Meilin had thought to herself that if things were going well and they had no complaints, the women wouldn't have had such a nice time at the celebration after all.

Meilin studies the advertisements: 'Maids from Hunan wanted'; 'Looking for Mainlander babysitters'; 'Domestic help required – Sichuan natives preferred'. There are so many! Surely she can find a job. She carefully tears out the page and puts it in her pocket. She leaves the rest of the newspaper behind. Perhaps it will bring good luck to someone else.

The next day, Meilin brushes her hair neatly and puts on the summer dress that she made from a pretty yellow and green floral print. The dress is simple, but it fits just right and she loves it. She wants to wear something special instead of her usual tunic over trousers. On the newspaper clipping, she has circled four adverts: three are clustered in the Da'an district and one is on Qidong street, in Zhongzheng. All are good locations for Renshu's school.

She starts in Da'an. At the first house, no one answers. At the second, when the door opens and she holds up the paper, the person inside says, 'Too late, already filled!'. She makes her way to the third house. Here, the woman seems interested and Meilin is hopeful. But when the woman explains that Meilin would have to live somewhere else, the conversation ends.

She heads towards Qidong Street. It's hot. Her forehead feels sticky and her dress has become rumpled from all the walking. She'll try one more and then, if she's unlucky, maybe Peiwen can let them stay for just a few more days.

All the houses on Qidong Street are in the Japanese style. Meilin walks slowly past each one, admiring delicate flower gardens, until she stops at the number she noted. She straightens her dress, brushes off the dust from the day, and holds her head high. She unlatches the gate and follows a pebbled path with stone lanterns up to the door. A willow tree shades the porch and a small acer grows beneath. She hears running water. Meilin rings the bell, admiring an octagonal window with partially frosted glass.

When the door opens, she is greeted by an older woman, soft-featured and stout, with wet hands and a kerchief tying back her hair. Her kind eyes and big smile put Meilin at ease. When Meilin explains she has come about the advert, the woman nods, then ushers her into a small entry hall and points at a pair of slippers.

'Please wait while I tell Madame Huang,' she says, disappearing behind a sliding wood-and-paper door. Meilin can smell meat and fresh rice cooking. She exchanges her shoes for the slippers and surveys her surroundings.

A landscape painting of cloudy mountains graces the entry. Black ink on yellowed silk. Tang dynasty, most likely. In front of her, a huanghuali table boasts an incense burner, a carved trinket box and an intricate sandalwood fan. She longs to pick up the fan and hold it to her nose, inhaling the scent. Seeing such treasures rattles Meilin, summoning too many memories. She stifles her urge to sob and looks down. The sliding door opens and the older woman motions Meilin down a long wooden corridor that creaks as they walk. On one side, full-length windows open to a stone garden. On the other, white sliding walls edged in black conceal the rooms behind. At the corridor's end, the woman slides open another door and gestures for Meilin to enter.

The main part of the room is sunken lower than the walkways. Meilin notices that the tatami mats on the floor are concealed by a soft, luxurious rug. On a sofa with red and yellow silk cushions and fine upholstery lounges Madame Huang. Her mixture of elegance and disdain reminds Meilin of Wenling. There is a similarity in Madame's manner as she regards Meilin, her expression both lazy and critical.

When she speaks, Madame's voice is sharp, with a strong Sichuan accent, firing off questions that only a Sichuanese could understand and answer. Meilin is grateful for the time she spent learning the dialect while in Chongqing. In fact, part of her delights to hear Madame using the familiar colloquialisms. Meilin suspects Madame's manner is mostly performance, testing her mettle. Meilin holds her composure and answers back.

Yes, I can make that dish.

Yes, I know where to get those vegetables.

Yes, I can launder and mend.

Yes, I can sew. At this, Meilin holds up her finest embroidered purse. Madame Huang's eyes shine.

'Well,' says Madame, 'I suppose we'll try you out. You'll be better than those locals.'

Meilin holds up her hand.

'What is it?' Madame is irritable.

'I have a son. He's a good boy, studies hard. He's quieten and polite. Can he stay here, too?'

Curiosity piqued, Madame's lips tighten. 'A boy? He'll have to help in the gardens. What did you say his name was?'

'Dao Renshu. Renshu,' Meilin whispers.

'Renshu,' Madame says, thoughtfully. 'How old?'

'He's nearly finished at Jianguo High School. He's studying for the joint entrance exams.'

'Very well, then.' Madame nods her assent. 'Now, speak with Cook Chin to find out what she needs from the market. You must clean and press the washing so I have my best qipaos ready for the dinner at General Fan's on Tuesday. And can you adjust these curtains? I don't like the way they fall – they're too long, and make the room feel heavy.' She gets up and pulls open a bureau drawer, taking out a bolt of blue-green silk. 'You must do something with this. I have been saving it since we arrived. My last maid was hopeless. I wouldn't trust her with my worst silk, let alone my best.'

Just as Madame exhausts her list, the older woman returns with a tea tray. Meilin bows and backs out of the room.

While Meilin changes back into her street shoes, the older woman sidles up and puts her arm around Meilin.

'Call me Auntie Chin. Madame is thrilled you're here. Never mind her brashness, she means well. The General mostly keeps to himself and his work. Stick with me and you'll be fine.'

Meilin heads back to the juancun, tired but relieved.

It takes longer for Meilin to say goodbye to Peiwen than it does to pack their few belongings. She leaves behind anything that Peiwen could use and takes only their clothes, Renshu's books and her sewing basket.

'Visit us often,' Peiwen says, grasping Meilin's hand, not wanting to let go. 'You are always welcome here,' she adds, even though both know that is no longer true.

'Thank you,' Meilin says, and squeezes Peiwen's hand.

*

At the Huangs', Auntie Chin shows Meilin a small room to the side of the kitchen that is for her and Renshu. Three tatami mats cover the floor. A large window faces the street, and its window-sill is low and wide. In the corner is a small table with a lamp and an electric fan. Meilin turns both on. The air in the room stirs softly, the light inviting. Meilin arranges Renshu's books on the windowsill. On the table, she puts his inkstone, his brushes, paper and a new inkstick.

She reflects on how quickly, once again, their circumstances have changed. While she doesn't know Madame and the General yet, she feels like she is on familiar ground. The scents from the kitchen, the banter between Auntie Chin and the gardener, and Madame's concerns remind her of the Dao family compound.

When he sees the room, Renshu's face breaks into a broad smile.

'Here,' Meilin says, gesturing to where a pair of thick, soft coverlets lie. 'Here are beds that will not move in the night; here is a desk that stays standing all day. Here are walls that do not sway with the winds or let the rain and cold leak through.'

'Is it just temporary?' he asks.

'I don't know, but it is just for us.'

The room at the Huangs' becomes a retreat for Renshu in the final months leading up to the Joint College and Universities Entrance Examination. While Meilin spends her days learning her new job, Renshu studies in that quieten space, its fan cooling the air and its shades drawn against bright sunlight and distrac-tion. On the day of the exam, he finds great satisfaction in being able to answer every question. When he gives in his paper, he knows he has done his absolute best.

His results are good: he receives an offer to study engineering at National Taiwan University. He rushes home to tell his ma. Breathless and bursting with joy, he picks her up and whirls her in a circle.

Once he puts her down, she exclaims, 'I'm so proud! It's what you said you wanted on the day of the Lantern Festival in Shang-hai. You have made it happen! Do you remember?'

Renshu nods, and notices his ma is teary. 'Ma, are you sad?'

'No. Yes. Of course not. It's just' – and she wipes her eye – 'I wish your father could know. I wish *my* father could know.'

Renshu hugs her gently. 'Me too,' he says.

'When I think of all that we've gone through, during all those years when I scarcely dared to imagine the future. It's . . .' She sniffs and shakes her head. Whatever it is she wants to say, she can't seem to summon the words. Finally, she just pulls him close and embraces him again.

Later that night, Renshu reflects on his ma's reaction. It dawns on him that when he goes to university, they will be apart for the first time in his life.

Renshu is granted a small scholarship and work-study job at the library to help with his fees. He finds housing in a men's dormitory near the campus, sharing a room with three other students. The NTU campus lies southeast of Zhongzheng, surrounded by rice paddies and narrow footpaths, away from the commotion of the city. Even though it's less than an hour's walk from Qidong Street, it's a different world.

On the first night in the dormitory, Renshu is restless. It is strange not to hear his ma's soft breathing. He wrestles with his blanket, hoping he isn't disturbing his roommates. From the bunks across the room, alternating snores indicate Pao Dafei and Liu Zhaohui are asleep. Above him is Li Hotan. Pao, who Renshu recognises from Jianguo, is studying physics. Li and Liu, like Renshu, are engineering students. They knew each other before coming to university, both having lived at the same juancun in Hsinchu. Renshu sighs and flips his pillow over.

'Are you asleep?' whispers Li Hotan.

'Not really,' Renshu whispers back.

'Me neither.'

'It's just, I guess, odd, to fall asleep.' Renshu pauses, not wanting to say he misses his ma. 'In a new place,' he finishes.

'I know what you mean. I'm used to my siblings sleeping right next to me.'

'Where are you from, Li Hotan? I mean before Hsinchu?'

'We were in Kunming.'

'And before that?'

'Our hometown was near Wuhan. And you?'

'We are from Changsha. We went to Chongqing, then Shanghai. Then here.'

'Hmm,' Li says, acknowledging so much with a murmur.

Renshu yawns.

'Dao Renshu?'

'Yes?'

'Pao said there's a good noodle vendor by the main university gate in the early evenings. Let's go tomorrow after classes.'

Renshu smiles in the dark. 'I'd like that.'

On the first day of lectures, Renshu joins a flock of students walking along the Royal Palm Boulevard. Everyone wears freshly pressed white shirts, khaki trousers or knee-length skirts, and polished shoes to start the year. He is amazed to find himself surrounded by so many young people, all hoping to rebuild the Republic. By the end of the day, his head spins, and he's glad when it's time for the evening meal with Pao and Li.

They, too, have found the day both overwhelming and inspiring. Renshu relaxes as he realises he's not alone in feeling intimidated by this new life. The talk ranges from imitating the mannerisms of a mathematics professor, to speculating which courses will be the most difficult, to eyeing pretty girls at a table nearby. After many bowls of noodles and a little too much to drink, they eventually stumble home, singing songs.

As the year progresses, Renshu thrives. He is fascinated with physics, with engineering and problem-solving. And, like most everyone else, he continues with his English language classes. Given the ever-strengthening links between the US and the Republic of China, knowing the language will better his chances for just about everything.

Li Hotan and Pao Dafei become great friends. They all have memories of the War of Aggression and the Civil War. Even though they don't discuss them much, this shared past bonds them. Each knows how lucky they are to be here.

Pao, despite his solemn demeanour, has a wicked sense of humour. His family came to Taiwan from Guilin shortly after Retrocession, so he has known Taipei the longest. When they all go out, Pao does most of the talking. He has a knack for knowing where the best food vendors will show up. Li Hotan, on the other hand, is personable and handsome. Girls are always bringing him dumplings or asking for help with their assignments.

Together with Pao and Li, Renshu spends long evenings studying, taking breaks for noodles or shaved ice from the stands along the Liugongjun canals. Sometimes they watch American movies at the cinema and flirt with female students. While Renshu's too shy to say much to the girls, he is delighted to be in their company.

Most weekends he visits the Qidong Street house. His ma and Auntie Chin are always happy to see him, and even Madame and General Huang occasionally say hello. But each time, as his visit draws to an end, he feels the pull back to his new life at the university.

Once Renshu starts university, Meilin reminds herself that he's only a short distance away. This is the future they both wanted. She is proud of his achievements, proud that he will be a scholar. But she didn't expect this sideswipe of sorrow she feels now that he has started to make a life on his own. As much as she tries to brush it away, she can't dismiss the feeling that their bond, which has held them together through fires, bombings and betrayals, is starting to weaken.

Meilin pushes aside what she can't change and instead focuses on her work. As the months pass, Meilin notices that the Huangs have all the luxuries one could want: teas, wines, brandies, tobacco, cosmetics, silk. Although she wonders where these luxuries come from, Meilin knows better than to ask. The only enquiries she makes are what dishes Madame and the General would like to eat, which flowers she should put in the porcelain vases, and when Madame needs her qipaos ready for glamorous soirées.

However replete they are with luxuries, though, they are

running low on rice. The Huangs do not want to rely on the US wheat subsidies like common military folk. The last maid, a local girl, had procured a large amount of rice. In fact, it was because she boasted that she could get rice that Madame Huang had hired her. As the stockpile shrinks, Meilin's worry increases. Will they dismiss her if she cannot replenish the supply? She doesn't want to find out.

Auntie Chin says she's heard that Mr Tsai in the market sells rice, but it's overpriced and full of grit and sometimes even bugs. Somehow, the Benshengren girl got good rice from him, but Auntie Chin doesn't know how she did it.

'Those Benshengren.' Auntie Chin shakes her head in disgust. 'They should be grateful we saved them from the Japanese. Instead, they cheat us and refuse to speak properly.'

Meilin thanks Auntie Chin and heads to the market.

On the way, Meilin thinks about how different it is to live in the city, among the Taiwanese. At the juancun, most residents were so certain they would be returning to China, they never bothered to venture beyond the compound. Like Auntie Chin, many of them looked down on the Taiwanese as a Japanised race that needed to reconnect with the Motherland. The few Benshengren Meilin had met didn't seem to like the Chinese from the mainland, either. Waishengren, people from outside the province, they called them. Outside the juancun, she senses it even more.

Meilin knows that, as a new face to Mr Tsai, she'll get just one chance to make a good impression. So, before approaching him, she lingers near his stall, watching the interactions. Whenever someone comes up to Mr Tsai speaking Mandarin, he acts as though he doesn't understand. This is intriguing. Mandarin is the official language. Mr Tsai must know what these people want. But he maintains a blank face. When they shout and insist, writing the characters on a piece of paper and waving it in his face, Mr Tsai says he has no more rice, or that his shop is closed. He refuses to sell them anything. Or he offers a small, overpriced scoop of broken rice, riddled with gravel.

But when someone speaks Taiwanese, Mr Tsai's face opens.

They chat for a long time. Only after this exchange do they hold out their bags for Mr Tsai. He fills their sacks with new crop rice.

After a little while, Meilin slips away. She won't try to buy rice yet. She carries on with her errands, thinking about Mr Tsai. Meilin has always had an ear for languages. In Shanghai, she had picked up enough Shanghainese to blend in. And in Chongqing, she'd gotten much better prices in the market when she switched to Sichuanese. She thinks of how Auntie Deng and Uncle Liang howled at her early attempts. Yet they became her friends and, in time, her lifeline. Meilin smiles to herself, but then her reminiscence is clouded by the memory of the Great Tunnel disaster. It's been fourteen years. If that hadn't happened, maybe the family wouldn't have splintered. Maybe they'd all be here in Taiwan together. Liling would be twenty-three, maybe even a mother herself. Meilin sighs and shakes herself out of her daydream. No rice will come from sad memories. It's clear: now that she lives outside the juancun, she must learn Taiwanese.

Her errands bring her to Yongle fabric market in Dadaocheng. Meilin wants to find buttons and braiding for Madame's latest dress. A highlight of working for the Huangs is that Madame has a sewing machine that she not only allows, but expects, Meilin to use. After selecting what she needs, Meilin browses up and down the stalls, looking for bargains. Her eye falls on a light green cotton printed with small pink flowers. On impulse, she buys a few yards and heads home.

On her way, she notices a pair of women walking in the opposite direction. Over their arms, each carries a woven rattan basket filled with piles of linens. Curious, Meilin turns and follows. Where could they be going?

The river. They are heading to the Tamsui. Once there, they join other women washing clothes on the shore. They all seem to know each other and share a sense of camaraderie that Meilin misses. Some have children, who help or play in the water. It reminds Meilin of how women in the juancun would gather to do the washing, exchanging jokes and gossip, making the burdensome task light. She listens carefully, trying to make out the words; these are Benshengren women, happily speaking in

Taiwanese. At first, Meilin is surprised. Overeager to enforce the government's Mandarin-only policy, the ever-present military police are likely to arrest anyone they hear speaking Taiwanese. But here, Meilin reflects, the splash and gurgle of the river covers the women's voices and grants them a small freedom.

When the weekly drudgery of doing the laundry next arises, maybe Meilin will bring her basket to the Tamsui and see what she can learn.

The river water ripples over a shallow pebble bed. Meilin dunks in the clothes, watching them darken. They lose their crispness and become heavy. She rolls her shoulders, which ache from carrying the basket for so far. Squatting, she scrubs a bar of soap into the folds of fabric, coaxing the suds into a rich foam. Nearby, other women wash and rinse, slapping the clothes on the large stones to get the water out, then wringing them into tight coils stacked into their baskets. That first day, a few eye her suspiciously, and no one speaks to her. Still, no one tells her to go away.

The wet washing – even when wrung out – is so much heavier on the way back. Meilin spends a precious coin to hire a pedicab back to the Huangs' house.

Week after week, she returns, and becomes more accustomed to the work. Washing changes from being her most dreaded chore to part of her weekly rhythm. A few women at the river start to recognise her, ask her name, become friendly. She picks up a few phrases in Taiwanese and some of the women, in appreciation of her efforts, teach her more. When she asks why the Benshengren don't like the Waishengren, they look away and change the subject. They reassure her that they like her, she's different. But eventually, with the rushing waters muffling their whispers, they tell her about the events of February 28, 1947, two years before Meilin and Renshu arrived in Taiwan. Meilin pieces together the story of 228 bit by bit. They tell her how a Benshengren widow was selling cigarettes in defiance of the tobacco board monopoly; they recount the widow's refusal to stop when asked, and the way the crowds supported her; with disgust, they tell about the cowardly officer who fired a shot into the crowd, killing someone by accident, followed by the not-so-accidental killing of thousands of civilians. Since then, thousands have been persecuted by the Kuomintang. Kidnapped, disappeared, killed. *This is taboo, no one can talk about this*, they say. But everyone does: everyone aches to tell how someone they know, someone they loved, was brutalised. As always, Meilin listens. She didn't know. She wants to weep with them, for their losses, for their suffering. She begins to understand the animosity she felt when they first arrived in Taiwan.

Through the whisperings and fellowship at the river, Meilin becomes friendly with a younger woman called Lin-Na, who lost her mother in the 228 massacre. Meilin says that she, too, knows what it is to lose family in someone else's fighting. Over time, the two become close. Sometimes Meilin brings extra food for Lin-Na and her cousins to share. When Lin-Na admires the Madame's clothes and Meilin reveals that she sewed them, Lin-Na asks Meilin to alter some of her own clothing. Lin-Na has a stall in the Yongle fabric market, and she offers Meilin good deals on some of the nicest bolts of cloth.

When only a few days' worth of rice remain, Meilin confides in Lin-Na that she needs to be able to buy rice, but fears that she'll only get the worst kind because of her accent. Lin-Na introduces her to Mr Tsai, and by the end of that day, Meilin not only has a new supply of rice, but she has also made a friend in Mr Tsai.

Chapter Thirteen

Taipei, Taiwan, January 1960

Renshu is on his way to meet his friends for celebratory noodles. His feet are light, like springs, full of possibility. He reaches down and runs his finger along the edge of the envelope in his pocket, tracing the perforated ridges of the stamps.

Last year, when he was finishing his final exams and preparing for military service, Renshu began to imagine a life beyond NTU, beyond Taiwan. Inspired by the announcement that Li Zhengdao and Yang Zhenning had won the 1957 Nobel Prize in Physics, Renshu and his classmates began to dream of going to the US for graduate school.

Renshu has done well, and his professors have encouraged him to continue with his studies once he finishes his mandatory service. To help in the fight against communism, the Government has been recruiting top students in technical fields to study in the US. Renshu knows his ma would be thrilled for him to become a professor. Although she might not have imagined him going to America, it is clear to Renshu that this is the future.

He investigates the requirements. The challenge of going to the US for graduate study has many steps: he must complete a four-year degree, complete his required military service, demonstrate proficiency in English, prove political aptitude and suitability, gain admission to a US graduate programme, find a sponsor and financial means, and obtain a visa.

Piece by piece, he has been working on this problem for a long time. After graduating from NTU with high honours, he is now completing his conscription. And today, Renshu has another piece in his pocket: an offer from the graduate programme in mechanical engineering at Northwestern University, Evanston, Illinois, USA.

At the noodle place, his friends are already celebrating. Pao has been accepted at NYU to study physics, Liu will be going to the University of Wisconsin for electrical engineering, and his friend and academic rival Li Hotan holds a letter from Columbia.

'Dao Renshu! Where will you go?'

Renshu brandishes his letter from Northwestern, and joins them in a toast.

Renshu turns his attention to the next step in the process. To get his visa, he needs proof of a US bank account containing 2,400 US dollars. Renshu's friends have connections. Fathers in the government, rich relatives in Hong Kong. Some already have family in America. They will all be able to find those funds. Twenty-four hundred dollars? Renshu doesn't even have twenty-four cents! But there must be a way. He couldn't have got this far otherwise.

He brings the letter to Meilin.

'Ma, I have news,' Renshu starts.

Meilin puts down the pair of trousers she is mending and looks up. Strands of silver are starting to shimmer in her bun.

He hands her the envelope.

She, too, runs her fingers across the stamps. Turns it over, opens it, takes out the paper. It is all in English; she hands it back. 'What is it?'

'It's an offer of admission to graduate school at Northwestern University, in mechanical engineering.'

She is looking at him, smiling, but still puzzled.

'In America.'

'America!' A parade of emotions passes across Meilin's face: disbelief, pride, uncertainty, sadness. For many months, Renshu has dreamed of this opportunity, but only now does he understand that it might break her heart. She blinks and shakes her head in amazement.

'What's next? How does it work?' she asks.

He explains to her about the bank account.

She nods. He wants to go. She wants him to go. But they don't have the money.

It is the Year of the Rat and the Lis are having a Lunar New Year party at their villa. They have asked the Huangs if Meilin could come to help serve the guests.

At the party are government officials and high-ranking military, as well as the influential and elite – at least those who managed to flee the mainland with their material wealth intact. Women coo over earrings and necklaces, admire one another's outfits. Men exchange handshakes and hearty greetings. Meilin enjoys standing on the periphery and feasting her ears on the chatter. Apparently, the new fashion will be for shorter qipaos. Meilin brightens to hear this: shorter styles mean that she can save the scraps from the dresses Madame will want to alter. She'll sew them into purses, slippers or maybe even silk underwear. Now the gossip drifts to who is expected tonight. There are excited whispers about one of the guests, a retired civil servant. Apparently he was bold and brash in his youth, but this recklessness has paid off and he was decorated by the Generalissimo.

Yet however much glamour is in the air, Meilin hears longing in these voices. Everyone has suffered. No one left China unscathed, no matter how much gold and jade they smuggled with them. Nothing in Taipei is ever quite as good as what they left behind.

Another wave of guests has arrived. The party has become louder, merrier. Hurrying back and forth from the kitchen, Meilin refills platters with fresh, hot dishes. The wine has loosened tongues, which now remark on this eleventh year of the Generalissimo's five-year plan to retake the mainland. In the parlour, seated on plush cushions and at low zitan tables, groups of men play mahjong, chess and go. Someone quips, *How is it that they can be such masters at these games of strategy, and still have lost the Motherland?*

After several hours, Meilin's feet are tired, and most of the food has been eaten, the wine drunk. She is carrying a tray of dirty plates and empty glasses to the kitchen when she hears his voice in the parlour.

She stops, strains to listen. Doesn't hear it. She must be mistaken.

No. There it is again. She'd know that voice anywhere. She knows its tenor, its timbre. She puts down her tray and peeks into the room.

She freezes. She must be seeing a ghost. She retreats into the kitchen.

Clearly she's having a hallucination. Second-hand nostalgia and opium smoke are clouding her mind.

'Suimei, go find out the name of the gentleman in the smart suit at the mahjong game.'

'A little old for you, don't you think?'

Meilin ignores the teasing and pushes the girl along. 'Go, ask someone his name.'

The gesture is unnecessary. Of course it's him.

Suimei soon hurries back, pronounces his name.

Meilin sinks down.

'Do you know him? You know him! Oh, he's so sophisticated. How do you know him? Tell me!'

Meilin must be careful. 'No.' She shakes her head. 'He's not who I thought he might be.' She hopes this will throw Suimei off her trail. She needs to think about this.

From an alcove in the corner, she watches him. He must be in his late fifties now. He walks with a slight limp. His suit hangs loose on his shoulders. His cheekbones are more prominent and his cheeks more sunken. He is somehow both softer and rougher. He reminds Meilin of Hongtse.

What about Wenling and Lifen? She looks around. Wenling must not be here. She would dominate the room if she were.

The last of the evening glitters away. People make wishes for a prosperous year. Glasses clink to a glorious return to the mainland, but the toasts are as empty as the bubbles in the champagne.

It is only when the guests are leaving that he walks over to Meilin.

He puts his hand out to touch her arm.

She jumps back and rubs her skin as if soothing a burn. Her stomach flips.

'You are real. It is you,' he starts.

She nods, unable to say a word.

'I know you are not a ghost,' he continues, 'because when I see ghosts, they are never surprised to see me. But you are as shocked as I am.'

Meilin still says nothing. She is more than tongue-tied; she can't even think.

'Somehow I thought I'd see you again,' he says.

'I need to help clean up,' she stammers finally.

'And Renshu?' he asks, his voice softening.

'Graduated from NTU,' she says. Her mouth is dry.

Longwei's face lights up. 'He's still here in Taipei?'

Meilin nods. Her pulse is throbbing.

Someone calls her from the kitchen. She looks over and sees Suimei waving, grinning.

'Mr Dao, sir, your car is here.' A footman stands with his coat and fedora, waiting to escort Longwei out of the villa.

'Thank you,' he says, placing his hat lightly on his head. 'Meilin, my disappearing and reappearing sister-in-law, let's meet tomorrow. Café Astoria, four o'clock?'

And with that, he's gone.

Soon after Meilin started at the Huangs', Madame, pleased with her work, gave her the beautiful blue-green silk she'd shown her on that first day. When Renshu left for university, Meilin had set up Madame's sewing machine on the table where he'd studied. With plenty of light, enjoying the electric fan and strains of opera from Auntie Chin's radio in the kitchen, Meilin made herself the nicest dress she'd owned in years. She's only worn it a few times, to a Hubei Native Place Association festival or the occasional party. Mostly, it hangs in the closet. From time to time, she holds the cool silk to her cheek and admires the soft shimmer.

The morning after the New Year party, she puts it on. Needs

a little adjustment, she thinks, tugging at the sleeves and around the waist. After changing back into her tunic and trousers, she makes the alterations, ripping out a row of stitches here, adding in new ones there. She tries it on again, twirling in front of a mirror, trying to see the back, wondering if she should adjust the hem.

'You look lovely, my dear,' Auntie Chin says from the door.

'Hmm. I want to look strong,' Meilin says.

'Strong?'

'Yes, strong like someone who has taken care of herself and her family. Like someone who can't be bossed around.'

'That kind of strong isn't something you look like, it's something you are. And you, Meilin, are. Where are you going?'

The dress will be fine, Meilin decides. She starts to brush her hair. 'I'm meeting—' She pauses. *Who is Longwei to her?*

'A friend?'

'Someone I used to know,' Meilin says, pinning her hair up.

'Well, I hope it's a nice reunion,' Auntie Chin says pleasantly, as she goes back to the kitchen.

I do, too, Meilin thinks.

Meilin told Auntie Chin she wanted to be strong, but she's jittery. On the way to the café, she calculates: it's been nearly thirteen years since Yichang. Thirteen years. Where does one begin? Does she say *I'm sorry for leaving?* But she's not. She's not sorry at all. She had to look for her parents, she had to try. What would have happened if she and Renshu had stayed? It's an impossible question. Does she say *I'm glad to see you?* Is she? She was shocked to see him at the party. She still is. Maybe there's nothing to say. Maybe she should just turn back. What good could come from this? No, she'll go. She looks up. She's at Wuchang Street; she's only a few doors away now.

There it is: Café Astoria. She looks through the rounded windows, intrigued by the treats on display, a tray of fluffy white candies with almonds catching her eye. As she enters, she is greeted by a wonderful whiff of confectionery. A staircase leads to the tables. Smoothing her hair, she heads up.

He sits alone, his fingers fussing with a corner of the menu. She notices that the top of his head is balding. When he looks up, he smiles and, despite everything, Meilin can't help smiling back. A forgotten sensation flows through her; here is someone who knew her before, someone who remembers her life with Xiaowen. Someone who understands what she lost, and who she could have been. Whatever the outcome of their conversation today, she's grateful for this moment of deep recognition. He stands and pulls out a chair for her. His hand trembles slightly as he sits down.

'I was worried you might not show up.'

'I was worried, too,' she says.

He chuckles. His laugh seems more rounded than she remembers, just like his shoulders. She feels herself relax, just a little.

Longwei insists on ordering chocolate cake and dark coffees. His wallet, though fat with notes, is shabby, and the edges are soft and worn.

To her surprise, he asks very little about the years since Yichang. She doesn't volunteer anything.

He does, however, ask about Renshu.

Meilin anticipated this. She shows him a photo of Renshu taken during his conscription. His eyes are serious, his cadet's uniform smartly pressed, his hair short under the cap that is almost too big for his head. Longwei studies it carefully. When he raises his eyes, she sees they are glassy.

'He looks just like Xiaowen.'

'I know,' she says.

Handing it back to her, he sketches the outline of his story.

Where was he? Shanghai, Nanjing, Chongqing, Chengdu, Taipei.

How did he move? Trains, jeeps, steamboats, motorcycles, cars and, finally, a plane.

And his career? It was good for several years. But it didn't take a military genius to see that the Generalissimo didn't want advisors or strategists, only yes-men. Longwei has been a lot of things, but never a yes-man. To disagree with Chiang was to write one's own obituary. After the Generalissimo's five-year plan stretched into six, then seven, Longwei knew it was time. There are many secrets to being a good gambler, but the key is knowing when to walk away. When he saw the opportunity, he took a post of high rank and low power. Then, as soon as would be respectable, he retired while his reputation was still intact.

In all his talk, he hasn't mentioned what Meilin most wants to know.

'And what about Wenling and Lifen?'

There is the smallest hesitation before he speaks. 'We were only in Shanghai a short time before I was relocated to Nanjing. There, we looked for her family, but their home was abandoned. We didn't find anyone.'

Meilin closes her eyes.

'When I had to return to Chongqing, she didn't want to go, of course. "This time," she said, "this time, let me take Lifen and go back to Shanghai." I couldn't say no. I planned to join them after the war.'

Although her own memories of Shanghai are painful, she understands why Wenling loved the city so much. She wonders if Lifen grew out of her scowling resentfulness and into some greater ease with herself. But Longwei's tone is ominous.

'What happened?' she asks.

'Once Shanghai was no longer safe, I arranged for them to come here. They were supposed to be on the *Taiping* when . . .' He falters.

Meilin gasps, recalling the horror she'd felt after hearing two ships had collided on a dark January night, each having turned off their lights to avoid enemy detection. 'They drowned?'

'Maybe, maybe not. Their names weren't on the manifest. I don't know.' He stirs a small spoon in his coffee, as if the clink and swirl might reveal something more. 'I sent her money for the tickets, but maybe she decided to go to Hong Kong instead? Maybe they stayed in Shanghai? I don't know. Their footprints are lost.'

'Did you place missing person adverts? Did you look?'

'Of course I looked! In Taipei, in Hong Kong, and up until

communication was cut, I even put notices in the Shanghai papers. Nothing.'

'I'm sorry. I am so sorry,' Meilin murmurs. In the presence of Longwei's grief, wounds that had grown numb feel newly raw. She reaches out towards Longwei's arm and gives it a squeeze. He gently pulls away to take out a handkerchief, then blows his nose and shakes his head.

'Did you ever think of looking for us?'

He picks up his coffee and takes a sip, watching her over the rim. 'I didn't think you wanted to be found.'

She feels the colour rising up her cheeks. He puts the coffee down and reaches into his pocket for a handful of sunflower seeds. He starts cracking them with his teeth, and Meilin can hear him sucking the salt out of the shells. His teeth seem enormous. She puts her hand on the side of her coffee cup. It is cold.

'Why did you leave?' he finally asks. 'I would have looked after you and Renshu. After all that we went through, you must have known that.'

She doesn't say anything.

'Didn't I always bring you supplies? Wasn't there always enough for Renshu's books and uniforms, for your cloth and thread? Ever since Xiaowen was lost, was there ever a time I didn't look out for you?'

There are too many questions. She can't answer any of them. She can't return his gaze.

In the long seconds that follow, something wakes in Meilin. A small voice that counters this dragon roaring his righteousness. Maybe she didn't want to be looked after. Maybe she hadn't needed Longwei's overbearing shelter as much as he wants to believe. From the distance of more than a decade, it's easy for him to protest his good intentions. She doesn't entirely trust him. She never has. *Call his bluff*, says the voice.

Meilin murmurs something to herself.

'What? Look at me to say what you have to say,' he booms. But then, 'Meilin.' His voice breaks over the syllables of her name.

'I said' – and she slowly raises her eyes – 'I said, "So help us now."'

He stares at her.

Though her knee trembles under the table, she keeps her eyes even and lips calm.

He lets out a low whistle and shakes his head slightly.

'Come, let's go.' He pushes back his chair.

They walk along the night market. Hawkers are selling snacks, offering fresh noodles and hot tea. Longwei pauses at a stall filled with books, maps and trinkets. He picks up a brass vase with a lapis inlay of a phoenix, turning it back and forth in his hand. Then he puts it down and continues browsing.

'What are you looking for?' Meilin asks.

'Just looking. Sometimes I find something special. Vases, jade, calligraphy. I am beginning to understand why my father collected those treasures.'

'Why? What do you think Old Hongtse was after?' She'd always thought it was about money: more ways to spread his investments.

'Maybe he wanted beautiful objects, the kind that outlast foolish humans. The artistry that goes into something like this' – he lifts the lid from a red lacquer jewellery box with an intricate carving of a willow and river – 'isn't changed by political machinations or intrigue. When all those are over, this will still be beautiful.'

'It's about more than beauty,' Meilin says.

'How so?'

'It's about strength, too. Endurance. An object can hold on to memories and stories in a way that people, that generations, cannot.' Where is her own scroll now? She hopes it has been passed on to other, kinder hands.

Longwei shakes his head at the seller's raised eyebrows and puts the lid back on the box.

Meilin continues along the road home.

He walks by Meilin's side, offers her a protective arm.

'Are you courting me, Old Man?' she teases as she takes it.

'Only for the past twenty-five years.'

Even though it's dark, she hears the smile in his voice. To her surprise, she is smiling, too.

'Here we are,' she says brightly when they reach the Huangs'. She puts one hand on the gate and one on his arm. 'Come back for dinner with Renshu. He will be delighted to see you. Next Saturday?'

With a squeeze on his arm, she signals goodbye, closing the gate behind her.

Chapter Fourteen

Taipei, Taiwan, February 1960

After collecting the fish from the market, just as his ma asked, Renshu heads to Qidong Street. The Huangs are away in Hsin-chu, so Auntie Chin is taking the weekend off. Meilin has asked him to help prepare dinner for a guest. She has also told him to bring all his documents for America. What is she thinking?

She opens the door just as he's about to knock.

Renshu hands her the fish, along with a punnet of fresh straw-berries. She beams at the strawberries and takes the food into the kitchen as he changes into slippers.

'Did you bring your papers, too?' she calls.

'Yes, Ma. Who is your mystery guest?'

She emerges from the kitchen, drying her hands on her apron.

'Renshu,' Meilin says. 'Uncle Longwei is here in Taipei.'

'Uncle? Here?' Renshu exclaims in disbelief. He hasn't thought of Uncle for years. 'How? How did you find each other?'

Meilin tells him about the party.

Renshu doesn't recall when they stopped looking for Longwei and the family, but part of him never stopped hoping they'd find them, one day. He shakes his head in amazement. 'I wonder if we've crossed paths and not even known it? And Auntie Wenling and Lifen, are they coming tonight, too?'

'Renshu,' she starts, and with the change in tone of her voice, he knows.

'What happened?' he asks.

'They were supposed to be on the *Taiping* the night it sank.'

He sinks down into a seat, crestfallen to have found and then lost his aunt and cousin again in the space of a minute. Then he thinks of Liling and the deep-rooted ache she left behind.

'Renshu, we can ask him to help us.'

'But we never went back to the boat in Yichang,' he hesitates. 'Isn't he angry?'

'I don't know. Maybe not anymore. Even if he is angry, he still might help. Come, we need to prepare the food.'

Longwei arrives wearing a charcoal grey Western suit and a dark maroon fedora. In his hands are gift bags that he sets down once he sees Renshu. Even though Renshu is twenty-five, not thirteen, it's still a surprise to meet his uncle's gaze at eye level. Longwei laughs out loud with joy and, to both Meilin and Renshu's shock, gives him a huge hug.

'You are marvellous,' he says, his eyes scanning Renshu, as if trying to take him all in. 'A marvellous young man! Congratulations on your many honours from NTU, your father and my father would be so proud. I am proud to be your uncle.' Renshu stands up straighter.

Longwei turns to Meilin. 'He's even more handsome and glorious than in the photo.'

'Come, come in, have you eaten?' she says. Though brisk, her tone is affectionate.

'I brought these for you.' Longwei picks up the bags and presents them to Meilin. A bottle of brandy and a box from Astoria Café. Renshu peeks over Meilin's shoulder as she looks inside: it is filled with the pillowy white almond confections. 'Russian soft candies,' Longwei says.

The evening evaporates as they devour Meilin's food and exchange stories. Meilin and Renshu rarely drink, but Longwei pours brandy for them all, and the conversation flows. Even so, there are some topics they navigate carefully. Meilin glosses over the destruction of her family's compound and the Shanghai years, and Longwei doesn't press for details. When their bellies are full, Renshu clears the table. From the kitchen, he listens to his ma and Longwei talking and laughing. It is as if a whole new dimension of her has come to life, a fullness that he hadn't realised had become muted. He brings out the strawberries, Longwei's special candies, and fresh plates.

When he sits back down, the conversation sobers.

Longwei clears his throat. He still has his smoker's cough. 'Renshu, your ma says you hope to go to the US for graduate studies. What a magnificent opportunity. Tell me more.'

Renshu nods, suddenly nervous. He takes out his paperwork and begins to explain all the requirements.

Longwei keeps his eyes steadily on Renshu, not looking at the documents that accumulate in front of him in a small pile.

Meilin sits with her hands folded in her lap, motionless, watching Longwei.

When Renshu finishes, Longwei pages through the papers: the offer of admission, the statement of approved political screening from the Security Bureau, a certificate of excellence from the Ministry of Education's English proficiency exam, the mostly completed visa application, and, finally, an incomplete form. Renshu needs proof of a US bank account with funds to cover expenses and tuition, an estimated 2,400 US dollars.

Renshu is restless. When it comes to the money and the visa, they all know that Longwei is the only one who can aid them. What is Uncle thinking? Will he help?

The clock in the hallway chimes ten o'clock.

'Uncle,' Renshu says, rising from the table, 'I am sorry, I must go now. I have to get back to the barracks.'

Longwei picks up the documents and taps them on the table, straightening them into a tidy stack. 'Leave the papers with me,' he says. 'What good fortune that our family is together again.'

'Thank you for the many ways you have always helped us,' Renshu says to Longwei, keeping his voice neutral and sincere, before leaving with a bow.

After the door closes, Meilin and Longwei sit in silence. The Huangs will return tomorrow from Hsinchu, and Meilin still has preparations to make. But she's not ready for the evening to end yet. Just for tonight, she can imagine that this is her house. Meilin reaches towards the brandy bottle to refill their glasses.

Longwei grasps her arm. 'Marry me, Meilin.'

'What?' She stares at him and tugs her arm free, setting the brandy back down.

'I mean it. Marry me.'

She laughs, then realises that he's not joking.

'We've shared so much loss. Who else could understand?'

Meilin brings her hand to her mouth, holding back a wild torrent of questions. Is he mad? What could he be thinking? Is this a trick?

'Say something.' Is that fear in his eyes?

Even when he's had some of her best interests at heart, there was always more at play.

'Say something,' he repeats.

It's never wise to give a gambler what he wants on the first ask.

'Help Renshu first.' She studies his face. She knows she's pressing on an old wound. She could tell by the way Longwei watched Renshu tonight that he still loves his nephew, still longs for a son.

'Marry me,' he says again. 'Everything will be so much easier.'

Easier? When has *ease* ever been the measure of his methods? Or hers? Through all her years of struggle, getting remarried has never appealed to Meilin. Her independence has been too hard won to relinquish to some man. But this isn't some stranger: this is Longwei, who, in many ways, knows her better than anyone.

'Longwei, please help him. This is his chance.'

Keeping eye contact, Longwei stands, then reaches for his blazer and fedora. He takes his time putting them on. Finally, he picks up the documents and rolls the papers into a loose scroll that he holds in one hand. 'Beautiful dinner tonight. Thank you.'

Meilin's heart is in her throat. She stands, too, wondering if they have asked too much, if she should have said yes to his proposal. She walks him to the door, uncertain what to say, massaging the knuckles of one hand with the fingers of the other as Longwei changes back into his street shoes.

Standing in the doorframe, backlit by the lantern outside, he leans forward and lifts an errant curl from the side of her face, tucking it back behind her ear. Then he gives Meilin a half-bow and heads out into the night.

*

They wait. As days turn to weeks, March passes. Then it is April, and the humidity rises as their hopes drop. By May, Meilin doubts everything. Did she hand Renshu's future to someone who will squander it? Might Longwei give the papers to someone else, along with his money? Should she have accepted Longwei's marriage proposal?

Aside from Longwei's response, whether good or bad, there are so many other ways in which this opportunity could fall apart: the visa could be denied, there might not be enough boat tickets, the government could change its mind, the money could come too late. A summer typhoon could wash away the offices and all the paperwork. She finds herself imagining one disastrous scenario after another.

Renshu has just finished a training drill, sweating in the June heat. He'll be glad when his compulsory service is over. Though he knows it's his duty to be ready to defend the Republic, he hates the thought of battle. He isn't a bad shot, but the drills leave him shaky, even if the targets are only black silhouettes. When they practised hand grenade deployment, he was sick and had to leave the field. Because he had demonstrated excellence in all other areas, his commanding officer grudgingly let him off the hook. Whatever happens with his visa application, he is determined not to stay in the military.

As he approaches the barracks, he sees Longwei, leaning on a motorcar and smoking a cigarette. Longwei's stance suggests that it has been years since he stood at strict attention for anyone. Renshu rushes over, his heart beating faster. Good news? Bad news? Why has his uncle come?

Longwei takes a last drag, then throws the cigarette butt down and extinguishes it with his foot. 'Renshu, let's walk.'

As Longwei enquires about his training, his ma, her health, Renshu is very proper. He gives short, clipped answers. His stride is straight and disciplined.

'Relax,' Longwei finally says. 'This is a friendly visit, not an examination.' He looks at Renshu. 'You know, you look just like your father.'

Renshu doesn't know what to say.

Longwei sighs sadly and shakes his head. 'And are you a patriot, too? Do you wish to become as great a soldier as he was?'

'Uncle, if necessary, I would serve the Republic with honour and diligence, but—'

'But what?'

'I wouldn't choose a career in the military.'

Longwei purses his lips and furrows his brow slightly.

Renshu worries that his candour was foolish. Perhaps he should have been more diplomatic.

'I was in the military for many years.' Longwei reaches into his pocket for his cigarettes and lighter. 'But I can understand your position. After my time on the battlefield, I found other, better ways to fight. After all, there is always an enemy and always a war, but one does not always have to be a soldier.'

He offers Renshu a cigarette.

Renshu shakes his head.

Longwei shrugs and lights his own cigarette, takes a long inhale and exhale. 'What about working for the government? Do you dream of returning from your studies in the US to be a civil servant?'

Does this mean Longwei has decided to help? Renshu's unsure how to answer. While not unpatriotic, he'd be reluctant to work for the KMT. He's heard about far too many beatings, mysterious disappearances and other difficulties for those who voice unpopular opinions, even within the ranks. Though affiliation with the government seems like a good thing, it would come at a price. His ma has always taught him that it's better to stay uninvolved.

'Clever boy,' Longwei murmurs. 'Not too quick to answer, to please. You look like your father, but you think like your mother.'

Renshu stares at Longwei.

'Above all else, Meilin is pragmatic.'

Is that a compliment or a condemnation?

'What was my father like?' Renshu decides to avoid the question, if he can't be honest.

'Xiaowen? Xiaowen was . . .' For a few paces Longwei considers, then responds. 'He was also clever. With books, with art. He had an eye for quality.' Then, in a bittersweet tone, 'He was a good man.'

Renshu smiles, glad to hear this.

They continue walking. Renshu steals a look at Longwei. As a child, he idolised, even loved, his uncle. Longwei, who always seemed so full of confidence and swagger, looks weary now. Silvery tips poke through his short hair; there are extra folds of skin around his neck and jaw. Longwei turns and looks back at Renshu.

'Your ma,' he starts, uncertainly.

Renshu raises his eyebrows, and nods, encouraging Longwei to go on.

'Did she ever—' He pauses, backing away from his own question.

'Did she ever what?' Renshu peers at the older man's face. Inscrutable.

'In the years we were all apart, did she ever mention me?'

'Of course, Uncle. We looked for you everywhere in Shanghai. She looked for you when we first got here, too, reading the newspapers, asking around. We wanted to find you, but eventually, we had to . . .' His voice trails off. Give up? Leave the memories behind? He doesn't want to say either of these things, although both are true.

Longwei shakes his head and gestures, as if waving away the topic. Although Renshu has answered his uncle's question, he has the feeling Longwei hasn't asked what he really wanted to know.

The conversation shifts to other topics, and soon they have looped around the compound and are back near the barracks. At the car, Longwei squints at Renshu, taking him in one more time. 'Arrange your boat ticket to the US,' he instructs, then gets in.

Renshu stands in shock, watching Longwei drive away.

It's going to happen. He's going to America. All those years of hope and struggle and hard work. All those pieces of the puzzle that he painstakingly assembled. Dumbfounded, he looks around. He hears laughter from the barracks, where the soldiers are glad to be off duty for the evening. Catching their energy, he whoops aloud. He can't wait to tell his ma.

*

Renshu gets a ticket on the next cargo ship, pleased that many of his classmates will be travelling on the same boat. The journey to America will take months. But a week before the departure date, even as Longwei tells him to finish packing, he produces no papers.

The final days pass in a flurry. Meilin avoids conversations with her neighbours, as she doesn't want to jinx their good fortune. There is too much to do – clothes to sew, suitcases to find and fill.

Where is Longwei?

The night before the boat is due to leave, when the wait has gone from worrying to excruciating, Longwei finally turns up with a sealed envelope.

'This has Renshu's passport, visa, sponsorship letter and bank information. All the necessary documents are here. Keep it all together, keep it sealed.' He turns to Renshu. 'When you get to immigration, hand all the papers to the officials. Make sure you get them all back. I've included contact information for Chen Yuming, the son of an old friend of mine. He also studies at Northwestern, and he'll help you. Keep all the papers in a safe place.'

He hands Meilin the envelope. It's lighter than she expects. Is this thin sheaf of papers strong enough to carry her boy across the ocean? Meilin gives the envelope to Renshu, who takes it and embraces Longwei. Caught off guard by this burst of affection, Longwei stumbles slightly, then embraces Renshu back, murmuring in his ear, 'Study hard and don't get involved in politics.'

Renshu nods.

Longwei then takes Meilin's hand in his. 'For family,' Longwei says.

'For family,' she agrees.

Keelung Harbour, Taiwan, July 1960

He is waving from the boat, surrounded by his classmates. They are the best students from the top universities. They are the luckiest of the lucky. The most talented of the top. Her boy stands among them.

Meilin thinks of departing Changsha twenty-two years ago,

driven away by fear and fires. She was younger then than he is now. There was no knowing what lay ahead. Today, he looks towards his future with hope. The wind snaps the flags on the boat to attention.

They have been one another's only constant. When everything else was uncertain, they found certainty in each other. She always believed that Renshu would be okay. He was a good boy, and he has become a good man. She hopes that he will be happy. That he finds a good life. That he feels safe and loved.

She raises her hand, waves it once.

He waves back. Triumphant, elated. A friend next to him throws an arm around his shoulder. Renshu gestures towards Meilin and his friend sees her. He, too, gives her a huge grin. She waves again. The boys wave one last time, then disappear into the crowd of passengers.

The crew is taking up the gangplanks, horns are sounding. All around, people cheer and wave, but Meilin stands still. He's going to America, the beautiful country. It is what he wanted, what he dreamed of. When she sees Renshu again, if she sees him again, he will be filled with a home she doesn't know. He will speak a language she doesn't understand; he will have eaten foods she has never tasted, and seen sights beyond her imagining. He will be so far away, further than he has ever been.

She feels like she is breaking apart – whether from joy or sorrow, she can't say. A kindly woman next to her says, *We are so proud of our boys, aren't we?* Meilin nods and tears roll off her nose. She has never felt more bereft.

PART FOUR
1960–1968

Chapter Fifteen

'We need to go. Dao Renshu's going to cry.' Li Hotan holds out his hand for a handshake.

A long, silvery Greyhound has just pulled into its bay at the Port Authority Bus Terminal and passengers are boarding. Renshu's suitcase and satchel sit at his feet. It's time to say goodbye to his friends Li, Pao and Guo.

The voyage took nearly two months, making stops in the Philippines and Hawaii, and passing through the Panama Canal before finally docking in New York. About thirty students sailed on the ship, each with a dream of America. Renshu spent countless hours with Li Hotan, Pao Dafei and Guo Yao, playing card games, telling stories and comparing hopes. Now it's time to go their separate ways. Li and Pao will stay here in New York City, for their studies at Columbia and NYU. Guo will soon board a bus to Boston. Renshu is the only one from this group headed to the Midwest.

Renshu grasps Li's hand, blinks hard and swallows. He is filled with gratitude for Li and Pao. 'I'm not going to cry,' he protests.

Li clasps his other hand around Renshu's. 'Of course not. Me neither,' he says, blinking hard. 'Zaijian.'

'Zaijian,' Renshu says. Then, 'See you again,' tasting the words in English.

The bus rumbles west through the crimsons and oranges of a summer sunset and into the night. Through the length of Pennsylvania, Renshu dozes fitfully. When the bus struggles up a hill, the revving engine and shifting gears jar him awake. Going down, the turns in the road and the squeaking brakes jostle him.

No matter which way he shifts in the seat, he feels stiff and squashed. Eventually, he falls asleep in an uncomfortable slouch.

Renshu wakes to a sore neck and a gnawing stomach. Blearily, he watches the land pass by his window. Last night's hills and valleys have flattened out into farmland that stretches for miles. Some fields, already harvested, have been shorn bare. Others still wave with row after row of sweetcorn, the green stalks tipped by gold. There are no labourers working the land, no lines of bamboo hats, scythes and baskets. Instead, huge tractors and mysterious equipment crawl across the fields, digging several furrows at once. Where are all the people?

Passengers are starting to wake around him, coughing, stretching. He doesn't know anyone here. When they stop for breakfast and a fuel break, everyone scatters in different directions. Renshu, afraid of becoming lost, must not let the bus driver out of his sight. He buys what the driver buys for breakfast, he sits where he can see his green uniform. When the driver uses the toilet, Renshu does, too, rushing, so that he doesn't get left behind. He cannot be left here, wherever here is.

Back on the bus, the hours pass. In the seats behind him, a woman gripes: *Joshua, stop teasing your brother. No, Evan, no more snacks.* Across the aisle, two women look through a photo album. *That's Charlie, he's the one that Nancy was after at the picnic. Oh, yes, and that's Cousin Darren.* So many new names. Renshu has a new name, too, for his American life.

It had happened one evening, not long after they sailed from Taiwan. Western names kept bubbling to the surface of the dinner conversation, followed by cackles of laughter and applause. *Peter, Stephen, Benjamin, Alexander, Jerry.*

'And what about you? What will your name be, Dao Renshu?'

He didn't understand what they were asking.

'You need to choose a different name, a Western name,' Li Hotan explained. 'I shall be' – and he paused until all eyes were on him – 'Andrew Li.' He extended his arm in a flourish, enjoying the ceremony.

'Why would I choose a different name?'

'It's easier that way. When you fill out papers, when you open a bank account, when you meet a girl – an American girl, maybe – if you have Western name, it's easier for them to pronounce and remember it.'

Renshu blinked. He said nothing.

'In America, when you meet someone, you don't say your family name first, but just this name,' said Guo.

'A name is a calling card. A name is a handshake. A name is an entry on to the stage,' someone else added.

'It's how you start an introduction. "Pleased to meet you, I'm Andrew."' Li Hotan held his hand out to Renshu.

More names, more guffaws. They scraped their chopsticks against empty bowls and continued their banter long after the meal had ended.

A few weeks into the journey, Renshu had lain awake one night, restless. He'd risen and turned on the small lamp above the desk in the cabin he shared with three others. They stirred, but no one woke. His eye fell on the book Li had been reading. *Walden* by Henry David Thoreau. Renshu flipped through until he found a sentence where he had no need for his English dictionary: *Heaven is under our feet as well as over our heads.* The sea beneath was unsteady, the sky above was endless. This seemed to be as true a statement as any. Henry.

From his satchel, he took out a piece of paper, an inkstone and inkstick, a brush and his fountain pen. He emptied the remaining drops of tea from a mug into the tray of the inkstone and rubbed the stone back and forth, watching the ink darken and pool. With his brush, in careful strokes, he wrote *Dao Renshu* down the right side of the paper. He put the brush down and waited for the ink to dry. Then he uncapped his pen and wrote *Henry Dao* in a horizontal line on the left side. He folded the paper and put it in his pocket.

Still wide awake, he went up to the deck and stood, resting his arms on the railings. A night-time captain nodded to him, but didn't ask any questions. No matter how far Renshu looked, there was no land in sight. He was somewhere between China and Taiwan and America. The stars shone like they had never been dimmed by smoking buildings or the heavy haze of humidity. The sea was still. No moon, no wind; only a quieten ticking of the ship's engines.

He was no longer Dao Renshu. He was not yet Henry Dao. Hovering somewhere above these two names, he stood on the deck and watched the horizon until the eastern sky began to colour.

'Evanston? Ah, you're gonna need the el.'

Renshu draws back. Did the bus driver just tell him to go to hell?

'But I am going to Evanston, Northwestern University.' Renshu holds out his ticket.

The driver peers at Renshu's ticket while loudly working a piece of chewing gum from one side of his mouth to the other. 'Buddy, they sold you the wrong ticket. Look.' He points with his stubby forefinger, dirt caked under the nails. 'Port Authority Bus Terminal, New York, to Chicago Bus Terminal, Illinois.' He jabs his finger at the word *Chicago* for emphasis, leaving a greasy smudge. 'This is the end of the road for me. Like I said, take the el.' And he turns and walks through a door labelled 'Do Not Enter'.

You go to hell. Renshu scowls at the closed door.

Now what? He's lost somewhere between his friends in New York and his destination in Evanston, and doesn't know a single person in between. After rehearsing his question and working up his courage, he asks at the ticket counter. Elated that the woman understands him, her answer speeds by and he doesn't catch the details. He's too embarrassed to ask her to repeat herself. 'Okay,' he says, and walks back to the waiting area. It's hot. He takes off his heavy coat, which is far too warm for the late summer heat, but too bulky to fit in his suitcase.

He stares at his suitcase and satchel. Should he walk? He doesn't know what direction to go. He doesn't know the distance. Is he near? Far?

He studies the boards with timetables. There are listings for

New York, Philadelphia, Indianapolis, Milwaukee. Nothing about Evanston.

'Can I help you? Are you lost?' asks a young man with glasses and dusty brown hair. He wears a tan V-neck sweater over a red-checked shirt and dark brown trousers. Like Renshu, the man has a single suitcase and a satchel. There is a reassuring openness in his manner.

'Yes, yes,' Renshu says. Flustered, he looks down at his ticket, then back up at the man.

'Where do you want to go?'

'Evanston, Northwestern University,' Renshu manages to say.

'I thought that might be case,' says the man, nodding. 'Me too. C'mon. We'll take the el.' He motions for Renshu to follow him out of the door.

Renshu looks up and down the road. No rickshaws or carts, no cheerful ringing of bicycle bells. Cars fill the streets. Horns blare, people shout. Everywhere are street signs and shop signs and newspaper stands, but Renshu can't stop to work out what they say. He must keep up with the man. There is a rumbling overhead. Astonished, Renshu looks up through dark green metal arches to see a train. A train! In the air?

'Hey, this way. Got some change?'

The man is dropping coins into a turnstile. Renshu is relieved to see the cost is in coins and not bills. Renshu reaches into his pocket, counts out the fare, and pushes the bar to go through. They rush up a staircase to an elevated platform just as a train arrives. It's crowded. They squeeze in and stand, holding overhead straps to keep from stumbling as the train lurches away over the streets.

The man holds out his free hand, 'I'm Richard. Richard Addison, and this is the "L", short for elevated train.'

'Henry,' whispers Renshu.

'Pardon?' Richard leans forward. He can't hear over the squealing and shifting of the train.

They turn a corner and Renshu almost falls. He steadies himself, takes a breath and says it more loudly, returning the handshake. 'Henry. I'm Henry Dao.'

Evanston, Illinois, September 1960

Longwei's contact, Chen Yuming, or, as he calls himself in America, Charles Chen, is a little older than Henry and has an easy manner and friendly smile. He's been at Northwestern for about a year studying economics. He looks vaguely familiar. Perhaps he was finishing at NTU when Henry was first starting? Chen agrees this is possible, but he's been in the US for a few years now. Before starting graduate school, Chen was in Chicago helping with his uncle's business. He still goes down to visit quite often. A room in the boarding house where Chen stays is available, and Henry gladly moves in after Chen puts in a good word for him with Mrs Patterson, the landlady. Henry and Chen are the only Chinese in the house; the majority of the other boarders are Americans. They are welcoming, but mostly keep a polite distance, even from each other. Everyone is focused on their work or studies.

At the boarding house, Henry has a whole room of his own. Not shared with anyone. His books are on his desk. His clothes are folded and put away in the dresser. There are still a few empty drawers. In the closet hang his coat, a few dress shirts and a blazer for special occasions. At the bottom sits an extra pair of shoes. When he first arrives, he turns the lights on and off several times, just for the luxury.

The street outside is lined by large trees. Oaks, elms, maples. The shapes of the leaves fascinate him. There are no twisty, sprawling banyan groves reclaiming anything in their path, or delicate, fan-shaped ginkgo leaves brushing the air. Every so often, a car drives by. A mother pushes a buggy up the sidewalk. So quieten. So different from the bright heat of Taipei, the palms and azaleas of the boulevard at NTU, or the merry night markets. It is strange, this sense of heat without a sea nearby. Air without the scent of salt or fish.

Chen shows Henry around the neighbourhood, tells him where to get second-hand copies of textbooks, advises him on the paperwork for international students. It is Chen who helps him get a job in the cafeteria as a bus boy, so he can eat for free as well as earn some money. With the job and the money from Uncle Longwei, Henry has enough for rent, books, supplies and blue aerogramme letters to write to his ma once a month. As long as he is thrifty and works hard, money will be no problem.

Henry's studies command most of his attention and energy. Months pass in a routine of going to lectures, studying and working at the cafeteria. In his letters to Meilin, Henry tries to describe American football, doughnuts, pizza, and the way the trees reach and arch over his road, describing the autumn as a tunnel of gold. When the weather turns cold, Henry wears his thick coat and new boots, walking through the spicy crunch of fallen leaves.

It isn't until the winter that his first waves of homesickness arise. Somehow the excitement of all that was new has carried him through the first semester, but in the early months of the year, with bitter winds howling off Lake Michigan and short days offering only the weakest of sunlight, his longing for his ma and the comforts of Taiwan intensifies.

On the evening of the Lunar New Year, Henry sits at his desk with a half-finished letter for Meilin. For months, he has been trying to find his way around his new language with a frozen tongue. He reaches for his Chinese–English dictionary. It is as thick and heavy as a brick. The thin pages sound like moth's wings as he flips back and forth, looking for words to understand this kind of cold.

When he writes to his ma, the Chinese characters flow like a river down the page, thawing his words: *Ma, the winter snows are fierce and sharp. I don't remember ever seeing snow in Taiwan. The winds are like screeching demons that shake the trees. The bare branches scrape my windows in a fury. Some days, I wear two pairs of socks and both of my sweaters and I still feel cold! Today is the Lunar New Year, I wonder what you are doing. Are you making radish cakes for the Huangs? Sharing a fish and gossiping with Auntie Chin? Do you remember when we lit lanterns and made wishes in the streets of Shanghai? Ma, I miss you.*

Henry puts down his pen and stands up, stretching his arms,

then wanders over to the window. He pulls back the curtain and feels a cold draugh steal into the room. Outside, the street lamps are blurry and yellow. It is calm, except for the occasional bright movement of headlights coming down the road or red tail lights receding.

In Taipei tonight, firecrackers are flying and dragon dancers are weaving through the streets to drumbeats so loud and deep that you can feel them in your belly. A flurry of red envelopes is exchanging hands. Spilling from open shopfronts are pyramids of oranges and pomegranates, boxes of kumquats, nuts and candies carefully arranged and tied up with red strings. Outside the temples, people will be buying bundles of paper money and joss sticks to burn, and thick red candles to light. Everywhere, red paper lanterns with gold tassels will hang in the street. Conversations will swell and break into laughter, the sounds of families reuniting with relatives and friends. Here in Evanston, he rubs at the fogged-up windowpane and cranes his neck to see if he can see any stars. Nothing; just the shoulder of thick clouds.

Not long after, however, comes the spring. Small blossoms dot the campus and tiny leaves appear. Students shed their layers of coats and hats and scarves. Instead of a hurried dash through the frigid air from boarding house to campus and back, Henry strolls, welcoming the warmth, the longer days. Green lawns reappear from under melted snowbanks, and tulips and crocuses brighten his walks.

When summer comes, he takes a job washing glassware for a chemistry laboratory and studies for his upcoming qualifying exams. Soon the year spins around to another autumn, another new set of graduate students, new housemates. A few more Chinese students arrive, and though there are no vacancies at the boarding house, Chen befriends them as well. There are enough Chinese students on campus now for small gatherings, and a Chinese Student Association is formed. Henry's second Lunar New Year away from Taiwan is spent in the company of new friends.

That year, Henry completes his master's degree. His hard work and excellent academic performance result in an offer of a fellowship to continue as a doctoral student. If he accepts, his fees and tuition will be waived, and he will earn a stipend as a research assistant. He had always thought he would return to Taiwan after his master's. That was what his offer was; that was what Longwei's financial help would cover. But a chance to do a doctorate? And to know that he has earned the opportunity through his own efforts? And maybe he'll even have some extra money to send back to his ma? How can he say no?

On the other hand, how can he say yes? If he stays, that means four or five more years, at least, before he sees his ma or uncle again. Who will take care of them? Will they take care of each other?

Lately, his ma's letters describe a world that is harder and harder for Henry to recall. She tells him about Peiwen's twins, who have new jobs, and that Baobao, the baby, has been accepted into Jianguo High School. But his images of Taipei are becoming blurry. He no longer remembers how the different lanes and alleyways connect. Meilin's news – once so evocative, carrying the smells in the market, the sounds in the streets, the voices of the neighbours – diminishes into written characters on a thin sheet of blue airmail paper. Dao Renshu is fading. Staying in America will make him even more hazy.

Something flutters in the periphery of his thinking. A story. One of his ma's stories. He hasn't thought of it in years. It's the one about the old man from the frontier with the horse. *This fellowship*, he thinks. No matter what he decides, it will be both a blessing and a curse.

Chapter Sixteen

Evanston, Illinois, November 1963

It's a Friday morning, late in November. In his graduate student office, Henry is at work on a calculation that has plagued him all week. He woke up with an idea for a different approach and now, immersed in thought, he senses this is a promising path. Henry loves cracking a puzzle: the gates open, cogs turn, the equations march down the page and his understanding starts to fall into place.

Henry's doctoral research specialises in aerospace engineering. If there was one thing that Henry understood in China, it was that whoever ruled the skies ruled the world. When he thinks of those early years in Chongqing, he feels a profound helplessness. No matter how big their outrage or how fierce their guns, the Chinese on the ground had little or no chance when the Japanese dropped their bombs. Gravity itself was on their side. In the end, it was science – better science, American science – that halted Japan. Now there is another war, a cold one, and the race is not just to rule the skies, but the stars and the moon as well. Where there is fear, there is also opportunity. Henry is not one to pass up opportunity.

His stomach growls. It's nearly noon. Happy with the morning's progress, Henry puts his papers away and heads to the boarding house for lunch.

Climbing the steps up to the porch, he sees through the big picture windows that the living room is packed. It's odd to see people there in the middle of the day. Typically, it's just Mrs Patterson watching her soaps until a handful of students arrive for lunch. But there's a crowd around the television. Mrs Patterson, eyes glued to screen, is sobbing.

'President Kennedy's been shot,' someone says.

On the TV, a camera pans across a conference room with rows of tables set for a banquet. But no one sits. Men in smart suits and women with elegant hats are milling around. *There are many stories coming in as to the condition of the president. One is that he is dead. This cannot be confirmed.* The camera zooms in on a waiter in a white tuxedo and a black bow tie wiping his face with a handkerchief. The picture shifts to a newscaster in shirtsleeves in a newsroom. Behind him, people are rushing around. Phones ring. He starts to speak: *The word we have is that the president is dead. This is not officially confirmed.*

Mrs Patterson shakes her head. 'Terrible, terrible. This can't be happening.'

Henry glances at the other students. Everyone is transfixed.

The newsman is talking about a priest and last rites; he is saying the police have a suspect in custody. Then he interrupts himself: 'Our correspondent in Dallas, Dan Rather, confirms that President Kennedy is dead. There is still no official confirmation of this, however.'

No one is certain what is fact, what is rumour.

The newscaster is saying something about an ambassador, then stops mid-sentence and looks to his side. Putting his glasses on, he picks up a piece of paper. 'From Dallas, Texas. The flash, apparently official. President Kennedy died' – he takes his glasses off as he speaks – 'at one p.m., Central Standard Time' – he looks up and to the side – 'two o'clock Eastern Standard Time, some thirty-eight minutes ago.' Looks down, puts his glasses back on. Shifts some papers.

Mrs Patterson weeps. The room begins to quiver with fearful murmurs. Is this part of a greater attack? Is it the start of a war? Who has done this? Why? The telephone starts ringing. The TV reporting continues. Someone else turns on the radio. More news. The telephone rings again. People drift into other rooms, the kitchen, the porch, the street, outside, anywhere away from the horror.

How can this be happening? Henry thought he had left this kind of tragedy behind in China. This is not supposed to happen here in the beautiful country. What does Henry do now? Go back to his office? Call his ma? Chen's down in Chicago again, so he can't ask him. Henry's not hurt, but the world itself seems broken: it's not the same place it was just a few hours ago. Someone brings a tray filled with mugs of hot coffee into the room and passes them around. Henry drinks his too quickly and scalds the roof of his mouth.

Over the following days, the news is always on. People are reeling with sorrow and shock. The suspected assassin is arrested and then shot while being transferred to the county jail. Classes are cancelled, flags fly at half-mast. The country, the world, is stunned. When Henry first arrived in America, he wondered where all the people were. But now, on the TV, he sees them, drawn out by tragedy, as if America is bleeding into the streets.

A few nights later, Henry awakes to the smell of smoke. Bells clanging. Shouts, screams.

He pants. His heart races. More smoke. Sirens wailing.

He jumps out of bed and reaches for the leather wallet where he keeps his passport and emergency cash. He pulls on a sweater, his warm winter coat, wool socks and boots. More sirens are coming down the road.

'Wake up! Wake up!' He bangs on his neighbour's door. 'You need to get out!'

No answer.

He bangs again. 'We need to run to the shelter. Where's our shelter?'

A crackle of flames taunts him. No time to wait.

He rushes down the stairs. Why is no one else awake? Coughing, he hopes he won't gag on the smoke. He runs down the steps and into the front garden. Where are all the people?

He scans the sky. It's dark, but there's no mistaking the silhouette of planes in the distance. The air thrums with their approach. Down the street, flames light up the sky. Houses are crumbling, wails cut through the night. Bombs must have already been dropped. He squints up again. The planes will double back for another attack. Where's the shelter?

'Mr Dao?'

He turns. Mrs Patterson stands on the porch in her slippers, with a housecoat thrown over her nightgown.

'Where's the shelter? We need to hurry, we need to get everyone out before the planes come back!' he shouts.

'Mr Dao.' She comes down the stairs and scans the sky. 'There are no planes.'

He looks up again. He's certain. 'But the sirens, the fire—' He gestures at the flames. Adrenaline pulses through his arms.

She peers up and down the street. 'What are you talking about?'

He looks again. All is dark and quieten. There is only the hum and flicker of the street lamps. He sniffs. 'Don't you smell the smoke, Mrs Patterson? Where is it coming from?'

She shakes her head disapprovingly as she sniffs, too. She notices his boots, trousers, coat. 'What did you think was happening?' she asks.

'I just . . .'

'What's all the commotion?' The man from the room next to Henry's walks out. He comes not from the house, but the back garden.

'You too?' she exclaims in exasperation.

'I couldn't sleep.' He shrugs. 'Came out for a smoke.'

'See?' she says to Henry. 'It was only Mr Wetherall, up at an ungodly hour to smoke a cigarette. Mr Dao seems to have had some sort of episode,' Mrs Patterson says.

Henry winces at her condescension. But he saw the planes, he heard the fires. He really did.

A cigarette? He doesn't understand.

Since the assassination, Mr Wetherall has been playing the same record again and again. Classical piano seeps into Henry's room. It cuts through the pervasive atmosphere of grief, through Henry's own confusion. *What is this music?*

Although they've nodded 'hello' in the corridor for close to two months now, Henry has been too shy to speak to the man. After that night in the garden, he feels even more sheepish. Also, though he's been here three years, the fear of being misunderstood remains. When speaking to Americans, Henry's stomach tenses as he watches them take in his words, relaxing only after their response indicates understanding. But there's the music again. *What is it?* He resolves to ask. Before he loses his nerve, he knocks loudly on the door.

The young man answers immediately. He must be over six feet tall, but slouches in his doorframe, suggesting ease and self-possession.

Henry starts: 'The music—'

Before he can get his sentence out, the man apologises. 'I'm sorry, does my music disturb you?'

Henry considers the question. This music has interrupted his studies and demanded he pause. It has made him want to listen again and again, paying more attention each time.

'Yes, it does. I like it very much.'

Looking relieved, the housemate laughs. 'I suppose Chopin can be both disturbing and likeable. It's the only thing I can bear to listen to right now. I'm so sickened by the news.' He extends his hand. Henry notices how long the man's fingers are, the way the joints and knuckles stick out. His handshake is firm and quick. 'I'm Guy Wetherall. I'm in the graduate programme in composition at the music school. And you?'

'Henry. Graduate student in engineering.'

Guy nods.

'What is the music?' Henry asks.

Guy says something quickly, including a few words that don't sound like English. Reluctant to ask him to repeat himself, Henry asks how to spell the name. Guy opens the door wider and motions for him to come in.

A record player rests on a wooden milk crate turned on its end. Inside the crate are several records. The open closet is stuffed with shirts, trousers and jackets. The bed is unmade, and pillows have fallen on the floor. The desk is littered with music scores, scattered at different angles.

Guy picks up an album cover from the desk and hands it to Henry. It shows a painted portrait of a young man in a dark jacket, red vest, white shirt and bow tie. Henry wonders if this is the composer or the musician. On the cover is written 'The

Chopin Ballades' in light, watery blue, followed by 'RUBIN-STEIN' in a bright orange.

'You can borrow it if you like. Do you have a record player?'

Henry shakes his head.

'Oh. You know you can listen to records at the music library, don't you?'

Henry didn't know this. He asks Guy to wait as he hurries back to his room for pen and paper. He carefully copies the words 'Chopin Ballades' and 'Rubinstein' and thanks Guy.

'No problem,' Guy says, closing the door.

Soon, the record starts again and Henry hears Guy humming along.

The next week, Henry visits the music library. Behind the reception desk, a young woman sits reading, with bobbed brown hair and a dark green cardigan. Absorbed in her book, she doesn't notice Henry approach.

'May I listen to this record, please?' he asks, holding out the slip of paper with the album name.

Her head jerks up, her green eyes alarmed. 'Sorry?'

Henry blushes. Was his question unclear? He asks again.

'Oh.' she relaxes. 'You surprised me, that's all. Let's see.' She tucks a stray lock of hair behind her ear and reaches for the slip of paper.

He holds his hand to his cheek. It's still warm.

She scans the paper, then glances at him, before rising from her seat. She's nearly as tall as he is. 'Let me show you,' she says, walking to a wooden cabinet with many tiny drawers. She pulls out the long drawer marked 'C' and flips through the cards. When she has found what she's looking for, she takes a tiny pencil from a box and notes down a series of letters and numbers.

'When you want a record, first look it up in the card catalogue and write down the call numbers,' she says, showing him the slip of paper. '*Then* you bring it to me and I'll get your record.' A smirk plays at the corners of her mouth.

Feeling vaguely chastised, Henry follows her back to the desk. She looks over her shoulder. 'Wait just a minute.'

She disappears through an open door. He rises on his toes, seeing if he can glimpse her through the doorway.

Soon she returns with the album, her head cocked to the side. 'This one?'

Nodding, he reaches out for it and she pulls back a bit.

'Library card?'

He fumbles in his wallet and holds out his student ID. She takes it, then raises her eyes to his and smiles.

'Here you are, Mr Dao.' She hands him the record and gestures towards an empty carrell with a record player and headphones. 'We hold your card until you return the record.'

As he listens to the music, he sits very still, absorbing the sounds, eyes closed. It is as if Arthur Rubinstein is playing just for Henry. After the first side finishes, he picks up the record by its edges, flips it over and replaces it on the turntable. He lowers the needle down to the shiny black edge and waits for the music to begin again. The afternoon dissolves as he listens to the record a second, then third time. The music washes away the anguish he has felt over the past weeks. Beyond that, it subdues a longing in his belly, his arms, the soles of his feet. There is nothing patriotic or militaristic in this sound. No one can claim its allegiance. It belongs only to itself, the notes tumbling into his ears like waterfalls, drenching him in their urgent beauty. The ballades tell stories of heartbreak and loss, of persistence and passion. They speak of all that he cannot voice in English, Chinese or any language.

It had been a bright autumn afternoon when he entered the library. Now the sky is scarlet and purple with dusk. Even though Henry's hands and face are cold as he hurries home, he doesn't notice. He's thinking about Chopin's Ballades and picturing a pair of smiling dark green eyes.

Henry starts to visit the music library every Sunday. He always looks for the same librarian and asks for the Chopin.

'Here you are, Mr Dao,' she says, handing him the record.

'Thank you.' He wonders what her name is.

Eventually, she starts pulling the record out from the shelves as soon as he approaches the desk.

After a quieten Christmas and New Year's spent at the boarding house, Henry is eager for the semester to begin. When he goes to the library on the first Sunday back, his heart leaps when he sees the librarian.

'Happy New Year, Mr Dao.'

'Happy New Year . . . what is your name?'

'Rachel Howard.' She holds her hand out.

'Henry,' he replies, taking it.

'I know,' she says, with a sparkle in her eye.

Rachel. Rachel, would you like to go for a walk with me? Rachel, do you like doughnuts? Rachel, do you like the movies? He'd practised in his head all break, but in the end, he becomes tongue-tied, and just asks for the Chopin record once again.

Chapter Seventeen

There's a knock at the door. Henry opens it to find Chen in snow boots, with his coat unbuttoned, scarf hanging loosely around his neck.

'Are you sure you don't want to come down to Chicago? My cousins would love to see you, and there's always plenty of food to eat.'

'Tempting, but no. I've got to stay here this weekend.'

'Okay, okay. I tried my best,' Chen says to the ceiling, holding up his hands in surrender. 'You'll have to answer to my auntie next time you see her.' Chen looks around the room. 'So what *will* you be doing tonight? Please tell me you won't be seeing in the Year of the Dragon in the company of this guy.' Chen picks up *Classical Electrodynamics* by J. D. Jackson and waves it around. 'Trust me. He's no fun at all.'

'Nah, not tonight.' Henry laughs. 'I thought I might go to a party.'

'The Chinese Student Association party? That was last week.'

'This is just an informal gathering. Lots of students from Taiwan.'

Chen steps into Henry's room. Closes the door. 'Who's the host?' His voice is suddenly serious.

Henry bites his lip, trying to recall the name. He didn't know the host. Arthur Lai, a fellow NTU graduate, although they didn't know each other at Taida, passed the invitation to him. 'Someone named Hu. Yes, Joseph Hu, I think.'

Chen frowns. 'I don't think you should go.'

'Pardon?'

'I said, don't go. You don't know this Joseph Hu. He could be making trouble.'

Henry laughs. Chen must be teasing. 'Trouble? What kind of trouble? Do you know him?'

Chen doesn't answer his question. 'You're here with government sponsorship, right?' he says.

'We all are.'

'Yes. So stick to the official Chinese Student Association events. It's safer that way.'

Henry looks at Chen, incredulous. Something has soured in the air between them.

'You don't know who is organising this, who will be listening. If word gets back to the wrong ears that you were there – even if you don't say or do anything – there could be a problem. Don't go.' Chen's earlier joviality has vanished.

'It's just a party.' Henry bristles.

'A party is never just a party.' Chen buttons up his coat and leaves.

Henry stares at the door, wishing he had thought of something to say in response. Now Chen's words roll around the room, echoing off the walls. Even though the curtains are drawn, and rolled-up towels line the cracks where the window meets the sill, a cold draught creeps in and drifts over the floorboards, accumulating like invisible snow in the corners. Henry checks his diary for the address again, then closes his books, puts away his pen and pencil.

He pulls his boots on. Then gloves, scarf, coat, hat. He's still not used to needing so many layers. He heads out, locking the door, and steps into the crisp, cold night. The icy air catches in his throat; he coughs and winds his scarf around his neck one more time. Henry is troubled. Why is Chen so concerned? Long-wei's parting words come to mind: *Don't get involved in politics.* Henry has been careful since he arrived here. But this isn't politics, it's a New Year's celebration. Crunching along in old snow, Henry quickens his pace and tugs his hat down lower, trying to cover his ears more fully. Sure, Chen has been a friend, but he doesn't know everything about Henry either. The cold cuts right through his boots, and his toes feel numb. At a crossing, Henry raises his head to check the street signs. It starts to snow. Lit by the headlights of oncoming traffic, the snowflakes look like thousands of tiny lanterns.

Entering the cold, bright lobby of the apartment building, he stamps his boots and leaves footprints on the damp doormat. A sludge of wet leaves has accumulated at the bottom of the steps. As he heads upstairs, the patches of snow clinging to his coat melt, and voices float down. After four flights, he comes to a corridor with a door open into an apartment, shoes and boots spilling out into the hallway. The room is packed with people and merriment.

'Henry! Henry – Happy New Year!' a familiar voice calls. With a blast of warm air from the room, Henry's glasses fog up. For a moment he is enveloped in scents of garlic, soy sauce, ginger, scallions and sizzling pork. He is surrounded by a sea of Mandarin with occasional waves of Taiwanese. He understands some Taiwanese, but he never learned it well enough to speak it fluently. All of the lectures at NTU were in Mandarin, and although there were Taiwanese students in his classes, he hadn't known any of them personally. The Benshengren and Waishengren students tended to stay separate.

As he takes off his layers and wipes his lenses clear, he feels the comforting wash of words he doesn't have to reach after and intonations he knows without hesitation. Again, the voice calls out and he squints through the crowd to see Arthur Lai motioning him over to a table full of food. Henry's fingers ache and burn as they warm up.

Settling down to a plate of dumplings, long noodles, fish and broccoli, sticky rice cakes, watermelon seeds and peanuts, Henry fills with a contentment he hasn't felt since the dinner before his bus out of New York. Someone offers him a mug of jasmine tea. He blows across the top of the surface, cradling the mug in both hands.

Sipping his tea, Henry takes in the room. There are students in clusters everywhere: some from his department, some he's seen at events in the student centre. There are a lot of people he's never seen before. It's so different from his first winter, when he and Chen seemed to be the only Chinese students around. Just as Henry is realising that he doesn't see anyone from Chen's circles, someone sidles up to him to chat. It's the host himself, Joseph Hu. At first, Joseph's questions seem like harmless small talk: What is he studying? When did he arrive? What does he think of America? Joseph seems to be half listening, half monitoring the room, nodding at people who pass by, waving hello, all the while reassuring Henry, *Go on, go on, I'm listening.* Henry's tea is almost gone. Only the dregs remain, strong and slightly too bitter. Henry suggests maybe Joseph wants to go talk to his other guests? Joseph waves the suggestion away – 'You are my guest. Besides, I see them all the time' – and starts to ask more questions. Which university did Henry study at in Taiwan? Who was his advisor there? When did he do his conscription? The questions tip from inquisitive to insidious. Where was he stationed? Did he know this person? What about this person? Chen's words come floating back: *Be careful . . . a party is never just a party.* The mug is cold in Henry's hands.

Dodging the last of Joseph's queries, Henry gestures at his empty plate. He thanks Joseph for his generosity and wonders if he might have just one more serving of scallion pancakes?

'Of course, eat your fill! We'll talk more later.' Joseph claps his hand on Henry's back.

Henry doesn't respond. He heads to the table.

The room that seemed inviting an hour ago has become stifling. The cut glass bowls that sparkled with festivity now look cheap and flashy. The laughter in the apartment rattles like tin cans.

The platter that had been stacked with scallion pancakes is now empty. On the plate next to it, a few dumplings languish, cold and limp. Small beads of grease have congealed on their wrappers. Henry's not that hungry, after all.

This party, despite its comforts, bristles with a troubling undercurrent. Henry has walked into a den of unclear allegiances. Whether it is due to Chen's words earlier, Henry's own cautious nature, or a combination of both, he is sure he must leave. Immediately.

He makes his way over to Lai, who is happily caught in an argument between two girls about whether to release paper lanterns tonight; one says it is too early and they should wait for the full moon, the other says they should do it now since they are already gathered. Lai claps his hands and says, 'Let's do both!' For a moment, Henry wants to be drawn in, to joke and flirt. But he sees Joseph from the corner of his eye, and his uneasiness outweighs his longing to stay. Henry taps Lai on the shoulder.

'I'm going.'

Lai stops mid-sentence. 'Don't you want . . .?' He gestures at the table laden with half-eaten platters, stacks of soiled plates, bottles of all sizes with all kinds of drink.

'No, I need to study. See you later. Happy New Year.'

'Okay. Happy Year of the Dragon, my friend,' Lai says in a theatrical voice that makes the girls giggle. One of the girls looks at Henry. Her glance is sly, but he catches it. Her eyes slide across the room, telegraphing a message to Joseph.

While Henry laces up his boots, Joseph comes rushing over. The host presses a sesame candy in his hand and a red envelope. 'Happy New Year, Dao. Will we see you again soon?'

Henry ignores the question, wishes Joseph a Happy New Year and leaves.

He buttons his coat and puts on his scarf and gloves as he hurries down the stairs. He pulls his hat over his ears and steps outside. The snow is falling in thick, heavy flakes. All the tracks from earlier in the evening have been snowed over.

A few blocks away, Henry wonders if he overreacted. He takes the envelope and candy out of his pocket. He sucks on the candy and opens the envelope under a street lamp. It holds a notice for an upcoming meeting, with a date and address. 'Please come!' written in English at the top, in urgent black ink.

You don't know who will be listening.

Snowflakes smear the ink and soften the paper.

Don't get involved in politics.

Henry looks over his shoulder, tears the invitation into pieces and drops them. They flutter into the wet snow.

The sesame candy tastes harsh, with a metallic, tooth-breaking sweetness. He spits it out into the snow, too.

*

When Chen returns from his cousin's in Chicago, he asks, 'So, did you end up going to that New Year's party? I've been wondering.'

'Just for an hour or so. I left early,' says Henry.

Chen nods approvingly.

'Why do you ask?'

Chen doesn't give a reason. Instead, he says 'Look, I'm heading back to Taipei after I finish my degree. I won't be around to keep an eye out for you. Don't go anywhere or associate with anyone that could put you on any kind of government blacklist.'

'Blacklist?'

'Yes. Blacklist. I'm not kidding. Those guys won't even give you a chance to explain yourself. No hesitation, no mercy.'

'But we're in the US.'

'True, but we're here on the goodwill of the KMT. And our families are still in Taiwan.'

Chapter Eighteen

Evanston, Illinois, February 1964

'Musicology,' Rachel says. 'The study of music in various contexts –
historical, cultural, philosophical. How it shapes who we are. How
we live, how we love.'

After weeks of resolving to ask her out and instead only asking
for the Chopin, Henry has finally managed to invite Rachel out
for dessert. She agreed so quickly that, in his flustered delight,
he couldn't think of anywhere to go. She suggested a popular
student diner just a few blocks from campus.

Now, over steaming mugs of coffee and large slices of pecan
pie, she speaks non-stop about her studies and her love of music.
Though she speaks quickly, Henry understands every word. He
is charmed by her lively manner, the way she reels off new ideas
and names of singers he has never heard of.

'Sure, I appreciate the greats – Beethoven, Chopin, Mozart –
but what I really like is folk music. American folk music. Woody
Guthrie, Peter, Paul and Mary, the Weavers. All of it. So I'm
here for my master's degree, focusing on American folk music
traditions during and after the Great Depression. Do you have
favourite folk songs from China?'

He closes his eyes and hums the opening notes to 漁光曲, the
lullaby his ma used to sing him.

'Oh, it's beautiful! So lyrical and soulful. What is it about?'

'The fishermen, out on the water, looking at the clouds and
the waves. They try to catch the fish with an old net, on an old
boat. They work hard every year. It's a hard life.'

'What's it called?'

'Song of the Fishermen.'

'I'll look for a recording,' she declares. 'We might just have
one. You never know. It's a huge collection.'

Henry takes a bite of pie. He's shocked at the sweetness, but relishes the roasted pecans.

'Actually.' Rachel leans forward and whispers. 'I've come to Northwestern to escape.'

Henry sits back in alarm.

'My parents, Simon and Deborah Howard, are such good, upright citizens of St Louis. But too old-fashioned. If I had gone home right after graduating from Mizzou, I'd be on a set track: marry an eligible boy from a suitable family, have a few kids, join the country club, attend summer socials and winter fundraisers. Dull, dull, dull.' She slumps back in her seat and stares at the ceiling. Then she straightens up. 'I don't want such a sheltered, predictable life. There's a whole world out there to see, don't you agree?'

Henry nods, but actually, he can't imagine why anyone would want to run away from stability.

'After the war, my parents wanted to concentrate on building their lives in St Louis. My father worked his way up the ladder at his office, and my mother loved the new way of life: two cars, a big house, summer holidays at Branson. Her highlight of the year is the Christmas window display at Famous-Barr. I like it well enough, but there's got to be more to life than floating Santas and engagement announcements. So here I am. For two years, at least.'

Henry's pie is almost all gone.

'Anyway, enough about me. Tell me about you,' she says.

As simply as possible, he tells her about his early years, relaying only the barest facts. 'Eventually, we made it to Taiwan. I worked hard, was lucky, came here, met you,' he finishes.

'You must have seen so much. Been so brave. I admire that.'

Henry's not sure what to say. It's not as if he chose to grow up in such turmoil. It's just what life was like. They did what they needed to do in order to survive. That's all.

'Your mother must be amazing to have kept you safe through all that.'

Yes, Henry thinks, *she is*.

'Tell me more,' Rachel presses, eyes shining.

'Next time,' he says, finishing his coffee. 'Our pie is finished and it's getting late. May I walk you home?'

Coffee and pie are soon followed by a visit to the movies, then a week after that, a dinner. With Rachel, Henry learns the joys of holding someone's hand, sharing ice creams, having impromptu picnics. She possesses an enchanting confidence he has never seen before. In Rachel's eyes, life isn't just something to survive, it's an adventure in wonder and beauty. When Henry's with her, he forgets that English isn't his first language. The clenching in his stomach disappears. In its place, laughter returns.

He likes the way Rachel says his name. 'Henry Dao, Henry Dao, come sing with me?'

He is too shy to sing, but when she holds out her hand, he takes it. She sings him songs from Broadway musicals, from Ella Fitzgerald and Duke Ellington, the songs of Joan Baez. He likes that when Rachel sees him, she sees Henry Dao, the doctoral student in Aerospace Engineering at Northwestern, a man with a bright future. Dao Renshu is someone else, far away.

He loves that she doesn't know, can't know, what he'd most like to forget. With Rachel, he can let down his guard because he is with someone who, in her ignorance, her innocence, offers safety.

In many ways, falling in love with Rachel is falling in love with America.

Evanston, Illinois, May 1964

Henry stands in the student union, looking at notices on a bulletin board. A flyer for a symphony concert has caught his eye: Chopin's Piano Concerto No. 2. Chopin! Although Rachel has introduced him to so much new music, Chopin is still his favourite. What would it be like, Henry wonders, to sit in the audience as the music comes alive, pouring from the instruments?

'Henry, long time no see! How are you?' Henry looks up. It's Arthur Lai.

Arthur walks over, his hand extended in greeting. After a brief catch-up, Henry realises how much he has missed his friend's warmth.

'Hey, Joseph has organised a gathering next weekend. You should come. Very informal, you know, just an afternoon softball game and a potluck afterwards. Good food, good fun.'

Chen's warning jumps to mind, but Henry dismisses it. He'd overreacted last time. Everything has been fine. A softball game certainly seems harmless enough.

Arthur looks at his watch. 'Ah, I need to go.' He takes a pen from his pocket and writes on a piece of paper. 'Here.' He hands it to Henry. 'Here are the details. See you there.'

Henry studies the slip of paper. It is the same date as the concert. He looks again at the concert flyer. In addition to the Chopin, they are performing *Appalachian Spring* by Aaron Copland and Dvorak's Symphony No. 9, 'From the New World'. He's pretty sure Rachel has mentioned the other two works, too. There will be other softball games, but what are the chances of another concert with these three pieces? He decides to buy the tickets.

The week after the concert, Chen knocks on Henry's door and comes in, closing it behind him. He holds out a photo of a softball game and asks if Henry can identify anyone in the picture.

It's the game Arthur invited him to.

'What's this for?' Henry tries to keep his voice neutral.

'My uncle in Chicago. We're just trying to get a sense of the Chinese community here.' Chen's tone, too, has a careful nonchalance.

Henry studies the photo. Joseph Hu sits at a picnic table, talking to some students whose backs are to the camera. In the corner, at home plate, ready to bat, stands Arthur Lai. The girls Lai was teasing at the party sit in the bleachers. He doesn't know their names. Henry's trapped. Chen knows that he should be able to identify Joseph Hu. Henry points and says he was the host of the New Year's party.

'Anyone else?'

Henry squints at the batter. It could be Arthur, but it might be someone else. He's wearing a hat and the resolution is blurry. It really could be anyone.

Henry shakes his head and hands the photo back to Chen.

After Chen leaves, Henry notices his hands are shaking. Had the concert been another day, he might have been in that photo.

Had it been a mistake to trust Chen so much? In China, his ma was always scolding him for being too trusting. But Chen has been a good friend. He would have struggled to survive without Chen in those early days. Can he keep the good part of their friendship and step away from the events of the past few months?

Henry tries to concentrate on his work. Chen doesn't mention the photo again. Between finishing his studies and his frequent trips to Chicago to see his uncle, he's busy. The matter seems forgotten.

Later in the summer, Henry runs into Arthur in the bookstore.

'Did you hear?' Lai lowers his voice. 'Joseph Hu has run into some troubles. A government agent in Taipei paid his family a visit. They told his father that Joseph needed to be more patriotic here.'

'What?' Henry thinks of Chen's photograph. 'What did they say he did?'

'Apparently his name was on a list of students who were trying to organise pro-Taiwanese democracy events in the US.'

'When was this?' Henry hopes Arthur can't hear his heart beating.

'I don't know. But I do remember Hu voicing some pretty strong opinions at his late-night parties. Not exactly pro-KMT sentiments,' Lai muses. 'After Joseph got the warning, he said he was in a country that protected freedom of speech. He didn't think the KMT could touch him, but I heard his father was brought in for more questioning.'

Henry shudders. He can't think of a single time that questioning by the KMT has ever ended well.

'Why are they harassing his father? He's not the one with the big mouth.'

'The father needs to discipline the son,' says Lai.

Henry swallows nervously.

'It gets worse,' Lai continues. 'Joseph needed to renew his visa because he wants to stay for a PhD. He brought his passport to the consulate in Chicago and now it seems to have been "lost".'

'Ah, it probably just takes time for the paperwork to go through.' Henry tries to dismiss his unease.

Lai raises his eyebrows. 'It's been nearly two months. He can't enrol next semester without his passport. He can't leave the country, either, but he can't work legally. He's stuck. He's at their mercy until they give it back.'

'Wow . . . poor guy,' Henry murmurs. His mind is racing. He's thinking of the photo. Even though Henry didn't identify Lai, someone else might have done. Is there a way he can warn his friend without appearing to incriminate himself? 'We have to be so careful about what we say or do.'

'I know,' agrees Lai, shaking his head. 'I hadn't realised.'

Henry says he's late for a meeting. He rushes out of the bookstore.

That night, Henry can't sleep. His stomach is a writhing nest of uncertainty. Did he play a role in Joseph Hu's troubles? What about Lai? Is he in danger, too? Worse, what if Chen finds out that Henry didn't identify Lai when he could have? Would Chen turn on Henry? What if any of this gets back to Meilin? Or Longwei? His mind whirrs with worry. How naive to think that just because he was in America, he was safe.

For the rest of Chen's time in Evanston, Henry can't quite look his friend in the face. He excuses himself from invitations to go down to Chicago, to go out for meals, to see movies. To avoid running into him around the boarding house, he listens for when Chen leaves his room and waits until he sees him walking up the road before departing on his own errands. On the rare occasions they do cross paths, he forces himself to be cordial but is careful not to reveal any information about his activities. Once or twice, Chen has knocked at the door, asking if everything is okay. Henry assures him he's fine, but busy with research. Each time, Chen nods knowingly, approvingly, and Henry is at a loss to understand what this could mean. Henry knows he hasn't done anything wrong, but he's cautious. It's too easy to blunder into something.

After Chen's departure, Henry keeps a measured distance from the different Chinese student groups. He forgoes the comforts of language and food for the safety of anonymity. Invitations peter away and eventually stop coming.

In early August, Rachel suggests a day trip to Chicago, to which Henry eagerly agrees.

'What shall we do?' he asks.

'You surprised me with the Chopin concert. Now it's my turn to surprise you,' she says, and won't answer any questions.

They take the L down to the city for a picnic in Grant Park. Afterwards, she leads him over to the Art Institute. There's an exhibit: Treasures from the Ming and Qing dynasties. She says she thought he'd enjoy it, and she's curious, too, to learn more about China. Touched by her thoughtfulness, Henry takes her hand, and they go in.

Is this real? He goes from case to case, mesmerised. There are intricately carved presentation boxes of cinnabar and lacquer, ceremonial vessels inlaid with mother-of-pearl cranes and peonies, an eighteen-armed porcelain figure of Guanyin seated on a flowering lotus, a trio of luminous white jade vases, a lavishly embroidered priest's robe with phoenixes, bats and clouds in a thousand different colours. Is this China? Is this where he comes from? The exhibition seems like a dream. The Chinese words for the objects are at the tip of his tongue, but he can't say any of them, no matter how loudly they resonate in his mind. It is unsettling to see scholars' tables and chairs with footrests cordoned off, cloisonné garden seats in glass cases. Strange, too, the empty rice bowls, the clean, cold serving plates and dry spoons lined up motionless under gallery lights. When were these objects last warmed by human touch?

None of it feels like the China he remembers. He knows a China of perpetual dislocation, a sky filled with enemy planes, a world of screeching sirens, monks chanting, buildings collapsing and smoke – always smoke. His China stumbles with hunger, with devastation and heartbreak, with citizens wailing in the streets. What is this country of refined elegance that stares from behind these panels of glass?

He comes upon a scroll, fully unrolled. Goosebumps rise on his arms. It is quieten, but his heart starts beating loudly in his ears. An old, odd ache stirs in his gut. He sits down on a bench and is flooded with memories of his ma's voice. For a moment, he is by her side again in the late afternoon light of Dao Hongtse's antiques shop.

He closes his eyes, trying to think of the last time he saw their scroll. Was it in Shanghai? She'd said she sold it. He recalls how she showed up with tickets for the *Taiping*. At the time, he didn't question her. He was just a boy. Someone touches his shoulder. It's Rachel.

She sits down and leans against him. He puts his arm around her. It has been a long, full day. He rubs his eyes, shakes himself and focuses again on the scroll in the case. Leaning forward to see the title and inscription, he reads '*Peach Blossom Spring*, attributed to Qiu-Ying (c.1494–c.1552), poem of Tao Qian (365–427).'

'Rachel! I know this story!' He leaps up and pulls her over to the beginning of the painting, at the far right of the case. Moving slowly to the left, he tells her Meilin's account of the sleepy fisherman who awoke surrounded by peach blossoms. Henry squints at the details, enjoying the tiny ducks on the water, the stroke of each pine needle, the blues and greens of the mountains in the distance. He tells how the blossoms led to a crack in the rock – here, Henry points at the back of a small figure entering a cave – that led to a marvellous land. For centuries, the land had been protected from war. The people welcome the fisherman into their world of peace and plenty.

Then he pauses. They have only looked at half of the scroll; the story continues. He goes over and rereads the placard at the beginning of the display. Puzzled, he stares at the calligraphy. It is an old, artistic style, difficult to decipher. Yet, there are more lines to the story:

Eventually, the fisherman missed his family. As he prepared to go home, his hosts said, *Don't bother to tell the others about us, and don't try to come back. It is impossible to return.* The fisherman thanked them for their kindness and left. As he went, he marked the path carefully. At long last, he reached his home village. Everyone asked where he had been, and of course, he told them all about his discovery. But when they went to seek this miraculous land, even though his markings were clear, the trees, cave and land had disappeared. For years and years, many searched for Peach Blossom Spring, including the wisest and the eldest of scholars, but no one ever found it again.

Henry rereads the lines, not quite believing. His ma hadn't told him the whole story. Henry thought the fisherman had stayed in Peach Blossom Spring forever. But no, he'd left and lost his paradise. She'd only told him half the story. Why did she leave out the ending?

For so many years, he had understood the tale as a story of hope and new beginnings. Discovering the full version triggers an upheaval of memory. Now broken images wash over him, the ones he tried to forget: Mr Xu's traitorous grimace, his ma's hands, chapped and bleeding after digging through rubble, the boat sailing away from Yichang without them. These memories pull him back and back into the troubled past, where the floor crumbles beneath his feet. A rush of shouting, pushing, shoving deafens him. He's in the Great Tunnel again and the air isn't right, the lights keep going out. People are clawing and screaming, but no sounds come forth. *Liling! Liling!* He tries to cry out but he's gagged in an eerie, stifling silence. He can't see her, he can't hear her, he can't save her.

'Henry, are you okay?'

Unsteady and shaking, he sinks back down. He grips the edges of the wooden bench, and its solidity reminds him where he is. His pulse starts to slow. He loosens his grip, closes his eyes, tries to calm his heart. 'I'm okay. I'm okay,' he repeats. *Why did she only tell half the story?*

Rachel peers into his face. 'Hey,' she says. 'Let's walk, let's get some fresh air.'

Outside, they make their way through Grant Park. After a few moments, Rachel turns and looks at Henry curiously.

'You know, just now at the exhibit, that was the first time you've ever told me much about your mother. We always seem to talk about here and now, but I still want to know about your childhood. What can you tell me?'

Something has loosened the tight lid he usually keeps on his past. Once he starts, the words flow out of him. He hopes that speaking his memories aloud will reconstruct what has just been shattered in the museum. It feels strange to say the names of the people and towns of China again. It's like he's describing someone else's life. As he tells his stories, Rachel grows quieten. Part of him forgets she is there.

They sit down near the fountain. 'My ma had this hand scroll, like the one in the museum. She carried it with us, wherever we went. She used to tell me stories from it.'

'Like "Peach Blossom Spring"?'

'Yes, stories like that.'

'What happened to it?'

He shakes his head. The loss of the scroll strikes his core. 'She had to sell it,' he whispers, his voice weak. He pushes away the memories. If he looks at them, he'll see how big his sorrows are. In China, as long as they kept moving, they were surviving. As long as they were surviving, they didn't have to think about what they had left behind. It's the looking back that terrifies him.

'We survived. We got out. We were lucky.'

'Henry?' Rachel is looking at him with such tenderness, such love. Behind her, the fountain splashes and glitters in the late afternoon light.

'Hmm?'

'Don't you ever get homesick?'

Homesick? He doesn't even know what he could call home. 'I miss my ma. I miss the food.'

'I see a lot of signs on campus for different Chinese student groups. Do you ever go to any of the events?'

He shakes his head. Trying to explain his ambivalence is too daunting. 'I went to a few, maybe. Then I needed to study,' he says. At the mention of his studies, his composure starts to return. He is good at learning. Being a student, a scholar, is an identity he both aspires to and feels comfortable with. He stands up, breathing more easily, and they start to walk towards the water.

'So, what about the future?' she asks. 'Will you stay here or go back?'

Henry is silent for a long time. Then, 'My ma—'

'She must miss you so much. Does she hope you'll come back?'

After every question, a long pause.

'There are opportunities here I wouldn't have there.'

The breeze has picked up. A red-tailed hawk soars above Lake Michigan.

'I think,' Henry says, watching the bird spiral up higher and higher, 'I think for right now, my life is here.'

He turns towards her. She looks back at him without the weight of so many miles, so much sadness and loss. There is, in her expression, the kind of light that could lift him. A passage-way that only opens once. He steps through.

'Hey, there's an ice-cream vendor over there. Let's get some.' Henry reaches for Rachel's hand. 'No more old memories. We'll make new ones.'

She squeezes his hand and keeps hold of it. They head back towards the museum. A few steps later, he stops her.

'I told you many things today,' he says. 'But here is all you really need to know.'

He holds up his index finger and motions that she should hold hers up, too. Then he brings their fingers together and says, '*Yi*. One.'

'*Yi*,' repeats Rachel.

He raises his middle finger, and she does the same, fingertip to fingertip. '*Er*. Two.'

'*Er*.'

Ring finger to ring finger. '*San*. Three.'

'*San*,' she whispers.

Then he shifts his hand and interweaves their fingers together. '*Wanwu*. Everything.'

'*Wanwu*.'

He pulls her in close. His lips are on her neck. Her other hand traces his shoulder blades, and she taps out a steady, tender rhythm: *Yi, Er, San, Wanwu*.

Chapter Nineteen

Taipei, Taiwan, February 1965

Auntie Chin knocks at Meilin's door. 'A letter from Renshu!' she cries, waving the light blue aerogramme.

Meilin jumps up.

'Arriving on the Lunar New Year, too. What a good omen,' Auntie Chin says, handing her the letter.

Meilin nods in agreement. Eager to read Renshu's latest news, she turns the letter over in her hands.

'Meilin?' Auntie Chin has asked her something she didn't hear.

'Sorry?'

'I said, "What are your plans for tonight?" How will you be celebrating the Year of the Snake?'

'Oh, yes. I'm going to the Lis' with Longwei.'

Auntie Chin shakes her head with amusement. 'One wouldn't know that the first time you went to that party, you went as help, not as a guest. My, how things have changed,' she says as she heads back to the kitchen.

Whenever one of Renshu's aerogrammes arrives, Meilin's heart leaps. She wiggles the tip of her sewing scissors under the sealed edge of the letter, then makes a clean slit along the crease. As she reads the letter, weeks of worry and wondering recede. Over the next few days, she reads it several more times, savouring new details with each reading, like a second or third infusion of tea leaves. In today's letter, Renshu mentions a new friend, an American girl called Rachel. This is the first time he's mentioned a woman. Meilin feels the peculiar ping she's come to know, that of watching her son grow into a man from a distance. She tucks the letter into her handbag to share with Longwei later.

Since their reunion five years ago, Meilin and Longwei's friendship has grown steadily. With time, she'd introduced him to the Huangs as her brother-in-law. They knew him already from their own social circles. When Peiwen met him, she found him very impressive. Afterwards, Meilin told him not to take himself so seriously and he laughed. He, too, has introduced her to some of his associates. She often attends parties as his guest and enjoys the ceremony and celebration that entails. But each time, she is glad when the evening finishes and she slips back into her familiar room at the Huangs'.

After Renshu first left for America, Longwei tried once more to convince Meilin to marry him. They were walking at New Park, and Meilin had shared Renshu's first letter home. Something about their mutual joy in witnessing Renshu's new life must have encouraged him.

'Meilin, I meant what I said that night. Will you marry me?'

'Longwei, stop.' She put her hand on his arm. 'You have helped Renshu immensely, and for that, I will always be grateful. But we aren't, I cannot—'

'Why do you still work as a maid?' He interrupts. 'You could stay with me. You would never have to work again.'

From the outside, Meilin knows, she appears to be a middle-aged widow, working as domestic help. But inside, she's found tremendous freedom for herself. Once she's done the housework, which isn't much, she can spend her time as she wishes. She won't give that up.

'Longwei, you have done enough for us. I couldn't accept such kindness.'

'It's not out of kindness, Meilin.' Frustration makes his voice sharp. 'We are the only ones left. Why not be here for each other?'

'We *are* here for each other. Why do you need something more?'

He had scowled, muttering about her stubbornness, and let the matter drop.

Still, Meilin cherishes Longwei's company. When she has news from Renshu, he's the one she most wants to tell. His reactions, whether joyful or troubling, anchor her own myriad emotions. When she knows she's scheduled an outing with him, the days before pass with a lightness of anticipation, and the days after are filled with the comfort of having been together.

When Longwei arrives at the Huangs' to take Meilin to the party, he gives Meilin a small bag, quite heavy.

She looks inside: rice, salt and oil.

'A little sentimental, don't you think?' she laughs.

Longwei shrugs from beneath his fedora.

'Thank you,' Meilin says. 'Neither a single grain nor drop will go to waste.' She gives him a quick embrace. His cheek is smooth and smells of aftershave. Meilin flushes and turns so he cannot see her face. 'I'll put these away, and then let's walk over to the Lis'. It's a wonderful night to walk through the streets.'

Many have come to the Lis' tonight. Throughout the evening, people ask about Renshu. Meilin notices how Longwei glows with pride whenever he speaks about his nephew. Conversations drift from topic to topic – which businesses have done well this year and which are struggling, what brand of TV one should purchase, now that Taiwan has its own broadcast channel, and debates about the new museum up in Shilin holding the Palace Museum treasures, rescued from the Japanese and the Communists. Some argue that it is right to celebrate their glory and display them. After all, the treasures are the cultural soul of China. Others see the museum as proof of Chiang's tacit concession that they aren't going back.

On the way home, Longwei and Meilin chat as they stroll in the dark, amiable. When they are close to Longwei's apartment, he invites Meilin in for one more toast. It's been a lovely evening and, wanting to make it last just a bit longer, she agrees.

A manservant greets them at the door. Longwei confers with him briefly then ushers Meilin into an elegant lounge.

'Sit, sit.' He gestures at a pair of scholars' chairs on either side of a low, rectangular kang table.

Soon the manservant brings a tray with a bottle of baijiu and a pair of small porcelain wine cups painted with plum blossoms.

Meilin takes off her coat, drapes it on the back of her chair and sits, exhaling a contented sigh.

Longwei fills both cups and nudges one towards her.

'Happy New Year!' he says, lifting his wine.

'Happy New Year!' she echoes, and they clink the small cups and drink.

'Longwei, a letter from Renshu came today,' Meilin says, reaching into her purse for the aerogramme.

Delight spreads across Longwei's face. For an instant, she sees a hint of Xiaowen in his expression. 'May I see?'

'Of course.' She hands it to him and watches as he scans down the columns of characters. His eyes grow wide as he takes in Renshu's news.

'So, he's met a girl. Good for him,' he says.

Meilin takes another sip of baijiu. Her head feels a bit clouded.

'Meilin?'

'Yes?'

'Can I . . . I know you don't want to marry me, so I'll stop asking. But can you tell me why? Why is it so hard to consider?'

Again? 'Xiaowen was my husband. Xiaowen—'

'How many years has it been? And I'm still competing with a dead hero,' he mutters.

'It's not that, Longwei,' she says. 'Xiaowen and I were so young. I'm a different person now. You have done more, been more to me than a brother. But—'

'What is it?' he asks, laying a hand on her forearm.

She looks up, startled by his intensity.

Over the years, she has seen his expressions shift from haughty to angry or prideful, lighthearted with the children, etched with pain when Liling died. Now she sees something new, something softer. Neither beseeching nor demanding. A depth of understanding, of sorrow. A sense that his dark eyes, perhaps for the first time, are not broadcasting demands or desires or dominance, but seeking connection.

Tenderly, she lifts his hand off her arm and holds it.

She opens her mouth as if about to speak. To answer him, for him to understand, Meilin would need to explain about Shanghai, about the antiques seller, the scroll. But when she thinks about what happened, before she can even utter a word, her heart starts thudding, her stomach feels weak. What if Longwei says what happened was her own fault? What if he becomes angry that she kept the scroll secret? He might say none of it would have happened if she hadn't left them in Yichang. Would she lose his respect, his friendship? She could not bear that. Better to live with this impasse than risk these questions.

She looks down and shakes her head, then squeezes his hand and lets it go.

Longwei leans forward and kisses her once, very softly, on the cheek.

Meilin rises and says it's time to leave. Longwei jumps up to help with her coat.

He holds it out and she slips her arms in the sleeves. When she turns to face him, he wraps his arms around her shoulders, embracing her goodnight. Then he pulls her closer. The sharp tang of alcohol emanates from him. His lips seek hers. She turns her face towards his, meeting his kiss. For a moment, she swells with fierce, tender passion. Then, suddenly, Longwei morphs into the leering face that has haunted her nightmares. Bile rises to her throat. Meilin is trapped again, pinned underneath Mr Li's rapacious pawing and heaving.

Meilin pushes against Longwei's chest. Her coat makes it hard to move, but she manages to put a free hand on his forearm. The raised ridge of his long scar feels raw under her palm. Curling her fingers, Meilin digs her nails into the scar, as hard as she can. 'No!' she shouts.

Longwei yelps and pulls back.

She stumbles backwards, knocking over a chair.

She keeps her eyes on him. He is breathless, his face flushed with interrupted desire. How did this escalate so quickly? Meilin's knees are shaking. Her heart pounds, the pulses rising through her chest and booming in her ears. She resists the urge to cradle herself and stands motionless.

They stare at each other in silence. *Don't break eye contact*, she tells herself.

'Meilin.' His voice quivers with anguish.

She holds up her hand in warning. She steps back, shakes her head. 'Elder brother.'

He grimaces at her formality.

'I will always love you as your sister, as your friend. But not, not . . .'

'Not anything more,' he says, and his intensity dissolves into defeat. He slumps down into his chair. Turns his back to her and stares into his empty wine cup.

Meilin exhales. She rubs the side of her arm where he held her too tightly, then wipes away the sweat that has blossomed above her lip. Her eyes rest on Longwei's back. It looks smaller than when the evening began. There is so much sadness in the curve of his shoulders. She steps towards him and her hand lingers above him momentarily. *Could there be a way?* she wonders. Then she pulls her hand back, buttons up her coat, and lets herself out.

Chapter Twenty

Henry is staring at the towels in the bathroom at Rachel's parents' house. There are so many, all of different colours and sizes, layered and stacked on the bars. He's not sure which to use. But he's certain there is a right answer. He doesn't want to embarrass Rachel or himself by using the wrong one. Everything about this beautiful house makes him feel nervous.

It's his first time meeting the Howards. Though he and Rachel have been together for more than three years now, she has always insisted that they both need to be sure of what they want before she'd bring Henry home.

After Rachel finished her degree, she got a job at Northwestern, helping to develop the collection at the music library. Henry was delighted she had decided to stay, despite other opportunities. He didn't want to lose her. From time to time, they had spoken of marriage, but there seemed to be so many obstacles. He was uncertain what his prospects would be after completing his degree, and wanted to know he could offer her stability and support. Every so often, she was called home to St Louis by her parents to meet with 'this or that boy'. Each time, she came back assuring Henry that her heart was his alone, and she was simply letting her parents exhaust their options. Perhaps most troubling, interracial marriages were illegal in Missouri. As much as Rachel didn't want her parents' meddlesome matchmaking, she did want their blessing, and with it, a wedding in St Louis.

But then, fortune smiled on them.

Earlier that spring, Henry's advisor had asked him about his career plans, encouraging him to consider staying in the US. With the recent changes in the immigration laws, he explained, non-citizens with special skills, such as advanced degrees in science and engineering, would be eligible for permanent residency leading to citizenship. *Think about it. We need promising talent like yours to stay, working against the threat of the Reds. There are a lot of good jobs out there for you.* The conversation soon progressed to technical questions about Henry's research, but Henry kept his advisor's words in mind. However enjoyable or rosy his life in America, Henry is always aware that Chiang Kai-shek's government could call him back at any time. As an American citizen, he'd be beyond the long arms of the KMT.

Then, in June, the US Supreme Court overturned laws banning interracial marriage. Rachel had come running up to him after work, waving the newspaper. 'We can get married!' she'd cried. 'We can get married anywhere in the country!' In the wake of Loving vs Virginia, they quickly got engaged and planned a trip down to Saint Louis to meet Rachel's parents and seek their blessing.

They had arrived earlier this afternoon. When Deborah and Simon came out to greet them, Henry noticed a slight hesitation before Simon offered his hand. Deborah's face fell, and then she smiled, perhaps a bit too brightly, before insisting on addressing him as 'Mr Dao'.

'Rachel didn't say that you were an Oriental. When she said her friend's name was "Dow" I thought she meant Dow of Dow Chemical. Never mind. How handsome you are. How charming.'

Dinner, too, was awkward. After they had eaten, the conversation turned to gossipy news about who was engaged, who was married, who was expecting children, and so on.

'As we're on the topic of weddings,' Rachel said, nudging Henry.

Henry carefully wiped his mouth and laid the cloth napkin on the table. He rose and walked over to Simon and Deborah. With his hands behind his back in a stance of respect, he addressed Rachel's parents. 'Mr and Mrs Howard, Rachel and I would like to get married, and, today, I ask for your blessing.'

Silence.

Deborah's brittle grin diminished to something still resembling a smile, but smaller. Simon's expression was opaque, his head faintly nodding as he looked Henry up and down.

'Oh,' said Deborah. 'Oh,' she said again, shaking herself. 'Where are my manners? That's . . . what surprising news, darling.'

'Mmm hmm,' Simon said, coughing. 'Something caught in my throat,' he muttered, picking up his glass of water and draining it.

'Let's have dessert,' Deborah suggested as she rose from the table and started collecting plates.

Henry turned to Rachel, hoping for some indication of what he should do next.

'It's fine,' she mouthed. 'I love you.'

Rattled by their cryptic response, Henry had excused himself to use the bathroom. Perhaps they needed a moment to take the news in.

Now, still perplexed by the array of towels, Henry shakes the water from his hands as best he can, then wipes them dry on the back of his trousers. He looks at his reflection in the mirror, straightens his collar, and heads back downstairs.

Just outside the dining room door, he pauses. Voices are leaking through.

'Rachel, are you trying to make some kind of point here?' Simon's voice borders on exasperation. 'Okay, point made. You know you don't have to marry the Ebers boy. Of course, we would have been very happy, and Mr and Mrs Ebers would have been thrilled, and of course, William Ebers is crazy about you. But really, it's okay. We'll stop pushing. But don't throw your life away just to make a point.'

'Daddy! This is not about William Ebers. That's not it at all. I want to marry Henry. We love each other. We want to make a life together.'

'Honey,' Deborah says, 'we're not prejudiced or anything, and I'm sure your Mr Dao is a perfectly nice man, but there are lots of perfectly nice men out there who are more our type.'

'Our type?' Rachel hisses. 'And what in God's name do you mean by that?'

'Don't be difficult, Rachel. You know exactly what your

mother means. Besides, I don't believe this kind of marriage is even legal here.'

'But it is! Haven't you been paying attention? Just last month the Supreme Court decided unanimously – unanimously – to overturn laws banning interracial marriage.'

'Legal doesn't mean moral,' Simon grumbles.

'For years, you've been after me to get married. But I told you, I needed to wait for the right person and the right time. That person is Henry. That time is now.'

'Yes, the time is certainly now,' Deborah quips. 'But why him?'

'Because when he looks at me, he sees more than an eligible wife. Because I love the way he looks at the world. He doesn't take anything for granted; he appreciates everything. Even though he had a difficult childhood growing up in China during the war, that doesn't hold him back. In fact, I think it makes him more determined to do his best, and more grateful for every small joy. I love how completely absorbed he becomes when he's passionate about something. And he knows how much my music means to me. He doesn't expect me to give it up after we get married. When we have children, I'm sure he's going to be a wonderful father. He makes me feel happy, he makes me feel understood. Because I love him.'

There is movement inside and footsteps towards the door.

Henry jumps back just as Rachel storms out.

Shock registers on her face and she slams the door behind her. 'Oh God! How long have you been standing there? What have you heard?'

Henry shakes his head, unable to reply.

'I'm so sorry. Don't worry about my parents. They don't understand yet, but they will. They're being awful, but they think they're being protective. They're afraid I'm making a mistake, but I've told them I'm not. I love you. You know that, don't you?'

Henry, flustered, manages to say, 'I just . . . I just didn't know what towel to use upstairs.'

'Oh,' Rachel replies. 'Oh, I'll show you.'

*

Later, Simon and Deborah present a smiling front and say they are happy for the couple. Deborah wants to know if they have a date in mind. If they want June – and who doesn't want a June wedding? – she'll need to get going on venues and invitations. And has Rachel thought about her dress yet? Of course, they'll have the reception at the country club. And the guest list. Oh, there's so much to do, Deborah fusses.

Everyone is pleasant enough for the rest of the visit, but Henry can't get the bad taste out of his mouth. Part of him is shocked that Rachel would disagree so openly with her parents. At the same time, that she would stand up to them for his sake makes him love her even more. Once they are on the road back to Evanston, he brings up the conversation he overheard.

'I am not my parents,' Rachel assures him. 'I was never ever interested in any of their plans for me. I'm my own person and they need to accept that.'

'But I don't want to start off with any bad feelings.'

'It will be okay. They'd be like that with anyone they didn't choose themselves. Once they get to know you, they'll warm up. I think my mother is already a little bit enamoured.'

Henry blushes. As they'd said goodbye, Deborah had kissed his cheek and handed him a plate of homemade cookies for the road.

'As for my father, really, his bark is worse than his bite. You know that expression? He'll come around. I'm sure of it.'

Henry glances at her. She doesn't seem to be that bothered. Maybe this is how the Howards act? Faced with no other choice, he takes her word for it.

Taipei, Taiwan, April 1968

Meilin leaves her new apartment and heads over to Peiwen's. When the Huangs were relocated to Hsinchu last year for the General's work, Meilin stayed behind. As fond as she had become of the Huangs, she didn't want to leave Taipei. They helped her find a small flat in Da'an district, where she helps out the family upstairs, the Hsus, who are cousins of Madame. With their pay, her savings, and the occasional cheque from Renshu, it's enough. An added benefit: it's much closer to Peiwen. When Meilin has news, she can be at her old friend's house in minutes.

Peiwen and her family still live at the juancun. But the original bamboo and mud walls have been replaced by brick, and they have added another storey and an extension out the back. Plus, they now have electricity and plumbing. As always, Peiwen is happy to see her. On the table in front of Peiwen is a box of clear plastic flowers, small, coloured bulbs, and long strings of green wire. Her fingers deftly connect a bulb and a flower to the wire, then she moves on, attaching another bulb, another flower. The string of Christmas lights grows as they chat.

'Meilin! Such news! Congratulations! Are you going to go to the wedding?'

Meilin shakes her head. It's too far and too expensive. Renshu said he would send her a ticket, but she wrote back that she wouldn't know anyone, doesn't know the language. She told him to save his money, to focus on his life there.

'You must be so proud, so happy!'

'Of course! It's what he wants, and she seems lovely.' Meilin's voice falters. 'Here, let me show you the photo he sent.' She busies herself searching through her basket.

'There. There it is.' Meilin produces a black-and-white photo of Renshu and Rachel.

'Beautiful, just beautiful,' Peiwen says, studying the photo. 'Such a nice boy. This Rachel is a lucky woman.'

As Peiwen shares the latest news of her own children, Meilin picks up a string of lights to help out. She wants to distract herself. Both women understand the finality of Renshu's news. He really won't be coming back to Taiwan now, not even for a Chinese bride to take to America, as some have hinted he might. Peiwen shows her how to couple the lamps and flowers, then snap them into place. She's done ten boxes already this morning, she says, and gestures over to the corner, where boxes of completed lights are stacked up. Later, Huifang will drop them off at the warehouse before going to her nursing shift. They are hoping to earn enough extra cash to buy a second-hand bicycle for Baobao.

Now Peiwen starts gossiping about other juancun residents. She tells Meilin how old Lin shot himself last March. On the one hand, it seemed to come from nowhere, but then, he never was happy here, having been forced into conscription by the KMT in the last days of the war. He left a farewell note saying he had no family, no wife, no country and no reason to live. While Lin's story isn't unusual, it still saddens Meilin. She holds the string of lights loosely in her hands, wondering how things would have turned out for her and Renshu had they stayed in the juancun after all. Blessings and curses, she thinks to herself.

'And speaking of marriage,' Peiwen continues, 'did you hear that Hou and Yang have married Taiwanese women?'

'Married? At their age?' Meilin exclaims.

'You've got to understand. These guys are so lonely. The government's marriage ban for soldiers stole their best years and chances. And now that the prohibition has finally been lifted, they have an opportunity to move on. Those who left families back on the mainland don't know if they're alive or if they'll ever see them again. You can't blame them for wanting to start a new life here. Of course, there are hardly any single Waishengren women around.' At this last comment, Peiwen looks at Meilin pointedly. 'You know, Meilin, you could have offers in two minutes if you wanted.'

Meilin puts her first completed light string in a box and busies herself starting another.

'Don't you ever want the companionship? Especially since Renshu's been in America? What about Longwei?'

Meilin hesitates. Although Peiwen is a dear friend, Meilin never told her about that night with Longwei, whom she has been avoiding since her move. Sensing her uncertainty, Peiwen gets up.

'Let's have some tea,' says Peiwen.

Meilin follows her friend to the kitchen, where she fills the kettle from a tap and lights the small stove. There's a new, long white-tiled counter, and Peiwen has made cheerful yellow curtains for the big window. While Peiwen fusses with cups and tea leaves, Meilin starts to tell Peiwen about Longwei's most recent proposal. But towards the end, she loses her nerve and glosses over the details, just mentioning that he tried to kiss her.

Throughout the telling, Peiwen is quieten. She arranges the teapot and cups on a tray and heads back into the sitting area.

'Why not let him kiss you? He adores you,' she says finally, handing Meilin her tea. 'Anyone can see that. Why not have a little romance?'

Meilin stares at her tea. The leaves are opening, the liquid is golden, its aroma nutty and comforting. She considers how to answer. After a long silence, she decides that she cannot explain, not even to Peiwen. She cannot voice her fears, her shame. She takes a sip of her tea. 'I'm too old for such things.'

Peiwen looks at her, wrinkles her brow. Opens her mouth to argue, but then seems to reconsider. 'Have you told him about Renshu's engagement?'

Meilin blows out a sigh and opens her eyes more widely. She is close to tears. 'Not yet. Will you come with me?' She knows this is a favour she can ask of Peiwen.

'Let me get my things. We'll go together.'

Shortly after that New Year's celebration, Longwei became very involved with the new National Palace Museum and rarely contacted Meilin. Maybe he, too, felt the need for some distance. She updated him about Renshu from time to time, but most often at a gathering or with other friends. Occasionally he'd offer another invite, asking her to attend the opening of a special exhibition or a party. She'd accept, but as soon as the formal ceremonies concluded, she'd leave early. Theirs is a fragile balance. Those old wounds remain tender. Still, they have both lost too much, too many, to let anything else slip away.

Now, he welcomes both Meilin and Peiwen into his house. Meilin is surprised by how much he has aged since she last saw him. His hair is all white and very short around the ears. He is bald on top. Veins pop out from the backs of his hands. He moves with as much dignity as ever, but more slowly, and with a silver-tipped cane. When they tell him the news of Renshu's engagement, his mouth twists into a funny kind of smile. 'At least somebody in this family wants to get married,' is all he says.

St Louis, Missouri, June 1968

Despite her parents' reservations, Rachel is determined, elated and in love. Just as she predicted, Simon and Deborah slowly become accustomed to the idea of Henry as a son-in-law. When he graduates and becomes Dr Dao, they warm up considerably. When he receives a prestigious job offer at one of the country's top research laboratories, they send champagne and flowers. By the time the wedding invitations are in the mail, Deborah is bursting with tearful pride about her handsome, brilliant, talented son-in-law. Even Simon admits that he has never seen his daughter so happy.

The night before the wedding, Henry and Rachel have dinner with Henry's friends Pao Dafei, Li Hotan and Li's wife, Jingyuan. Pao has borrowed a car from a colleague to drive them all down from New York for the event. Jingyuan, also a Taida graduate, has recently arrived in the US to pursue a doctorate in chemistry at Columbia. Throughout the evening, the conversation flips between Mandarin and English, as they catch up on all that has happened since the beginning of their graduate school days. When Henry translates for Rachel, occasionally his friends jump in and correct him, teasing that he's leaving out all the good parts.

'Did you hear about Liu?' Pao asks Henry towards the end of the meal.

'Liu Zhaohui, our classmate from Taida? Didn't he go to Wisconsin to study electrical engineering?'

Pao nods.

'It's not a great story.' Li has switched into Mandarin. 'Apparently, he got really involved in the Taiwanese Student Associations.'

The hair on the back of Henry's neck bristles.

'He went back to Taipei for a funeral and then was detained. They took his passport at the airport and he couldn't leave.'

'Because he was involved with a student group?' Henry baulks. Rachel leans towards him quizzically, responding to his change in demeanour.

'Supposedly he also attended a meeting about Taiwanese independence in Chicago, and his name got back to the government. I thought you might have heard something because Evanston is so close.' Li finishes, still speaking in Mandarin.

Henry wonders if Chen's uncle is still in Chicago. He considers saying something about Joseph Hu. Li and Pao are his oldest friends. He trusts them completely. But that doesn't mean he needs to tell them what happened to people he didn't really know anyway. He shakes his head. 'No, I hadn't heard that about Liu.'

Pao mentions that he has heard about a few other students in New York whose political activities have caused their families trouble back in Taiwan.

There is a subdued pause. Best to stay out of politics, they all agree.

'Everything okay?' Rachel asks, concern on her face.

'Yes, just some news about a classmate,' Henry says, neglecting to translate the conversation.

When dessert comes, they chat in English. Henry's friends howl with recognition when Rachel tells the story of how they met and Henry's persistent requests for the Chopin record. Eventually, the friends start reminiscing about Taida, the food in Taipei, and other classmates they have lost track of. It is so good to be among friends who understand being caught between cultures. At some point, Henry even tells a joke.

Amid the uproarious laughter, Rachel tugs at his arm. 'What's so funny?' she asks.

He hadn't noticed they had drifted back into speaking Mandarin again. He tries to translate, but the joke isn't funny in English.

Rachel manages a vague smile. 'You're so talkative with your friends. So funny,' she remarks. 'Who knew?'

He blushes. Is she angry?

'There's still so much that I don't know about you. Henry

Dao, you are a never-ending mystery. I'm glad we have a lifetime ahead of us so I can learn.'

In the church, Li Hotan stands beside him as best man, and Pao Dafei acts as an usher, alongside Rachel's brother, Robert. Henry is grateful that his friends are there, along with a few research colleagues from Northwestern. Initially, he was shy about inviting his colleagues, but Rachel insisted. He's touched that they've made the drive down for the ceremony. It's reassuring to see familiar faces among the church pews filled with guests in wedding finery. But once the music starts and Rachel is walking down the aisle with Simon, everything else is a blur. It's a simple ceremony followed by what seems like hours of photos, a receiving line, and an afternoon reception at the country club.

After the meal, Robert clinks a spoon against his wine glass and stands to make a toast.

'I'd like to propose a toast to my little sister, Rachel, and her new husband, Henry.' The room grows quieten. 'It took my parents a while to get used to the idea of this marriage. But I liked Henry right away when I met him. I told my parents, "At least she's not marrying a coloured man." ' Robert pauses, hoping for a laugh. There are few titters. His wife Wendy shouts, 'Robert, just finish the toast!'

'As we have got to know Henry, we have learned that he is kind, patient and wise. Also, he's brilliant. Have I mentioned that he's brilliant? He is Dr Dao, an engineer. He's working to help us defeat the Reds. He's not a Commie, in case anyone is worried. He's from Free China, not Red China. He's one of the good guys.' Robert nods approvingly at Henry, then Pao, then Li.

'We're glad you have found each other. I honestly thought Rachel would never get married, but I have been proven wrong. So, let's all raise our glasses to Mr and Mrs Henry Dao on this happy day.'

'Hear, hear!' shout some of the louder, more inebriated guests. Robert drains his glass and sits down.

Rachel is very red. It's hard to say whether from fury, embarrassment or too much champagne.

Li Hotan stands to make his toast. 'Henry and Rachel,' he says, facing them. 'May you have many children and few troubles. Congratulations!'

He holds up his glass, and everyone drinks.

Once the mingling starts again, Deborah sidles over and takes Henry by the arm. She parades him around, showing him off to all her friends.

'Dr Dao, this is my dear friend Mary Ellen Carter.' Deborah gestures towards a large blonde woman in a beige floor-length beaded gown.

'My, you are handsome, aren't you?' Mrs Carter says, looking over the top of her glasses at him.

'I'm Ethel Stonebridge.' An angular brunette in a smart green suit holds out her hand. 'And I think our Rachel has done very well. Very well.'

'Ah, Ethel. Of course, Ethel wants to meet you, too,' Deborah says, with a tinge of annoyance.

'Mr, er, Dr Dao, I thought it was such a shame they knocked down Hop Alley and the Old Chinatown for the new stadium,' Ethel says, as if continuing a conversation they've been having all evening. 'All those Chinese families and businesses down there.' Ethel shakes her head. 'Where did they all go? Do you know?'

'Ethel! Just because Rachel's new husband is Chinese doesn't mean he knows all the Chinese in St Louis,' Mary Ellen scolds.

'Well, of course not, Mary Ellen,' Ethel snaps. 'But he must know a few.' She turns back to Henry. 'What about the Wangs? Do you know them? My Richard wouldn't trust anyone else with his suits and shirts. I can't think of anyone who has ever had a bad experience with Mr Wang. Or Mrs Wang, for that matter. Good people. Hardworking. Not like some of those families down there.'

Out of the corner of his eye, Henry can see Pao, Li and Jing-yuan sitting at a table laughing.

'I do not know the Wangs, but they sound very nice,' he says gently to Ethel. 'It was a pleasure to meet you both. Please excuse me.' He gestures towards the other side of the banquet hall and makes his way over to his friends.

'Dao Renshu! Congratulations on a wonderful party and a beautiful bride!' Li leaps to his feet.

'Sit, sit,' Henry says, and seats himself at the table.

After a few more stories and a few more jokes, Li is reaching for his jacket. 'I'm afraid we must say an early goodbye. There's a long drive ahead, and Pao's colleague needs the car first thing Monday morning.'

Rachel, who has been chatting with school friends, comes over to Henry's side and he puts an arm around her.

'It's been wonderful to meet you,' she says to Henry's friends. 'Thank you for coming.'

'Congratulations again, Mrs Dao,' Li Hotan says.

Rachel grins. Henry kisses her cheek.

'I'll walk you to the car,' Henry says, giving Rachel a squeeze and letting her go.

After their final handshakes, the three get into the car. Watching them, part of Henry wants to call out *Wait! I'm coming, too!*; to go with them to New York City, back to a familiarity he only now realises he has missed. It's not rational, it's not real, this longing. His life, his new wife, are here. A job and a future await. But as the car leaves and Li Hotan waves out the back window, another piece of his past – a joyous one – speeds away down the road.

PART FIVE
1968–1989

Chapter Twenty-one

Los Alamos, New Mexico, September 1968

The autumn after their wedding, Henry and Rachel move to northern New Mexico for his job at Los Alamos Scientific Laboratory. Driving in from the east, they are bewildered by the dramatic landscape. Arid plains rise to cliffs and mesas of sculpted volcanic ash. The final stretch of their journey follows a winding, twisting road that clings to the sides of the hill with an elevation gain of over a thousand feet. In awe, they arrive at the town that was kept a secret during the Second World War, the birthplace of the atomic bomb. Henry is amazed to think that he will work at the very place that ended the War of Aggression.

Nestled on plateaus just below the Jemez Mountains, Los Alamos has a population of about 15,000 people, most of whom are families connected with The Lab, as they call it. Some of the brightest scientific minds of the Western world have assembled to work on defence and energy research, eager to keep America ahead of the Soviets in the Cold War. The jobs are well funded, the town is safe and the schools are good.

Henry enjoys his job. As is the case for most of his colleagues, his research is classified, so he cannot discuss what he does outside of work. He doesn't mind, although it is an adjustment after the atmosphere of intellectual freedom at Northwestern. They hope to start a family right away and then, once the kids are older, Rachel will explore better options for her career. Santa Fe, just under an hour's drive away, is a vibrant, cultural city. Rachel is curious to learn more about the Hispanic and Native American traditions that contribute to Santa Fe's atmosphere. It's unlike any other place she's ever lived or visited.

While trying for a baby, Rachel looks for work in town. She soon finds that for women not working in the sciences, the job options in

Los Alamos are limited. Aside from schools, a few shops, a hospital and a library, the main employer is the laboratory. The majority of the workforce there is male. Many of the scientists are young and newly married. Most of their wives, whether or not they have children, are also seeking meaningful work. In short, the town has an excess of intelligent, highly educated women competing for a small number of jobs. Once all the nursing, teaching and library positions are soaked up, there's not much left but secretarial work. Rachel tries this for a few months, but finds it mind-numbing.

The first year passes and Rachel does not become pregnant. She's nearly thirty. She thought she'd have a few babies by now. Instead, she is far from family, far from what she trained to do, far from who she thought she'd be at this point in her life. Henry watches Rachel's frustration and doesn't know how to help.

When, during the second winter, Rachel finally becomes pregnant, they are overjoyed. Their life as a family is ready to begin.

Los Alamos, New Mexico, October 1970

Henry is sitting at his old desk in his new home, completing his US citizenship application. Rachel is away for the day, shopping with a friend. She wanted to get a few more supplies before the baby's arrival. 'I know we're mostly ready,' she'd said, 'but I'm just nervous.' Henry is, too. Especially after trying so hard for so long. The thought of becoming a father both thrills and terrifies him. How does one *be* a father? How will he learn? With a twinge of sorrow at the blankness of his memory, he wonders what his own father was like. Then he thinks about Longwei. Longwei always seemed to know what to do, even when the world was falling to pieces. As far as Henry could remember, the only time Longwei ever faltered was when Liling died. The memory stops Henry in his tracks. *What if something were to happen to his baby?* He can't bear the thought. He promises himself that he will protect his baby, no matter what. He will do everything possible to make sure this child won't know loss.

He looks at his paperwork again and realises he needs details from his original visa. From the back of his bottom desk drawer, he retrieves the envelope Longwei gave him before he left Taipei. Taking out his Republic of China passport, Joseph Hu comes to mind. Henry has decided he won't set foot in Taiwan again without the protection of an American passport. Even though he never did or said anything anti-KMT, he still fears someone might one day target him. As for Charles Chen, even if he was a good friend, he must have been connected to the KMT. Henry never wants to be in a position again where he could be asked about other Chinese. With the security of US citizenship, he will be able to breathe more easily – and, with time, he hopes to extend that safety to his ma.

Searching for the information he needs, he shuffles through the papers. An unexpected name catches his eye. He spreads out all the documents on the table and examines each one. They all say the same wrong thing. This must be a mistake.

He thinks back to when he arrived in America. Standing at passport control, he gave the envelope to the official. The man went through the papers, entering some details in an official-looking ledger. When the man was satisfied with the forms, he slid his eyes from the black-and-white photo to Renshu's face. He stamped the passport and visa, put the papers back, and returned the envelope to Renshu.

'Welcome to the United States of America, Mr Dao,' the official had said. Renshu had quickly flipped through the papers, checking that the bank account letter and the invitation from the university were both there, then he'd put the envelope in his briefcase.

Those first months, whenever any documentation was required, he'd simply handed over the whole envelope. Whether an administrator at the university or a clerk at the bank, no one ever questioned the contents. Everything seemed to be in order. He hadn't needed the papers since then. Moving from apartment to apartment during his student days, then across the country, he had always kept the envelope safe. Why hadn't he looked more carefully a long time ago?

He recalls the flurry before leaving Taiwan. At the last possible minute, Longwei had arrived, deliberate and ceremonious as an emperor. There had been no time to read the papers over. And hadn't the envelope been sealed? Renshu had taken everything and left. He'd trusted it would be okay.

And it had been okay. More than okay. He'd sailed across the ocean and through the formalities. He'd started his life in America, found work, found a fellowship, found Rachel, started a career. He couldn't have hoped for anything more.

But who does this paper say he is?

He must speak with his ma. He calls the Hsus' house. While it rings and rings, he looks again at the papers in disbelief. He smooths the pages and runs his finger under the names.

'What is it?' An agitated voice asks.

The time difference. He'd forgotten. He glances at his watch. Nearly noon here . . . It's about 3.00 a.m. there. He apologises, then realises he has spoken in English. He switches languages, and explains it's Renshu.

'Renshu!' More exclamations come rattling down the line.

'Wait,' he shouts, stopping Mrs Hsu just before she runs downstairs to wake Meilin.

'Will Mrs Hsu please give my ma a message?'

'Your ma? I'll go get her.'

'No, no. Tell her I will call later, ten a.m.?'

'Okay, okay! Ten a.m.!'

'I have to go. It's expensive to call.'

'Yes! Expensive!'

And the line goes dead.

Henry hangs up. He looks at the photo of his younger self. Dao Renshu. So green. But his nostalgia is soon replaced with anger at the young man's naivety. Renshu was too trusting of too many. Henry has learned the virtue of caution.

Taipei, Taiwan, October 1970

Meilin waits by the Hsus' phone. They have all gone out to school, to the market, to work. Their apartment is quieten. She's been up and worried since 6.00 a.m., when Mrs Hsu told her that Renshu had called in the night. She tugs at the cloth on the table, smoothing out the wrinkles. Why did he call? Is someone hurt? Sick? All morning, she's been watching the clock creep forward to 10 a.m.

Outside, the air resounds with hammering, shouting, drills and jackhammers. Throughout the city, the old military villages with their crowded, crumbling rooms are being knocked down to make room for modern apartment buildings with reliable electricity, big windows and indoor plumbing. The alleys, once strung with bright banners of drying laundry, have been paved over into busy streets, wide enough for two-way traffic. By mid-morning, the noise of construction competes with a cacophony of motors, horns and bicycle bells. Bamboo scaffolding has replaced the wobbly fences that used to keep in chickens and children. And inside the scaffolding, concrete structures rise and rise. Taipei seems to be erasing and rewriting itself before her eyes.

When the phone rings, Meilin seizes it quickly. The phone slips from her fingers and bangs on the table, momentarily dangling by the cord. She grabs the black handset. 'Renshu?'

'Ma.'

They speak so infrequently. Each time, Meilin closes her eyes to concentrate on the contours of Renshu's voice, trying to discern all that is underneath his words. Over the years, she has sensed him growing bigger and stronger. She's imagined fuller shoulders in his deeper resonance, a stronger jaw in his proud news, his graduation and fellowships. A broader chest, bursting with joy when he told her Rachel was expecting their first baby. But today, in the single syllable, she hears hesitation, sadness. As if he has shrunk back to being a child.

'Is everyone okay? Is Rachel okay? The baby?'

'Yes, yes, she's fine. Just tired. Not long now.'

Meilin opens her eyes and smiles in happy anticipation of her grandchild.

'Ma?' There it is, again, that note of sorrow.

'Yes?'

'It's about the visa Uncle arranged when I left Taiwan.' His voice dwindles.

'What is it?' She holds the handset more tightly, trying to hear more.

'I was looking up some details for my citizenship papers. And Ma—' Renshu pauses. After a silence, he speaks quickly, 'Ma, he has listed himself as my father and Wenling my mother.'

She sits back as if struck.

Marry me. Everything will be so much easier. Realisation washes over Meilin like a cold, engulfing wave.

'Ma, are you there? Did you hear me?'

'I'm here.' Her voice feeble. 'Really?'

'It says "Father – Dao Longwei, Mother – Xue Wenling".'

Oh, what have you done, Old Man, what have you done?

'Your name is nowhere on any of my papers.'

She squeezes her eyes shut and winces, trying to shake off this bad dream. This can't be happening. Why would Longwei do this?

'Can we fix it?' Renshu asks.

How? It's been more than ten years. How did this go unnoticed for so long?

'Longwei must have thought things would be easier for you with his name there.' She wants to convince herself as much as Renshu. 'And he was right, wasn't he?'

'But your name isn't here,' he repeats, barely audible.

Static crackles on the line.

Meilin gathers some words. 'It's just a formality. I'm sure of it. There was so much at stake, he was trying to make your passage as smooth as possible, give you the best chances. Besides' – speaking quickly to fill that awful silence – 'he loves you. He has always loved you. In many ways, he considers you his son. It's not such a big lie,' she murmurs, but even as she says it, she feels sick to her stomach.

'But why didn't he put your name down?'

Marry me, Meilin. She can't bear to tell Renshu of Longwei's many proposals, of the night he kissed her, of the ways she has kept him at a distance ever since. What good would it do for him to know?

'I don't know.' She is glad her son cannot see her tears.

'What should we do, Ma?'

What can they do?

'Complete your application. Use their names and send it in, right away. You must keep the documents consistent. You need the citizenship. Your baby needs an American father.' She takes a deep breath, summoning all her strength. 'I am your ma. Longwei knows that, you know that, I know that. The rest is just paperwork.'

Renshu clears his throat. 'Okay, Ma. But will you ask him why?'

'This call is too expensive now.' She can't bear to keep talking.

'Ma, please, will you ask him?'

'Take care of Rachel. You call me when the baby comes.'

'Of course. Ma, please?'

A pause.

'Okay,' she finally promises.

'Zaijian.'

'Zaijian.'

She puts down the phone and sits in a daze, squinting at the bright day. Sunlight glares off panes of sheet glass that are being fitted in the building across the way.

Downstairs in her own rooms, Meilin tries to console herself. No one's hurt. No one's sick. Still, she feels robbed. She promised Renshu she would speak with Longwei, but she's apprehensive. The fragile understanding they've built has been pulled out from under her feet.

She tries to recall when she last saw him. Lunar New Year? No, she was with Peiwen's family this year and didn't go to any of the Native Place Association parties where she would usually see him. Before that? It would have been at the Mid-Autumn Festival, maybe a year ago, but she can't recall actually seeing him then, either. She needs to see him. Now.

Meilin stands outside Longwei's apartment. She must be resolute. She will be unwavering and face the man who gave them so much, but also has taken so much from them. She straightens her shoulders, steels herself. She will demand that Longwei amend Renshu's papers. She will neither plead nor threaten, but she will not be denied. She will reclaim what belongs to them.

She knocks and waits.

Yang, Longwei's manservant, stooped and grey, opens the door. His eyes widen with surprise to see her. He bows and nods, then hurries away to tell Longwei.

Meilin steps in and closes the door softly behind her. The staleness of unwashed dishes and dusty floors saturates the air. The curtains are closed against the brightness of the day. All the dread and resolve she felt on the other side of the door veers into worry. Something's not right. The apartment is too quieten.

Yang returns and gestures at the slippers by the doorway. He waits without comment while Meilin changes out of her street shoes. She follows him down the hallway. The floor creaks with each step. When they reach Longwei's bedroom, Yang opens the door and stands back, ushering Meilin in.

A table near the bed holds a tray with the morning's breakfast dishes: a porridge bowl, a teacup, a spoon. Longwei is a vague shape in the bedclothes. Where is the man of linen suits and silver filigree cigarette cases? The smooth talker who made things happen? Propped up by pillows, his once swaggering torso disappears into softness. His cheekbones reveal the shape of his skull.

She steps close to the bed. His eyes, which had been shut, flick open.

'Who's that?' His gaze is rheumy and his voice is weak.

'It's me, Meilin.'

'Hmph.' Longwei grunts. He lifts a pair of thick-lensed glasses to his face with a shaky hand and peers at her again.

'No,' he finally says, smacking his lips. The creases at the corners of his mouth look dry and flaky. She picks up the water glass and offers it to him, but he waves it away, almost knocking it out of her hands.

'No?'

'No, you are not Meilin. She is much younger than you.'

Meilin bites her lip.

'She has a boy. That boy is always hungry for sesame sweets

and wanting to catch crickets. Where's the boy?' he demands in a ragged, uneven wheeze.

She doesn't know how to begin to explain. She looks at her hands, and her determination crumbles. How can Longwei have been reduced to this?

When she looks up again, he has nodded off.

Regret swamps Meilin the minute she leaves the house. How could she have let her fears blind her to the fact of his ageing, of all they still had to lose? Was she mistaken to keep her distance? For years it has seemed like not just the right thing to do, but the only thing. Now the fearsome dragon she had dreaded is barely a bump under the sheets. For how long has she been hiding from someone who no longer exists?

Over the following months, she visits several times. Each time, he asks who she is. He doesn't believe her. He thinks she is Wenling. He thinks she is a maid. He thinks she is a nurse. He asks again and again, *Are you my wife?* Only once does he recognise her. 'Meilin, Meilin,' he sighs. 'You were always so stubborn. Why so stubborn?' She struggles to answer. During this delay, his coherency disintegrates. What could she have said?

When she tells Renshu that Longwei is too old, too ill, to ask about the paperwork, Renshu doesn't want to let it go. He insists that Longwei owes them an explanation, that Longwei must fix the mistake. 'Leave it,' she says. 'Why are you still carrying this?'

Hovering like a ghost is the possibility that it might have been different had she agreed to marry Longwei. Would he have told her what he had done? Would he have changed the papers? Maybe it never occurred to him that it would cause problems. People were always changing names and relations back then. If she had married him, would she be listed, on some official's document in some obscure ledger, as the mother of her son?

The questions are endless and unanswerable.

Eventually, Meilin wonders herself into the realisation that answers won't change what's been done. She's always told Renshu that regret is too heavy to carry. And yet, it's impossible to have complete conviction that you've made all the right decisions. No one is that lucky or that naive. Maybe, Meilin thinks, it's that you have to carry your regrets until you've made peace with them. Only then can you lay them down.

Renshu writes with other, happier, news: his successful citizenship ceremony, his rewarding work, the birth of his daughter. It had been a difficult birth, and there won't be other children, but this makes Renshu treasure her even more. Meilin's heart swells with every emotion when she learns the child's name: Lily. Though his life is distant and her days are marked with longing for her boy, she sees he's become a good man, a happy man. When a photo arrives with Renshu, Rachel and Lily, Meilin learns a new kind of mother-love, that of seeing her boy become a father. Touching the side of his face in the photo, she recalls the afternoons in Hongtse's antiques shop, the air of terror and triumph in Chongqing. Over all those miles and years, there were many times she had almost lost him, but she never did. Paperwork can't undo what they have lived.

Shortly after the New Year, Meilin brings the photo of Renshu's family to show Longwei. At some level, she's sure he will understand who they are. She hopes so.

'Happy Year of the Pig, Longwei,' she says, entering his room.

He opens his eyes with a start. For once, he looks straight at Meilin with an eerie clarity. 'Xiaowen. You must write to Xiaowen,' Longwei says.

At the mention of her husband's name, Meilin's heart flutters.

Longwei grasps Meilin's hand with both of his. They are cold and light, delicate as twigs. He wheezes heavily, winded from the exertion. In a quavering voice, he continues, 'Tell him. Tell him I looked after them when he didn't come back. Both of them. Tell him I kept my promise.'

Despite his frailty, Longwei's grip is firm. Meilin swallows hard and after a moment's hesitation, nods.

'I loved her, too.' His voice is stronger now.

Meilin is speechless. He releases her hands and falls back on the pillows, closing his eyes in exhaustion.

'I loved her, too.' Longwei begins to cry.

They sit. The only sounds in the room are his sobs and the light rain outside.

Meilin reaches over and places a hand on Longwei's thigh. It feels bony and spare under the blankets. She massages it gently. 'I know,' she murmurs.

And she does. Their connection has been gradual, grudging, and, now she sees, immense. There is no other word for all that they have shared.

Over the following days, he eats less and less. He mumbles about boats and trains; he asks about the kerosene shop. He is lost. A mind in the shadows. A body seeking stillness. He drifts in and out of sleep. Meilin sits with him, hour after hour, unwilling to leave his side. Soon, he withdraws into a stupor and, not long after, a final silence.

Chapter Twenty-two

Los Alamos, New Mexico, December 1978

During the early years of Lily's life, Henry experiences a previously unknown contentment. In Lily, he witnesses childhood unfolding in a way he's never seen before. It is steady, sheltered, safe. Lily lives without fear, without hunger or threat of displacement. He wipes away only tears from falling off her bike or scraping her knee.

Since Longwei died, Henry has considered moving Meilin to the US, but a fear that his uncle's shoddy paperwork might cause issues for his own citizenship holds him back. He tries to reassure himself: he is a US citizen; he has worked his job for many years with good reviews. Still, caution abounds. His work is classified, and he needs his security clearance to be as simple as possible. The fewer questions raised, the better. He continues to keep one wary eye on Taiwanese events – Chiang Kai-shek's death in 1975, and the passing of the mantle to his son, Chiang Ching-kuo, makes Henry nervous. He's not sure what to expect. On the one hand, as a young man, Chiang Ching-kuo was connected to the Communists. On the other, he makes promises of democratisation for Taiwan. This ambivalence only adds to Henry's unease.

Knowing it's better to be practical than patriotic, Henry is grateful for his job. Governments have always needed military and security strategists. There is always a war somewhere. He's never known it to be otherwise.

In this so-called Cold War, Henry isn't shooting anyone. He's not dropping any bombs. He works on the theory and design of weapons and defence systems, spoken of only in the company of other scientists and engineers, and this invisibility suits him.

He's not responsible for the existence of this knowledge. Instead, he sees himself and his colleagues as guardians of a great power. He hopes his research will be sufficient to demonstrate to any enemy that the actual deployment of these weapons is unnecessary, that it would result in MAD: Mutually Assured Destruction. 'It's a mad, mad world,' one of his co-workers is fond of saying. Henry isn't sure if that is a joke or a lament.

Of course, there are occasional moments that give Henry pause. When he and his colleague, Tom Benson, present their findings, Henry has noticed that some people always direct their questions to Benson, not him. Initially, this was a relief, but after eight years on the job, he doesn't need an interpreter, especially when he has been the project lead. Once, he thought he over-heard a new staff member complaining about his accent, but he could have been mistaken – there are many internationals in his group, although he is the only Chinese. Sometimes there are well-meaning comments about how he 'must do things differ-ently' in his country. *This* is my country, he thinks.

Gradually, Henry has developed a sixth sense for how to talk with his in-laws. Speak too little, and they whisper comments to Rachel about his English comprehension. Engage them for too long, and sooner or later, he is expected to answer any and all questions about China, Korea, Vietnam or anything remotely Asian. *Henry, you must understand these people, right?* Rachel rationalises their talk as attempts to connect with him and dis-misses his discomfort. They're trying to reach out, she says, can't you meet them halfway? As long as the discussion is about Lily, baseball or the weather, he listens, and even offers a joke or two. But as soon as the pleasantries end and conversation flags, he finds a way to excuse himself.

As the years pass, he pushes aside these minor irritations and focuses instead on the joys in his life: a wonderful wife in Rachel, smart and gregarious, the perfect counterpart to his natural reti-cence; a healthy daughter, Lily, full of curiosity and innocence; enough salary to provide for them as well as to send some money to his ma every month; the stability to have a mortgage, a car, even a piano. He enjoys the merry chaos of birthday parties, the spectacle of music recitals, the chance to give Lily roller skates for Christmas. He has taught his daughter how to ride a bike, how to swim.

Isn't each of these a victory in itself?

It's Friday evening, a week before the Christmas holidays. Lily's in the kitchen, singing Christmas carols to herself as she glues colourful strips of construction paper into a chain for the tree. Earlier that afternoon, when they put the lights on, she had studied the side of the cardboard box. 'Daddy, it says "Made in Taiwan". Just like you, right?'

'Yes,' he had said, as he adjusted the string of lights to reach the higher branches. Now he and Rachel relax on the couch, watching the news and enjoying the twinkling glow. Halfway through, the usual programme is interrupted with a special report from the White House. President Jimmy Carter sits at a desk looking very serious.

'Good evening, I would like to read a joint communiqué that is being simultaneously issued in Peking, at this very moment, by the leaders of the People's Republic of China . . .'

From the kitchen, Lily is belting out 'Up on the Housetop'. Henry stands and turns the volume up.

'The United States of America and the People's Republic of China have agreed to recognise each other, and to establish diplomatic relations as of January 1, 1979. The United States recognises the government of the People's Republic of China as the sole, legal government of China.'

Henry continues watching with a sense of mounting disbelief.

'The government of the United States of America acknowledges the Chinese position that there is but one China and Taiwan is part of China.'

It has never occurred to Henry that the US would derecognise the Republic of China. After decades of supporting the ROC, how could America turn its back like this? What will prevent the Communists from storming across the straits and swallowing the island? What will happen to Taiwan?

Worse, what about his ma? Will she be punished for her Nationalist connections to Longwei? Or her son in the West?

He turns and looks at Rachel. Her face is pale.

'What about your mother?' she whispers.

'I don't know. I have to call her.' He glances at his watch. It's morning in Taipei.

Meilin answers right away and assures him she's fine. But she says there were reports of an angry mob near the American embassy. Policemen tried to hold them back, but the protesters outnumbered the officers. The police were probably sympathetic to the crowd's fury, too. Everyone feels betrayed by the US. It's been thirty years since she has felt this frightened.

Los Alamos, New Mexico, January 1979

'You want to bring her here?' Rachel asks.

Henry nods. 'People are leaving Taiwan. Who knows what Beijing will do when the embassy closes? She's got no one there. We've been thinking about this for years. Now is the time.'

'Where would she live?'

'With us, of course!'

'But she doesn't speak English.'

'She can learn. She can help look after Lily; you can go back to work. You've been talking about retraining as a librarian. It could be an opportunity for you, too.'

'I haven't been a student for years.'

Rachel's reluctance surprises him. 'You'd be great,' Henry says. 'I know you could do it. What's the problem?'

'She doesn't know anyone here. What will she do? How will she spend her days? Won't it be disruptive?'

Disruptive.

Henry thinks of all the nights his ma woke him in the dark; the way he stopped asking questions and just knew that if she roused him, that meant it was time to go. Meilin is no stranger to disruption.

'I think she'd be glad to be with family. Rachel, it's not safe for her in Taipei.'

'Look, I've got to collect Lily,' Rachel says, picking up her purse. 'Why don't you see what we need to do? We'll figure something out.'

As the car drives away, Henry looks around the kitchen: the refrigerator door boasts Lily's cheerful drawings of dogs; on the wall are family snapshots from over the years; on the table sits Rachel's crystal vase, holding paper narcissus buds. His American life. Henry knows that, even with all the joys Lily has brought them, Rachel is not that happy here in this small town. Her radiance has faded. He misses her. Maybe, if Meilin comes, that will give Rachel a chance to do more of what she loves, like when they first met.

Henry has written Meilin's name at the top of the form. In the space for sponsor, he writes his own. In the space labelled relationship to sponsor, he writes 'MOTHER'.

It asks for her date and place of birth. Henry leaves it blank.

It asks for her parents' names. Henry leaves them blank.

The rest of the form asks about his own citizenship, his address, her address. He completes those details. There are a lot of pages. Towards the end, it asks for proof of identity and relationship. His eye rests on a list of acceptable documents:

1. Birth certificate with names of mother and child, place and date of birth.
2. Government-issued identification, such as passports or household registration cards showing kinship.
3. Other official, notarised, government-issued documents, with their names and relationship.

He has none of these. Maybe his ma has something in Taipei? He starts a letter to Meilin. He explains that, through the family reunification provisions, she can live with them, but he needs some documents. Then he copies out the list from the application. He finishes with updates about Lily's schoolwork and piano lessons, and encloses a cheque for $200. He signs the letter *Renshu*.

Los Alamos, New Mexico, February 1979

'Daddy, you got something from Nainai.' Lily waves a big envelope at him.

He feels hopeful.

Lily hops from foot to foot. 'Is there something for me?' she asks. Still standing, he shakes the envelope over the table. Along with a letter, a small crocheted lace doily in the shape of a flower and a sheet of puppy stickers falls out. He hands them to Lily.

'So pretty!' she exclaims.

He unfolds the letter. As soon as he sees the characters, a lump of frustration builds in his throat. Tears push their way forward. He puts it back down after a cursory glance.

'What is it? What does she say? Is there anything else for me?'

Henry shakes his head. He pulls a stack of disused Fortran cards from his briefcase and hands them to Lily.

'Ooh, cards! I'll draw a picture for Nainai that you can send back.'

'Yes. Good idea.' He cuts his sentences short to keep the emotion out.

The letter. He sits down and picks it up again. His hands are shaking too much, so he places it back on the table. Henry cradles his elbows and leans forward as he reads his ma's words.

Renshu – I have no records from your birth. All the family tablets were left in Changsha. What didn't burn with the house was probably destroyed by fighting. Even if they survived, we have no way to get them. There are no household registration records with our names in Taiwan. We used names from Peiwen's family, remember? Please forgive me. It was the best decision, the only decision, at the time. You don't need to send so much money to me. I am just fine. You must save for Lily's school and for your household. The distance between us is far, but I am happy knowing you and your family are safe and healthy. That is all that I want. – Ma.

Henry curses. How can there be no documentation showing that his mother is his mother? And why does he need papers and forms to prove this? In frustration, he slams his fist on the table, and the vase of lilacs next to him tips over.

Water pools across the table. He jumps up and grabs the letter, knocking the vase to the floor in his haste. It shatters, pieces scattering and skidding. He looks down at the drowned lilacs and broken glass. It was Rachel's favourite vase.

'Daddy?' Lily stands at the door.

'The vase fell over,' Henry says, his pulse still throbbing. 'It was an accident.'

'Are you okay, Daddy?'

He doesn't want that scared look in her eyes. 'Yes,' he says carefully. 'I'm okay. But I'm angry.'

He kneels to pick up the glass.

'At me?'

'No, not you, Little Girl.'

'Then who? Nainai? Mommy?'

He shakes his head. 'Just angry.'

In the end, Henry writes down that Meilin Shui is his aunt. He writes a letter that says she will live with them; he can provide for her. That his family needs her and she needs them.

'Maybe you could say that she is "a close aunt who raised me, practically a mother",' Rachel suggests.

He adds this, and hopes that 'close aunt' will be good enough. He mails the application.

Henry's habit of scanning the post for a blue airmail envelope with his American name carefully written out in his mother's penmanship, raised lines of Chinese characters bulging through from the other side, shifts to anticipating an official kind of envelope, something from the government.

Spring turns to summer, and Meilin writes to say that more people are leaving Taiwan. Peiwen's daughter Huifang and her family are headed to Australia, to be with her sister, Huiqing. Peiwen and Yuping have managed to get visas to the US and will join Huibao in Pennsylvania. The Hsus have emigrated to

Canada, where their daughter now lives. Mrs Hsu's parting words to Meilin were that if she couldn't go to the US, she should try to move somewhere else in Taipei. If the Communists come, they will certainly come to these apartments. At the very least, she should destroy any letters and papers that connect her to Renshu.

When the official government response finally comes, it is not the full-sized manilla envelope stuffed with packets and further forms that Henry expected. Instead, Rachel hands him a thin, simple envelope. Filled with foreboding, he pauses.

'Whatever it says,' Rachel says, 'she is your mother. Nothing will change that.'

There is the sound of rustling paper as Rachel picks up and smooths out the letter he has crumpled and tossed aside. She reads aloud, mostly to herself: 'Unfortunately, aunts, uncles, cousins or in-laws are not considered immediate relatives. Therefore, we cannot grant Mrs Meilin Shui an immigrant visa on the basis of family reunification. She is, of course, welcome to make an application to visit your family on a temporary tourist visa, or put in a general application for the annual quota of Chinese Immigrants to the United States of America.'

He keeps his back to her. Hearing the words aloud has solidified the reality.

'Henry,' Rachel starts, and puts her arm around his shoulder. He stiffens and pulls away. She lets her arm drop, but stays by his side.

'What now?' she asks, staring out the window with him.

'I don't know.' Henry stares at the bald patches of dirt in their overlooked garden.

'We'll try again,' Rachel says, determination in her voice. 'There must be a way. We could talk to an immigration lawyer? Get a temporary visa and convert it to a permanent one? Maybe there are other types of visas? Someone, somewhere will have an idea.'

Over the next weeks, they research other options. Can they demonstrate that Meilin has expertise in science, maths or engineering? No. Does she have the capital and experience to establish a self-sustaining business? No. Is she a political refugee? Not anymore – at least not in the eyes of the US government. Would she be coming as an investor? No. Would she be filling a job for which qualified US workers are not available? At nearly sixty-seven years old, probably not.

They are advised that, if she falls into none of these preferred categories, they should apply for one of the remaining direct immigration visas. Approximately two hundred of these are available each year. However, as there is a backlog, the waiting period for approval may be significant, in some cases stretching into years.

'We've done everything we could, we really have.' Rachel adds the final letter of advice to the pile of paperwork they have accumulated.

Henry knows she's right. But knowing this brings no consolation.

Not an immediate relative. The words swim and blur as his eyes fill. Meilin is his ma. *Not an immediate relative.* Henry wonders if his English has failed him.

Taipei, Taiwan, August 1979

Meilin is waiting. At exactly 10.00 a.m., the phone rings.

'Renshu?'

'Ma.' His voice sounds like a flag that has lost the breeze. None of his news surprises her, but she couldn't have predicted how a distance she has carried folded up inside for so long now expands. What began as a growing sense of separation in Keelung Harbour almost twenty years ago has swelled to become an ocean she cannot cross.

'What about a tourist visa? You could come and stay for a few months, see how you like it?'

A welcome predicated on leaving? Flying so far just to come back?

'Maybe,' Meilin says.

Renshu continues, trying to fill a space that has been drained of hope. He is saying something about the possibility of visa rules and quotas changing.

Does she want to step into another country? Begin again in another language? New food, new people? Start over, like a child, at nearly seventy?

What Meilin knows is life in Taipei. She can find somewhere else in the city to live. Who would bother an old woman with no ties to anyone? She has her savings; over the years Renshu has sent money for anything she could want. For years, now, she has spent her mornings in the park, meeting the same friends for tai chi and gossip. Even though the city has grown beyond recognition, she can still find all that she wants in the market. Her life here is hers and it is enough.

'Renshu,' Meilin interrupts, 'do you remember our hand scroll?'

He stops speaking. His half-formed dream vanishes. 'Of course. We loved that scroll.' A warm timbre has replaced the thin strain of worry in his voice.

'Do you remember the end?'

'Mmm . . .'

In the quieten, Meilin hopes he is imagining the final scene, where the scholar-traveller rests in the shade of cherry blossoms, writing and reciting poetry, while small birds flit and chirp among the branches above.

'Renshu, I am fine here. Your life is there now, with Rachel, with Lily. Never mind about the papers, the visas. I'll tell you what I want instead.' She pauses.

'What?' His voice is both cautious and curious.

'An orchard. Plant an orchard, Renshu. Promise?'

A long pause.

'Okay, Ma. I promise.'

That night, Henry dreams in Chinese.

He is high in the mountains. He has travelled by foot and is weary, oh so weary. While climbing, he approached with hope, but now that he has arrived, loss echoes everywhere. The terraces are overgrown with weeds. Piles of stones slump where once there were buildings. No one has been here for a long time.

Among the ruins grows an orchard. Where did the seeds come from? A passer-by dropping fruit, a gift from the birds?

Henry dreams an orchard. He dreams soft clouds of blossoms, boughs full of pinks and whites, reaching their arms to blue skies, promising bounty. The blossoms' scent will carry an elixir for happiness, a balm to soothe his sadness. He imagines fruit swelling under rain and sun, caressed by warm breezes. At summer's end, he wants to sink his teeth into ripeness, straight off the tree, bursting with sweet, tart juices. He wants to devour a year's growth in a few happy mouthfuls.

Cherries, peaches, plums. He will tend them all, transform this land into his own Chinese hand scroll. A refuge. An orchard.

When he wakes, he pages through seed catalogues. He pauses at the pictures of trees in full leaf, his hand resting on the photos of dark, glossy fruit. His mouth begins to water as he completes the order form, writes a cheque, addresses the envelope and licks a stamp.

Henry has ordered two baby cherry trees.

Henry curses as the shovel hits another stone.

'Break my back,' he says, shaking his head, wiping his face with the edge of his sweat-stained T-shirt.

'What are you doing?'

He looks at her: messy pigtails, uneven bangs. Dirt in the creases of her knees, her brown legs sticking out from under her red sundress. He reaches out to rumple her hair, then digs the shovel in again. Hits stone once more.

'Are you digging a hole all the way to China?'

The ground is pocked with loose gravel. It holds little moisture and less promise. He removes big chunks of tufa, piling them up next to the pit where he will plant his cherry tree.

'Last year, in Miss Stanford's class, we read a story about someone who dug a hole so deep it went to China. She said it was a *fable*, which means it's not exactly true, but not exactly false, either. I wonder which part was true and which part wasn't.'

The soil is thin and meagre in this land of plenty. Here, where rain is scant and the ground cracks in the summer, where thunderclouds build false hope every afternoon. The moisture is absorbed by the thirsty air before it can reach the parched land.

Still, Henry dreams an orchard: cherry, peach, apricot, plum; stone fruits with their vibrant colours and flavours of sun. He keeps digging. Maybe past the topsoil, past the volcanic rocks, the soil will become rich and nutrient-filled. When he reaches clay instead, he curses.

'So, are you? Are you digging a hole to China?' She is still there, sitting on the ground, inspecting the rocks he has unearthed.

'Maybe, Little Girl. Maybe.' He tosses the shovel into the pit and goes inside.

The trees arrive by special delivery. Lonely little sticks poking out of small burlap sacks. They look like orphans from a kinder, lusher land, clutching their only belongings. Henry swallows his disappointment and concentrates instead on the tags attached to the branches. He squints at the print beneath the photos.

'Are those supposed to be cherry trees?' Lily asks.

'Yes.' He can't think of anything to add.

'They look like sticks in the mud.' She plays with the frayed edges of the sacks. 'Have you ever heard of that?'

He shakes his head.

'*A stick in the mud* is someone who doesn't want to have fun and doesn't want anyone else to have fun, either.'

Henry doesn't say anything. After Lily goes inside, he carefully lowers one of the trees into the hole. The hole is almost deeper than the tree is tall.

'You need some enriched soil and compost. The soil here isn't good enough to support fruit trees.' Rachel joins him in the garden.

He glowers. Who *buys* dirt?

'At least add some peat and woodchips. That would keep the moisture in.'

He ignores her.

'Those trees will need nutrients, fertiliser, food. They won't grow otherwise.'

Henry doesn't trust soil from a plastic bag. If he digs deep enough, he's certain he will find good earth. He shovels dirt and rubble into the hole, trying to support the tree, patting down the light soil and watering it with the garden hose.

The other tree he carries to the front yard, to a hole he has dug near the end of the drive. There are two towering cottonwoods already, but he wants a cherry tree there, too. The hole is only deep enough to hold the rootball of the sapling, and there's not much space between it and the cement drive, but he plants it anyway.

'That's the worst possible place for a cherry tree,' Rachel criticises, following him. 'There is no light and it's right near the edge of the driveway.'

He brushes past her with the hose.

The next day, she backs the car into the tree twice, first rushing out of the drive on the way to the grocery store, and again later on her way to pick up Lily from a friend's.

'Why can't you be more careful?' he complains.

'Why can't you plant the tree in a sensible place?'

The cherry tree at the end of the drive never takes root. After being run over and replanted too many times, its few buds wither and fail to open. By September, it is a brittle and dry stick in the mud. It doesn't last the winter.

Chapter Twenty-three

Los Alamos, New Mexico, March 1980

This year, Lily's in fourth grade, and she has the best teacher. In Miss Gibson's classroom, there are interesting maps on the wall showing other continents, like Asia and Africa and South America, with photos of the people who live there. There are posters of mountains, deserts, jungles, rivers. Each Monday, on a bulletin board titled 'What I Noticed Last Week', Miss Gibson writes things like 'Emily shared her seat with Joanne' or 'Daniel included Freddie in the kickball game'. Her handwriting is perfect. All the letters find their places in the right order and right size on the name tags on each desk. No one's name is too long or too short for the space. Each name seems to glow when she writes it out.

Last year, when Danny Henderson teased Lily, saying she had slanty eyes, and chased her at recess yelling 'Egg Foo Yung!' and 'Ancient Chinese Secret!', the teacher told him to knock it off and that it wasn't Lily's fault she was different. But even though the teacher made Danny stop, Lily felt worse than ever. Miss Gibson isn't like that. She makes it so the kids don't tease in the first place. Danny hasn't said one mean word or made any horrible faces so far this year. To anyone.

It is Friday afternoon, and Miss Gibson welcomes everyone back to the classroom after lunch for a special activity. On the blackboard she has drawn a tree trunk and a few branches in white chalk.

In the trunk of the tree, she writes 'Ellie Gibson.' Higher up, the trunk divides into two. She picks up a green piece of construction paper that has been cut in the shape of a leaf. Miss Gibson writes 'Anna (mom)', then sticks it on the right branch. She picks up another leaf, writes 'Charles (dad)', and sticks it on the left branch.

'Can anyone guess how this works?'

'Those are names of your family?'

She nods. 'We are going to make our family trees. Each person in your family has a leaf on the tree. One side holds the leaves from your mother's family, and the other holds the leaves from your father's family. All families look different, just like all trees look different. But they all have leaves.'

Miss Gibson goes over to the supplies table and holds up a sheet from a stack of brown paper. 'You can draw your trunk and branches on this, and' – gesturing to smaller stacks of paper in light and dark greens – 'you can cut your leaves from these. Shall we get started?'

Always eager, Lily takes some sheets of paper. She starts by drawing the trunk and branches. She carefully cuts out several leaves, then starts to write. She starts with her mom, then continues with that side of the family, sticking on leaves for her grandparents, uncle, aunt, cousins.

Lily looks at the other side of her tree. She picks up a leaf and writes *Henry Dao*. Then she thinks of those blue airmail envelopes from her nainai in Taiwan. What is Nainai's name? She stops. She doesn't know. All around, Lily sees other trees filling with leaves, big and small. Kids are asking Miss Gibson where to put uncles, cousins, aunts, great-grandparents, second cousins. But Lily is stuck. Her cheeks warm with shame. She doesn't know the names. Her dad never mentioned anyone else. Are there others?

'This is stupid,' someone says from the back. Lily glances over. It's Danny.

Miss Gibson goes and speaks to him in a hushed voice.

'No, it's boring,' he says and crumples his brown paper into a ball.

Only Lily notices. Most of the other kids have finished, and the room is getting louder. Small leaves start sailing through the air. Miss Gibson says something to Danny, then walks to the front of the room. 'Clean-up time. Five minutes until the bell.' She circulates again, praising and asking questions, pointing out scraps of paper to tidy, transmitting warning looks to boys who are teetering on hilarity.

Lily stares at her paper.

'How's your tree coming along, Lily?'

Covering her dad's side with her arm, Lily launches into an explanation of her mother's side. If she talks enough, there won't be time for Miss Gibson to ask about the empty half. She tells Miss Gibson about Grandma Deborah, who thinks she should wear more dresses, and her Grandpa Simon, who calls her 'gook', and she's about to move on to Uncle Robert when Miss Gibson stops her.

'He calls you *gook*?' Miss Gibson sounds horrified.

'It's a nickname. He's always called me that. Is it bad?'

'Umm . . . tell me about the other side of your tree,' Miss Gibson says.

Keeping her eyes down, Lily slowly reveals the bare branches with only two leaves. 'I don't know anyone else,' she mutters.

'It's okay, Lily. It's been a long afternoon.' When Lily looks up, she notices that Miss Gibson's smile is strained and her eyes are a bit glassy.

Lily nods and blinks back tears. She stuffs her paper into her bag and heads out to the buses.

When she gets home, Lily takes the crumpled paper and smooths it out on the kitchen table. She studies the tree. She knows that her dad was born in China, then moved to Taiwan, then came to the US. She knows his mom is in Taiwan. That's all. She's never met her. Her dad doesn't speak Chinese to her mom, or to anyone, really.

Sometimes, Lily feels like there's something she's supposed to know that she doesn't, or something she's supposed to be that she isn't. When she asks her dad about his past, he says he doesn't remember. Her mom has told her not to ask, that it upsets him because it was hard to grow up during the war. They must, her mom emphasises, focus on the family they are now.

She hears the front door open. Her mom is home. Should she put the paper away? Lily's mom is humming to herself as she puts away her coat, opening and closing the closet. Now she's coming down the hallway. Lily sits motionless.

'Oh! Lily, you gave me a scare. I thought you would be with your friends at the park. It's gorgeous out, now that spring is finally here.'

Tears start rolling down Lily's cheeks.

'What is it? What's wrong?' Rachel comes over to hug her daughter. Lily buries her face in Rachel's shoulder, sobbing out the story of the afternoon, her frustration.

'Oh, honey.' Rachel holds Lily, murmuring soft reassurances, but she offers no answers to Lily's questions about Henry.

Leaning on one elbow, chin in her hand, Rachel considers the tree.

'You've done a brilliant job with my family. I love how you made each person's leaf a different shape.'

'Mom, what's a *gook*?'

'What? Did someone at school call you that?' Rachel immediately sounds angry.

'No, but Grandpa Simon does. Is it bad?'

'Grandpa.' Rachel taps her fist to her mouth, working out what to say. 'Grandpa doesn't mean anything bad when he says that, but he shouldn't. It's not a nice word to call anyone. People sometimes use it to make fun of people who are Asian or who look Asian.'

Lily bursts into fresh tears.

'Oh, Lily. Oh, Lily . . .' Rachel rubs her back and continues looking at the paper. After some time, she says, 'I like how you've arranged the little leaves for Uncle Robert and Aunt Wendy's kids. And putting the twins on the same stem is so clever.' Her fingers rest on the names of Lily's youngest cousins.

'But . . .' Lily indicates her father's side of the tree.

Rachel nods. 'I know, sweetie. Let me talk to your Dad.'

That night, after Lily is asleep, Rachel comes into the living room. She holds out Lily's tree like a banner for Henry to read. He puts his book aside.

'Lily's schoolwork? Very nice,' he says, not sure what he's supposed to see.

'No, it's not.' Her finger taps the side with only two leaves.

Henry leans closer to see his name written on one and 'Nainai' written on the other.

Rachel puts the paper down and crosses her arms. 'When I came home she was really upset because she couldn't add any other leaves, and doesn't even know her own grandmother's name. Henry, she wants to know more. It's her family, too.'

Henry sits back in his chair. 'Some families are small.' He shrugs.

'That's not the point. The point is that she doesn't know about your background, and she wants to. I understand you don't want to talk about the past, but Lily should know her own grandmother. I'd like to meet her, too. Besides, having a small family is all the more reason to hold everyone close. Don't you want your mother to meet her grandchild? Don't you want to bring everyone together, even if only for a visit?'

Taipei, Taiwan, April 1980

Meilin sits in the courtyard of Lin-Na's house and reads over Renshu's latest letter. He wants her to spend the summer with them in New Mexico. Rachel needs to be away for a few weeks for a librarian training course. Lily wants to meet her nainai. Would Meilin come and help out while Rachel is gone?

She is thinking about the opportunity when Lin-Na comes and joins her in the shade. Meilin tells her friend about Renshu's news.

'Wah! Are you going to go?'

'I'm not sure yet.'

'Really? Why not? How long has it been since you've seen him? Don't you want to meet your grandchild and daughter-in-law?'

'Of course I do, but it's such a long trip. I'm . . .' Meilin hesitates, not sure what this feeling is that holds her back. She thinks of the logistics: passport, planning, plane travel, going to another country, where, once again, she doesn't speak the language. But it's not just the hassle; it's all those years of living so far apart.

What if they no longer recognise each other? What if the reunion makes them feel even more distanced?

'If it were me, I'd be jumping on a plane to go see them.'

'Hmm?'

'Go! Then you'll know what it's like where they live. You can imagine their house, their foods, the trees and streets. If I had family in America, I'd go and see the Golden Gate Bridge and the Statue of Liberty. Why not?'

'Maybe you're right.' Whatever her worries, Meilin admits, the alternative – of not seeing Renshu and his family – seems far worse. 'It's just for the summer. He says if I like it, we can try to find another way for me to stay.'

'Would you want to?'

'I don't know.' Meilin looks around. In the cool and shady courtyard, Lin-Na's husband has set up a small pond with gold-fish and a fountain. 'I like it here.'

Once her plans for emigrating to the US fell through, and the Hsus and Peiwen's family had left Taiwan, Meilin sought out her old friend at the Yongle fabric market. The Benshengren woman had always been friendly, but Meilin hadn't seen her as much since moving to the Da'an apartment. Meilin hoped to sell Lin-Na some of the silks and cottons Mrs Hsu left behind.

Lin-Na was happy to buy the fabrics and asked how Meilin had been.

When Meilin explained that she was, once again, looking for somewhere to live, Lin-Na had offered a space in her home until Meilin found something. Lin-Na's family quickly grew so fond of Meilin they insisted she stay. After six months living here in Dadaocheng, she is practically one of the family.

Despite widespread fears, the PRC didn't immediately invade Taiwan. And although the American flag no longer proudly flies downtown, a new office has been established, the American Institute in Taiwan, down a drab back alley. It seems that the US, despite courting Beijing with one hand, hovers protectively over Taiwan with the other.

But in Taiwan, it's been industry, not military, that has been striding forward. Businesses have sprung up all over the island, making computer peripherals, electronics, cameras. Trade and investment between the US and the ROC booms. Over the past decades, the island's economy and infrastructure have grown. Many who left Taiwan to study in the US now return, bringing their business connections and technical expertise. Many of those who stayed in the US have fostered collaborations back home in Taiwan. The little island is becoming a mighty tiger, an economic miracle. Taipei is constantly growing.

Meilin watches this burgeoning economy and can't help but think that Old Dao Hongtse would approve. Money, trade and commerce are mightier than ideology and more devastating than swords. *Kerosene is good business: everyone needs heat, everyone needs light.* Now it is electronics and computers that everyone needs.

The next week, Meilin writes back to Renshu. *I will come.*

Meilin grips the armrests as the plane leaves the ground.

She is uneasy seeing the land far beneath her feet. The houses get smaller and smaller, the roads become squiggles. For the first time in years, she thinks of the bombs falling in Chongqing. She remembers always looking up at the planes. Now she looks down. How easy it would have been for those Japanese pilots, not having to look anyone in the eye, not even having to see the people below! As easy as dropping a handful of pebbles on dirt.

The flight seems endless and Meilin cannot find any comfort in her seat. The recirculated air has a cold, sterile taste. Every minute takes her closer to Renshu, but at the same time, every minute takes her further away from all that she has come to know.

Los Alamos, New Mexico, June 1980

Of course, he recognises her the minute she steps through the airport gate. But she's different; smaller, greyer. She's sixty-eight, and the twenty years since he waved goodbye from Keelung Harbour have softened her shoulders, her cheeks, the skin around her eyes. Her hair, as ever, is pulled into a simple bun at the nape of her neck. She wears a brown knitted vest over a light blue silk tunic. Her trousers are simple. He is sure she has made all her clothes. Her eyes, though, still have that gentle kindness and deep intelligence. She reaches up to welcome Rachel. Their embrace is awkward, but affectionate. When she sees Lily, her smile grows even wider.

Then it's a barrage of sensations: the brush of his ma's soft cheek, the rough wool of her vest against his palm, the smell of camphor in her embrace. He feels the cool silk of her sleeves, the grasp of her fingers on his back, her voice in his ear – right there, not through a hard plastic telephone handset, but *right there*, where he can feel the vibrations of her saying his name. For nearly two decades, he has been far away from these textures, scents and sounds of home. His eyes swim with the immensity and immediacy of it all.

'Welcome, Ma,' he murmurs.

'Mmm, Renshu.' She nods into his chest.

Nainai is staying in Lily's room. During her visit, Lily will sleep on a mattress in her father's study. He cleared a shelf for her and she has filled it with a stack of library books, some stuffed animals, a Hello Kitty notebook, coloured pencils and stickers.

Nainai brings gifts from Taiwan: glittery barrettes with butterflies and pearly beads; a tin full of mooncakes; a small satin purse with a single snap, containing a jade elephant and a gold bell; a plastic box filled with Chinese vocabulary flashcards; the miniature toothpaste tube and eye mask from the flight. Lily loves it all.

Nainai has brought a jade pendant in the shape of a pair of plums for her mom. It has a red string running through its small gold loop. Rachel admires it, then says, 'Oh!' and goes to their bedroom. When she comes back, the pendant hangs from the gold chain Henry gave her for their tenth wedding anniversary. Henry gives her a kiss on the cheek. Nainai nods in approval.

Then, for her dad, Nainai unpacks a porcelain teapot with bamboo handles and two blue-and-white porcelain teacups. Each has a domed lid and sits on a small saucer. The cups have a pattern like evenly spaced grains of rice. They have no handles. Her dad's face lights up as he lifts and admires each one. Finally, Nainai hands him a cylindrical red tin of tea. He takes the lid off and inhales happily.

'Are you hungry? Tired? Would you like a rest?' Rachel asks.

Renshu translates and Meilin nods: a little hungry and yes, a rest would be good. After eating a bit of rice, Meilin goes to her room to lie down. She falls asleep to the sounds of Rachel getting Lily ready for bed and Renshu washing up in the kitchen.

She wakes early, disorientated by the dim light in the room. She pulls back the curtains to see pine trees, and in the distance, mountains. The air feels dry, and she's a bit light-headed. Hearing movement downstairs, she puts on her slippers and a dressing gown, and heads down for something to drink.

Renshu is awake. When she comes into the kitchen, he fills the kettle and sets it on the stove. While it heats, he taps a few tea leaves into the cups. The kettle whistles. He pours the water right up to the rims, letting it spill over the edges, then puts the lids on. She slides into a seat at the table.

'I like Rachel,' she says, as he sits down across from her.

He smiles and peeks under the lid to see if his tea is ready.

'And Lily reminds me of Liling. Not just her face, but her whole manner.'

She lifts the saucer and sips her tea. Finally! The taste soothes her parched throat. Hot, pungent, and comforting.

They are quieten for a few moments.

'You know, she's about the same age Liling was when we lost her,' Meilin reflects.

'Wow, you're right. I hadn't thought of that.' He leans forward on one elbow, holding his chin in his palm, shaking his head.

'I wonder what kind of woman she'd have grown into,' Meilin muses. 'Lively, I'm sure. Stunning, too. You could always see Wenling's beauty just ready to burst through in Liling.'

'When I was first at Northwestern,' Renshu says, 'I went to Chinatown in Chicago a few times with Chen. Sometimes, maybe in a restaurant or on a crowded street, I'd think I could see Liling.

I knew it was impossible, but still, I'd be scanning faces for the rest of the afternoon, looking for her.'

'Imagine what Wenling would think of her handsome nephew doing so well in America!' Meilin exclaims. 'She'd either be very jealous or very proud, I expect.'

'Probably both,' Renshu laughs.

Meilin reaches out and squeezes his hand. 'I miss them all,' she says.

'Me, too.'

Again, they are quieten for several minutes.

'Ma?'

'Hmm?'

'The story of Peach Blossom Spring—'

'You remember it? One of my favourites!'

'Of course I remember. But, Ma, when you told it to me so long ago, you didn't tell the whole story. Why?'

'I didn't?'

'You left out how, after the fisherman returns home, he can never find Peach Blossom Spring again. No one else can, either.'

'Oh,' she says, sounding surprised. 'I wonder why I did that. I don't know.' She furrows her brow, as if to summon the Meilin and Renshu of so long ago, their fears, their hopes. She shakes her head and repeats, 'I don't know.' She traces the edge of her tea saucer with her index finger. After a few moments, she says, 'I guess the thing about Peach Blossom Spring is that if you are fortunate enough to find it, you are also unfortunate, because then you have to decide what to do. Do you stay, and forgo all else? Or do you return home, with the understanding that you'll never find it again? Is it a blessing? Is it a curse?'

Renshu doesn't answer. Soon they hear footsteps running overhead and down the stairs.

'Nainai! Good morning!' Lily shouts, bursting into the room, giving her a big hug. 'What shall we do today?'

Once she's recovered from jet lag and become more accustomed to the dry air, Meilin's visit passes pleasantly. They visit a few attractions in Los Alamos. At the science museum, they see models of Little Boy and Fat Man, the bombs that were dropped on Hiroshima and Nagasaki. Each is only about ten feet long. At five feet in height, Fat Man is barely taller than Meilin. Little Boy is even smaller. Meilin puts her hand on the cold metal casing, painted white. Far away in China, while she and Renshu had lived and mourned and fled and lost and feared, here, in this very place, in this town with too much light and not enough air, scientists had worked to create destruction. She wouldn't have wanted the war to last any longer. And yet, there must be better ways of finding peace.

They also visit the Bandelier National Monument and show her the caves and ancient dwellings of the Pueblo people. Later, they visit the Plaza in Santa Fe. Meilin loves looking at the Native American jewellery for sale in front of the Palace of the Governors. She likes the silver beaded necklaces with charms of bears, birds and turtles carved from turquoise, coral and lapis. She buys gifts to take back to Lin-Na. Rachel and Lily take her to a fabric shop in Santa Fe, and she is amazed at the selection. They stock up so she can sew pyjamas and knit afghans for the winter.

About a week after Meilin's arrival, Rachel leaves for her course. She'll also spend a week in St Louis visiting her parents. Meilin respects Rachel's ambition, and she's proud that Henry wants to support her career. She also likes that she is playing a small part in helping Rachel see her parents.

After dropping Rachel off at the airport, Henry, Lily and Meilin make a trip to the Chinese grocery store in Albuquerque. Although it's nowhere near as nice as the markets in Taipei, they fill a trolley with tins of vegetables, packets of dried mushrooms and noodles, spices, tofu, bottles of dark soy sauce, sesame oil and oyster sauce, chilli flakes and a fifty-pound bag of rice.

Nainai takes up residence in the kitchen. She is always at the table chopping, preparing, cleaning, knitting or drinking tea. The stove is never quieten, never clear. Lily loves that there is always something bubbling, waiting to be eaten or not quite ready yet.

Chop, chop, chop, Nainai's big cleaver minces a pile of mushrooms and pork. Scrape, scrape, it brings together the fillings.

Chop, chop, chop again, until all the pieces are mixed into a pale pink paste with creamy white bits of garlic, small green flecks of scallion and ginger fibres. She adds some salt, massages it in with her fingers, scrapes the mixture into a pile. Chop, chop, chop.

'Jiaozi,' says Nainai.

'Jiaozi?' repeats Lily.

Nainai nods and rolls out a ball of dough into a thin sheet. Then she picks up a water glass with the rim floured and presses out a perfect circle. She lifts it carefully from the board and puts it to the side.

'Lily,' she says, handing her the glass. Lily likes it when Nainai says her name. It sounds so pretty in her voice. Nainai rolls more dough and Lily presses out more circles. Nainai dusts them with fine flour so that they don't stick to one another.

When all the circles are ready, Nainai places a spoonful of filling on one. She dips her index finger into a shallow bowl of water, then traces the edge. She folds the wrapper over the meat mixture, lining up the ends, then pinches them into a serrated seam. She puts the jiaozi in an empty steamer basket lined with cabbage leaves. 'You try,' she says, in English, handing Lily a circle.

Lily's seams aren't even and her wrapper keeps tearing. Some of her dumplings have too much filling, while others have too little. Never mind, Nainai seems to say, and she pinches them closed all the same, adding them to the bamboo basket.

Henry can hear Lily and Meilin in the kitchen. Lily speaks to Meilin in English and Meilin responds in Chinese. Despite the different languages, they seem to have a lot to say to each other.

'Come eat!' Meilin calls from the kitchen.

'Daddy, come on!' Lily calls.

In the kitchen, there are steaming bowls of rice with chopsticks, and a small fork for Lily. The table is filled with dishes he hasn't had for years: braised lotus root, stir-fried snow pea leaves, sea cucumber, a whole fish, pork with water chestnuts and mushrooms, beef noodle soup and a mountain of dumplings.

They eat.

*

While Henry gets Lily ready for bed, Meilin starts scrubbing the dishes with warm, frothy suds. Despite the long journey, she's glad to be here, to see Renshu's American life. Coming back into the kitchen, he grabs a towel to help.

'It's good to have you here, Ma.'

'Mmm.' She hands him a dripping plate.

'I'm sorry that we haven't found a way for you to stay.'

'Shh.' She gives him a big pot to wipe dry. 'I've been able to meet Lily and I see how much Rachel loves you. You're very lucky. We're all lucky.' She starts rinsing off the chopsticks. 'Almost done,' she says.

As he puts the dishes back in their cabinets, he remarks, 'It could have been different if Uncle hadn't left your name off my papers.'

She fills the kettle and puts it on to boil, turning her back to Renshu.

It could have been different. There are so many ways in which it could have been different, so many junctions. In the end, there's nothing to be gained by this kind of thinking. 'Longwei did what he thought was necessary,' she says.

'He should have been honest.'

'Renshu! Nothing was straightforward then. We all had to make difficult choices. You know that.'

'No!' Henry argues. 'He stole something that wasn't his to take. He broke our bond!'

'Lower your voice, you'll wake Lily!' Her hands are shaking slightly as she gets the cups ready. When she pours hot water into the first, the excess flows over the top, filling the saucer and splashing on to the counter. 'It's only paperwork, Renshu. You have your citizenship, your family, your life in America. Leave it alone. We asked him to help, and he did. If he made a mistake, then forgive him.'

'Why are you defending him?'

Meilin doesn't answer.

'I cannot forgive him for leaving off your name. I'll never understand why he did.'

Meilin is silent for a long time. She rubs her cheek and eyes.

Understanding has always been how Renshu makes meaning. Explanations offer comfort. But here, there are none. 'We can forgive without understanding. Sometimes we must. Maybe that's what forgiveness is – accepting someone's actions, even if there are no good explanations.'

Meilin picks up her teacup and takes it to the sink. 'It's late, Renshu. I'm going to sleep now.' She leaves him sitting at the kitchen table.

'Nainai, tell me a story.'

Meilin understands what the girl is asking, but doesn't know if she can do what she wants.

'Please?'

Meilin puts down her knitting and stands up. Lily follows her to the study, where Meilin picks up the box of Chinese flashcards. She will try.

After several minutes, she finds 'horse' and 'old man'. She puts the two cards out in front of Lily.

'Is this a story about an old man and a horse?'

Meilin nods, and looks for a card to show loss. She can't find one.

Lily looks at her expectantly.

Meilin finds the card for good fortune but not the one for disaster.

Lily tries to guess the story. 'Does the man ride his horse? Does he go to fight battles? Was he once a soldier and now he's old, spending his days peacefully? Is the horse his best friend?'

Meilin feels defeated by Lily's questions. She doesn't have enough language. 'We ask Daddy,' she finally says.

Meilin and Lily come into the kitchen where he sits, reading the newspaper. Lily is expectant, excited. His ma's face has that combination of helplessness and imperiousness that means she wants him to do something.

'Tell her,' she says in Chinese, 'tell her the stories from when you were little.'

No.

He makes a non-committal snort and looks back down at the newspaper.

'Renshu.' She puts her hand on the print. 'It's important. If you don't tell her, how will she learn what matters?'

'She doesn't need to know.' He pulls the paper out from under her hand.

'What do you mean?' Meilin argues. 'Of course she needs to know.' She glances at Lily, whose smile is changing to an expression of worry.

'No, she doesn't!' he snaps, getting up from his chair. 'What is the point of telling her all those sad stories? I wish I didn't know them myself.'

Meilin steps back. 'I didn't mean *our* stories,' she says. 'Although she will, one day, want to know those, too,' she adds quietly. She puts her arm around Lily. 'I mean the ones I told you as a child: the rooster, the pear tree, the old man who lost his horse . . .'

'Oh.' His face relaxes. And then, vaguely: 'Maybe later.'

Rachel returns from her course, excited about a career in library science. When Rachel seems a bit taken aback by all the unfamiliar items filling the refrigerator, Meilin wonders if she's overstepped. Never mind – there's only a short time left before her return flight. Meilin is glad to have come, but she's ready to go back to Taipei. She misses the fountain and goldfish in Lin-Na's courtyard. She misses the fresh vegetables from the market, and the warm, thick air.

Renshu asks if she would like to stay longer. Should he keep trying for a permanent visa? His voice is full of hope, but Meilin knows that for her, Taipei is home.

'Renshu, this is your Peach Blossom Spring, not mine.'

His expression sobers, crestfallen.

Meilin continues. 'We have feasted, we have celebrated. Now it is time for me to return home.'

'Okay, Ma,' he finally says, his voice a hoarse whisper. 'Okay.' Somehow, Meilin's visit has increased the distance between his past and his present. What he thought would build a bridge has, instead, widened an abyss. Part of him is relieved she wants to return to Taipei, and that part of him will always feel guilty.

The day before Meilin returns to Taiwan, Meilin and Lily pull Lily's red wagon to the plant nursery down the road. They buy big bags of mulch and enriched soil, and drag the wagon home. Cutting open the bags releases a rich, earthy smell. They dig in with their bare hands. The dark, damp soil crumbles in their fingers. They use it to fill the hollows around the struggling cherry tree in the backyard, tamping down the earth with a shovel. They spread the mulch around its base and water the tree generously. A few weeks later, the tree begins to stretch and grow.

Chapter Twenty-four

Los Alamos, New Mexico, September 1980

Rachel and Lily are moving Lily's things back into her bedroom. Lily sets down an armful of books as her mother snaps a fresh fitted sheet on to the mattress.

'Why couldn't Nainai stay longer?'

Rachel shakes out a top sheet and spreads it over the bed.

'I don't think she wants to be all by herself in Taipei,' Lily continues. 'Why can't she stay here?'

Now, Rachel tucks in the edges of a light blue blanket. Lily watches her mother straighten the bedspread and fluff the pillows in their clean cases.

'Mom? Did you hear me? Should I ask Daddy?'

'Oh, no, no,' Rachel hastens. 'Don't bother him. He finds it all too upsetting.'

'But why?'

Rachel sits on the bed and pats the covers, motioning for Lily to join. 'When your Daddy was growing up in China, it was wartime. He and Nainai had to move around a lot. Eventually they went to Taiwan because it was safer.'

Lily already knows this. But she stays quieten. Maybe her mom will say something new.

'Things were better in Taiwan. Your daddy studied hard and got a scholarship to come to America.'

'What was he like when you met him?'

'Very handsome. Very shy.' Rachel laughs.

'How did you meet?'

Lily likes the way her mom's face softens as she tells the story. 'From the moment he asked for that Chopin recording, I liked him. There was something so different about the way he looked at the world. As if everything mattered. As I got to know him and learned what he had lived through, I realised that his is an old soul. An old soul with fresh eyes. And he was so handsome. Who wouldn't fall for someone like that?'

'A real love story!'

'Yes,' Rachel says softly. 'It was.'

'But why doesn't he want to talk about it? It's a good story with a happy ending. And I still don't see why Nainai can't stay.'

'Somewhere in all the moving around, some papers got confused. The governments think Nainai is his aunt, not his mother, so she can't stay.'

'Why doesn't he just tell them there was a mistake? Can't it be fixed?'

Rachel sighs. 'We tried to fix it, but we couldn't. That's what makes him so sad.'

'Oh.' Lily has seen this sadness in her father. The last thing she wants is to make him sadder.

'Well, I'm glad Nainai came to visit.'

'I am, too.'

Lily begins to hound Rachel for more information about China and Taiwan. But Rachel doesn't know much herself. She goes to the library to ask for recommendations, and the librarian points her towards a flyer. A Chinese Language and Culture course will be starting soon at the community centre. The course seems like a perfect compromise. Rachel mentions it to Henry, saying she understands that he wants to leave his past in the past, but Lily has a desire and a right to learn about her heritage. Initially, Henry is reluctant, but Rachel insists.

Lily loves the classes. She cannot believe her good fortune. Most of the other kids are Chinese, a few are half-Chinese. She's thrilled to make friends who look like her, even if just a little bit, even if they go to different schools. Teacher Li, whose children are at university, is gentle and generous. Everyone feels included.

Rachel likes the classes, too. Sometimes, while Lily's in class, Rachel sits outside and chats with the other mothers. She enjoys the solidarity and friendship, especially with the women from mixed couples. They commiserate about the long drives to the

Chinese grocery store down in Albuquerque, where their husbands work their way down one aisle and up the next, examining every single vegetable and box of tea. They compare notes about the mysterious packets and tins of sharp-smelling, shrivelled-up, dark foods that fill the cupboards and refrigerator. It feels good to exchange stories of misunderstandings and long-distance calls, about the sometimes joyous, sometimes anxiety-inducing arrival of light blue aerogrammes in the mail.

Los Alamos, New Mexico, June 1981

Henry stands facing his cherry tree, which has grown as tall as Henry himself. At his feet is a roll of netting from the garden store.

In the spring, Henry and Lily had watched with joy as blossoms appeared for the first time. Their excitement grew with the arrival of leaves and tiny green fruits. Every so often, Lily's impatience would get the better of her, and she'd taste one. She'd cringe, wrinkling her nose. 'Too sour!' she'd cry, in both disgust and delight. Now the cherries have finally started to expand and ripen.

But they weren't the only ones watching and waiting. At some point, the birds had made their move. In one day, they'd descended and stolen the best cherries.

Henry's trying to figure out how to protect the remaining fruit.

'*Laoshu* – mouse. *Xiongmao* – panda. *Shizi* – lion.' Lily runs up. She must be shouting words from her Chinese class. He didn't hear them arrive home. He can't articulate why, but the classes make him uneasy.

'*Laoshu, xiongmao, shizi*! Mouse, panda, lion!' She dances around him.

These are nothing to build sentences with, Henry thinks. Words like pebbles.

Lily doesn't care. To her, each word is a jewel.

He throws the netting over the branches. He is trying to be

gentle with the tender shoots and leaves, but he needs to pull the netting tight.

'Daddy! I learned the character for tree, *mu*. It even looks like a tree.' She traces the character 木 on her palm. 'Then, if you put two of them side by side, it becomes the character for a small wood, *lin*, 林. And finally, if you squish three trees into your character box, one on top and two below, you get *sen*,森, a forest. If you put person and tree together, you get rest, *xiu*, 休. Rest is a person by a tree.'

Her tones are all flat, sounding wrong in her mouth.

'I remember another word! *Niao*! *Niao* means bird. Nainai taught that to me when she was here.'

'Go get the hose,' he says to her. 'We need to water the tree.'

She wanders off, '*Laoshu, xiongmao, shizi, niao* . . .'

He inspects the netting.

'How do you say cherry?' she asks when she returns, lugging the long green garden hose behind her.

'*Yingtao*,' he says, carefully enunciating the tones.

'*Yingtao*,' she repeats, perfectly echoing his words.

He holds the hose and watches the water's arc splatter at the base of the tree.

'Do you know what else?' she says. 'The character for the sun, *ri*, looks like a box with a line. Sort of like a sun. And moon, *yue*, looks like sun, but with longer lines near the bottom.' She holds out her palm and traces the characters for sun, 日, and moon, 月. 'Putting sun and moon together gives you *ming*, bright, 明.'

'Go turn off the water.'

The tap off, the tree watered, Henry winds up the hose.

Lily follows him up the stairs and into the house.

'I love this language, Daddy.'

Los Alamos, New Mexico, January 1982

'Guess what? Guess what we did.' Lily bursts into the room, and before Henry can reply, she continues. 'We made banners for Chinese New Year!' She unrolls a red scroll of paper, where she has painted in black brushstrokes, in English: *1982 – Year of the Dog*. The characters 恭禧發財 have been printed, cut out and glued on, alongside stickers of lanterns and firecrackers. Hand-drawn dogs decorate the edges, accompanied by liberal doses of glitter and gold ribbons.

'The characters say *gong xi fa cai*.' She taps each with her index finger. 'It means "wishing you joy and prosperity".'

'Very nice, Little Girl,' he says. The purple mimeographed characters, glued at slightly odd angles, look out of place in his American kitchen.

'Can we go?'

'Go where?'

Lily has been talking and he missed her question.

'The party! There's a Chinese New Year's Party, and everyone and their families are invited. I want to go. Please? Please?'

Henry looks over at Rachel, who hands him a photocopy of a hand-drawn invitation. Along either side is a sketch of a vertical banner with a New Year's couplet written in Chinese calligraphy. Each banner has been coloured in with a red crayon. A red diamond-shaped sticker with the gold character for 'blessings' sits proudly at the top.

Below, in English: 'You and your family are invited to join us for a celebration of language, culture and food to welcome in the Year of the Dog. Bring a potluck dish and we will all share our good fortunes.' The date is a Saturday a few weeks from now.

'Maybe,' he says, folding the paper and putting it in his pocket.

'Oh, I hope so.' Lily waves her banner back and forth. Bits of glitter fly off and alight on the floor as she twirls. 'Can I stick it up on my door?'

'Yes, good idea.' Henry pulls open a drawer and rummages past scissors, pens, and stamps to find a roll of tape. He hands it to her and points her upstairs.

He refills the kettle and puts it on the stove.

In the hallway, Rachel fusses with her keys, coat and purse.

'So, what do you think?' she calls. 'Should we go?'

Henry peers into his tin of oolong. Not much left. He tips a small handful of rolled-up tea leaves into his mug.

Rachel comes into the kitchen. 'It could be nice to get to know the other families. Some of them are like us.'

'Like us?' Henry looks up.

'Chinese daddy and Caucasian mommy.'

'Oh.'

The kettle starts to burble on its burner.

'Henry, let's go.'

The sounds of Lily dispensing long, large strips of tape filter down into the kitchen. Henry glances at the ceiling.

'Lily, that's enough tape! Don't waste it,' Rachel shouts.

'I'm *not* wasting it!'

The kettle shrieks. Henry turns off the gas and pours water directly on to his leaves, covering his mug with the lid from a peanut-butter jar to hold in the heat.

'Okay, okay, we'll go. We'll see what it's all about.'

When the Saturday arrives, Rachel is putting plastic wrap over a platter in the kitchen. It holds a mound of something studded with walnuts and ringed by Ritz crackers.

'What is that?'

'It's a cheeseball.'

'A cheeseball?'

'It's an appetiser, for the party. You spread the cheese on the crackers and ta-da! Delicious! We always used to have one on New Year's Eve growing up.'

Henry doesn't say anything. He shakes his head as he goes upstairs to get changed. He'd really rather stay home tonight. He hears Rachel telling Lily to put her shoes on. It's just a party, he tells himself.

'恭禧發財! Happy New Year!' A broad-shouldered man in a pressed suit greets them at the door. His black hair is slightly silvered, and his proud and handsome face is creased. Henry detects traces of a northern accent. Beijing? 'Edwin Huang,' the man says as he extends a hand to Henry. 'I don't believe we've met.'

Huang's handshake is firm, insistent. His gaze seems to be

searching for something in Henry. Not even over the threshold, Henry wonders if coming was a good idea.

'Henry Dao,' he says.

Edwin's eyes rest on Rachel. 'Your wife?' he asks in Chinese.

'Yes, this is my wife, Rachel,' Henry answers in English. He loosens his hand to put his arm around Rachel.

'Pleased to meet you,' she says, and Edwin nods.

'Lily has been enjoying the Chinese classes so much,' Rachel starts.

Edwin turns to Lily and repeats his greeting: '恭禧發財!'

Teacher Li, who has been lingering near the door, anxious that her pupils show off their learning, whispers to Lily, '*Hong bao* . . .'

'*Hong bao na lai*,' Lily stammers and Edwin beams.

He produces a red envelope from his breast pocket and presents it to her. She graciously accepts with both hands, just as Teacher Li instructed.

Rachel still holds her platter. A Chinese woman in a dark maroon qipao is heading towards them. 'Oh, that's Patricia, one of the mothers from the classes,' Rachel whispers. Henry can hear the relief in Rachel's voice to see a familiar face. Patricia takes the platter.

'Welcome! So nice to see you. Let's take this to the kitchen.'

Rachel hands her coat to Henry and follows the other woman. As they walk away, Patricia looks down at the dish. 'What is it?' she asks.

'A cheeseball.'

'A cheeseball?'

As Henry hangs up the coats, he surveys the room. Red and yellow streamers stretch along the walls, embellished every few feet by paper lanterns decorated with tassels and plastic ornaments of dogs. On the tables are red and yellow carnations and imitation mini-firecrackers. How many people are here? Maybe forty? Although a few faces are vaguely familiar, he doesn't know anyone well. He had no idea there were so many Chinese in town. Henry is not sure where to stand or what to say.

Some of the Chinese wives wear qipaos; others wear stylish Western outfits. Everyone seems to have jade or gold jewellery. Rachel wears a plaid dress with a big white collar that shows off the jade pendant Meilin gave her. The wives are fussing about the food, bringing out dishes. Rachel, usually so at ease, seems uncertain how to help. She chats with one of the Caucasian wives.

Lily has been enticed over to a table where kids are decorating paper lanterns. Girls with shiny red ribbons in their pigtails and boys with short haircuts cluster around, jostling one another.

Someone comes over to Henry and introduces himself as David Tian. He says he is neighbours with Tom Benson, Henry's colleague, and that he's glad to finally meet Henry in person. Tian's easy manner relaxes Henry and, over beers, they speak about when they came to the US, where they went to graduate school, how they came to be in Los Alamos. At some point, without realising it, they have shifted into Chinese. Henry detects Tian's Sichuanese accent.

'Are you from Chongqing?' Henry asks.

'I was born there after my family relocated during the War of Aggression. Hard times.' He shakes his head.

For a moment neither speaks.

'Are your family still there?'

'Some. Most of us went to Taiwan.'

Henry nods. He figures that Tian is a little younger than he is, maybe the age of Peiwen's youngest son. Tian slaps his knee when they discover they both went to National Taiwan University.

'I knew it! Another Taida alum. There are a few of us here tonight. Huo! Lin!' Tian calls to a pair of men.

Over jovial introductions, they swap stories about their undergraduate years. Neither Greg Huo nor Steve Lin were in Henry's class. They are younger, but they recall common professors and favourite haunts. Soon they all lapse into a happy reminiscence of eating danzai noodles. Henry can almost taste the savoury meat sauce and black vinegar.

'Those noodles are from my hometown, you know. Great things come from Tainan,' Lin says.

'Happy New Year to my fellow Taida graduates.' Huo holds up his beer, and they all raise their glasses.

Their merriment has caught the attention of Edwin Huang.

'It is wonderful to see old classmates and make new acquaintances, isn't it? It makes me hopeful to one day reunite with my own classmates, from my Kunming days at Lianda,' Huang remarks. 'Come, eat. The food is ready.'

Lily's plate is divided into neat thirds, where she has served herself egg-fried rice, fruit and cucumbers. Rachel's has a green salad, bread, devilled eggs, meatloaf and a generous helping of her cheeseball. But Henry's plate is piled high with bamboo shoots and bitter melon, cold sesame noodles mixed with shredded pork, scallion pancakes and tangy fish with tofu and peanuts. He has also served himself a bowl of beef and noodles in a rich broth.

The room is getting louder, and there is a clatter of chopsticks and soup spoons as everyone eats and exclaims over the dishes. Conversations are a mix of English and Chinese, peppered with accents and regional dialects. Lily bolts her food and runs off to play. Rachel pokes at her plate.

Henry reaches over and touches her hand. 'Aren't you hungry?'

'Oh, I'm fine. I'm enjoying the atmosphere.'

He looks down at his own empty plate.

'It's nice you can have all these special dishes I don't know how to make,' she says.

'They're okay,' he says, his stomach rumbling for more. 'It's a lot of unusual ingredients. Too much trouble to make at home. Maybe just once in a while, it's nice to have.'

Rachel stands up, eyes bright. 'I'll go see if they want a hand with desserts.'

Someone taps Henry's shoulder. 'Join us for a smoke?' It's Tian.

As Henry goes to get his jacket, he pokes his head into the kitchen and sees that the women have separated into Chinese- and English-speaking groups. Rachel's engaged in an animated conversation. He catches her eye and signals he's going outside.

On his way out, he overhears two Chinese women talking about the classes. He pauses. At first, it sounds like they are arguing about Teacher Li. When he listens more carefully, he realises they are both in agreement that the classes need more rigour. He reflects this is probably true. One of the women complains that there is too much emphasis on fun, as if Chinese was just a cultural curiosity. The kids have no real grasp of their history or heritage. The other says it's time for proper Chinese lessons. And, she continues, having mixed-race children involved dilutes everything. It's essential that the parents speak Chinese at home, and how's that going to happen when only one parent can?

Henry's face flushes. He's heard enough.

The sharp night air is a relief. For a moment, Henry closes his eyes and breathes deeply. Tian, Huo and Lin stand in a huddle, smoke rising from their cigarettes. They are joined by a few other men he doesn't know.

Tian waves him over, holding out a box of cigarettes. Henry declines, thinking of Longwei's nasty lifelong cough. They are talking about the upcoming delegation of scientists that will visit from the PRC.

'China is changing,' one of the men says. 'This could be an opportunity to re-establish contact. A lot of people didn't get out when our families did. There are colleagues, friends, teachers still there. We could help them now.' The speaker pauses and clears his throat. It is Edwin Huang. 'Deng is a different creature from Chairman Mao, and even Premier Zhou. He sees the importance of science and technology.'

'Different, but still Communist,' someone quips.

'The thing is,' Tian counters, 'you've been here a long time, Huang. A lot of us came with the support of the Nationalists. If they hear that we're welcoming a PRC delegation, they could blacklist us. I don't want to jeopardise my family or betray any colleagues in Taiwan.'

'Not all of us came here with a Nationalist blessing,' Lin mutters.

'But if we don't welcome them, will we be seen as uncoopera-
tive? The US government is trying to build on the mainland's
split with the Soviets. This is our chance to help shape the
changes.'

Henry squints to see who is speaking. He doesn't know the
man and realises he can't tell where he's from, because the man
is speaking English. In fact, everyone has switched to English,
thus obscuring tell-tale accents and idioms.

'They're just visiting. It's not like they're going behind the
fence,' Huo comments. From their earlier conversation, Henry
knows that most of Huo's research is theoretical and unclassified.
'There have already been successful astronomy and oceanography
exchanges. A lot of collaboration and cooperation is possible,
beyond ideology. Doesn't the spirit of scientific enquiry rise above
politics?'

It's seductive, this thought of scientific internationalism, but
Henry's not certain that anything is above politics. He rubs his
hands together to warm them up, ready to go back inside. In fact,
he's ready for the evening to be over. Although the talk is cordial,
sides are being taken.

'Why don't they invite a delegation from the ROC?' Tian
says, stamping out his cigarette. 'If Deng says, "One country,
two systems," then I say, okay, one country: the Republic of
China.'

A female voice comes from the doorway. 'Gentlemen, your
smoke break is over. Come inside for the presentations.'

Waiting for the children to line up, Henry reflects on how this
night takes him back to a time before graduate school. The
families, the noise, the shared food, all these echo the early
years in Taipei when they lived in the juancun. But in those
days, they were all looking in the same direction. Tonight, it
feels like facing any one way means turning your back on
another.

Rachel appears and takes a seat by Henry.

'Some people are so nice,' she says, as she sits down, 'and
some are not. But I had a really nice chat with Maisy and

Darren's mothers, so that's good. I'm ready for the evening to be over.' She yawns.

The lights dim and the kids file on to a makeshift stage in the front of the hall.

They start singing Chinese folk songs, which sound nothing like Henry remembers.

Henry's mind wanders. He contemplates the men's arguments on whether and how to welcome the delegation. Polite applause breaks his thoughts as the kids finish singing. Next, Teacher Li announces there will be short speeches about each animal of the Chinese zodiac.

'The *whole* zodiac?' Rachel whispers.

'It will go fast,' he says, 'and then we'll leave.'

As they progress through pig, rat and ox, Henry goes through the arguments again: welcome the visitors and, by association, the PRC? Oppose the visitors, favouring the Nationalists? Oppose both? No, there's no sense in making bad feelings in all directions. Welcome the visitors with an open heart but a discerning eye?

Tiger, rabbit.

Dragon.

This evening has summoned Henry's past. The conversation he had with Uncle Longwei on their long-ago walk at the barracks rises from his memory.

'*Renshu, as you move through the world, stay awake. There's always a game being played. And there's always'* – here he had leaned forward, *close enough that Renshu could smell the garlic on his breath* – '*a point where the game shifts from the pieces on the table, to the people in the room. Pay attention to the edges. If you get too drawn in, you might not notice when the stakes change.*'

'I get it,' Renshu had said. '*Stop while you're ahead, don't be too greedy.*'

'*No. It's not about greed. The important thing is to stop while everyone is playing the same game.*'

Snake. Horse.

Henry can feel a much larger disagreement between Tian and Huang brewing. The earlier conversation will soon be taken up again, now with more liquor, late-night bravado and nostalgia.

Goat.

Both men have made assumptions about Henry's own loyalties, too.

Monkey.

The rules are changing. It's time to stop playing the game.

Rooster.

After the skits, Henry decides, they will go home. He'll point to the late hour and Lily's bedtime, an early start tomorrow or a busy day ahead. He has a litany of good excuses. He will use them all.

Dog.

'I was born in the Year of the Dog,' Lily says.

She's at the podium.

'Let me tell you about people born in the Year of the Dog,' she reads from a piece of paper. 'People born in the Year of the Dog are honest and loyal. They make good friends and partners. Everyone looks to a Dog for advice and help. They love helping others and can sometimes be a bit stubborn.' She puts the paper down. People start to clap.

'Actually,' she says, and the applause stops. Rachel grabs Henry's hand in alarm.

'Actually, I love dogs. So, I'm glad I was born in the Year of the Dog. People talk about favourite kinds of dogs, special breeds and pedigrees. Sometimes people think that purebreds are the best. But I like mongrels better. After all, that's what I am. A Chinese-American mutt. And everyone knows that mutts have the best personalities.'

Lily stops. For a moment, no one says anything. The entire room stares at Lily, and then faces turn towards Henry and Rachel. Henry feels his cheeks burning. Rachel looks pale.

Teacher Li hurries up to the platform.

'Thank you, Lily. Sit down now.' She steers Lily back towards her seat. 'Let's thank all the students for their entertaining and informative speeches.'

Applause scatters through the room, brushing away that blistering silence.

As soon as conversations resume, Henry rises from the table. Rachel and Lily hurry behind. Henry barely stops for long enough for them to grab their coats.

It's time to leave. They won't be back.

Chapter Twenty-five

Los Alamos, New Mexico, January 1982

On the drive home, Lily talks non-stop about the food, the songs and the skits, declaring and redeclaring what was the best part. Her paper lantern rustles as she shifts in the back seat, fogging the window with hot breaths. Her finger squeaks along the glass and she traces out the Chinese characters for 1982, muttering *yi jiu ba er* to herself. Eventually, her murmur fades and is replaced by the quieten, regular breathing of sleep.

Rachel gazes out the window, absorbed in her own thoughts. From time to time, the car floods with light from oncoming traffic.

Henry is glad the party is over. From the moment Edwin Huang grasped his hand, he'd been reminded of the tensions of his graduate school years. The disagreement about the visiting delegations could split into a great divide, and Henry doesn't want to get caught in the middle.

As China normalises and the Taiwanese independence movement gains steam, he fears that he or his ma will somehow get squeezed between these two forces. It's not good that his papers are unclear. It's not good that he never knew what Longwei's connections to the KMT were. The situation, although far away, is still volatile. He fears that all his good fortune is accumulating like a debt, and one day fate will come to collect.

'I think Lily should stop going to the Chinese classes,' Henry says.

'What?' There's a sharp surprise in Rachel's voice.

'I said, we should take Lily out of the Chinese classes.'

'Because of what she said?' Rachel laughs. 'Aw, she's just a kid, and no one—'

'No. She can't go anymore.'

'Oh for goodness' sake, Henry!' Rachel slaps the dashboard.

Lily stirs. Rachel looks over her shoulder, but the child doesn't wake. 'Henry, she loves those classes. Can't you see that? Can't you see how happy it's made her to have something, someone to identify with? Why can't you let her have this one thing?'

A low profile. He needs to have a low profile, and in these classes, Lily sticks out.

'You said yourself that some of the people there weren't very nice,' he starts.

'Some of the people *anywhere* won't be very nice. That's true no matter what language you speak, or what holiday you're celebrating.'

'I heard some of the wives speaking in Chinese in the kitchen,' he explains. 'Rachel, they don't like Lily. They don't like that she's not all Chinese. They—'

'I know, I was there.' She cuts him off. 'I don't need to speak Chinese to understand scorn. Henry' – she leans forward, looking to see that he understands – 'I'm not looking for their approval. They don't speak for everyone, and there were a lot of nice families there. Lily's teacher, Patricia, the other mothers. We all agree the classes are great.'

He drums the steering wheel, trying to think of another way to articulate this feeling of vulnerability.

'Outside, they were talking about the delegation that's coming to visit from the mainland.'

'What does that have to do with anything?'

'So many opinions,' Henry continues, speaking over her. 'One wants to welcome them, another doesn't, another wants to talk politics, another wants to protest. Everyone is an expert.'

'So?'

'With these classes, they know who is in the community. They want to know who stands where.'

'What are you talking about? Who are "they"?' Her voice is rising.

'Shh,' Henry cautions.

'You're being unreasonable.' Her voice drops to a fierce whisper. 'People were talking. So what? They probably won't even remember the conversations tomorrow. Everyone's entitled to their own opinion.'

'Not everyone.'

'Yes, everyone,' she counters. 'Disagreements are allowed. It's a free country, you can say what you want. For God's sake, Henry, stop being so frightened! You're an American citizen.'

He lashes out. 'But my ma isn't!'

'Oh . . .' Rachel's voice changes in the single syllable. 'Oh.' Softer, now.

He turns the car into their drive.

'Lily doesn't need it.' He turns off the ignition and pulls up the safety brake. 'She doesn't need a language that will only take her away from her mother.'

On Monday, Tom Benson stops by Henry's desk.

'I hear you met David Tian this weekend.'

Henry's pulse quickens.

'He's a great guy, isn't he? I thought you two would get along. I don't know too many of the Chinese here, but I imagine it's nice to have someone to talk to.' Henry half acknowledges Benson's remarks. 'Did you know many of the Chinese there?'

Where is this conversation headed?

'Tian introduced me to a few others who went to the same university as I did. Different years, though. Otherwise, no, not really.' Henry shrugs. 'Not too much time to chat. We had to leave early. My daughter was very tired after such an exciting evening. Sweets, firecrackers, lanterns. She wore herself out.'

'Kids.' Benson smiles before continuing. 'So, this delegation of Chinese visitors. Are you going to be part of the welcoming committee? I heard they were looking for translators.'

Henry looks again at his colleague. Beneath Benson's easy manner and generous laugh is an impeccable intellect; insightful and precise. He never says a word more than is necessary.

'Ah, we already bought tickets to visit my wife's family this summer. It turns out it's at the same time as the visit.' Henry is surprised at how easily the excuse forms. It's not a falsehood – it's just not true yet.

'Understood.' Benson nods. 'I've got a team meeting soon. Talk to you later. I'm really pleased you met Tian.'

'Hurry, Mom, we're going to be late!' Lily has her shoes and jacket on and is waiting at the door. 'I don't want to miss anything. Teacher Li said we're learning about the four treasures of Chinese calligraphy. Come on!'

'Lily, come here,' her mom calls from the kitchen.

Lily is apprehensive. Rachel sits at the table. Lily remains standing at the kitchen door. 'What's wrong? Am I in trouble?'

'No, honey, you're not in trouble. But . . .' Rachel hesitates.

'But what?' Alarm bells ring in Lily's head. Something's not right. Her mom looks apologetic.

'Lily, we aren't going to Chinese class today.'

'What?'

'Your dad and I have decided that it's better if you don't go anymore.'

'What? Why?' Lily pauses, taken aback. Then: 'Did I do something wrong?'

'You didn't do anything wrong. We just . . . you, you do so many things, piano, soccer, choir, girl scouts. It's all too much.'

'I'll quit piano and girl scouts. I don't care about those things. I want to learn Chinese! Mom, please?' Lily's voice wavers. 'You can't just take this away for no reason. That's not fair!'

'I'm sorry, Lily, but your father really doesn't think it's a good idea.' Rachel gets up to try and comfort her.

'Is this his idea? Where is he?' Lily looks out the kitchen window and sees her father in the back garden. 'Dad!' she shrieks.

'Lily, don't—' Rachel starts, but Lily has already stormed outside.

Lily bursts out of the back door. Henry squints. Tent caterpillars are crawling all over his cherry tree.

'Why do I have to stop my Chinese classes?' she demands.

'You don't need to know that language,' he says, pulling down another branch and frowning at the wriggling mass of insects.

'But I want to learn it.' Now she is right beside him, breathless with fury.

'No, you don't want to know Chinese.'

'Yes I do! Please, Daddy?'

'No, it's better if you don't. That way, no one can tell you things you don't want to know.' Henry releases the branch and glances at the sky. Storm clouds are building.

'I *want* to know,' she argues. 'I want to speak Chinese. I want to be able to talk more with Nainai. I want to learn about the country you came from.'

The country you came from. It doesn't exist anymore. 'Listen to me.' He turns to face her. 'Don't trust Chinese people. I know. I learned the hard way. Just stay away.'

She comes closer to him and shouts, 'You're not being fair! People are nice there. They're my friends!'

'No!' he thunders. 'They are not your friends! No more classes!'

She recoils as if struck. She looks at him with a hurt he's never seen before. Instead of saying another word, she bites her lip and lifts her chin in defiance, then runs inside.

He reaches up and shakes a branch. Some caterpillars fall to the ground, others still cling to half-eaten leaves. He snaps off the branch. The door opens again. Rachel comes out and walks over to him.

'Can I ask you something?' she says.

He drops the branch and starts stamping on the caterpillar nest.

'What do you want for her?'

'What do you mean?' he asks, without stopping.

'You can forbid the classes, but you can't prevent her questions. She's going to want to know about her heritage someday.'

Henry stares at the house, where they hear Lily pounding out the opening of a Rachmaninoff prelude. It sounds like she is punching the piano.

After a moment, he says, 'I'd rather she be angry with me than know too much that will hurt her. If I told her all she thinks she wants to know, she wouldn't be able to unknow those things.'

A cascade of chords alternates between right and left hands, crashing down the keyboard. Lily has jumped to a loud, fast, angry section, striking extra notes on the edges of each chord.

'Do you remember how, when she was little, there were always things she wanted to do – climb trees with weak branches, jump down from the jungle gym? Dangerous things?'

Rachel gives a slight nod.

'And we said no,' Henry continues. 'Maybe she'd fuss, but eventually, she'd stop. Whatever it was, sooner or later, she'd forget. This is the same. What she wants – what she wants to know – she doesn't need it. She doesn't need to know all that misery, all that sadness. In time, she'll forget she asked.'

'Henry, she's not a small child anymore. I don't think this' – she gestures towards the house – 'is going away once she cries herself to sleep. I'd listen to her while she's still talking to you.'

Henry examines another branch. Where did this damn infestation come from?

'Isn't there something you could do to meet her in the middle?' Rachel suggests. 'Maybe teach her some Chinese yourself? Take her to Taiwan to see your mother?'

Henry shakes his head emphatically. No, he doesn't want Lily to speak the language. And as much as he would like to see his ma, he doesn't want to draw any attention to her or to himself. He can't go back, not now.

'There must be something. You've got to compromise a little. God knows I've learned to compromise in this marriage.'

'What do you mean?' he snaps, turning to face her.

Rachel looks at him in disbelief. 'What do I mean? This' – she gestures around – 'this place, with mothers full of snobbery and small-mindedness, this town with no interesting work for me, this is not my idea of a fulfilling life. I've worked hard, looking for ways to be happy. Have you even noticed?'

Henry winces. *No, not really*, he admits to himself.

'And with these classes, we finally found something that works for both me and Lily. She was thrilled, and I was just starting to make some real friends, and now you've put an end to it.'

'Lily can join a different club. You can find other friends.'

'That's not the point!' Rachel shouts. 'Look, I understand it's a delicate situation and you're concerned for your mother, but we're your family, too. Doesn't our happiness matter to you as well?'

'Of course.' He dismisses her outburst. 'But there's no comparison between the danger of the classes and whether or not you get to have coffee with some kid's mom. Don't you understand how serious this threat is?'

'No,' Rachel says, frustrated and furious. 'No, Henry, I don't understand.'

Henry stares at her. She glares at him, then turns and walks away. He looks down. Caterpillars are crawling all over his boots.

From the house, the piano notes are still stumbling over one another, the music coming undone. An immense dissonance rolls through the air as Lily puts her entire arm down again and again, smearing the keys. The lid of the piano clatters shut, followed by the sound of the stool being knocked over.

She's going to want to know about her heritage someday. Heritage. The word sticks in Henry's mind. Later that afternoon, he goes into his study and opens the dictionary. 'Something that is handed down from the past, a tradition.' What tradition could he pass down? A broken country? Suspicion and betrayal? Miles and miles of misery? Who would leave such a legacy to a child?

Why not give Lily freedom instead? In place of sad stories, Henry will give his daughter a blank page. He cannot imagine a more generous gesture. Never mind that she doesn't want it, cannot understand its value at the moment. In time, she will.

Los Alamos, New Mexico, March 1982

'Can I go the library on my bike? These are due tomorrow.' Lily holds up her library books. Most weekends, she spends a few hours working her way up and down the aisles of the children's section in the library, finding a new stack of stories for the week ahead. She loves how reading is like travelling through space and time. There are so many places she's read about that she'd like to see in real life one day.

Rachel yawns and raises her head from the book she's reading. 'Have you done your homework?'

Lily nods.

'And piano practice?'

'Yes, this morning when you were out walking with Mrs Bennett.'

Rachel knits her brow. Then: 'Wear a jacket, it's chilly. Be back by four o'clock.'

'Thank you!' Lily gives her mom a kiss and hurries out the door.

Lily checks her watch: there's just enough time. She cycles as fast as she can, locks her bike outside the library, and goes in the automatic door. Inside, she slides her books on to the returns desk and heads to the children's section. But today, instead of her usual long, lazy dawdle along the shelves, she grabs two books at random and heads to the check-out desk.

The librarian, Mrs Trujillo, smiles at her as she stamps the books. 'Quick visit, Lily,' she says.

'Uh-huh.' Lily nods.

'These are good ones, you'll have to tell me what you think next time you come.' She hands Lily the books.

'Yes, Mrs Trujillo.'

She runs the few blocks from the library to the community centre and slips into her seat just as Teacher Li is passing around a container with calligraphy brushes. Between each pair of students is an inkstone, a dry stick of ink, and a small bottle of water.

'Lily, welcome!' Teacher Li's voice brightens. 'We've missed you! Never mind, you can catch up. Just follow the others.' She raises her voice to shush some tittering. 'Now, let's remember how we begin to practise Chinese calligraphy. First, you need to sit very evenly and calmly.'

She instructs the class to put their feet flat on the floor and hold their backs straight.

Lily adjusts her posture and copies Teacher Li's instructions, making her hand into a fist to measure the proper distance between the edge of the table and her belly. Teacher Li then tells them to place their arms on the table, close their eyes, and take a few deep breaths, inhaling and exhaling loudly.

Once the lesson begins, Lily is mesmerised. She loves the feel of the inkstick scraping against stone as it mixes with the water. She loves the way the brush drinks the liquid from the dark pool. It feels magical when the brush tip meets the paper and the ink makes its mark. Teacher Li has given them special paper marked with boxes so they can practise their numbers. Lily fills a whole page, then another, and another.

Some of the kids start painting smiley faces. Others use the brushes to paint their fingernails black or trace the bones leading from their knuckles to their wrists. A few water bottles tip over and some of the girls squeal, blaming the boys. Lily ignores them all.

Too soon, the hour is over and Teacher Li is collecting the materials. Lily reluctantly puts her brush in the jar of water to clean it and gets up to leave. It's 3.30 p.m. Plenty of time to get back to the library and cycle home.

She's kneeling to unlock her bike when someone taps her shoulder.

'Where were you?' She turns around. It's Thomas Lu, one of the boys who was messing around during the Chinese lesson.

'Yeah, we thought you weren't coming back,' adds a boy whose name Lily can't remember. Evan? Eric? While she's not certain, she's sure there's a mean gleam in his eye.

Lily frowns at them, looking around for some of the other, nicer kids. She doesn't see anyone.

She doesn't like how Thomas looms over her. She stands.

'Just busy.' She shrugs.

'Oh, I thought you'd be too chicken to show your face again after the New Year's party,' he sneers.

What was wrong with the New Year's party?

'What are you talking about?'

'I'm a mutt, a mixture, a mess-up,' he says, in a high voice. 'I'm Lily and I like the Year of the Dog, because I am one.' He holds his hands up like paws and minces around.

'Shut up!' Lily yells, and pushes him.

'Ooh, watch out, she's gonna fight you,' Eric jeers. He pulls on her backpack straps, and she stumbles.

Now Thomas comes towards her. His face is no longer mocking, but furious.

On another day, she would have been frightened. She would have run away or tried to say sorry. Instead, she regains her footing and stares him in the face.

He's shouting something at her, but she's too angry to listen. She was so happy to be back in the class. She's not going to let these dumb boys ruin it all.

Without thought, she swings her fist and punches him as hard as she can on the nose. There is a crack and her fist throbs from the impact. She pulls her hand back and rubs her knuckles. They feel like they are on fire.

Thomas cries out. His hands have flown up to his face, and blood trickles from his nostrils.

'Shit, man!' Eric squeals. 'Are you okay?'

Lily is shaking and speechless. What has she done? She didn't mean to . . . to what? To hit him? The thing is, she did mean it. She's not sorry. Not one bit.

Thomas is howling, and there's blood all down his T-shirt.

'C'mon, Thomas,' Eric says, pulling his friend away. 'You're going to be in so much trouble,' he says to Lily as they leave.

Lily doesn't care. She looks down at her fist. It's starting to swell, and it's her writing hand. She picks up her backpack and gets on her bike, riding one-handed all the way home.

'Lily! It's nearly four-thirty!'

'I know, I'm sorry I'm a bit late. I got side-tracked.' Lily hides her hand behind her backpack.

'We were worried. You have to keep an eye on the time. How else are we going to trust you?'

'I'll be better next time,' Lily says, and goes upstairs.

In her room, Lily flips through the new library books. They're not very good. Next time, she'll have to leave earlier, so she can choose better ones. When the phone rings, she stiffens and strains to hear her mom's conversation, noting how her tone changes.

'Oh hello, Mrs Lu! How are you?' Rachel sounds pleasant and surprised.

'Really?' Surprised, but not so pleasant.

'Oh, there must be some misunderstanding. She's no longer taking the classes.' Reassuring, like when she knows she's right and is just waiting for the other person to see their error.

'Today? No, she was at the library.' Defensive.

'Oh . . .' Slower. Taken aback.

'Oh, I see.' Deadly calm.

Lily closes her eyes.

'I'm so sorry. We will be speaking with her.'

Lily puts her head in her hands.

'Thank you for letting us know. Bye now.'

Lily counts three seconds before her mom calls for her dad. Then she starts counting again and gets up to twenty before she hears the footsteps coming down the hall.

'Lily.'

'He started it! He pushed me! He was saying awful things!'

'You should have ignored him,' her mom says.

'No! There were two of them, I couldn't. They were being mean. They shouldn't get away with it!'

'They may have been wrong, but violence is not the answer,' Rachel says.

'We're supposed to stand up to bullies!' Lily won't let the argument go.

'Lily, you *broke* his nose!'

Lily giggles. She doesn't mean to, but it escapes her before she can stifle it.

'You weren't even supposed to be there in the first place!' Rachel scolds. 'Never mind the boys' behaviour, you lied to us about where you were going. We trusted you and you went behind our backs. That's what's even worse.'

'I really wanted to go to the classes,' Lily moans.

'You will apologise. You are grounded, for the rest of the school

year. No parties, no friends over, and no bike rides to the library.'
Rachel says this in a tone that says the matter is over.

Lily looks at her dad. He has said nothing the entire time. He just shakes his head in disappointment and leaves the room. Lily feels even worse.

'I just wanted to learn. I just wanted to be a part of something,' she whimpers.

Henry, though not at all pleased with Lily's lying and sneaking around, is secretly delighted that she broke the little shithead's nose. It sounds like he deserved it.

Chapter Twenty-six

Taipei, Taiwan, December 1983

Meilin censors her letters to Renshu. She doesn't tell him what she has come to understand about the Cultural Revolution on the mainland or the White Terror in Taiwan. She doesn't write about the growing Taiwanese pro-democracy movement. She doesn't write anything that could put either of them in harm's way. There are too many busy tongues, envious eyes, grasping fingers. She doesn't tell him how people have been sneaking back to the mainland to look for friends and family. Once passports became available for ROC citizens, people started booking trips to Hong Kong, Singapore or Europe in order to sneak back into China. They all want to find what they left behind so long ago.

She doesn't tell him how Peiwen's neighbour from the juan-cun, Old Wu, returned to Xi'an and found only sadness. Names of places had changed, entire villages had been razed or flooded, records had been lost, ancestral tombs smashed to pieces. Old Wu wept at all the violence done to the living and the dead. Among all the people, he didn't recognise a single face. And what would be the point of telling Renshu about how those who did return and find their loved ones had their hearts broken in ten thousand other ways? Families had been split and spread out across the country. Many discovered that their fathers and mothers had suffered cruel struggle sessions or their brothers and sisters had been summarily executed for having Nationalist ties or overseas relatives. Others told of friends who died from beatings, malnutrition, untreated diseases. And all too often, for the most brilliant intellectuals and artists, suicide or madness had destroyed their light.

Even successful reunions were tainted. There's the story of Madame Zhao, who sold a gold bar and a jade bracelet to buy tickets to Shanghai. She wanted to find her sisters. She found them, but after a joyful homecoming and celebratory meal, suspicion and jealousy crept into the air; they wanted more from her, they didn't believe her when she said that times had been hard in Taipei, too. Their family had been targeted because of the daughter with black connections, the sisters said, and there was no need to name names. There was only ever one daughter who had left China. Madame Zhao cut her trip short and returned to Taipei two weeks early.

Despite these reports, people continue to dream of the mainland. Everyone hopes their situation will be different. But one after another, when they return to Taiwan, no matter what they say, Meilin can tell that China wasn't what they thought it was going to be.

Though stories like this fill her days, from gossip at the market to heartfelt talks over tea, Meilin never mentions a word to Renshu. She only tells him what he needs to know.

What does he need to know?

That she is well (even if she isn't; her eyes bother her, and arthritis makes it too difficult to sew).

That she is safe.

That she has enough.

That she misses him and thinks of his family often.

That she is glad they are healthy and happy.

Los Alamos, New Mexico, March 1984

He notices it at Monday lunchtime.

Yesterday, Rachel and Lily had taken his car down to Santa Fe for an oil change. Afterwards, they were going to go shopping and out for dinner, coming back late. He was already in bed when he had heard the door open, a rustle of bags, murmurs, and finally, quieten.

When Rachel came to the bedroom, he feigned sleep.

Since Lily's stopped going to Chinese classes, Rachel has been colder with him. Lily's initial outrage has morphed into

eye-rolling and shrugs. Rachel assures him this is just the beginning of the teenage years, but he can't shake the feeling that
something has broken between them. Still, he'll accept Rachel's
aloofness and Lily's sulking. Continuing the classes would have
led to greater trouble.

In the morning, he hadn't thought to look at the back of the
car. Lately, he has been leaving early, before Rachel and Lily
are up, before traffic builds. In fact, Henry has adjusted his
entire schedule to be about half an hour ahead of everyone.
Early to start, early to lunch, early to leave. This way, he avoids
unexpected office conversations. With the normalisation of
relations with China, more and more delegations have been
visiting the laboratory. Each visit makes Henry increasingly
nervous. The fewer chances for unstructured discussion with
anyone, the better.

But now, crossing the parking lot, he notices something white
on the back bumper of his car. Has someone marked it? He wonders if it was vandalised in Santa Fe. Many people in town have
requested licence plates that don't say 'Los Alamos County' so
their cars won't be targeted when they go to the artsier city.
Maybe he should get those plates, too. He hastens, sickened by
the sense of a transgression.

But no, it's a bumper sticker. Rachel must have allowed Lily to
put it there. Henry laughs at himself in relief. It's just a string of
teddy bears holding hands, with something written across the
bottom. Even though she should be too old for them, Lily still
loves teddy bears. He draws closer to read the text: 'TEDDY
BEARS OF THE WORLD, UNITE!'

Henry freezes. A communist slogan. He has driven through
town, on to the worksite, behind the fence, and into a classified
area with a communist slogan blaring out from his bumper. It
marks him as a traitor, proclaiming a loyalty to a system that he
has worked his whole life to oppose.

'TEDDY BEARS OF THE WORLD, UNITE!'

How long has it been on the car? Who has seen it? As he
arrived early, it's possible that every single person at work has.
Will he be taken in for questioning? He's desperate to remove

the sticker, but he can't be seen in this parking lot, pulling prop-
aganda off his car. That would incriminate him even more.

He unlocks the door and slides into his seat. Pulling out, he
wonders if it's better to go home on the empty, winding back
roads, or by the main road so he'll get home faster. He opts for
the shorter journey; it's still before the lunchtime rush. The
three-mile drive seems like three hundred. Once home, he backs
the car into the driveway. Turning off the ignition, he leaps out
and rips the sticker from the back of the car.

Putting it straight in the garbage could still be incriminating.
He hurries to his study to get his scissors. He cuts the sticker
into thin ribbons and then cuts the ribbons into tiny pieces. Bits
of bear ears and paws accumulate in a pile, along with capital
letters in cartoonish writing. He slices the exclamation point
into three pieces. He exhales, then realises he needs decoys to
mix in, should anyone piece together enough of the sticker to
figure out what it had said. Frozen peas. He grabs a big bag
from the freezer and empties the peas into an aluminium bowl.
The bowl rings out as each pea hits the surface. Henry starts to
shred the plastic bag.

When the sticker and the frozen-pea bag are a pile of confetti,
he sifts through the scraps. No one would be able to separate
snippets of the Jolly Green Giant from the remains of the communist bumper sticker. He spends the rest of his lunch hour
driving to different trash cans in town, sprinkling a few bits of
confetti in each. He finishes just in time to get back to work.

Back at his desk, Henry's stomach rumbles. He has completely forgotten to eat lunch.

'Where's my bumper sticker?'

Rachel is washing dishes. She shuts off the water and turns to
Lily.

'What?'

'My bumper sticker. The one we got in Santa Fe. It's not on
the car anymore.'

Rachel dries her hands and heads towards the door, Lily
following.

They stand and look at the back of the red Honda Civic. In place of the cheerful line of teddy bears, there is just a rectangular outline of dust.

When Rachel looks away, Lily knows that she knew already.

'You knew, didn't you? Why didn't you tell me? Where is it?'

'Daddy didn't like it.'

'Argh!' Lily exclaims. 'Why?'

'He said it was a communist slogan and people would think he was a communist if he had it on the car.'

'Commu-what? What's that?'

'Communist. Like Russia or China.'

'But he *is* from China. Besides, it was just teddy bears.'

'He's from Taiwan, not China.'

'*You* said he was born in China and grew up in Taiwan.'

'Yes, but we just say he's from Taiwan.'

'Why is he so weird about everything?'

'Careful,' Rachel warns. 'He grew up in really difficult times.'

'But that's not now. That's the past, and in a country thousands of miles away that he likes to pretend doesn't exist. Besides, what does that have to do with a bumper sticker?'

'Lily, stop.' Rachel's voice is hard now. 'You can get another one and put it somewhere else. Drop it.'

'Oh, who cares?' Lily mutters, leaving the room. 'It was just a dumb sticker.'

Later that week, the phone rings and Lily rushes to answer.

'Hello? Hello . . . Oh! *Hen hao, hen hao. Ni hao ma?*'

Henry starts when he hears Lily speaking Chinese.

'Dad, phone!'

Who could it be? Henry isn't expecting a call from his ma. As he takes the phone from Lily, he mouths, 'Nainai?' She shakes her head.

'Hello?' he says in English.

An unfamiliar male voice starts speaking Mandarin. Henry waves Lily away and adjusts the phone, missing the man's name. The caller says he is a graduate from NTU and now studies in America.

'Who is this?' Henry asks, still speaking English.

The man says the surname Yang and continues, saying something about building community. Henry thinks through his friends from graduate school. He can't recall any Yangs. It's hard to concentrate on the man's words. A thought jumps into Henry's mind: could this be related to Lily's bumper sticker?

'How did you get this number?' Henry interrupts.

The caller says something vague about Chinese surnames in the phonebook. Henry realises that the man hasn't said where he is calling from. Now he is asking Henry if he's heard of the pro-democracy movements in Taiwan, asking if Henry was aware of the 'Voice of Taiwan' phone line. Henry doesn't know what the man wants or who he is speaking for. *Don't show your cards when you can't tell what game is being played.*

His hands tremble. 'Not interested!' he shouts into the handset, and hangs up.

When the phone rings again, he doesn't answer.

Lily appears around the corner.

He shakes his head and lets it ring.

The next Saturday afternoon, Henry sits in his study, puzzling over a calculation for work. He hears Rachel's car arrive home, back from dropping Lily off at a friend's. There's the jangle of keys at the door, the rustle of paper bags, and soon her footsteps down the hall. Rachel knocks on the door as she opens it.

'Okay, I've updated the bank, the utilities, the school and my family about our new, unlisted phone number,' she says. 'Lily understands she's only to give it out to friends we know. You've told your mother, right?'

Henry grunts an acknowledgement.

'I've told most of my out-of-town friends, too. Do we need to tell anyone else?'

'No, no one else.'

'What about your friends, Li and Pao? You'll want to call and tell them, right?'

'No, they're big-shot professors now, they have forgotten me.'

'Henry, they're your oldest friends. Don't you want to keep in touch with them?'

Henry shrugs.

'I don't understand you,' Rachel sighs, exasperated. 'You used to enjoy doing things. We used to laugh a lot. We used to talk a lot. Now all you want to do is hide in your study. What happened?'

Henry bristles. 'What's the problem?' he says. 'You have a place to live, plenty of food, a car of your own. I have a good job. Lily is healthy and doing well in school. Why are you complaining?'

'Because you've changed. It's like you've folded in on yourself and you keep me out.'

Henry stares at her.

'There are supposed to be two people in a marriage, you know. But lately it feels like you're not really here, like you want to be invisible. We've been married nearly sixteen years, Henry, and you've become more unknowable, not less. The thing is' – her voice starts to quaver – 'I gave up a hell of a lot to support you and your career. And you don't even seem to care. Do you?'

Henry is stunned. Even if he is locking her out, as she says, it's only to protect her and Lily. He looks back down at his calculation. *Aha!* There's a mistake in his algebra. He picks up his pencil to make the correction.

'Henry! Argh! Forget it – just forget it.'

She stomps out of the study. He hears her pick up her purse and keys and slam the door. The car drives away.

He curses. She's overreacting. He continues to work on his calculation for the rest of the afternoon.

'Where's Mom?'

Lily is standing at his study door. It's sunset, and the golden light makes a halo around her. He must not have heard her come in. It's nearly 6 p.m.

'I don't know. Maybe she went shopping?' he suggests.

Seven p.m. passes, then eight p.m., and Rachel is still not home. Around 8.30 p.m., Henry makes some fried rice with scrambled eggs and tomatoes. Lily stands next to him in the kitchen, rinsing lettuce and chopping carrots for a salad.

When they sit to eat, Lily asks, 'Did you and Mom have a fight or something?'

Henry can't bear to meet Lily's gaze. 'She's just upset,' he tells his plate.

They finish the meal in silence.

In the morning, Rachel still hasn't returned.

'She'll be back,' Henry says.

Lily looks at him mournfully over her bowl of cereal, then continues reading her book. Rachel hates it when Lily reads at the table. They finish breakfast in silence.

'I'm late for the bus,' Lily says, slipping her book in her backpack and getting her coat.

All day at work, Henry is distracted. Where is Rachel? When is she coming back? What if she doesn't? He has never considered that she might actually leave. She'll be back, he reassures himself again. But maybe he should go home early, just in case Rachel's not there and Lily needs someone. Then he remembers that Lily has a key. She has been coming home by herself after school for years. Still, he leaves work a bit early, picking up some supplies for dinner, just in case.

Rachel's car is in the driveway. He hurries into the house. She's sitting at the table. She looks up at him, not smiling.

'Where's Lily?' he asks, putting the groceries down.

'She's at Connie's. She always goes there on Mondays after school.'

'Oh.' Was he aware of that arrangement?

'Henry.'

'Rachel, I'm sorry. I—'

'No. Listen.' Rachel holds up her hand and continues. 'All yesterday and today, I've been walking around Santa Fe, trying to figure out how to fix this – how to fix *us*. And finally, this afternoon, I realised that I can't change you. I don't know how. I can't protect you when I don't even understand what you're so frightened of.

'But Henry, I won't continue like this. I'm sick of trying to give you what you need and having you just shut me out.'

Henry holds his breath. What is she saying?

Tears are in her eyes. She wipes them away and steadies her voice. 'When we first came here, Los Alamos seemed like a good place, but now I just feel trapped. I miss being in a bigger place. I need more than part-time shifts at the public library. It's not enough anymore. I want something more, something different.

'Soon Lily will be in high school, and then college, and what will be left for me? I love being her mom, but I can't only be her mom and your wife. It's not fair to anyone if I keep trying to make you and Lily my everything. I need a life of my own, too, and there's nothing here.'

Is she leaving him? Henry's heart beats faster. What would he do without Rachel?

'I'm going to look for a full-time librarian job down in Santa Fe. I'll keep applying until I find something good. Something challenging, where I can grow, where I can have a profession, not just a job.

'I've thought about this,' she continues. 'Lily's old enough to look after herself after school, and on the days she's involved in activities, she can cycle. She might have to help out around here more, but that will be good for her.'

Henry studies Rachel's face. He can see how much this means to her. There is an intensity, a determination in her that he hasn't seen in a long time.

'We said "for better and for worse" and I won't break those vows, but I won't desert myself either. I need this. For me.'

Henry's so relieved Rachel's not leaving him that he can't stop nodding. He's nearly crying. 'If you want to work in Santa Fe, that's fine. We'll work something out. I'm just glad you came back.' He holds his arms open to embrace her. 'And I'm sorry.'

When the next school year starts, Rachel's new job keeps her in Santa Fe until late most evenings.

Initially, Lily feels a bit lost. It's odd to leave for school in the morning after her mom has already gone to work, and it's odd to come home to a quieten house. Until now, her mom has always been around, taking care of meals, shopping, cleaning up. There are so many things she'd seamlessly handled.

Eventually, Lily grows to like having more responsibility and more independence. She figures out meals for herself and her dad, does some of the shopping, gets around town on her bike. With her free time, once she's done with homework and practising piano, Lily reads. She has outgrown the children's section, and the librarians have introduced her to Jane Austen and the Brontë sisters. She imagines herself growing into someone with Elizabeth Bennet's wit, Jane Eyre's resilience and Catherine Earnshaw's fiery passion.

Her mom is happier, but so busy. Her dad seems to have mellowed, but he's also more withdrawn. On weekends he retreats to his books and music. Lily, too, retreats to reading. It's like the three of them are orbiting around the home they share, but they are no longer in sync.

Lily has stopped asking him about his past. It's not that she doesn't care – more that she's given up. It's easier not to argue with him. Besides, she's got a life of her own. High school is a welcome change from the awkward, gangly middle school years. She loves the buzz of more clubs, more people to meet, more challenging classes. She finds a welcoming group of friends in choir and joins the literary magazine. As long as she keeps her grades up, her parents don't seem to mind her extra activities.

At school, she's run into a few of the kids from the Chinese classes, but that was so long ago, everyone seems to have forgotten about them. She still has the box of Chinese flashcards Nainai brought. Even though she's unsure how to pronounce the words properly, and doesn't know who she'd speak with anyway, they feel like a connection to something important. Occasionally, when her dad gets a blue aerogramme from Taiwan, she'll run her fingers along the thin paper, wishing she could read it. If she asks how Nainai is, he always says something vague and predictable, like: 'She's fine and she hopes you are studying hard.' Someday, Lily thinks, she'll find a way to see Nainai again.

As high school continues, Lily's studies come to have a

two-fold purpose. She works diligently and does well, because this is a part of who she is, who she has always been. But in addition, her academic performance becomes a different way of communicating with her father. She takes advanced sciences and calculus and, whenever she's stuck, she asks him for help. These are questions he answers happily.

Towards the end of her senior year, she is accepted at Rice University in Houston. Lily is thrilled. She wants to create a new sense of self, in a new city, a new state. She's tired of this town where she's lived her whole life. Itchy for experience, she wants to see the world. Rachel's happy because, although Lily will be in another state, it's not too far: just one state over, in Texas.

'Very nice, Little Girl, that's a good engineering school,' Henry says.

Rachel adds: 'Yes, since you've got the ability, you should really look at their engineering programme. If I had the chance to do it again, I'd get a technical degree.'

'Do EE; there are always jobs for electrical engineers. Good security for the future,' her dad says.

But Lily isn't thinking about jobs and marketable degrees. She's mostly looking forward to the adventure of a fresh start. For the rest of the summer, her parents continue encouraging her to major in engineering. It's a topic they seem united on, for once. And because Lily likes most subjects and hates disappointing her parents, it's easy enough to agree.

Los Alamos, New Mexico, June 1989

It's a Saturday afternoon, a week into the summer holidays. A last, long summer at home in Los Alamos before Lily starts at university.

Lily walks into the living room. Her dad is sitting on the floor, playing solitaire, half-watching a TV programme. His hair is thinning and the top of his head is bald. She sits down on the sofa to watch, too.

Suddenly, the show is interrupted. Henry glances up.

The screen shows crowds teeming somewhere at night, fires blazing in the background. A man lies face-down in a cart, his T-shirt stained with blood. A tank stands among smashed barricades before the camera switches to close-ups of people on bicycles. Against the sounds of shouts, sirens and the insistent snapping of gunshot, the announcer reads: *As the world watches and listens in horror, the peaceful pro-democracy movement in China comes to a violent and bloody end, crushed by waves of Chinese military forces. Hundreds of unarmed civilians, hungry for freedom, mowed down in Beijing by gun-firing soldiers.'*

The screen cuts to the broadcasting graphic: 'Special Report – CBS News.'

Henry watches in horror, clutching his unplayed cards in his hand. Lily's chest starts to ache from holding her breath.

In the middle of the night, the announcer continues, tanks had entered Tiananmen Square in Beijing, shooting indiscriminately at the thousands who had gathered in student demonstrations. The footage shows throngs of soldiers in full uniform and green metal helmets fighting civilians. In desperation and defiance, people are throwing bricks or waving sticks and cattle-prods. *'Thousands of combat troops from the People's Liberation Army now occupy Tiananmen Square in Beijing. The students are gone. The air reeks of gunpowder.'*

The report continues, but a curtain comes down over Henry's face. He tosses his cards on the carpet, stands up and shuts off the TV.

'I was watching that!'

He gives her a look she knows means *this isn't up for discussion.* But she's so close to starting life on her own terms, she challenges him anyway.

'Are you just going to turn it off and ignore it? Act like tanks didn't just roll into that crowd to start killing people?'

'You don't know,' he says. 'You don't know anything about this situation. You don't know anything about the people there, and who is seeing what and who is—'

'But what could justify mowing down peaceful protestors? Tanks and troops advancing on university students? Students!

This is wrong. What kind of government does this? Don't you care?'

Lily's questions hang in the air. Neither speaks.

'How can you just turn off the TV?' she says, eventually. 'Don't you want to do something?'

'What can I do?' His hands fly up in a gesture of despair. 'I cannot help them. I cannot even help my own mother. Stay out of it. You don't know the whole story.'

'That's exactly the problem. I don't know the whole story. I don't know your whole story; I don't know *my* whole story. How am I supposed to know who I am if so much is off limits?'

Henry stares at her, shocked. Seeing her father's surprise, Lily continues. The release is overpowering. Now she is shouting and can't stop herself.

'Why do you always push away anything connected to China? Why won't you tell me more about your past? What are you so scared of?'

He looks at her for a long time, not saying a word.

'You don't even know, do you? You've spent all these years being so afraid of everyone and everything, and you can't even give me one good reason why.'

'Okay, okay. I will tell you. What do you want to know?' There is a wild surrender in his eyes and, for an instant, Lily wishes she hadn't asked, fearful of what she has provoked. But she can't loosen her grip on this chance to finally, maybe, understand him.

'Everything. Tell me about China. Your China.'

'My China?' His eyes widen in disbelief, as if she has uttered an impossibility. 'My – I—' he starts, but cannot continue.

He falters and leaves the room.

Back in his study, Henry sits at his desk, shaking. When he closes his eyes, he is bombarded with images of his final days in Shanghai, of suspected Communist sympathisers shot dead in the street, the scramble to get away on the boat.

When Lily looked at him just now, he saw, perhaps for the first time, not the child he has spent so much of his life trying to protect, but a young woman filled with anger and love. He was reminded of his ma's fierceness. *What are you so scared of?* Lily's voice echoes in his head.

Everything. Everything, he wants to say.

He's afraid for Meilin. Any militaristic show of strength by China feels like a threat to Taiwan. This monstrosity at Tiananmen reminds him, yet again, of his ma's vulnerability and his own helplessness. A son is supposed to help his mother, and he can't. Despite his fancy degrees, his American citizenship, his job, all his measures of success, he can't help his ma, and this, he knows in his bones, is an unforgivable failure.

The image of the tanks advancing rolls through his mind. Lily's right, it's not fair, but he still doesn't want her to see it. He doesn't want her to get involved, even from this distance. He doesn't want her to know this can happen to students.

What are you so scared of?

He's afraid for his life here. He reminds himself his job is secure; his papers are fine. But he is still haunted by Longwei's name. He can never know whether or not he's walking on false ground. If unrest simmers in China or Taiwan, he is terrified something from the past will compromise those he loves.

It's not just that he's scared: he's shrinking. Long ago, he split his world into two: Renshu's world, and Henry's. For years, the division has been pulling him apart, stretching him. It's too hard to hold two countries, two dreams. He has already left behind so much of his life as Renshu. He can't risk losing the life, the family, he has built as Henry.

He closes his eyes, puts his head in his hands.

Over the next few weeks, Lily replays the argument over in her head. She keeps returning to the moment when he left the room. *There he goes again, walking away instead of facing things.* Initially, it is her rage, her indignation that drives her back to that moment. She's certain she has a right to know more, and she's furious and frustrated that he still – *still* – is so secretive. She's not a child anymore. What could possibly be so bad?

But eventually, the sharpness of her anger dulls, and she is left with the image of him faltering, shaking his head, and leaving the room. As her fury fades, she starts to see his anguish. He actually can't face those memories. Guilt hits her like a tidal wave. Through all her years of prodding, poking and insisting, never once did it occur to her that he wouldn't tell her his stories because he couldn't.

PART SIX
1989–2000

Chapter Twenty-seven

Houston, Texas, August 1989

Leaving the air-conditioned lobby and going outside is like walking into a wall of searing humidity.

'I will have melted by the time we get to the activities fair,' Lily says, wiping away a layer of sweat that has sprung up while waiting for the rest of her freshmen group to emerge.

They walk over to the Rice University student centre in a gaggle. Everything during Orientation week, or 'O-week', has been done in a gaggle. They toured the campus together, they went out for midnight dessert at House of Pies on Kirby Drive together, they squashed into a bus to Waterworld together, they went over the rules of the Honor Code together. Lily's met so many new people she can't keep names and faces straight.

As overwhelming as it is, it's exciting. Lily's on a high. Though she treasures her friends from home, by the end of high school, she sometimes felt trapped in cliques. Everyone thought they already knew everyone. Now she has a chance to define herself, instead of being defined by people who have known her since middle school, or even preschool.

The courtyard of the centre swarms with students in shorts and T-shirts. Upperclassmen have set up tables representing different clubs, and hand out snacks, free pens and stickers. Powderpuff Touch Football, Campanile Orchestra, The Rice Thresher Newspaper, Campus Crusade, Juggling Club. Lily drifts from table to table. So many groups! A red banner with 'Chinese Student Association' in gold lettering catches Lily's eye. Curious, Lily pauses. Someone hands her a pamphlet with a piece of candy in red foil. 'There's a welcome picnic in a few weeks – join us!' the young woman says. Lily fans herself with the paper, but that only moves the hot air back and forth.

She sees a shady spot on some steps and sits down. The coolness of the concrete is a relief. It's good to get out of the bright glare. She opens the candy and pops it in her mouth. Strawberry, with a soft filling. Her eyes rest on the pamphlet. She decides she'll go to the picnic. No one can tell her not to.

The highlight of life at Rice is her roommate, Anne Lin, a Houston native.

'Do you think they put us together because we're both Chinese?' Lily asked on the first day.

'Are you Chinese?' Anne had said, with a puzzled expression all too familiar to Lily.

'Well, half. My dad is Chinese.'

'Ah, okay, I can see it,' she said, nodding. 'Actually, my family is from Taiwan, not China. What part of China is your Dad from?'

'Umm, I'm not really sure.' Lily reddens, suddenly ashamed. 'But I know he was in Taipei before coming to the US. And my grandma still lives there.'

'Cool. Mine does, too.'

Even though Anne is a pre-med, biology major, they are in a lot of the same classes. Along with all the other science and engineering freshmen, they are taking the big three: calculus, chemistry and physics. She and Anne often study together, comparing notes and doing homework together. Early in the semester, they are up late one night, struggling over some physics questions.

'I wouldn't take this class if I didn't have to. How the hell is knowing about the trajectory of cannon balls going to help me be a better doctor?' Anne grumbles.

'Why do you want to be a doctor?' Lily asks, genuinely curious.

Anne shrugs. 'I dunno. I like bio. It's interesting. I think I'd like to be part of a family practice, helping people, learning about the body. I can see the endpoint. So the tough parts – like physics – are bearable. What about you? Why do you want to be an engineer?'

Lily thinks about it. She's never asked herself this question. 'Actually, I'm not even sure what engineering is.'

Anne laughs out loud. 'What?'

'Well, it's just that, since this year's classes are mostly intro sciences, I'll get a better idea next year when I take the engineering specific courses.'

'I guess that makes sense.' Anne yawns.

As the semester continues, Lily's favourite class is the required humanities course. The professor is funny and energetic, and he draws out interesting insights from every student. Though some science majors complain about the reading, Lily loves that every week brings a new book from a new writer. Small-group discussions are a welcome break from the never-ending homework sets and lab reports of her huge maths and science classes.

At the Chinese Student Association picnic, about twenty students cluster in the shade, which is only slightly cooler than being out in the sun. Most look Asian, but Lily notices a blonde girl in a sundress. In a circle of guys playing hacky sack, a couple look like they might be Hispanic or Indian. It's hard to tell, but on first glance, Lily doesn't see anyone else who looks part Chinese.

The wooden picnic table is laden with food. Someone has brought a Tatung rice cooker, just like her dad's at home. Though most of the food looks unfamiliar, once she starts to fill her plate, traces of memory rise. There are scents that Lily can recall from her dad's late night cooking sprees. There are flavours she recognises from his occasional weekend lunches. Sharp-tasting plum pickles and strange, soft brown mushrooms; slippery, almost rubbery, sea kelp that she chews and chews and then forces herself to swallow, not sure if she's eaten it properly. Crumbly, round pastry cakes with elaborate swirls, stamped with Chinese characters and filled with a slightly sweet, slightly grainy reddish paste. Salads of steamed greens dressed with soy sauce, black sesame seeds and scallions. Most of all, it reminds her of that long-ago summer with Nainai.

Lily lingers near the edge of a group who are swapping stories about Saturday Chinese school. One recalls a calligraphy teacher who would sneak up and snatch the brush from their hands if they were holding it improperly, leaving behind a tell-tale black streak. Another mentions the tedium of having to fill pages and pages each week, practising Chinese characters. They all groan in sympathy. Someone joins the circle, introducing herself as the secretary of the Chinese Student Association. She says her name is Elizabeth, and she's a junior studying pre-med and Asian history. She wanted to come say hello to all the newcomers. When she sees Lily, she pauses and says, 'Nice to see you. Non-Chinese are welcome to our CSA meetings, too.'

'But I am Chinese,' Lily stammers.

Elizabeth raises her eyebrows. 'Really?'

Lily feels herself shrinking. Now the others are looking at her, too.

'Well, half-Chinese. My dad is Chinese,' Lily manages to say, her voice trailing to a whisper.

Elizabeth looks her up and down, nods slowly, then issues a big smile to the group, shepherding in the attention of everyone standing there. 'Like I said, we welcome everyone.' Lily cringes at the saccharine sweetness in Elizabeth's voice. At that moment, someone calls to Elizabeth. 'Ah, duty calls. The president wants to talk.'

An athletic-looking guy with spiky hair and a Houston Rockets T-shirt stands up on one of the benches to get everyone's attention. He introduces himself as Chris Gee, the president, and talks about the club and their many upcoming activities. At the end, he makes a joke peppered with Mandarin. Everyone bursts into laughter. Lily smiles and nods, hoping no one will notice she doesn't understand.

'How was it?' asks Anne, who'd just wrinkled her nose and shaken her head when Lily asked if she wanted to join too.

Lily's not sure what to say. 'Good, I think.'

'You think? Did you like it?'

'It was nice. Lots of good food, lots of interesting people.'

Anne stretches her arms out over her open calculus textbook. 'Glad you had fun. Not for me, though.'

'Why not?'

'I had enough of that stuff when I was a kid. My parents were always dragging me to language lessons, parties, softball games. Whatever the event, it always ended in arguments. At some point,

I realised these were just occasions for moms to compete with other moms, brag about their kids, complain about their husbands, and rehash gossip from Taiwan.'

'Hmm.' Lily nods, wondering what that would have been like.

'Hey, tomorrow night some people are going to Chinese Café in Bellaire. You should come. I'm sure the picnic was nice enough, but Chinese Café is really good.'

'I've never been to a Chinese restaurant.'

'You're kidding. Never?'

'Nope. My mom doesn't like Chinese food. There was only one Chinese restaurant in Los Alamos, and my dad said it was terrible. Then, later, when we stopped talking to other Chinese people, he had even more reasons to stay away.'

'Wait, why did your dad stop talking to other Chinese people?'

'I have no idea, he just did. It was around the same time he made me quit Chinese lessons.'

'What? Your *dad* made you quit Chinese lessons?'

Lily nods.

'I wish my dad would have let me quit. Those classes were tedious.'

'Maybe, but I would have liked to learn the language.'

'Didn't he speak it to you at home?'

'He said it was better if I didn't learn it.'

Anne is thoughtful. 'Does your mom speak Chinese?'

Lily shakes her head.

'Then maybe it was out of respect for her or something.'

Lily laughs, a bit more bitterly than she intended. 'Or something.'

'You could learn now, though, if you wanted. What's stopping you?'

'I don't know,' Lily sighs. 'It would feel weird, almost like a betrayal. He was so against it. Besides, if I couldn't tell him I was learning it, what would be the point? If I couldn't even speak it with him?'

'That's messed up.' Then Anne smiles at Lily. 'If Chinese Café is going to be your first Chinese restaurant, then you're starting with the best. I bet even your dad would like it.'

*

After her initial embarrassment fades, Lily is drawn back to more of the CSA events. She hopes everyone will have forgotten what Elizabeth said. And anyway, it wasn't unkind. It was just an observation. But at each event, whether a movie night, or a festival celebration, or an outing to a Chinese restaurant, instead of making friends and learning about her heritage, she feels more and more out of place.

Towards the end of the semester, the CSA advertises a mid-finals study break. Lily goes along. People crowd around tables, eating platefuls of dumplings and agonising about exams and term papers. When the conversation shifts to scandalous stories about 'Love Boat' summers in Taiwan, trips on which they were meant to be practising Mandarin and appreciating Chinese culture, but instead were learning about sex and alcohol, Lily is uncertain how to react. When they laugh about infuriating their parents by answering Chinese questions in English, Lily has nothing to add.

But then students begin reminiscing about making jiaozi. Lily leans in. She remembers making jiaozi with her nainai. Yet, as they talk, she notices it is something most of them do with their families each Chinese New Year. She feels deflated: her family hasn't celebrated Chinese New Year in ages.

How is it that something she was sure would make her feel complete, would give her a sense of identity, ends up making her feel more alienated than ever?

Ashamed of her inability to relate, she leaves early.

When Lily gets back to the dorm, she flops down on her bed and stares up at the ceiling. 'I keep going to all these events, hoping something will fall into place, and it never happens. I don't fit in. Everyone seems to have had these common experiences that I didn't. Most of the time I don't even know what they are talking about. Have you ever heard of the Love Boat?'

'Oh God.' Anne shakes her head. 'That was so embarrassing. Every summer when we visited my relatives in Taipei, we'd see these Chinese American kids running around in the night markets and at the tourist spots, acting like fools. My aunties were constantly warning us to stay away from them, and clucking that we'd better not become so spoilt and Americanised, too.'

'See, I didn't even know what it was. And everyone else has an opinion about it.'

'But you said that not everyone in the CSA is Chinese, right? What about them?'

'They don't seem to care.' Lily props herself up on one elbow. 'Maybe because it's not part of their heritage. A lot of them are taking Chinese as an elective, or studying Chinese history. It's like they have no personal *shoulds* attached; it's just something they enjoy.'

'Lily, it's a club. If you don't like it, if it's not fun, don't go.'

Lily flops back down again.

'Lily, Lily, Lily. You can't earn your being Chinese or half-Chinese. It's like you're trying to prove something that isn't provable. Whether or not you speak Mandarin fluently, or have visited relatives in Taiwan or Hong Kong every summer since you were three years old, those things don't make you more or less Chinese. You do realise that, don't you?'

Lily doesn't say anything. She knows Anne is right, but hearing it put so plainly stings.

'What's the point in trying to be part of a group if it makes you feel this bad? If you want to know more about Chinese culture, take a class or read some books or something. You don't have to be *grade-A Chinese Student Association Member*.'

Lily swallows a lump in her throat. She feels foolish.

'Hey, if you want some real local culture, come two-stepping tonight. There's a group of us going to Pearland. How many months have you been in Texas and you still haven't gone? Three? That's the real disgrace here.'

'Uh . . .'

'Oh, don't make that face. You have to try it first. C'mon.' She stands over Lily and takes both her hands, pulling her upright. 'I don't suppose you have boots? Never mind, it doesn't matter. Now, what to wear?' Anne opens the closet.

'Can I go in jeans?'

'Jeans are good,' Anne says, rifling through the hangers.

Anne is right. Two-stepping is fun. And she's also right, Lily decides, about the CSA. When Lily comes back for her second semester, she stops trying to figure out how to be Chinese, and just tries to figure out how to be herself. It is easy to pass among the rest of the students as 'vaguely ethnic', which, in a city like Houston, is not uncommon. She puts a distance between herself and her heritage, a distance that slides, eventually, into indifference, so that when asked about her background, Lily will lightly remark, 'Oh, my dad's Chinese,' as if it were his affliction, not hers.

Chapter Twenty-eight

Houston, Texas, August 1990

Sophomore year, classes are more challenging. Lily's in new territory: computational thinking, differential equations, fundamentals of electrical engineering, materials and devices, and engineering lab. Last year's enjoyable humanities courses seem a distant memory. Everything feels so serious now.

Midway through the semester, Lily's up late at the computer lab, trying to finish a lab report that is due in the morning. She has had to wait for a computer to be available and now, at nearly 2 a.m., one is finally free. She just needs to add some data to her report, do the graphs, print it all, and she'll be done. She inserts her floppy disk into the computer and waits. Waits. There's a sinking feeling as the icon for her disk doesn't pop up right away, then an error message saying it's unreadable.

'Argh!' she moans. 'No, no, no, stupid computer!'

'What's wrong?' asks the girl at the computer next to her.

'Stupid computer, stupid disk. I can't get to my file and my report is due in' – Lily looks at the clock – 'exactly seven hours.'

The girl nods sympathetically. 'Go ask Tony,' she points at the help desk. 'He's really good at rescuing files from damaged disks. I don't know how he does it, but he's saved my files before.'

'Right.' Lily jams a straightened paperclip into the hole next to the disk drive to free her disk, then grabs it and hurries over to the help desk, where a guy with curly brown hair is reading a textbook.

'Can you help me? My lab report is due tomorrow and my files are all on this and it says it's damaged and it's my only copy and all my lab partners are asleep and—'

'Whoa, slow down. Here, let me see what I can do,' he says, holding out his hand for the disk.

He inserts it in his computer. She notices he has the long, lanky build of a basketball player.

'What's the file name?'

'Umm . . . circuits lab? Or lab four? I don't know, I just know I had it open this afternoon.'

He types something then shakes his head. 'Hmm . . .' He ejects the disk and inserts it into another computer, types again, leans back.

'Can you see anything?' Lily hops from side to side.

'This may take a while. Why don't you come back in about ten minutes,' he says to the screen. Then he looks up. He has huge hazel-brown eyes. 'What's your name?'

'Lily. Lily Dao.'

'Okay, Lily Dao, see you soon,' he says, turning back to the computer.

'Yeah, okay, sure.' She wanders outside, waits for a few minutes, gets a packet of M&M's from the vending machine, does a few loops around the engineering quad, checks her watch, then goes back. He's reading his book again.

'Did you fix it?'

He nods, reaching over to pick up a new floppy disk.

'Yup, I transferred your files on to a new disk. It'll cost you, though.' He points at a sign reading *New Floppy Disks, $1.50 each*.

She bursts into tears of relief as she counts out the change. 'God, I hate circuits and wires and all that stuff!'

Tony puts the change in the drawer. 'What's your major?' he asks.

'Electrical engineering.'

'Oh, of course.'

Lily sniffs and wipes away her tears. He's really good looking. 'What about you?' she asks.

'Me? I don't hate circuits.'

'No.' Lily laughs. 'No, I meant what's your major?'

He looks around the computer lab. 'Computer science.'

'Oh, of course. And you like it?'

'Why would I study it if I didn't like it? Here.' He hands her the disk.

'Thank you! You're a life-saver!' Lily looks at the clock: nearly 3 a.m. Just enough time to finish and, hopefully, get some sleep.

The next afternoon, she goes back to find Tony. After she turned in her lab report, she thought she'd crash out in bed and sleep all day. Instead, she lay awake, thinking of him, replaying their short conversation. He was funny and kind, and though he probably thinks she's a complete dork, she just wants to see him again.

'Lily Dao,' he says as she walks up. 'Do you have another ailing computer disk?'

'No, but I wanted to thank you for helping me.'

'Just doing my job.' But he gives her a huge grin.

'When you're done, do you want to, I don't know, go for a walk or something?' she blurts. She's never been so bold with a boy before. He raises his eyebrows at her in surprise. Her face feels warm and she tries to backtrack. 'I mean, I'd totally get it if you're busy, and really, I—'

'Yeah.' He nods, a spark of amusement in his eyes. 'Sure, I'd like that. Meet in the quad around four?'

'Great, yes, see you then,' she stammers, blushing, but smiling. She feels like skipping as she goes out the door.

They walk the three-mile outer loop of the campus. Twice.

On the first time around, they tell each other a bit about themselves. He's a senior, heading off to graduate school in the fall. His family is from Pittsburgh. Although you can't tell by his last name, Camberwell, he's Italian, on his mom's side. She's a physician. His dad's a computer engineer.

'So, do you take after your dad, with the computer stuff?' Lily asks.

'Actually, a lot of people say I'm like my grandpa, my mom's dad. When I was a kid, my parents were busy at their jobs, so after school I'd hang out with my grandparents.'

She watches his expression warm with fondness as he tells her about his grandparents' deli, a Pittsburgh community hub. It seems like he was part of a large extended family that included the whole neighbourhood. Maybe this is why he is so easy-going and helpful.

'What about you?' he asks.

She tells him a little about growing up in New Mexico. When he asks about her family, she gives her standard reply about her mom being Caucasian and her dad being Chinese. But soon, they're talking about other things: music, books, places they'd like to travel.

'I better go,' she says, as they finish the second loop. 'I'm going two-stepping with some friends later. Wanna come?'

He recoils in horror. 'No way, no country dancing for me.'

She winces, regretting her impulsiveness.

'But are you free Saturday night?' he asks.

'Where are we going?' she asks, climbing into his car.

'You'll see,' he says and pushes in a cassette tape. They drive out of the Houston city limits to the strains of U2's *The Joshua Tree*.

After about half an hour, they pull up to a country fair. It's charming and hokey. Strings of bare bulbs light up stalls with carnival games and rickety rides. The fair is full of people from the nearby town, out for the night.

'A country fair? How exciting! I've never been to one.'

'What? Did you grow up under a rock or something?' he teases.

'Something like that,' Lily mutters, wishing she had played it cool. 'How did you know about this, anyway?' she asks.

'I didn't. I had something else in mind, but when I saw the lights, I got curious.'

'I like that,' she says.

'What?'

'How you changed plans without even blinking; how when you saw something you liked, you went after it.'

He gives her a look that suggests he's holding back saying something more, then grabs her hand as they walk up to the ticket booth. Delight thrills through her, and she squeezes his fingers. As they wander, enjoying hot dogs and people-watching, Lily watches him, too. She likes the way he tells stories with his hands; the lope of his stride; the way his voice holds laughter just under the surface. When he almost wins a massive stuffed dog at a basketball shoot, he claims he missed the last shot on purpose so they wouldn't have a third wheel for the rest of the evening. 'Right,' Lily says. Later, Lily has her fortune told by Madame Esmeralda, who predicts many adventures, much heartbreak, miles of travel, and finally, true love. Giddy, and slightly rattled by Madame's divinations, Lily points to the Ferris wheel.

Tony grabs her hand and steers her over to the ride.

'Such an amazing night,' she murmurs when they reach the top. She looks back towards the lights of Houston, tentatively leaning into him.

'Mmm . . .' He puts his arm around her shoulder.

What happens next, she wonders? She steals a look at him. He catches her eye and winks.

It's getting late and the crowds are thinning. The fair will be closing soon, but Lily doesn't want the evening to end. Full of candy floss and funnel cake, they head to the car.

Tony turns the key in the ignition. The clock on the dashboard reads 11.30 p.m. 'Tired?' he asks.

'No, not at all,' she says.

'Do you still want to go, then? I did have a plan for our evening, remember?'

'Sure, let's go . . . Um, where?'

He doesn't answer, but hums along to the tape, which is now playing some kind of jazz.

It's nearly midnight when they arrive at a deserted beach in Galveston.

'Come on,' Tony says, and they head to the shoreline. The moonlight illuminates the line between water and sand. The rolling hush of the waves paints a completely different landscape from the glitter of the fair. Lily takes off her sandals, the soft sand sucking at her toes. Further down the beach, flames flicker from a single bonfire. The sea and sky feel open and full of possibility. Suddenly jubilant, Lily starts running along the water's edge and turns a cartwheel. Tony tries, too. Despite his lithe grace when upright and shooting hoops earlier, he flops over, legs flailing at awkward angles. Breathless and laughing, they sit and watch the waves.

Lily notices a glow from the crest of each wave as it crashes. 'What is it?' she asks, mesmerised.

'I don't know, some kind of bioluminescence, maybe?' Tony says.

'Biolumin-what? Nah, it's magic. That's what it is. Magic.'

They keep watching in silence.

'You're right,' Tony says, after a few moments. She feels him turn to look at her and she meets his gaze. 'It is magic.'

He leans in towards her.

'Wait.' Lily scoots away. 'It's . . . I've never—'

'You okay?'

'I've never – I've never kissed anyone,' she admits, feeling foolish.

'Never?' He sounds surprised.

Lily bites her lip, hoping she hasn't blown her chances.

'It's alright. We don't have to do anything, we can just sit,' he says.

'No, no. I want to. I want to kiss you, I've wanted to all night, but now it's this big moment, a moment I've thought about, and I just want it to be special, and it *is* special, but what if' – she knows she's babbling, but she can't stop – 'I bet you've had tons of girlfriends before and—'

'Mmm, not really,' he says. 'No one like you, anyway.'

'How do you mean?' she stops.

'I don't know. You're just – different. In a good way.'

Different, in a good way. She likes that. She turns back to watch the waves again.

'So how's it possible that someone as pretty and funny and sweet as you has never been kissed?' His warmth reassures her.

She sighs. 'Growing up in a small town everyone has known everyone forever. In high school, I had the same kids in all my classes. Like, I always sat between Josh Daniels and Robert Dooley. Sure, we hung out in groups, but I didn't really date. Now that I think about it, kissing any of those guys would be like kissing a brother or something. Ugh.'

He laughs. 'Well, Lily Dao, lucky for us, I'm not your brother.' Tony takes her hand and softly kisses her knuckles, looking up at her.

'No you're not.' She leans in, her lips meeting his.

When Lily's with Tony, she feels like herself. She isn't Lily who is trying too hard to fit in, or Lily, the struggling engineering major, she's just Lily. She didn't know it was possible to feel like this: every single cell alive and singing. A leap of joy when she sees him, a surge of warmth when he holds her hand, a river that carries her away when they kiss, when his fingers find her ribcage, trace her hipbones. When they are together, there is a warm knowing in her palms, in the soles of her feet: *this works, this fits, we are.*

They share impulsive drives to Captain Quackenbush's Intergalactic Café in Austin, just for the coffee milkshakes; walks among alligators at Bayou Bend State park; long Thursday afternoons at the Museum of Fine Arts, when galleries are free and air-conditioned; and cycle rides to the Montrose neighbourhood, ending at Bess's, which, Tony assures Lily, has the best lemonade and chicken-fingers in Houston.

She's drawn to his sense of purpose and confidence in all that he does. As they get to know each other more, she becomes a little envious of his unspoken, unchallenged belief in himself. How is he so sure about what he wants to do with his life? How is he so sure about *everything*? He seems to take for granted an unconditional kind of support from his family that she longs for from her own.

It's not that her parents don't support her, it's just that their expectations are clear: she'll get an engineering degree and a good job. And the more difficult the classes become, the less able she feels to meet this expectation. She's not sure she wants to, either.

The fall semester is drawing to a close. Lily is lying on the floor in her dorm room, listening to a mix tape, when Anne comes in from lectures and flops down on their beanbag chair. She picks up the cassette case and scrutinises it. 'John

Coltrane, followed by R.E.M., followed by Tori Amos, then Gregorian chants, Bob Dylan, Cowboy Junkies, Miles Davis, Leonard Cohen and Chopin? This is the weirdest mix tape I've ever seen.'

'Don't knock it until you've listened to it. It's good stuff. Besides, Tony made it for me.'

'Ah, Tony. You're two little lovebirds, aren't you?' Anne puts the cassette case down, then wrinkles her brow. 'Hey, I hate to sound all mom-like on you, but didn't you say you were going to spend the day studying for finals?'

'I will. Soon . . . Later.'

'Okay, but don't completely lose your head over some guy, however great he may be.'

'Mmm,' Lily turns over on to her stomach, idly opening a textbook.

In the spring, Tony gets accepted to graduate school at Cal Tech. After graduation, he'll be moving to California to do a PhD in computer science.

'Amazing!' Lily cries, hugging him. 'It's like a dream come true, isn't it?'

'Yeah,' he nuzzles her neck. 'It's good, really good.'

Then he looks up, soberly, 'What about us?' he asks, pointing at her, then himself, then back at her again. 'I really like you. I don't want this to end.'

'Me neither,' Lily says.

'We could try long distance,' he says.

'Shh . . .' Lily puts her finger to his lips. 'Let's talk about that later. Right now, let's celebrate.' She removes her finger and replaces it with her lips.

But as the weeks pass, their uncertain future troubles Lily. She likes Tony a lot. Maybe she even loves him, but this feels like too much, too soon. She's never even dated anyone else. Tony doesn't seem to understand her fears. He's used to things working out. Used to having an expectation and being able to meet it. He doesn't question himself, doesn't doubt himself. While initially enormously attractive to Lily, this becomes a sore point, and she slowly starts to pull away.

Distracted, Lily neglects her studies. She had only just squeaked through the fall semester exams without failing, and the spring classes are even more challenging. It's not long before she's lost in lectures and behind on homework. She's dreading finals.

It's a Saturday afternoon in April. Lily sits at her desk, books open in front of her, and stares out the window. It seems everyone else is outside enjoying the spring sunshine. There's a knock at the door, four taps in quick succession. Tony.

'It's open, come in.'

'Are you studying or are you feeling sorry for yourself?'

She shrugs.

'C'mon, come outside. Give the books a rest. How about a short walk?' He massages her shoulders.

She stiffens her shoulders and pulls away. He gives her a look. She knows he's disappointed, but she's so far behind and exams are fast approaching. Concern and annoyance compete in his expression. Concern seems to win out. 'Are you okay? Stressed out?'

'I'm fine,' she mutters. 'It's just a difficult semester. I have to study.'

'You look miserable.'

'I hate engineering,' she says, welling up.

'If you hate it so much, why are you majoring in it?' He looks puzzled.

She shifts in her chair, then picks up a pencil and doodles as she speaks. 'Okay, I don't hate it, exactly, but I guess I don't love it either. Getting an engineering degree is a way of connecting with my dad. We had so many arguments growing up about, well, about everything, and finally it seemed like school was the one thing we could agree on. I was good at it and he liked that I was good at it. So, when I decided to come here, we all agreed I'd study engineering.' She pauses, rubs her eyes with both hands. 'It's not forever, and once I've finished, I'll do something else. It's kind of a peace-keeping. If I get this degree, then he can be proud of me, and then I can go do what I want.' Lily glances at Tony, expecting sympathy, but he looks incredulous.

'That's the stupidest thing I've ever heard you say.'

'What?'

'When we met, practically the first thing you ever said was "I hate circuits", and here you are, miserable, studying electrical engineering, because of some fucked-up idea of being a good daughter.'

Lily draws back as if slapped. Her blood courses in her ears. 'You don't understand,' she counters. 'You accept, you *expect*, that you can do whatever you want.'

Tony throws up his arms in exasperation. 'Why shouldn't I? I've worked hard. I've earned it. I don't owe anything to anyone.'

'Really? Don't you? I guess that's where we're different. It's not just mine, this future. It's my father's, too. This is my way of honouring him. It might be my only way.'

'That's bullshit, Lily! I don't believe you,' he challenges, his voice raised. 'You don't even sound like you believe yourself. You sound like someone saying a line – one she thinks is the right line to say.'

She stares at him. She can't think, doesn't know how to respond.

'You get one life. Why do you want to live it for someone else?'

He shakes his head, fed up. 'I don't want to be with some pale, dutiful version of Lily who is trying too hard to be someone she isn't.'

'You arrogant prick!' she explodes. 'So now you know me better than I know myself? You've known me what, half a year, maybe? There's a lot you don't know about me. Not everyone sees life as clearly as you get to, Tony Camberwell. Why do you think you know who I am, what I want? You barely know me at all.'

Tony's eyes flash furiously. She can see the veins in his neck pulsing. They stare at each other. Then, a coldness. Then, a nod. 'Maybe you're right. I barely know you at all. I thought we had something special, something different, but I was wrong.'

He leaves before she can respond.

She looks down at her chemistry book. The words are blurry, and the paper swells and blisters as tears fall on the page.

You get one life. Why do you want to live it for someone else? Lily doesn't know. She has become so good at following someone else's agenda that she has forgotten her own. Tony's words ring in her ears. Her eyes well up every time she opens a textbook, and studying is impossible. Over the next few weeks, Tony leaves a few messages on the answering machine, asking her to meet up, then one hoping she'll come to graduation, then one last one before he leaves, saying goodbye. She ignores them all.

Chapter Twenty-nine

Houston, Texas, May 1991

Lily's final exams are disastrous. She fails four of her five classes and only just passes the fifth with a D. Academic probation, or possibly suspension, looms. She dreads talking to her parents and she doesn't know what to do. Ashamed, she drags herself to the required meeting with an academic advisor.

Dr Nancy Ashford's office is filled with bookshelves from floor to ceiling. She is an athletic, middle-aged woman with ruddy cheeks, round glasses and curly, unkempt hair. Her demeanour is serious, but kind. By way of introduction, she explains that she trained as a psychologist, and later became interested in academic counselling. She enjoys helping university students learn how to balance a demanding academic atmosphere with their own goals. She says she hopes Lily can use today's meeting to start to unravel what happened this semester. While Dr Ashford is talking, Lily keeps looking behind her at the bookshelves. In addition to many professional titles about higher education and counselling, Lily notices a shelf of novels and poetry: *The Collected Works of Emily Dickinson, Leaves of Grass, The Bell Jar, A Room of One's Own, One Hundred Years of Solitude, The Brothers Karamazov.*

'Lily?'

'Sorry?'

'I asked you what your major is.'

'Oh, um, electrical engineering,' Lily admits.

'Really?' The advisor's voice jumps in surprise. She holds up Lily's transcript.

'I know, I know, I just had a bad term. I got distracted. Next semester will be much better, I'll be more focused.'

'Lily, let me ask you something.' Dr Ashford takes off her

glasses and pinches the bridge of her nose. Her eyes look smaller and vulnerable. 'What interests you?'

Lily freezes. She's not sure how she's supposed to answer this question.

'You say your major is electrical engineering, but those are the classes you failed. We're looking at academic suspension for at least a semester, possibly a year. The thing is, your grades from last year are decent.' She puts her glasses back on and looks again at Lily's transcript. 'In fact, you got As and Bs in your humanities classes. Is it possible you might be better off studying something else?'

'I'm supposed to be an engineer,' Lily starts. Her voice feels weak.

'Supposed to be? Do you want to be?'

Lily is silent.

'I know that the reasons people choose majors can be complex and there are often a lot of factors at play. Considering your transcript, and listening to your voice now, it seems like you're uncertain. I wonder if you might use the time off to distinguish between what you want and what you think you're supposed to want.'

There's a huge lump in Lily's throat. She's not sure if she's being scolded. Tears start to spill, and Lily can't stop them. Dr Ashford pushes a box of tissues over to her. Lily takes one, wipes at her face, and wads the tissue up in her palm. She sniffs and tries to steady her voice. 'So is it for a semester or a year?'

'That's part of what we need to decide today. Typically, it's just a semester, and then you're on probation when you come back. But with engineering, not all the courses are offered every semester. It's tricky if you get out of sequence. Let's talk about this. Are there benefits for you in taking the full year off?'

'Maybe,' Lily says. The idea of time off is appealing.

'And how would you spend the year? Would you go home?'

Lily lets herself think aloud. 'No, not home. I'd stay in Houston. Before this, I already planned to live off-campus next year with friends. We had to sign a year's lease, so a few of us are already staying the summer anyway.'

'And what would you do?'

Lily's eyes rest again on the shelf of novels. 'Read a lot? I used to love reading so much. Work, probably. Definitely. I was going to look for a summer job, so maybe it could be for the year. A break from school and studying.' Her voice feels stronger now. Maybe this is something she wants. 'I used to always be able to earn good grades, but now . . .' Her voice trails off. She looks down at the moist tissue in her palm.

Dr Ashford shuffles through Lily's file again, paging through what must be her high school transcript, original application and letters of recommendation. She studies Lily. 'If you think a year is what you need, I'll support you. We need parental agreement, and then I can start to make some arrangements. Talk to your parents and then come back and let me know what you decide.'

Lily gets up to leave. Her mind is starting to spin with possibilities. What would it feel like to have that much time to figure out what she wants?

'Lily, whatever you decide, make sure it's your decision.'

'Yes. Thank you, Dr Ashford.'

Dr Ashford's suggestion feels right. The more Lily thinks about it, the more certain she is that she needs to stop the input of *shoulds*. The voices of her parents, friends, Tony, professors, are all noise. She needs enough quieten to hear herself.

She works up the courage to call home. She is determined to present her plan to spend the year in Houston, but not at Rice, as a decision, not a question.

After Lily explains, Rachel is, of course, reluctant. 'I don't know, Lily. Maybe you should come home for the autumn and start right back up again in the new year.'

'No, Mom. I want to stay here in Houston. I've already committed to a lease with my friends. I'll find a job to pay my part of the rent. You don't have to support me.'

'Lily, it's really important that you get your degree. A degree is a safeguard. I don't want you ever to be in the position where you have to depend on someone else for your income.'

'I'm not quitting. I'm just taking a year off. Part of it is because

I messed up, and part of it is because I need to figure out why I messed up so badly. Please, I've thought about it carefully and I really need this time.' She can feel herself wavering in her resolve. 'Just one year. Then I promise I'll go back and finish.' She bites her tongue and waits.

She hears her mom's sigh all the way down the phone. 'It sounds like you've decided you're going to do what you're going to do. What do you need from me, from us, then?'

'Your belief. Your trust.'

Los Alamos, New Mexico, May 1991

When Rachel tells Henry Lily's news, he is furious. At first, he is adamant that she go back to school as soon as she can; that she appeal the decision, retake exams, anything to stay on track. But Rachel is firm: he needs to let Lily find her own way. She's got a plan for the year, and they need to give her a chance. When he finally accepts that he can't do anything, he is crushed.

Henry keeps saying, 'I can't believe she's failed, she's dropped out.'

Rachel corrects him. 'She hasn't dropped out. She'll go back. She'll finish. We need to believe in her.'

But Henry feels like he's drowning in shame. He was supposed to carry on the Dao family name – he was the only one of Dao Hongtse's grandchildren who was the son of a son, the only one who survived. And where has he ended up? He has failed as a son. He cannot protect his mother and care for her in her old age. He has failed as a father. His child, his only child, has dropped out of university. Failed! After all that was lost and sacrificed, is this where the Dao family legacy ends?

In all these years, Henry's cherry tree has hardly ever produced much of anything. Each spring, the leaves are stingy and sparse. The harvest is resentful, offering sour, hard fruits that are stolen and then discarded by thieving jays.

After too many seasons of meagre blossom and scant harvests,

Henry chops down his tree. It falls easily, the trunk never having grown thicker than his wrist. He saws it in two, tosses the pieces into his wheelbarrow. He fills in the hole with dirt and abandons it. Not even weeds take root in that stingy soil. A hollow remains: a dry reminder of his orchard that refused to flourish.

Houston, Texas, August 1991

For Lily, the summer had been exhilarating, like she was getting away with something. She'd found a job at a bookstore in a converted theatre and enjoyed the camaraderie she shared with the other booksellers. Reading new releases, chatting with customers and immersing herself in the world of stories reminded her of all the time she'd spent in the library as a child. On the weekends, she and her housemates rode their bikes around the Montrose neighbourhood, up and down Bissonet Avenue, and over to River Oaks to gawk at the big houses. The weeks slipped by in late-night trips for pie or tacos on Kirby Drive, or visits to the Water Wall, where they stared up at sheets of water rushing down, down, down the semi-circular fountain and cooled off in the spray.

But now that the semester has started, Lily's out of sync with her friends. Her summer job at the bookstore has ended, and the days stretch out in front of her. She takes a few different part-time jobs, working retail and waitressing, but the hours are erratic and exhausting. Her pay with tips is just enough to make her share of rent and groceries. People at the tills or putting in orders seem to see right through her.

She misses Tony. She misses the way she felt when she was around him. Sometimes she'll spend an entire day off listening to that mix tape he gave her, again and again, as if the soulful lyrics of Tori Amos or Leonard Cohen could soothe, if not solve, her angst.

But sooner or later, she always finds herself returning to their last argument. It's not just the fact that they broke up that still upsets her; it's the way her sense of identity has been shaken. All through high school and the first year at Rice, she never had to choose between what she liked to do and what she thought she should be doing. There was enough space for both. But now, when she thinks about engineering, she feels overwhelmed and resentful. Tony's words knocked her off a careful tightrope act and she's unable to pick herself back up and continue. She hates that they fought, she hates that she has lost her first love and best friend, and most of all, she hates that he was right.

If you've lived your life mostly in response to someone else's wishes, however well-intentioned, when you first stand on your own two feet, you'll find your legs teeter like a toddler's, your voice wobbles. You have to learn for yourself, by yourself. *How do people know what they want? How do they find their way?* Lily wonders.

She thinks about Anne, who has never seemed to question whether or not she'll eventually become a physician. Sure, there are times when the classes are hard and she bitches about the MCATS as much as anyone else, but her goal is never in doubt.

'Take the year, think about what *you* want,' Dr Ashford had said. 'No one's stopping you from dreaming. Believe in yourself, Lily. Be confident.'

Tony was confident. Smug, even. She was fascinated by his sure-footedness in the world. He always seemed certain that what he had to say was worth saying, and that people would listen. This sure-footedness had to have come from somewhere. Did it come from knowing that the ground beneath his feet was secure? Did it come from knowing his family's story and his place in it? Do you need to know where you're coming from in order to think about where you want to go?

By December, Lily is so fed up with her erratic waitressing jobs that she's trawling the 'Help Wanted' ads again, looking for something more interesting and with a reliable schedule. One of her housemates, Pam, is a Houston native and mentions that the Montessori school where her mom works needs a classroom assistant starting in January. Intrigued, Lily submits an application and goes to the interview.

As soon as she enters the school, something wakes up in Lily.

A sense of excitement. She looks at some of the student projects posted on the walls. Unlike the schoolwork she recalls, these aren't variations on a theme. Every single one is different. Pam's mom explains that part of the philosophy of Montessori learning is that the work is student-motivated. Teachers step in to guide and help develop skills, but the students' own interests are the main drivers of learning. Lily spends the rest of the afternoon talking to teachers and students. She's struck by how passionate they are about learning and how little this feels like school.

Lily leaves that afternoon with a new job and mind brimming with questions: How do people learn best? What is the role of a teacher? A student? A learner? Where will you end up if you let curiosity be your guide?

It's just the job Lily needs. In it, she finds something that makes her feel alive.

The rest of the year passes quickly. As promised, she returns to Rice in the autumn and over the next few years, finishes her degree, not in engineering, but in education.

With a degree in education, she could go anywhere she wishes. Teachers are needed everywhere. Teaching is a job that won't tie her to a particular city, industry or part of the country. She could even go and teach English in another country. Why stay with the known when there's a whole world to explore? As fond as Lily has grown of Houston, she's ready to get away from the sprawl and muggy heat. Still, she has come to love the sense of a city. She relishes the energy of living close to so many people with different outlooks and lives. As she thinks about what's next for her, a conversation with Anne pops up in her memory.

They were sitting on the swing outside their college just before Anne left for medical school in Baltimore.

'I'll miss you! I wonder where I'll be headed next year after I graduate,' Lily mused.

'If you could go anywhere, where would you go?' Anne asked.

'New York City!' Lily blurted, surprising herself.

'What? Really?'

'Yeah. Don't you think there's a romance about it? It's a place to reinvent yourself. What is life, after all, if not a big adventure?'

'That's so cheesy,' Anne had said, forever practical and level-headed.

But one year later, that cheesy answer turns out to be something Lily can't forget. While a teaching degree and a life in New York aren't what she or her parents imagined, once Lily starts thinking about this plan, she can't stop. And she doesn't want to.

New York City. It's where so many stories have begun. It's where her father's US story began. Perhaps it is where her next chapter will, too.

Chapter Thirty

New York City, New York, September 1994

Lily finds a position in a small public magnet school in lower Manhattan, housed in a restructured and divided middle school. Each wing now hosts a smaller school with its own speciality. Her wing's speciality is science, but she teaches Language Arts.

The first year is tough. All day, groups of savvy, boisterous New York City middle-schoolers stream in and out of her classroom. Some days, she collapses at her desk after the last kid leaves, blinking at the strange silence after hours of non-stop noise. The forty-five-minute subway ride back to her Brooklyn apartment passes in a daze as she gears up for an evening of grading and preparing for the next day.

There are times she's so tired and disheartened by the constant grind that she's tempted to quit. Why didn't she stick with her engineering degree? At least circuits don't talk back and throw spitballs.

But deeper down, she knows this is her work to do. She's doing something that she likes, something that matters, and that, one day, she might even be good at. Even when things don't go as planned, which is most of the time, she's still fascinated by how people learn. She feels an instinctive determination to grow her knowledge that she never felt when she was studying engineering.

Her father did eventually accept her decision to forgo engineering, although he still urges her to take computer classes whenever they talk on the phone. Her mom was mostly relieved that Lily finished a degree at all. That Lily now has a profession and is independent has also helped to make peace.

On good days, Lily loves it. She loves the diversity of the student population, seeming to mirror the city itself. She loves the range of backgrounds and experiences they bring to their learning. Many speak languages other than English at home, and many are the first in their families to grow up in the US. A few of the students ask about her background, her last name. On the whole, they are unruffled when she tells them her father is Chinese and her mother is Caucasian. Many of them, too, are mixed race. She has a soft spot for the students who linger at the edges, and tries to find ways to draw them in. Without fail, they each teach her something she hadn't realised. Every student is different, and Lily devotes herself to learning about them, one individual at a time.

By the end of the year, for all the struggles, she's certain she has found her calling.

Summer flies by, and soon Lily is back at work, setting up her classroom. She's just finished stapling last year's short book reviews on to a bulletin board when there's a tap at the door.

An Asian woman she hasn't seen before enters, waving a stapler. 'Hi, do you have any extra staples? I've run out, and I've still got two bulletin boards to go.'

'Sure.' Lily heads over to her desk. 'Are you the new science teacher?' she asks, looking through her drawers.

'Yes, I'm Julie.'

'Julie Zhang?' As the woman nods, Lily continues, 'I saw your name on the new staff list. Welcome, I'm Lily. I teach Language Arts – and I can't find any spare staples. Here, just use mine.' She hands Julie her stapler. 'Is this your first teaching job?'

'No, thank God! The first year is so hard. I taught for a couple of years at a middle school in Queens, then went on maternity leave. When I was getting ready to come back to work, I wanted a smaller school and a part-time position. Isobel seemed enthusiastic and flexible when I interviewed, so I thought, why not? Besides, I like being in Manhattan. What about you? How long have you been teaching?'

'This is my second year. I started here last year. Yeah, Isobel's okay. Supportive, but she also asks for a lot. I guess it's part of being a small school. Don't be surprised if you find yourself doing some odd last-minute covers. But on the whole, the other teachers are great. And the kids – well, brace yourself for a lot of unsolicited opinions about the Yankees. And fart jokes.'

While they've been chatting, Julie's been looking at Lily as if she wants to say something. 'Hey, are you part Chinese?'

Julie's directness is refreshing. Usually, people approach this topic with a sequence of questions that slowly wind from polite formalities to what they really want to know.

'I'm half-Chinese,' Lily replies. 'And you?'

'All Chinese.' The way Julie emphasises the 'all' holds a suggestion of amusement. 'My son, Milo, like you, is half. My husband's family is from Pakistan originally, but they live in the US now. Which side is Chinese?'

'My dad's.'

'I see. Which part of China?'

'You know, I'm not sure.' Instead of feeling defensive or dismissive, Lily is surprised that she wants to say more. 'He was born in China, but he went to Taiwan when he was quite young. Sometime in the 1940s? Maybe during the war? I don't know. He rarely talks about his past. It used to infuriate me, but now I just figure that's the way he is. Everything is vague.'

'I know what you mean.'

This is the first time someone has responded to any of Lily's comments about her dad with something like understanding. It makes her want to keep talking, to know more.

'Julie, did your family go to Taiwan, too?'

'No, they left the mainland, probably around the same time as your dad did, and settled in Hong Kong. That's where I grew up. Do you still have family in Taiwan?'

'My nainai is there. She visited us once when I was little.' Lily pauses, growing thoughtful. 'I loved that visit. She was marvellous. Even though she didn't know much English, I felt like we understood each other. And she could boss my dad around like no one else. I've always wanted to see her again, but for some reason, we never went to Taiwan and she never came back. Like I said, my dad was vague about it. Anyway, what about you? How did you come to be in New York?' Lily asks, partly out of curiosity, partly out of an instinct to turn the spotlight away from her own experience. She's already shared more than she's accustomed to.

Julie explains that her family left Hong Kong for Toronto in 1987 when she was a teenager. Concerned about the upcoming 1997 handover to the PRC, they decided it would be safer to emigrate. She finished high school in Canada and came to NYU for college. 'And here I am,' she concludes, holding her arms out wide.

'Well, I'm glad you're here,' Lily says.

'Thanks, me too. Ah, I'd better go finish my boards.'

About an hour later, Lily is almost done setting up her classroom when Julie comes back, returning the stapler.

'Can I ask you something?'

'Sure.' Lily sits down and gestures for Julie to take a seat, too.

'What was it like to grow up with a mixed-race background?'

The question catches Lily off guard. No one has ever asked her a question like this, as if being mixed race is an interesting experience as opposed to a character defect. While she tries to figure out how to respond, Julie continues.

'My husband and I think a lot about how Milo will learn all his cultures: Chinese, Pakistani, and now, American. I speak to him in Cantonese, my husband speaks to him in Urdu, and we speak to each other mostly in English. What will Milo consider his native language?'

'I don't speak Chinese,' Lily says quietly.

'Oh, I mean, I wonder what the experience of being biracial will be like for him.' Julie clarifies, as if worried that she has somehow offended Lily, 'Will kids pick on him at school? Will he know where he's from? What will he say about his family? How did you handle it?'

'I don't know,' Lily says. 'It wasn't always straightforward. If anything, the Chinese part got lost. Whitewashed?' She gives Julie a half-smile. 'In a way, I think my dad found it too hard to be Chinese and American at the same time, so he let go of being Chinese.'

'How can a person stop being Chinese?' Julie wonders aloud.

'It would have been nice to grow up not seeing myself as two mismatched halves, but as a kind of whole. Maybe Milo will find a way to hold both his Chinese and his Pakistani heritages as precious. He doesn't have to choose between them, does he?'

'True.' Julie muses.

For Lily, it's odd to think about these kinds of questions after so many years. The bitterness and frustration they used to leave behind is gone. In their place, Lily finds a new thoughtfulness.

Julie glances at the clock. 'Hey, I've gotta get going, I need to run some errands. It's been really nice to meet you, Lily. See you on Monday!'

As Lily's second year of teaching progresses, she finds it much easier than the non-stop intensity of the first. While there are still rough days, she doesn't make as many rookie mistakes. She makes new ones, instead. But, she's getting better at thinking on her feet.

One Friday early in the year, when her last lesson ends with ten minutes to spare, Lily knows she needs to come up with something quickly, before chaos breaks out. On her desk is a book of folktales from around the world. She opens to a random page and begins to read aloud a Jamaican story called 'The Race Between Toad and Donkey'. The rustling of papers and shifting of chairs dies down. When she finishes, the class is quieten and there are three minutes left before dismissal. 'Read another?' someone suggests. The next story, 'The King's Son Goes Bear Hunting', is from Finland. She reads that, too, and it ends just as the bell rings.

It feels wonderful to read the stories aloud. The air in the room becomes expansive instead of stuffy and cramped. The following week, she decides to start the day by reading a folktale aloud to her homeroom class, and to end the day with another. For this, even the most fidgety students sit still, spellbound by the feats and foibles of tricksters, rogues, wisemen and fools.

Julie Zhang turns out to be a much-loved teacher and a great friend to Lily. When it's time for the annual parent-teacher conferences, Lily is especially grateful for her presence. During her first year, when the conferences began, the principal, Isobel, had asked Lily if she'd help translate for some of the Chinese families. As much as Lily wanted to help, she'd had to explain that she couldn't. Isobel's surprise, along with that of many parents who met her that evening and started speaking in Chinese, awakened Lily's regret and shame. This year, Isobel asked Julie.

'It's great that you were able to help out with translating,' Lily says to her, when the evening has ended and they are packing up.

'I'm so tired,' Julie says. 'My brain has been running in overdrive, trying to triangulate between parents, teachers and students, sometimes in three languages.'

'Three languages?' Lily asks.

'Cantonese is no problem, but my Mandarin's not that great. There were a couple of times when someone would ask me something in Mandarin, and when I didn't understand, they'd write out the characters. But then, if they used simplified characters, it got even more confusing. So we'd have to go back and forth between Mandarin, Cantonese, various characters and sign language. And then I'd have to relay that all back to the teachers. Phew!'

'Wow. I had no idea.'

'Technically, I probably shouldn't have done any of it. It's not in my contract, and the district has translators. Isobel put me in a tough position. She knew this was coming and she could have planned for it. When I confronted her, she said something about bureaucracy and waiting lists, and besides, it would be better as the kids already knew me.'

'So why did you agree?'

Julie shrugs. 'I know what it's like to be the kid in that situation.'

'Oh.'

'Right, I'm all done here for the night. Let's go,' Julie says, putting on her coat.

As they walk along the streets, Lily mentions that Isobel had asked her to help the previous year. 'It surprised me how terrible it made me feel, not to be able to help.'

'So she just assumed you spoke Chinese?'

'She's not the only one. Sometimes students, parents or even people in the park will just start speaking to me.'

'Did you ever learn any?'

Lily shakes her head. 'Not really.'

'Your dad never spoke it to you?'

'Nah. Maybe it made him too sad. Or maybe he thought he was protecting something, I don't know. He can be irrational about things.'

'Hmm.' Julie nods. After a few minutes, she says, 'You know, our parents' generation went through such hard times. Almost everyone I grew up with in Hong Kong whose parents came from the mainland had really difficult experiences during the war.'

Our parents' generation. Lily has never thought of her father as being part of an entire generation.

'I remember my dad telling a story about walking along the street in China during the Japanese occupation, before they moved to Hong Kong. On the other side of the street, he saw a classmate. Coming down the road was a Japanese soldier. Everyone knew that if you saw a Japanese, you were supposed to bow. But the boy wasn't paying attention, or wasn't quick enough, and was shot dead, right there. It happened so quickly, no one could do anything to stop it. My dad said he and his brother dropped to the ground immediately in case the soldier saw them, too. Luckily, the soldier left them alone, but it was so perilous. You could be killed for the smallest mistake.'

'Wow . . .' Lily says in disbelief, but there's something that's caught her attention: *there are more stories.*

'Those who survived saw things they wish they hadn't, things they'd like to forget. Probably your dad, too.' Julie stops to get out her MetroCard. 'Right. I'll see you tomorrow.'

'See you.' Lily waves, watching her friend hurry down the subway stairs.

On the way home, it occurs to Lily that she knows almost nothing about China's war with Japan or the Chinese Civil War. She doesn't really know why people left China, or where they went, if not to Taiwan. Spooked and then wearied by her father's anxieties, at some point she'd given up. But now Lily's view of her father broadens. She starts looking for stories from her father's generation, from those who stayed in China and from those who left.

She starts with books. She wants to fill her father's silence with the voices of those who needed to tell their stories as much as he needed to forget his. *Wild Swans,* then *Woman Warrior,* then *The Joy Luck Club,* then every novel, biography or memoir she can find. In the Strand bookstore, she is amazed to discover the autobiographies of Han Suyin, a half-Belgian, half-Chinese writer and doctor who lived in China at the same time as her father. Each story has its own shades of sorrow and resilience. Each story fills in one more part of the perplexing puzzle.

Over time, she realises that the more she learns about others' stories, the less she needs to pinpoint her own. Like the final stages of assembling a jigsaw, at some point, she no longer needs the missing pieces to be able to imagine the whole.

Chapter Thirty-one

National Palace Museum, Taipei, February 1997

Her eyes rest on the figure of a monk in the market.

Around him swirl shouts and calls, clanking wagon wheels, squawks and hoots. Smoke permeates the air, layered with the scents of meats and spices. Palanquins pass with curtained windows, tassels jingling, the bearers keeping a quick pace. In another direction, a procession of horsemen and foot soldiers wave banners, proclaiming the arrival of a high official. Porters set down their shoulder poles, baskets heavy with fish on one side and vegetables on the other. Market sellers rush forward to make bargains and carry the fresh goods to their stalls.

The monk's eyes are closed. He does not stir when a coin clinks into his bowl or a dog snuffles at his knee. Nothing shields his bald head from the sun or the rain, the dust or the wind. Even the clumsiest of pickpockets could rob him. But no one does. His stillness transports him somewhere beyond reason and action and language. He trusts that what unfolds has a purpose, even if he cannot see it.

A tour group swarms around Meilin, crowding to see the scroll. The guide calls attention to various details with a long, black pointer, hovering over the red collectors' seals, the fine calligraphy in the codicils, the delicate brushwork and characteristic colours of the period. The tourists snap photos before surging towards the next gallery. A mother holds a toddler in her arms, singing softly as they stroll the length of the scroll. A small group of children darts back and forth, hunting for images of animals: ox, horse, dog, tiger, heron, deer. An older couple lingers, speaking in low voices, leaving long pauses. There is no need for them to rush; they have been picking up and putting down their conversations for years.

The gallery fills and empties, fills and empties.

It's not her scroll, of course.

Each time a new exhibit opens, sharing more of the treasures saved from the mainland, Meilin goes to the Palace Museum, hoping. She has lost count of how many scrolls she has seen. Each is breathtaking. Each is a miracle of survival. And each time, the depth of her disappointment that it's not her scroll still surprises her. Perhaps disappointment is the price of hope. Meilin has learned to welcome the moments when this old sorrow rises and comes near. She clasps it around herself like a shawl, drawing grief ever closer. This sadness, however thin and threadbare, is all that remains to connect her to a boy now grown, a man long dead, a life of waiting and a past slowly fading from sight.

Taipei, Taiwan, March 1997

The days, the years, have passed in a flurry of work and gossip. At Auntie Luo's stall in Yongle fabric market, there is an endless stream of brides choosing silks and satins for special qipaos, newly rich businessmen and women seeking tailored suits. Ever sleeker and more sophisticated, they still come to be measured and fitted. Meilin is cherished for her ability to choose shades and textures that bring out a person's best. She no longer recalls when she shifted from being a customer to working at Auntie Luo's. Like so many things about her life in Taipei, the borders have dissolved with time.

Meilin loves mornings in Dadaocheng, when the streets are quieten and the only people on Dihua Street are the early worshippers travelling to the City God Temple. There is a reassuring rhythm in the shopkeepers' daily rituals. They light red candles for the ancestors, feed goldfish in the ceramic pots that grace their shopfronts, and water the small jungles of potted plants under the eaves. Before the heat and crowds rise, before the shuffle of footfall and squeal of bicycle brakes fill the air, and before sacks of millet, rice and dried mushrooms bulge out into the walkways, she likes to stand and gaze at the red brick arches receding down the arcade. Some mornings, she thinks she can almost glimpse, at the furthest end, a young mother and her boy, walking past the vanishing point.

This morning, she has woken early. Before birdsong. The house is still. The only sounds are her own breathing and the soft clink of porcelain each time she sips her tea and then sets the cup back down on the saucer. If she sits perfectly still, she feels a static silence wrap the house like a blanket.

Outside, buds extend the ends of the branches. Time is rushing, rushing forward. All is growth, hurtling through the days, unfurling a riot of colour and scent, an acceleration of seasons. Wait, she wants to call out. Wait. There is something in her that wants to stay the coming of the light. She yearns to hold the darkness, the stillness, a little longer. Lately, she's been dreaming of frost. It has been decades since she's had a deep winter. She craves the silence of snow, a sleeping season, a rest.

Los Alamos, New Mexico, March 1997

Henry has just arrived home from work. Rachel meets him at the door. She stands and waits as he puts down his bag, unlaces his shoes and puts on slippers. He heads down the corridor into the kitchen, taking off his badge, watch and ring. She follows.

'Henry, listen.'

She hits the 'play' button on the answering machine. In faltering English, a voice that sounds far away says, 'We are look for Dao Renshu.' There is the sound of muffled Chinese in the background. 'For Henry, for Henry. His mother very sick. Come.' The receiver clatters at the other end and is hung up.

Henry's hand flies to his mouth. He sits down, squeezes his eyes shut, pushes his clenched fist against his lips. Rachel takes a seat across the table.

Before the news came, Rachel had been preparing for a national conference for librarians. She was thrilled to be invited and has been looking forward to it for months. She offers to cancel her plans and go with Henry to Taiwan, but he says no. He wants her to go to the conference. He knows how much it means to her. Besides, in Taiwan, she wouldn't know the language, the country. It will be hard enough for him without having to be a tour guide.

She bristles. She doesn't expect him to play tour guide, she just thought he might want support.

He's immediately sorry it came out sounding like that. But he's adamant: he needs to go alone.

After another round of arguing, Rachel reluctantly agrees. She calls Lily to tell her the news.

'Let me speak to him, Mom,' Lily says.

Henry gets on the phone. 'I have to go to Taiwan, Little Girl. Nainai is sick.'

'Dad, I'll come with you. I'll help.'

'No, no, you have work. You concentrate on your life there.'

'It's okay. I have sick leave saved up. This is important, and I'm sure my principal will understand.'

'No, you don't need to come.'

'Yes, I do. I do need to come. She's my nainai.'

He doesn't say anything.

'I'm booking a ticket. I will meet you there. She's my nainai,' she repeats.

He stalls.

The man who spent years arriving early for appointments and meetings, who planned ahead so he wouldn't have to rush, who double-checked, then triple-checked all his calculations – he stalls. He needs to return to Taiwan, he can no longer push aside this past life, but he's drowning in the details. He must ask for time off work, arrange his ticket, update his passport, exchange money, pack. What to bring? How long does he need to stay? Who else is still there? Time is dripping away. He knows she's ill, but surely his ma won't die before saying goodbye. He's doing his best, but there are too many things to do; he's not ready yet. He's not ready.

Henry is becoming Renshu once more. Again, he is overpow-
ered by events and time. He's caught in a desperate rush of
people trying to get on a train or off a boat or into an air-raid
shelter. 'Ma! Ma!' His shouts are lost in a crush of shoulders and
elbows and shoving, no one looking down to see a lost boy. What
will he do if he loses his ma?

Rachel helps. She helps draft his letter to request time off
work, explaining the situation. She helps him pack, sorts his
passport, coordinates tickets with Lily, takes him to the airport.

After he checks in, they sit side-by-side at the gate, facing
forward, waiting for the boarding announcements to begin.

'Henry.' Rachel turns to face him. 'Henry, look at me.'

He turns and she puts both her hands on his shoulders, the
way she used to calm Lily as a toddler. Her face is serious, her
tone determined.

'Henry, whatever happens, know that you've done everything
you could for her, for many years. I'm sure she's proud of you.'

He shifts in his chair. The gate is filling with travellers and
well-wishers. The boarding announcement begins.

'Go on, now. They're calling your row.' She embraces him
tightly, kisses the back of his neck.

'Thank you, Rachel. Thank you.'

Accelerating down the runway, the engines hum then whirr then
roar. Through the soles of his feet, Henry feels vibrations building as the wheels turn faster and faster. He closes his eyes in
anticipation of when the air pressure from beneath the plane's
wings exceeds the pressure from above. This is the exact point of
change. The instant when the force of lift overcomes the force of
gravity and the wheels lose contact with the tarmac, and the
plane leaves the ground.

Taipei, Taiwan, April 1997

Chiang Kai-shek International Airport. Henry disembarks,
fatigued from the overnight flight. He looks at the paper where

Rachel has written Lily's flight details and makes his way to meet her. When she comes through her gate, a pride rises in Henry, surprising him. She's a grown woman. It's not just her stylish haircut and clothes. It's the way she handles herself. She holds her shoulders straight and pulls a small suitcase behind her, scanning the crowd. When she sees him, her face breaks into a huge grin and he glimpses his little girl again. She runs over and hugs him. Though he'd tried to dissuade her from coming, now he's grateful she's here.

Waiting in the customs queue, they chat about their flights. Soon, tiredness overcomes them and they fall silent. Henry almost drifts off before the general shuffle of people shifting bags and cases prods him back to wakefulness. Someone is stamping their passports. They collect their suitcases. When they step outside, they are met with a wave of humidity thick with scents he had forgotten.

He flags down a taxi and hands the driver Meilin's address. It's in a part of Taipei that he's never seen. Looking out the window, Henry recognises nothing as the driver joins a fast-moving river of traffic. Chinese characters overflow the jumble of signs hanging from shopfronts and along the streets. In a chaos of fonts and sizes and styles, his mother tongue surrounds him. Everything resounds with a language and a life he left behind.

Taipei teems with wide roads, an elevated subway, gleaming skyscrapers. Engines roar and horns blare where he remembers bicycle bells and the shouts of hawkers. In the Taipei he knew, the streets were lined with wooden electricity poles, with wires radiating outward, bringing light and power into the buildings below. Now he sees few wires and poles, just buildings that go up and up.

Lily, despite the jet lag and long flight, is wide awake. All this newness pours into her and he sees, once more, the excitement of the child who followed him around in the garden, saying random words in Mandarin. She is transfixed by the city she sees out the window, continually tugging his arm, marvelling at the swarms of motorbikes, tiny streets packed with pedestrians and open shopfronts, ancient temples tucked between modern, multi-storey buildings.

When the taxi drops them off, he pays, awkwardly counting the notes, waving away the change. They get their suitcases and stand side by side. Henry rings the bell and waits.

Down the length of the Dihua Street arcade, he sees children in school uniforms on their way home, swinging their satchels in full loops, trying to rotate them fast enough so their pens and pencils and papers don't fall out at the peak.

'Dao Renshu? Lily?'

For a split second, he thinks it is Peiwen, then he remembers she emigrated years ago. This is Lin-Na, his ma's friend from the fabric markets. She is younger than he imagined, closer to his age than his ma's.

'Yes, yes. You must be Lin-Na. And my ma?'

Her face tells him the news.

'When?'

'Yesterday afternoon. We called your home, but no one was there. We left a message.'

His mind goes blank. It is as if something he has been reaching after for as long as he can remember has slipped away. *Yesterday afternoon.* He closes his eyes and tries to work out where he would have been. He can't. Exhaustion and adrenaline render him helpless.

'Oh! What was I thinking?' Lin-Na berates herself and opens the door wide. 'Come in, come in. Have you eaten?'

They step inside, hoisting their suitcases over the threshold. Scents of camphor and incense cling to the walls.

She gestures at two pairs of clean white slippers next to a line of shoes.

Lin-Na closes the door, then puts her hand on his forearm.

'This way.'

They follow her across a courtyard, past the kitchen. He glances in. All the pots and pans are hung up, the hob is off, the counters are clear. His ma's kitchen was never silent, never still. There were always knives chopping, pots and pans clanging, stews bubbling, doors opening and closing. Her full market basket would be on the table or counter, boasting its radishes, cabbages, long beans, dried mushrooms.

Lin-Na opens a door and motions them inside. There is an empty chair next to the bed. He sits. Lily stands behind him.

Meilin looks tiny. Her hair is white. Lin-Na and her family have bathed and dressed her. She wears a dark blue silk dress with black embroidery. She lies with her hands folded on top of her chest. Her knuckles have grown large with arthritis, curling her fingers. Spread across the bed, near her feet, is a white satin shawl. It is embroidered with coral, violet and golden butterflies that circle colourful peonies. It looks like her own needlework.

What would he have said if he had arrived in time to say good-bye? Would he have confessed his failures: the orchard he never grew, the papers he never fixed, the years he never visited? For a moment, he sifts through memories of movement and uncertainty, the threat of air raids, the cold dread of bombings. Would they have tried to remember something good about those years together, too? In all the sorrow that hardened into numbness, was there ever any grace? He runs his finger along the individual stitches of the peony petals, the butterfly antennae, then softly smooths his mother's hair. He thinks of her hand scroll and her stories. How she always seemed to have just the right one to tell.

A soft touch at his shoulder. Lily. He forgot she was there. She squeezes his arm and he puts his hand atop hers.

The door opens and Lin-Na comes in, bringing another chair. She puts it next to Henry and motions for Lily to sit.

'We loved Ma Mei, too. She was like another mother to me.'

'Another mother?' he echoes.

'I lost mine just after the war.'

He stands and faces Lin-Na. 'I am sorry for your loss.'

'And I am for yours.'

Henry looks down at his ma again. How could such a small woman have carried so much?

Lin-Na crosses the room and opens the top drawer of a dresser.

'There are some papers and belongings she wanted you to have.'

As Henry starts to look through them, the door clicks closed.

On top of a brown folder sits a small red satin purse and an envelope. Inside the purse are two gold bells. The envelope is full of cash. The oldest bills are soft and worn, folding more like fabric than paper. At the front are crisp notes, in larger denominations.

He opens the folder: his Jianguo High School certificate, his Taida diploma, each with a small black-and-white photo of him. A photo of him in the army. A framed photo of her and Longwei, maybe taken in New Park? Longwei wears one of his cream-coloured linen suits. She is in the same dress she wears today. It's difficult, even now, to look at Longwei. He flips the frame over and removes the back. He peels away the cardboard matting. The photo falls to the ground. Picking it up, he notices that stuck on its back is another, smaller photo: a black-and-white snapshot of a couple. The photo is old, the edges are disintegrating. The couple is young. The woman is radiant. She wears a traditional wedding dress and a simple but elegant phoenix coronet. She has Lily's face, Lily's expression of delight. Henry peers at the man's face, eerily like the one on his Taida diploma. It's not him, it can't be him – the style is too old, the clothes are too formal. He would have remembered having a photo taken like this. Then he understands. Hands trembling, he turns the photo over. In his ma's script: *Shui Meilin and Dao Xiaowen, Year of the Republic 22.* He turns it over again and looks into his father's face.

'Are those your parents?' Lily now stands by his side.

He nods, handing Lily the photo.

She studies it. 'They look so young.'

'My father,' he murmurs.

'Do you remember him?' Lily asks.

He shakes his head.

'What do you remember?'

He looks away, into the distance, as if looking into the past. 'A courtyard, with fish in a small pond. A puzzle with monkeys made of some special wood. If you held it one way, there were one hundred monkeys; if you turned it upside down and counted, there were only ninety-nine. I never understood that.' His voice trails off.

He goes back over to Meilin. He leans down to kiss her brow and caress her cheek. Then he stands and puts the small purse with the two gold bells in Lily's hand and folds her fingers around it. He leaves the room.

Lily sits next to Meilin. She can still see her gentleness and beauty, even in her quieten pallor. She wishes there had been more chances to be together. Tears roll down her cheeks. Lily is grateful for the time she spent with her grandmother, however short. She leans forward and whispers, 'Goodbye, Nainai. I love you.'

In the kitchen, Lin-Na is preparing a simple dinner of rice and pork with vegetables. Her husband, Ta-wei, has arrived home and sits, chatting with Henry. Lily joins them at the table. Lily's surprised by how ravenous she feels. She eats, and then can barely keep her eyes open. Lin-Na, Ta-Wei and Henry are in an animated discussion. Lin-Na has a map out and they are pointing at places, agreeing, interrupting, talking over one another. It is so strange to hear her dad speaking Chinese. He spoke it so rarely when she was growing up. He is far more talkative than she ever recalls.

'Go to sleep,' he says, when he catches her yawning. 'It was a big trip. Tomorrow, you see some of Taipei.'

In the morning, while Lily is still asleep, Henry tries to make arrangements for Meilin's cremation. But it's difficult to know where to start, who to call, what to do. After too many frustrating phone calls, he gives up for the day, overwhelmed.

Later, they head out into the city.

Walking in Taipei feels like trespassing in someone else's memory. He cannot find the city he once knew. It is buried, not under ruins, like the cities he remembers in China, but under prosperity, which is its own kind of forgetfulness.

The streets that he assumed would bring him to the juancun lead him to a new park and high-rise apartments. He thought this was how he walked home from Jianguo, but maybe he is mistaken. There is no trace of the old red-and-white gates leading to tiny alleys. Down a different road, he sees crumbling grey concrete walls, water-stained from decades of typhoons. There are dilapidated buildings with rusty corrugated metal roofs. Long abandoned, the remaining walls are tagged with faded graffiti. Much of the area is surrounded by cheap fencing in a half-hearted attempt to prevent vandalism.

Switching gears, he tries to find one of the dormitories where he stayed as a student. They start walking, but when they reach the end of the street, he hasn't seen the building. He figures he must have been distracted. He turns back and walks the length of the street again, but still somehow misses it. The third time, he keeps track of the numbers as he goes. When he comes close, he slows down, stunned to discover that a shop-front now stretches across the expanse where his dorm used to be.

'Let's go and see NTU,' he says.

Along the way, they walk through a park. Da'an Forest Park. *This wasn't a park*, he thinks, as they pass people out exercising. They pass a fruit seller with a pyramid of pears displayed on his cart.

'Oh, Dad, that reminds me of a story,' Lily says. 'At school, I read my students folktales from around the world every morning to start the day. One of my favourites is from China. It's about a pear tree.'

'Hmm?' Henry is only half listening. He is trying to remember what this area used to look like.

'Here, I'll tell it to you. Once, there was a farmer who had a bumper harvest of snow pears . . .' The line catches in his ear. As she tells the story of the monk and the pear, his whole body responds. His eyes fill. He can almost taste the pears he found in the hills above Yichang. When she finishes the final line, 'And the monk bowed, saying "I only needed one seed,"' Henry is overcome. He takes out a handkerchief and wipes his brow and eyes. All he can manage to say is: 'Very nice, Little Girl. Yes, I know that story. I haven't heard it in a long time.'

'Really? Who told it to you?'

'My ma. She loved stories.'

'Do you remember other stories she told you?'

'Maybe,' he says. 'I'll think about it.'

They turn down smaller streets, and the roar of traffic subsides, replaced by a hum of street sellers and bicycle bells. People sit outside their homes on ramshackle chairs, fanning themselves in the spring air. Laundry hangs from iron window grilles. A collection of potted plants makes a green oasis down a quieten lane. Near a small covered market, they pass a butcher's stall with hog legs laid out on ice. A woman kneels and swings a cleaver at a cut of meat on a wooden block. The blade slices through the bone with a single thwack.

This is more like the city he remembers. Soon they are at the Taida campus. The Royal Palm Boulevard is as grand as ever. They walk by the library, stand under the Fu Bell, watch students wobble by on bicycles. Best of all, the azaleas are in full bloom, reassuring him that not all his memories have disappeared.

As the days pass, Lily wavers between the sensation of being in a completely foreign place and an uncanny sense of return. There are tastes that awaken memories of Nainai's visit. The crumbly, nutty sesame cookies; the cool, mellow sweetness of grass jelly and red beans on shaved ice; the sour, sharp tiny green pickled vegetables whose names she never knew. It is as if something deeper than language welcomes her home.

At the same time, she is surrounded by new sights to marvel at, to remark on. A family of four darting through the busy Taipei streets on a single motor scooter. The theatre of haggling and bargaining in the open markets. The clever ways vendors tie packages with a single length of string to make it easy to carry them without a bag.

It's disorientating not to be able to read the text wherever she looks, or eavesdrop on the conversations that flow past her ears. Because she can't understand the language, she tries guessing the relationships between people in restaurants and shops. She has never been among so many Chinese and Taiwanese. She has never been in a place with so few Westerners. In some ways, Lily has never felt so out of context.

At the same time, a context for her father and his ways has jumped into relief. She sees him in the ways the people talk, their gestures, the cadence in their speech. When they are at a restaurant and he chats with the waiter, pointing at the menu, asking questions, coming to agreement, laughing, she watches. This man is totally different to the inscrutable, unhappy, often unreasonable father she recalls from childhood.

Her father, blurry for years, has come into focus.

It has been nearly a week. Henry must make arrangements for Meilin. He wakes early one morning and resolves to ask Lin-Na for help.

In the kitchen waiting for Lin-Na, he selects a saucer, cup and lid, and scans the shelves for tea. While the kettle boils, he opens a tin of Alishan oolong, bringing it up to his nose. Maybe here, in this roasty, verdant scent, he can find his ma. He pours a small handful of the rolled-up leaves into the cup and waits. He catches the kettle before it shrieks, pours the water over the leaves and watches them start to open, to stretch and bleed their colour into the water. Replacing the lid to let it steep, he finds the words he needs.

When she comes in the kitchen, Lin-Na listens without comment, occasionally sniffing or wiping a corner of her eye.

'Of course. I will do as you ask, Renshu. It is an honour and a duty to help Ma Mei travel to the afterlife.'

He nods his gratefulness. He can see her sorrow, and when Lin-Na says that his ma was happy here, he believes her.

In the late afternoon, Henry takes Lily to Longshan Temple. The temple is a marker, a reassurance that this is the city where he and his ma found stability, where their wandering ended.

Inside, they buy two large red candles and six incense sticks. They pass tables overflowing with elaborate flower displays, and plates of fruit, candy and cookies left for various deities. Students write entreaties for success on exams, leaving them alongside offerings of fruit and paper money. The rhythmic clanging of cymbals and bells cuts through the steady chant of afternoon prayers.

Lily follows her father to the back of the temple, passing a cluster of people throwing oracle shells. He hands her the candles. After she lights each from an existing flame, he puts one candle in each burner. They watch in silence as pools of wax glisten and then harden at the base of the burner. They stay until the attendant collects their candles, along with those of others who have come to pray. The attendant handles each candle tenderly. Without extinguishing any flames, she creates a new bundle of the freshly lit candles, then balances it on one of the stands. More people come with fresh candles to light. There is a ceaselessness in the lighting, burning, collecting and extinguishing of flames.

Together, they continue through the temple, looping back to the golden incense burner at the front. Here he gives Lily three of the incense sticks. He lights the other three and stands, holding them in front of his body, at shoulder height, hands together, head bowed. Lily does the same.

Dao Renshu allows himself to remember, to feel. The memories come out of order, like a box of photographs spilled on the floor. The boat to Taiwan, sailing paper boats with his yeye, his time in the military, Chongqing smouldering, ships on the river, Liling, getting his letter from Northwestern, hiding in the Great Tunnel, his ma's smashed family tombs.

Grief, finally acknowledged, convulses through him. Longing, regret, loss all come in waves. A wail, more powerful than he has ever known, rises from his lungs. There is something intoxicating in the wild release. When it ceases, he is spent, but lighter somehow, having put down a burden he didn't know he was carrying.

When he opens his eyes, Lily is still there, by his side. Their incense sticks have only an inch left to burn. They release them into the sand and ash at the bottom of the burner. The temple has changed pace. The wave of afternoon worshippers has come and gone. Longer silences stretch out between periods of chanting. The echo of oracle shells dies out before the next clatter of divination breaks the air.

They watch the final wisps of incense smoke rise and twist. A crescent moon glows behind the temple's colourful dragons and phoenixes, flourishing into the purple evening sky with their feathers and scales, talons and tongues.

That night, they sit and drink tea in Lin-Na's kitchen after everyone else has gone to bed. Lily lifts her saucer to admire the delicate blue-and-white peony design on the sides of her cup.

'*Gaiwan*,' he says.

'*Gaiwan*?'

'Yes. It means "lidded bowl". The saucer is for the earth, the cup for man, and the top for the sky.'

'It's so beautiful.' She puts the saucer back down and lifts the lid, checking the tea leaves and inhaling the grassy scent.

Unbidden, he turns to her and starts speaking. 'My grand-father, Dao Hongtse, had three wives.'

She looks at him, purses her lips, but doesn't say a word. She reaches over to her bag and takes out a notebook and pen. *Dao Hongtse had three wives*, she writes.

Lily stays silent, hoping he'll continue, not wanting to scare away the stories she's waited her whole life to hear.

He looks over at what she's written, takes a long sip of tea, and continues.

'The family had a shop in Changsha, in Hunan Province,' he continues. And slowly, slowly, he begins to tell what he remembers. The room fills with the names of cities she has never heard of, relatives she will never meet. On the pages of her notebook, she tries to catch all the scraps of memory that fall from his lips: the kerosene shop, a treasured cousin, a park with a peacock, a hand scroll, his ma's stories. He says that when the Japanese came, the family fled in the night. He says they walked and walked, all around China. Sometimes they rode on carts. He doesn't know who pulled them, or why. He never will. He says they crowded on to packed trains and rode them north. He says the Japanese, or maybe the Nationalists, blew up the railroads and bridges. He doesn't know who did it; only that then they got out of the trains and kept walking. He says they took steamboats up and down the Yangtze River. The river was clogged with sunken gunboats and treacherous rapids.

They met people who were kind-hearted and hard-hearted. They moved from city to city. All kinds of shelters, all kinds of jobs for his ma. They learned how to become invisible.

When the Japanese stopped, the Communists started. And the misery began all over again.

When he finishes, they sit quietly for a few moments. It is late. In his eyes, it is as if she can see the distance, the weariness. He arranges the teacups on the tray and stands.

He takes a big breath. 'Chinese history is sad, Little Girl,' he says, shaking his head. He picks up the tray and leaves the room.

Lily looks over her notes. She runs a finger down each page, feeling the imprint of the ballpoint pen. She's not sure how to begin to process what has just happened, but she knows that her father has finally given her a most precious thing: her heritage.

After seven days comes the cremation. There are no family tombs. There is no land Meilin calls her own. They entrust the urn of Meilin's remains to Lin-Na, who promises she will inter them with her own ancestors, further down the island in Chiayi.

On the last day of their visit, Henry takes Lily to Keelung, the point of his and Meilin's first arrival to this island. They go to Zhongzheng Park and climb up past the playing fields, past the Ghost Festival Museum, to the highest part of the mountain. At the top stands a huge white statue.

'Who is it?' Lily asks.

'Guanyin, the goddess of mercy, kindness and compassion.'

They both consider the statue's serene expression, her flowing robes, her air of calm wisdom. After some time, Lily says, 'This feels like the right way to say goodbye to Nainai.'

'Hmm,' Henry agrees.

They take in the view. Below lies the city of Keelung. Henry gazes at the harbour, the ships in port, the mountains – and somewhere, beyond where the water and the horizon meet, China.

Just before they head back down, Henry glances up at the statue again. In her hand, Guanyin holds a rolled-up scroll.

Chapter Thirty-two

Los Alamos, New Mexico, June 1997

The Cold War is thawing. With fewer contracts for major defence projects, the Laboratory starts making offers for early retirement. For nearly twenty-nine years, Henry has worked hard, always producing research of high calibre and at a steady pace. While he has never been completely at ease in Los Alamos, the past few years have felt increasingly restless.

His long-time colleague Tom Benson has recently retired, and Henry misses his friend's intelligence and candour. Occasionally, Benson still comes by the office to consult, but it is less and less often. The last time, just as Benson was leaving, he asked if Henry had had any troubles with his security clearance renewal. Surprised at the question, Henry had said he hadn't. Benson then explained that his neighbour David Tian mentioned that some of the other Chinese scientists seemed to be having minor difficulties. The procedure involved a lot more questions than the last time. When Henry didn't say anything, Benson wondered aloud if the delays could be related to the espionage case against Peter Lee. Did Henry know him? No, Henry didn't know him. He was quick to add that, except for that one New Year's party years ago, he hasn't been involved with the Chinese community at all. It's been easier that way. Benson had nodded and given his characteristic hum of approval and agreement.

Now, considering the terms of the retirement offer, Henry recalls this conversation. Without Benson around, Henry has found it so much harder to navigate the unspoken understandings in his research group. For years, he'd relied on Benson's cues and respected his perspective. Several of Henry's major projects are drawing to an end and continued funding looks slim. *It was a good job*, he thinks to himself. Then: *It was just a job. And now, maybe it's time to let someone else do it.*

When he brings it up with Rachel, he is surprised by how quickly she agrees. Despite her many friends, she has never loved this town. She's ready for a change. They decide to put their house on the market. It is one of the easiest conversations he's had with Rachel in years.

Henry starts packing for the move. On the top shelf of his bookcase, he finds his brushes, his inkstone, the nub of an inkstick. The bamboo of the brushes feels delicate; their hairs are split and dry. The inkstone cradles dust in its well. He rubs the surface to make it shine again, but dust remains in the crevices. His Chinese–English dictionary lies beside them. He reaches for the dictionary, feeling the heft of it in his palm. It has been used as a doorstop, a paperweight and an impromptu bookend. Its pages have yellowed, the glue on the binding is dry and cracked. Flakes of paste fall into his hands when he opens it. Tenuous, brittle threads connect the covers to the body of the book.

He thinks of all those blue aerogrammes going back and forth from New Mexico to Taiwan. How many hours did he spend trying to arrange his American life into neat vertical columns, searching his dictionary for characters that almost, but never quite, explained this world? Now, when he uses his dictionary, he travels in the opposite direction, looking up a character that he cannot remember, or searching for a word he learned in English and never knew in Chinese.

In all these years of building his English, his Chinese has leaked away. There are phrases he no longer utters, syllables his tongue no longer pronounces, entire lexicons he no longer speaks. A language may be infinite, but a person is not. Henry cannot hold on to every word, thought, idea, memory. He would be so full that he wouldn't be able to move.

He flips through the pages, at first idly, and then with a sense of purpose. He stops when he reaches the listing for 修, to repair, to regulate, to cultivate. He runs his finger down the column of related character combinations. There are so many concepts built with the character of 修: to build a house, to study at school, to prune trees, to renew a former friendship, to repair a boat, to build bridges, to cultivate virtue, to cultivate the heart. Here he pauses. 修心, to cultivate the heart. He closes the dictionary. He traces the characters on his palm. For the first time in years, his heart feels light.

Within a few months, Henry and Rachel move to Albuquerque. He leaves behind the daily bitterness of doing someone else's work and never looks back.

The city offers book groups, museums, coffee shops, concerts. Rachel delights in making new friends, drawing a wider circle of acquaintances. She joins the Newcomers' Club. It has been years since she has been a newcomer anywhere. Best of all, she is able to find a position working at the University Fine Arts and Design Library, specialising in their music collections.

Albuquerque is diverse enough that difference is common-place. A passer-by, if paying attention, might guess that Henry is Hispanic, Navajo, Chinese, Japanese, Peruvian, or possibly Tibetan. But people generally don't ask, and he doesn't explain. Instead, he comes and goes from the library and Chinese grocery store without being recognised. He no longer needs to scan the street, ready to duck into the hardware store or bank if he sees gossipy Mrs Riordan bustling down the pavement.

At the new house, Henry lets the garden grow wild. The sage-brush, yucca and tumbleweeds take dominion over the sandy soil. *Xeriscape gardening,* Rachel calls it. When Rachel brings home a small bag of peaches from the farmer's market, their sweetness reminds Henry of something that he can't put into words. He eats all the peaches in a single afternoon, tossing the stones into the backyard.

A glorious Indian summer stretches into early October, baking the ground. The cottonwoods and aspens shimmer bright gold on the eastern slopes of the Sandias. On its heels comes a hard winter. From their new house, Rachel and Henry watch snow-storms come and go, hiding then revealing the mountains.

A sleep of snow covers the garden. Somewhere underneath, white tendrils start to reach through the dark.

The month of March warms and swells the ground. In the back garden, small shoots burst through the topsoil.

No one watches and waters. No protective hands whisk away the curious ants climbing up and down the unseen seedlings. Unsheltered, close and huddled together, as if to promise one another refuge, they share shadows to block the sun's glare. In defiance of April's furious winds, heartiness rises up the centre of their tiny trunks.

In early May, Henry pushes his wheelbarrow around the yard, filling it with dry cottonwood leaves that have blown into the garden. Behind a knot of tumbleweeds, he notices green growth. He untangles the weeds and stops.

Trees! Not sticks in the mud, but sturdy little saplings. He kneels to look and gently touches each branch, each shoot. The sticky buds leave sap on his fingertips. Each leaf is a green banner flying in the bright spring air. Unmistakable. The beginnings of an orchard.

'Rachel,' he says under his breath, then louder: 'Rachel, Rachel!' He runs into the house.

Together, they clear away the remaining leaves, dry grass and weeds. They don't discuss the miracle. Instead, they do the next thing necessary to help the trees grow. Henry gets his shovel and digs eight holes, evenly spaced and not too deep, with just enough room between them to allow for hope. When Rachel goes to the garden centre and comes home with bags of enriched soil, compost and mulch, Henry doesn't say a word. Together, they uproot the baby trees, and separate the clumps of roots and dirt. They lower the seedlings into the holes and shovel in compost and enriched soil. Rachel heaps mulch at the base of each tree and Henry waters them generously.

New York City, New York, September 1998

Four years in, and Lily has finally hit her stride in her classroom. This year is the best so far. She has found a balance of caring for her students and for herself. She's finally experienced and confident enough that she doesn't have to spend so much time preparing and marking her students' work.

When she came back from her trip to Taipei, the uneasiness that she had felt about herself for as long as she could remember started to fade. There wasn't a conscious laying to rest of those worries; it was more of a gradual shift into a peacefulness she hadn't ever known, a calming of an ingrained restlessness. Although her father has never mentioned his stories again, or even talked much about the trip, he seems much happier, too.

There's a circle of teacher friends she hangs out with, and she enjoys commiserating and celebrating classroom successes with them. But Lily's ready to have a social life outside of work. There have been a few guys she's seen on and off, but nothing serious. They are nice enough, but at some point, she usually starts daydreaming about how things will be when the relationship is all over, when she'll have her space to herself again.

On a whim, she decides to go to a Rice alumni night at a bar in Midtown. She's seen announcements come through the newsletter every so often, but until now, she's just been too busy.

She fusses while getting ready. It's been such a long time since she's gone to an event where she doesn't know anyone. What to wear? Not teacher clothes. Jeans? That doesn't seem right. She finally chooses a navy blue tunic dress and black leggings. Comfortable flats. Always.

When she arrives, she scans the room. A few faces are vaguely familiar, but there are none she can place. There are a lot of older alumni in suits and ties; they look like Wall Street people. Nobody ever wore a suit at Rice. It was all about shorts and T-shirts then. She doubts she'd recognise anyone wearing a suit now.

'Lily Dao?' The voice is filled with warmth and surprise.

She turns. 'Tony!' He's still got those unruly curls. His hairline is a bit higher and there are a few smile wrinkles near his eyes. He's not wearing a suit and tie. His look is classy and relaxed. Khakis, a maroon sweater, a nice collared shirt. It hadn't occurred to her that she might run into him.

He grins. 'At a loss for words?'

'I didn't know you were in the area.'

He smiles. 'I guess that's the point of these alumni things, right? Find out who's around.'

He really is still very handsome, Lily thinks.

'A drink?'

'Sorry?'

'Can I get you a drink?' he asks.

'Oh, yes, that would be great. Um . . . yeah, anything.'

He raises his eyebrows at her.

'Red wine,' she says, and is relieved when he doesn't ask for any more details.

While he's getting the drink, she looks around the bar. She still doesn't see anyone else she recognises. Tony comes back with a pint of Guinness for himself and a glass of wine for her. 'California Cabernet Sauvignon,' he says, handing it to her.

She nods and takes a sip. 'Very nice,' she says, hoping that's enough.

'So, Lily Dao, what are you doing in New York?'

'You don't have to keep saying my whole name. You can just call me Lily,' she says.

'Okay, Lily, what are you doing in New York?'

She likes hearing him say her name.

'I'm a teacher. I'm teaching middle school English at a magnet school.'

'An English teacher? Fabulous! That seems . . . just right.' He smiles. 'Do you like it?'

'Yes, a lot. It's hard work, but there's nothing else I'd rather be doing.' As she's saying this, she realises how much she means it. 'And you?'

'Ah, I'm doing a post-doc at Columbia.'

'Wow. Very impressive. Do you like it?'

He nods.

She nods. Sips the wine. Silence.

'Hey,' his voice softens. 'I seem to recall our last conversation wasn't – how can I put this? It wasn't exactly—'

Lily shakes her head. 'It wasn't great. That was ages ago. I had some growing up to do.'

'We both did. For a long time, I regretted what I said. I was sorry for how things ended.' He pauses, until she looks up. 'I *am* sorry for how things ended,' he says. His face is serious and open. There is a vulnerability in his eyes and he swallows, watching her.

'Me too,' she says, softly.

He glances around. The bar is filling up. He must be looking for other people to talk with. Soon he'll make his apologies and move on.

She wants to beat him to the punch. 'It's been great to see you. You're looking well, and it sounds like things are going fantastically.' He looks like he's about to speak. She speeds up so he can't cut her off. 'I always wondered, *whatever happened to Tony Camberwell?* And now I know.' She raises her glass and drinks a little too much, a little too quickly.

'Lily, do you want to go somewhere else? Somewhere quieter, to catch up?'

'Oh, sure. Oh. I mean, yes.' Flustered, she puts the glass down, delighted.

'Great! Give me a minute to grab my things.'

She watches as he weaves through the crowd. People like him, she can tell by the way they call out, the way they shake their hands. But he doesn't stop long to chat, he keeps moving to his coat.

'Let's get out of here.' He's back by her side.

She reaches for her purse and jacket and they step out into the autumn night air.

Several city blocks away, at an all-night diner, they talk the night away over scrambled eggs, hash browns, sausages and toast. He is as easy as ever to talk to. By the time they part, it's nearly 3 a.m. Outside her Brooklyn apartment, he gives her a hug, a sweet kiss on the cheek, and a promise to call soon.

True to his word, Tony calls. They meet again, and then again, and eventually they pick their friendship back up. Though they don't rehash their time at Rice, there is a sweetness in knowing that they carry for one another a knowing of who they were then, along with who they are now.

Once again, they are falling for each other. This time for keeps.

Albuquerque, New Mexico, August 2000

Lily and Tony are visiting her parents. As soon as they arrive, Henry shows them his trees. Over the past few years, he has pruned them and added stakes to stabilise their growth. The highest branches reach to Henry's chest. Having been given space, sunlight, water, food and care, they have spread their limbs wide.

'Peaches,' he says. 'I just threw the stones back here and now look: peach trees!'

Lily walks from tree to tree, fingering the long green leaves in wonder.

'First harvest.' Her father beams, tenderly stroking a small, plump peach.

Rachel calls them in for dinner.

The evening passes with an ease that bewilders Lily. The fears and regrets that have always shadowed her father seem to have lifted. Gone, too, are the unspoken resentments and frustrations that pervaded her childhood. After so many decades, old wounds are starting to heal.

That night, when they are getting ready for bed, Tony asks Lily if everything's okay, says she seems quieten.

'I'm fine,' she reassures him. 'It's just . . .'

'Just what?' He puts an arm around her shoulder.

'I never realised' – and her voice catches – 'I never realised that my father has such a nice smile.'

The following morning, Lily walks into the kitchen and sees a plate full of peaches sitting on the table. She picks one up. It nestles in the palm of her hand, heavy with juice and flavour. Leaf-dappled and promising sweetness, its red-orange freckled fuzz of skin yields just slightly when squeezed. It smells of summer.

Henry stands at the counter, washing more peaches. Bright drops of water bounce off their surfaces, pooling like tiny gems on the counter. The colander overflows with fruit. He takes down a wooden cutting board, its surface scored with years of tiny scratches, and starts cutting. The knife blade pierces through the flesh. With a practised twist of his wrist, he pulls sections cleanly away from the crimson stone. He peels off the skin in one gentle gesture, slices the peach, and picks up a piece. Juice drips from the fruit and he pops it into his mouth. He nods to himself. He puts the rest of the slices into a glass bowl.

'Welcome home, Little Girl,' he says, holding it out to her.

Epilogue

Albuquerque, New Mexico, April 2005

Henry's peach trees bloom. Bowers of blossom pile up to the sky.

Henry goes out to his orchard and sits. He wears no jacket or hat or gloves. His eyes are rimmed with grey. His few silver strands of hair glint in the sun. Henry's skin is smooth and wrinkled. There is too much skin for the bones inside.

He looks up, lost in a heaven of flowers. It is just as he had imagined so many years ago when he sat in his study, paging through catalogues, ordering those first cherry trees. It is, he murmurs to himself, more beautiful than any scene on any hand scroll, for he feels the cool spring air on his temples and his ears fill with birdsong and small rustlings of grass.

His ma's hand scroll and her stories. Can he remember them? Henry sits very still. As the sun moves across the sky and the shade shifts, the stories return. Slowly recalling them, he smiles to himself. Each is like a polished stone, its contours cherished and familiar. He thought he might have lost them, but he hasn't. They have always been within. Maybe he will tell them to his grandchildren when they next visit.

He considers his ma's version of 'Peach Blossom Spring'. For years, he thought she had told it incompletely, had somehow cheated him of the full story. But today, he realises something else. Perhaps it's not so much that his ma told it wrong, but that she told a different story. The original is a tragedy. The old fisherman from Wuling holds his dream, then loses it. And no matter how desperately he or the others search, no one ever finds it again. It is an endless, fruitless quest: an eternity of disappointment. But in Meilin's telling, once the old fisherman arrives, he stays. He learns to leave behind what he has left behind. Meilin never wanted the story to be a tragedy; she just wanted to find an ending. The story ends when there is nothing more to strive after. There is no more wanting. There is only the fullness of blossom, the caress of a breeze, a sky joyous with blue. This moment. This now. This peach blossom spring.

Acknowledgements

When I first started writing about my father's fruit trees, I didn't know I would end up writing a novel that spanned seventy years and tried to make sense of China's tumultuous twentieth century. My desire was to write a story that celebrated the abundance and happiness my father eventually found after a life marked by much turmoil.

Peach Blossom Spring is fiction. Although its characters and my family travelled along many of the same roads, the story is primarily a work of my imagination. When I was a child, my father said very little about his past. I knew that he was born in China, went to Taiwan as a youth, and came to America for graduate studies. That was all we needed to know, he assured us. But on Christmas Day 1998, for some reason I will never know, he told us a handful of his stories. I wrote down every word he said. Nearly twenty years later, I took those notes and began to piece together a narrative.

To bring a world to life that I had little personal experience of, I devoted myself to learning more about those who had lived through the same world events as my father. I am indebted to the writings, research and storytelling of Dominic Yang's *The Great Exodus from China*, Chi Pang-yuan's *The Great Flowing River*, Han Suyin's *Birdless Summer*, Madeline Hsu's *The Good Immigrants*, Jessica J. Lee's *Two Trees Make a Forest*, Q. M. Zhang's *Accomplice to Memory*, Joshua Fan's *China's Homeless Generation*, Helen Zia's *Last Boat Out of Shanghai*, Danke Li's *Echoes of Chongqing*, Mahlon Meyer's *Remembering China from Taiwan*, Rana Mitter's *China's War with Japan*, several of Diana Lary's books on twentieth-century China, Pai Hsien-Yung's *Taipei People* and Wu Ming-Yi's *The Stolen Bicycle*. I also owe much to the photography of Deng Nan-Guang, the films of Hou Hsiao-hsien and Edward Yang, and many academic papers, including research from Wendy Cheng, Zuoyue Wang and Pei-Te Lien.

In addition, I am grateful for helpful conversations with Dominic Yang, Danke Li, Phyllis Huang, Dafydd Fell and Biyu Chang. A special thank you to Clare Chun-yu Liu for inspiration, conversation, translations and introductions.

Thank you to Arts Council England for awarding me a Developing Your Creative Practice grant. The support from ACE was instrumental in funding a research trip to China and Taiwan that allowed me to retrace my characters' footsteps.

During my research trip, I had the great delights of working with Blue Lan as my interpreter, visiting Teacher Li at Blessed Imelda's, who answered my many questions about Taipei through the decades, and spending time with David Lin and Yowen Tsai, who generously shared family stories as well as delicious meals.

The story was improved by input from readers of various drafts and sections. Thank you to Jessica J. Lee, Yan Ge, Anne Chen, Linshan Jiang, Catherine Menon, Catherine Chou and Elisa Tamburo for your helpful contributions.

I feel extremely fortunate to have spoken with so many people in the course of my research. Their contributions make the book immeasurably better. Any errors are my own.

Because writing itself is a solitary activity, I've found that having a writing community is a lifeline. I have so much gratitude for the many occasions of coffee and craft with the Angles writing group in Cambridge, all my beloved Writing Circles participants, and the fellow London Lit Lab writers who first met Henry in my short story, 'Henry Dreams an Orchard'.

Deep appreciation to everyone at the Word Factory, especially Cathy Galvin and Paul McVeigh, for selecting me to be an apprentice in 2017, and Zoe Gilbert for being such a generous and encouraging mentor.

Much of *Peach Blossom Spring* found its way to the page during my time as the 2018/2019 David T. K. Wong Fellow at the University of East Anglia. Professor Jon Cook's insightful mentoring helped me articulate and explore many of the themes that emerged as the story developed.

It has been a marvellous privilege to work with Kate Stephenson, Ella Gordon and Serena Arthur at Wildfire and Helen

O'Hare at Little, Brown. I am in awe of how your vision, patience and editorial brilliance have transformed my manuscript into a book. Many thanks, as well, to copyeditor Tara O'Sullivan and cartographer Tim Peters. And for helping *Peach Blossom Spring* find its readers, I applaud the ace marketing and publicity efforts of Caitlin Raynor, Vicky Beddow, Stephanie Reddaway, Gabrielle Leporati, Lena Little and Ashley Marudas.

I will be forever grateful to my amazing agent, Clare Alexander, who knew before I did what this could become. Thank you for your support at every step.

And to my friends who have witnessed my writing and this story grow – Emma Rhind-Tutt, Pia Ghosh Roy, Nette Andres, Daphne Gerling, Bec Sollom, Yin Lim, Karen Littleton, Lynne Cameron, Lara Turner, Connie Hui, Rebecca Stevens, Suzanne Koopmans, Anne Clarke, and Ophelia Redpath – thank you. Your kindness and friendship mean so much.

A big hug to my Mom, Addie, and brothers, Michael and David. Thank you, 哥哥, for helping me find the right characters and for sending me Dad's copies of 三字經 and百家姓.

Lastly, to Nicholas, Juniper and Matthew. You are my world. Thank you. I love you all.